WILD WONDERFUL LOVE

"If only I could remember . . ." Jubilee said as she slowly began to turn around.

"We can pretend *this* is our wedding night," Chance whispered. "And the memories can commence at this very instant."

He did not give her a chance to voice her opinion of this suggestion as his lips descended and claimed her entire being with a kiss so demanding it left them both gasping for air.

"I remember what it's like to . . . kiss you," she replied. She tilted her head back in anticipation of his next kiss.

For a moment Chance could only stare at her in awe. Her moist lips were parted, and her long lashes fanned out across the tops of her cheeks like the gently fluttering wings of a butterfly. He did not want to kiss her again; he wanted to carry her to the bed and make love to her like there was no tomorrow; like he had only dreamt of doing last night.

"Why don't you show me how wonderful it . . . could have been, last night?" she murmured.

Chance did not have to be asked twice.

FIERY ROMANCE

CALIFORNIA CARESS (2771, $3.75)
by Rebecca Sinclair

Hope Bennett was determined to save her brother's life. And if that meant paying notorious gunslinger Drake Frazier to take his place in a fight, she'd barter her last gold nugget. But Hope soon discovered she'd have to give the handsome rattlesnake more than riches if she wanted his help. His improper demands infuriated her; even as she luxuriated in the tantalizing heat of his embrace, she refused to yield to her desires.

ARIZONA CAPTIVE (2718, $3.75)
by Laree Bryant

Logan Powers had always taken his role as a lady-killer very seriously and no woman was going to change that. Not even the breathtakingly beautiful Callie Nolan with her luxuriant black hair and startling blue eyes. Logan might have considered a lusty romp with her but it was apparent she was a lady, through and through. Hard as he tried, Logan couldn't resist wanting to take her warm slender body in his arms and hold her close to his heart forever.

DECEPTION'S EMBRACE (2720, $3.75)
by Jeanne Hansen

Terrified heiress Katrina Montgomery fled Memphis with what little she could carry and headed west, hiding in a freight car. By the time she reached Kansas City, she was feeling almost safe . . . until the handsomest man she'd ever seen entered the car and swept her into his embrace. She didn't know who he was or why he refused to let her go, but when she gazed into his eyes, she somehow knew she could trust him with her life . . . and her heart.

CHEYENNE TEMPTRESS

VERONICA BLAKE

ZEBRA BOOKS
KENSINGTON PUBLISHING CORP.

ZEBRA BOOKS

are published by

Kensington Publishing Corp.
475 Park Avenue South
New York, NY 10016

First printing: January, 1991

Printed in the United States of America

Chapter One

"Women vote! Now, that's about the funniest thing I ever heard! What are they going to vote on? Oh, let me guess." The young man pushed his floppy-brimmed hat to the back of his head and rolled his eyes upward in an exaggerated gesture. With a casual stance, he leaned back against the hitching post that stood in front of the roundhouse. His mouth curled into an impish grin when he added, "Women can vote on whether or not men prefer whiskey or brandy with their cigars. Or maybe they could vote on which end of the hen house they should—"

"Mr. Steele!" the elderly woman interrupted with an angry tilt of her head. With an expression as icy as the December wind, she leveled a steady gaze at his laughing face and drew a wool muffler up against her midriff, clasping her hands together within its warmth. Her fury did little to dispel the boy's taunting smirk, however. "You are treading on very thin ground, young man. I would advise you to—to—." Her words faltered when she noticed the arrival of another man. A rush of color began to creep through the hollows of her cheeks in vibrant shades of red, which clashed drastically with her heavy purple cloak and pillbox hat of the same dark color.

"Is this ornery nephew of mine giving you a hard time, Mrs. Crowly?" The man looked at the boy with a quick glance, then focused his attention on the woman

5

who stood before him. A small, dark gray bowler hat was perched on his head, which drew particular attention to his twinkling ebony eyes. He crossed his arms over his broad chest and struck a relaxed pose beside his nephew against the rail of the depot stoop. An expression as mischievous as the look on the boy's face came to rest upon his countenance. A smile touched the corners of his mouth and curved a thin black mustache, which framed his upper lip, into a curious tilt.

Mrs. Crowly gave a nervous chuckle when she tried to avert her eyes from the handsome face of Chance Steele. While she tried to control her giddy emotions, she silently reminded herself that she was a married woman, and far too old to be acting in such a foolish manner. Yet, every time she was in the presence of the dashing proprietor of the new saloon, she became flustered and unsure of herself.

"Your—um—" Mrs. Crowly looked around as though she was trying to remember what they were discussing until she glanced back at the young man who was watching her with a distinct expression of amusement. She straightened her shoulders, inwardly vowing to behave in a more dignified manner. "Your nephew was making light of the idea of women being granted the right to vote."

Without looking in the boy's direction again, a broader smile moved across Chance Steele's mouth and lit his dark eyes with a devilish twinkle. "Ah, yes, the suffrage issue." In an imitation of his nephew's previous gesture, he pushed his small hat to the back of his head, revealing thick raven-black wavy hair. Carefully trimmed sideburns outlined the contour of his handsome face and were touched with random strands of silver; a tribute to his age that only increased his extreme good looks. "I do recall hearing that our fair city is about to be visited by some, ah—" he paused as his teasing gaze lifted toward his nephew.

"A speaker for the suffrage, Mr. Steele!" Abigail Crowly finished with a tone of annoyance edging her

6

voice. Even Chance Steele's hypnotic smile could not distract the woman when her ire was aroused about this impending issue. "Miss Jubilee Hart from Washington, D.C.!" she retorted with a proud stance. "A representative of our cause. Why, Miss Hart has dedicated her life to unselfishly working for the rights of women all over our great country. It will be an honor for her to grace Wyoming with her presence."

"And it shall be an honor, I'm sure. Although, it is my personal opinion that the men of Wyoming will grant our lovely females the right to vote without any protests," Chance Steele said in a confident manner, which suggested he knew something the majority of the population did not yet suspect. Past experience had taught him that when his charm began to fail, it was time for retreat. "And," he quickly added, "If I can make my services available, or can provide any assistance for your upcoming rally, please feel free to call on me."

His disarming grin set Abigail Crowly's senses into a whirl again. "How very kind of you," she said in a tone shadowed with surprise. "Why, I doubt that most of the men will be as generous as you are toward our cause."

The smiling man ran his gloved hand down the front of the brocaded black silk vest that peeked out from between the lapels of his finely-tailored coat, then gave his shoulders a nonchalant shrug. "I'm a generous man." He glanced at his nephew and winked, causing the younger Steele to bow his head in an effort to hide his obvious mirth.

"I realize how busy you must be with the preparations for the grand opening of your new saloon, but I do hope you'll allow me to introduce you to Miss Hart when she arrives at the depot. And," she purposely turned her back to Jerrod Steele, making her intended invitation clear. "My husband and I would like to have you join us for dinner tonight."

"Dinner?" Visions of a bespectacled old maid flashed through his mind as he shivered with dread at the unpleasant thought. A hint of discomfort touched his raven gaze as he tried to invent a believable excuse for his whereabouts this evening. "I'm afraid I have to decline your kind invitation, Mrs. Crowly. I—I—" he focused a sorrowful look on the woman's flushed face. He hated to turn down a dinner invitation with the Crowlys. Not only was he indebted to Howard Crowly, but it was also good politics to be accepted among the leading citizens of Cheyenne. A man in Chance's precarious position needed to remain in the best of social graces at all times. But spending the evening in the presence of some old spinster from back East would be pure torture. "Jerrod and I have made previous plans, but perhaps another time?"

His regret was sincere as he declined the invitation. Still, it was his disarming smile which caused Abigail Crowly to blush profusely once again. "Anytime, anytime at all! How about tomorrow night?"

Jerrod Steele's forced cough did little to hide his amusement, yet his uncle did not give him the satisfaction of acknowledging his mirth. Chance's smile remained unwavering as he continued to stare at the woman. "Well, tomorrow? I—" his voice was cut off by the impatient howl of the approaching locomotive.

With great excitement, Abigail Crowly's attention was diverted toward the train. "She's here!" The woman reached out from the wooly interior of her muffler and squeezed Chance's arm before hurrying toward the passenger coach. "We'll count on you to be at our house for dinner tomorrow evening. But," she turned quickly to add, "If you change your mind about tonight, we'll be dining at the inn."

In her rush towards the locomotive, she did not wait for any further reply, and neither of the men made an attempt to say a word until the lady was well out of earshot. Then, Jerrod could contain himself no longer and he burst out laughing. "I suppose I shouldn't plan on you being home for supper tomorrow night?" he asked, then playfully slapped his uncle on the back.

8

"You may. I will not be an escort to some suffering old petticoat, no matter who invites me to dinner!"

A lazy smile remained upon Jerrod's mouth as his snickering ceased. The boy permitted the man to walk a short distance ahead of him, while he once again gloried in the pride that he felt toward his successful uncle. It never occurred to either the boy or the man what an odd couple they made as the two of them wove their way through the crowd waiting for the train to halt. The similarities in their eyes, hair and facial expressions made it obvious they were blood relatives. But Chance Steele, in his citified attire of silk and fine wool appeared to be worlds apart from the young man, whose lean form was clad in well-worn farm duds.

The planks of the walkway that ran in front of the depot were shiny with a thin layer of ice, which made walking treacherous and blinded the eye with bolts of light where the afternoon sun met with the frozen ground. A ferocious cold spell had moved into the area a month earlier, and would undoubtedly last until spring, but the hardy residents of Wyoming were learning to cope with the drastic weather conditions afforded by this rugged land. As for Chance Steele, he rather hoped it would be an extremely long cold winter.

The saloon keeper gave a contented sigh as his gaze swept across the expanse of the growing prairie town, whose rapid growth had earned it the title of 'The Magic City of the Plains.' Chance thought of Cheyenne as his town since he had been here at the beginning of its existence and had endured its rough infancy. In barely two years time he had watched — and participated in — this settlement's growth from a rowdy tent town, filled with railroad construction workers and cowboy drifters, to a prospering city of wealthy and prominent citizens. Chance Steele could not help but feel that he was among the most influential men in the area, and with the gala opening of his new saloon just days away, he would soon be one of the wealthiest occupants as well. His new position would be a far cry from

9

his early days in Cheyenne when he had lived in a tent while the railroad was being built. The first bottle of liquor he had served had been poured from the back of a trail-worn wagon. It was the same wagon that had transported him to Wyoming from his home in Mississippi. At times he found it hard to believe how his meager beginnings in this rugged territory had given birth to the success he was about to enjoy with the opening of his new saloon. Ah, but this was the land of opportunity, and Chance Steele grasped every opportunity that came his way.

A secure feeling came over the man as his gaze traveled along 17th street and settled on the sight of his first business endeavor. An elaborately carved sign, depicting the various forms of entertainment, adorned the top of the lavish establishment. Chance was certain the images of card players, voluptuous saloon girls and whiskey bottles would catch the eyes of weary gentlemen travelers when they got off the train. Once they entered the doors of the Second Chance Saloon they would discover a virtual paradise, the likes of which they would not find in any other establishment west of St. Louis, Missouri.

When the building of the Union Pacific Railroad had passed through this area in 1867, many of the liquor solicitors had relocated with the construction crews to Laramie, Wyoming—the next site along the pathway of the railroad tracks, which would extend from coast to coast upon completion. Foresight told Chance to remain in Cheyenne. Though many of the railway towns ceased to exist once the crews moved along to the new location, Chance had a feeling Cheyenne would continue to prosper. Still, he was taking a great risk. He used all of the profits he had obtained during the boom period, while the tracks were being built, to erect the elaborate building that housed his saloon. The huge structure was in the same location where he had first served drinks from his dilapidated old buckboard. By the time the building was finished, Chance's intuition about the town's growth had proven itself to be correct.

His saloon was already surrounded by well over a hundred businesses, which even included six doctors and seven lawyers. Becoming the proprietor of his own saloon had not been Chance's plan when he had traveled West. He had loaded up his sparse belongings and headed out of Mississippi, hoping to leave behind the life he had lived for the past seventeen years. He was weary of the riverboats where he had gambled away most of his life. The rocking of the stern would not lull him to sleep at nights, and he began to long for a sense of stability that the river no longer offered. A distant dream beckoned to him — the dream of owning land and putting down real roots for the first time in his life. The railroad was headed West, so Chance packed up his bags and signed on as a laborer for the Union Pacific. He was accustomed to working in the fancy state rooms of the Mississippi riverboats, and before his employment on the railroad crew his hardest labor was concentrating on the next deal of the cards. He would spend hours grooming himself for an evening with the lovely ladies who also made their living upon the floating pleasure houses.

By the time he had worked his way to Wyoming, he'd grown sick and tired of hammering stakes in the ground and of being covered with grime and sweat. Disillusioned by his new adventure, and the lack of the profits he had hoped to obtain by this time, he began to wonder if he had made a mistake by joining the railroad crew.

He studied the parade of solicitors who also accompanied the railroad crews, and it did not take him long to figure out where the real profits lay. Since there was nothing for the workers to do at night other than to drink and gamble away their wages, the saloon keepers were doing a thriving business. Chance Steele was a pro with a deck of cards, and he was also as smooth as silk when it came to dealing with the clientele of this type of business. It seemed only natural for him to

11

trade in his sledgehammer to pursue a gentler line of work. His plan to purchase land was put to the back of his mind as he took on the challenge of his first business endeavor. His qualifications were limited to his previous employment on the riverboats, but he was certain owning a saloon would prove to be profitable and fun . . . and Chance Steele was never one to miss out on a good time.

A pang of guilt accompanied this thought as Chance glanced at the young boy who stood beside him. Jerrod's arrival last month had made Chance once again assess the path his life had taken. With the wealth he had achieved in the past couple of years he could have purchased any ranch in the territory. Instead, he had used every last penny to build himself an establishment that could rival any saloon in the country. Yet since Jerrod had re-entered his life, Chance began to view this accomplishment in a more critical light.

A thoughtful expression drew the edges of Chance's thin mustache into a downward line as his gaze wandered out over the vast acreage beyond the boundaries of the bustling prairie town. Maybe he should start thinking more seriously about finding a suitable place for Jerrod to live now that the boy was his sole responsibility. But today was not the time to worry about such matters, Chance reminded himself. He turned back towards the locomotive and directed his full attention toward the passengers who were leaving the train. Mrs. Crowly was anxiously awaiting the appearance of her guest, but Chance was anticipating a few arrivals of his own. With the addition of St. Louis' finest courtesans, Chance hoped his new saloon would achieve a status of great renown. Then, Chance reminded himself sternly, he would think about purchasing some land and building a proper home for Jerrod and himself.

"So, do we have plans for tonight?" The mocking voice of the younger male cut into Chance's thoughts. Another deep frown burrowed across the man's countenance since it was evident that the boy was having a great time chiding his uncle about the old maid from the East.

"We do," Chance answered. He carefully repositioned the bowler hat upon his head, then ran his hand down the front of his shiny vest again. With a slight tilt of his head he motioned toward the door of the passenger coach. Jerrod's gaze followed his uncle's gesture in time to see the narrow doorway overflow with petticoats and curls, accompanied by the sound of excited female voices as the women began to descend from the plank in a disorderly manner.

In a moment rare to his exuberant character, Jerrod remained speechless. His open mouth and wide-eyed stare gave him the appearance of being younger than his sixteen years. When the young man's voice returned, he leaned towards the other man with an excited rush of words. "Lordy, Uncle Chance! They're beautiful! Why, there ain't a homely one in the whole lot, is there?"

A grin, which seemed to hover on the edge of indecent thoughts, moved into an idle curve across Chance's mouth. "I went to St. Louis and hand-picked each one of these fillies, personally. And, I do pride myself on being a good judge of beauty." He gave a sigh of self-satisfaction over his excellent taste as he added, "The cream of the crop, boy. And they're all ours."

The group of women paused at the end of the plank, uncertain of their destination beyond this point. Their loud chattering ceased while they glanced around in search of the man who had paid for their passage to this desolate place. When they spotted the mustached male moving toward them, a round of whispering and giggling broke out among the ladies. There had been much speculation among the group as to which one of his chosen dozen would be the first to privately entertain the handsome new boss. Now, as Chance Steele sauntered toward them, there was already an obvious undertone of jealousy and competitiveness among the ladies.

13

Chance's gaze moved over each of the women in obvious approval, but in the confusion of the moment, he did not recognize all of the women he had so carefully chosen in St. Louis. So when his wandering eyes happened upon two women who were still making their way down the plank, his first thought was that one of his 'girls' was straggling behind the rest. The older of the two women was dressed in sober gray and Chance dismissed her at once as the insufferable Jubilee Hart. It was the younger woman who drew Chance's complete attention. She was dressed every bit as flamboyantly as the other courtesans, but her vibrant fur-trimmed red cloak and plumed hat of red velvet lent her an aura of refinement, which the other prostitutes lacked. Strange that he couldn't remember this one . . . no, he'd remember, Chance told himself. Without taking the time to scrutinize his thoughts, Chance determined that the gorgeous blonde belonged to him. He had paid for a dozen women; perhaps one of the ladies had been unable to fulfill the contract and this beauty was her replacement.

As he waited for her to descend from the plank his mind began to envision this goddess walking down the curved stairway of The Second Chance Saloon. Ah, she would be worth a goldmine. But a strange twinge of possessiveness washed through him when he thought of other men handling this woman whom he had just set eyes upon. Maybe he should consider keeping this one all for himself. Women were scarce in Wyoming, and a beauty like this one would be rare in any part of the country. It was this sort of sensuous musing which involved Chance Steele when he reached the women. The blonde had separated herself from the older woman who had accompanied her down the plank, and was standing alone on the icy walkway. A noticeable line of displeasure drew her brows together and deepened the shade of her royal blue eyes. When the man approached her a look of astonishment swept over her face. But her expression immediately changed to aver-

14

sion when her flashing eyes traveled over his flashy attire. Chance Steele was so enraptured by his own fantasies of the lovely woman that he failed to notice her contemptuous expression. He bowed deeply from the waist, and stared suggestively at her.

"Chance Steele at your service, my lovely lady." Grinning broadly, he leaned forward until his face was inches from the frowning countenance of the woman. "And though it has not been my pleasure to have made your acquaintance before today, I can already tell you that your presence at The Second Chance Saloon will reap rewards far beyond what any of the other courtesans will ever know."

The woman's mouth fell open in astonishment but no sound escaped her parted lips. Before she could respond, he took firm hold of her arm and pulled her toward his group of 'ladies'. She felt like a lamb being led to slaughter, but she was too stunned to resist. The prostitutes, whose loud chatter had previously filled the air, fell into a dead quiet as they observed the approach of their new employer and his companion. They had encountered this woman when they boarded the train in St. Louis and had learned at once that she was not someone they cared to befriend. She had made her position clear concerning their profession the moment they had stepped into the passenger car. For better than half the journey she had preached to them about the evils of whiskey, gambling and prostitution, but to no avail. Though none of the prostitutes backed down from the outspoken woman, these 'soiled doves' were also wise enough to know that they were treading on dangerous ground. If she was as important to the women's suffrage movement as she claimed to be, then it was possible she could initiate a great deal of trouble among temperance groups as well. Temperance and saloons did not create a profitable mixture, so now they all wondered — what in the devil was their new boss doing in this haughty woman's company?

Chance Steele relaxed his grip on the blonde woman's arm once he had led her into the middle of his group of new employees. At once, she took advantage of his lax hold and pulled free. The rashness of her action alerted Chance to the hostility he had previously overlooked. A sick feeling began to move through him as he realized that he might have been mistaken about this woman's identity. When he glanced at the rest of the prostitutes, his grave error was confirmed by the shocked expressions on each of the women's faces.

"I—I, ah, I guess you are not one of my—"

With an angry reddening of the woman's face, she glared at the tall saloon proprietor. "Oh, you couldn't be more right!" Her arm swiped through the air as her finger pointed accusingly at the prostitutes, then leveled back at Chance Steele like a lethal weapon. "But it's apparent that *you* are the owner of the glorified brothel they have been bragging about ever since we left St. Louis." She pulled back her hand as if she was afraid he might grab her again, then she clenched her fists tightly at the sides of her velvet cloak.

"It was an unforgivable mistake," he said in his own defense. But even as he tried to explain his error, he reprimanded himself. A closer inspection of the lovely blonde revealed the obvious; she was far too fine a lady to be one of his strumpets. Her skin, though it glowed in high color was of a natural hue, unlike the brightly painted faces of the other women. He noted the way her soft curls cascaded over her shoulders before coming to rest upon the expensive red velvet cape. The golden fur which trimmed the finely-tailored garment matched the color of her gently arched brows. This lady was the embodiment of breeding and grace. She was utterly different than the women who had arrived from St. Louis to work at The Second Chance Saloon.

"The idea that you actually thought I was one of those—those—." Her words failed when she glanced toward the group. She could think of several names by which to address the women, but inwardly, she told herself that she need not resort to unladylike behavior.

There were other ways to deal with situations such as this, and Jubilee Hart knew exactly how to handle a man like Chance Steele. A fleeting thought of another gambler and saloon owner passed through her mind. The image brought back painful memories she did not wish to recall, but they fueled her fury at the man who stood before her.

"Miss Hart?"

The blonde turned abruptly and forced a feeble smile as she faced the woman who had just addressed her. "Mrs. Crowly?" she inquired. Another rush of heat reddened her cheeks with the embarassment she felt at being taken for a prostitute. When the older woman nodded slightly in acknowledgement Jubilee Hart sighed with relief. She moved out of the circle of prostitutes as quickly as she was able. "I hope this unfortunate incident will not affect the seriousness of my undertakings here," she said, reaching out toward the other woman.

"It was an unfortunate incident, I'm sure," Mrs. Crowly replied in a tone shadowed with embarassment. She avoided looking at Chance Steele and took the younger woman's extended hand, pulling Jubilee farther away from Steele and his troupe of prostitutes. When she felt they were a safe distance from the train depot , she paused and released her hold on the indignant suffrage leader. "I'm so sorry, Miss Hart," she whispered with a nervous shake of her gray head.

"Not as sorry as that despicable man will be," Jubilee answered as she smoothed down her red cape and glared back in the direction of Chance Steele.

With a helpless glance in the same direction, Abigail Crowly shrugged in exasperation. Though she sympathized with her new guest, she did not feel that Chance was entirely in the wrong, either. Abigail had been told the suffrage leader was lovely, but she was unprepared for the depth of the woman's beauty. Yet attired so richly, Jubilee Hart looked nothing like the dedicated woman her uncompromising reputation would suggest.

The elderly woman was unsure of what to say to Miss Hart, so she decided to say nothing more about the episode. She took a deep breath and forced a wide smile, which made her pale skin stretch like parchment across the prominent bones of her cheeks. "I can't tell you what an honor it is to have you here in Cheyenne," she said. Her smile remained in a fixed position, and she pretended not to hear the prostitutes' snickering and laughter. Abigail had dealt with such low creatures before, and she would not favor them with a response.

Calling upon all the dignity she could muster, Jubilee composed her expression and held her head high as she and Mrs. Crowly left the train depot. Her anger though, was silently consuming her like a blazing fire. She had already been taunted and harassed by those hussies on the train, then publicly humiliated by their boss the moment she had arrived in Cheyenne. She did not intend to let either of those incidents go without retaliation. But right now she had to concentrate on something else — the mission that had brought her all the way West to this forlorn territory known as Wyoming.

"Guess this just hasn't been your day has it, Uncle Chance?" Jerrod hooked his thumbs in the belt loops of his faded breeches while he watched Mrs. Crowly and her beautiful visitor walk away from the train station.

Chance Steele huffed with indifference, but his gaze did not leave the two women until they had disappeared from view. Making a fool of himself — especially in the presence of a beautiful lady — was not a common occurrence for the debonair gambler. "A woman like that could be a man's undoing, boy."

"Ah, anybody could made a mistake like like you did. She's too darned pretty to be a suffering — whatever it was that you called her." The boy whistled under his breath and gave his head an exaggerated shake to emphasize his meaning. Besides, as far as Jerrod was concerned, his Uncle Chance was above reproach.

A frown tugged at Chance's face as his glance met his nephew's for an instant. While he tried to force the incident from his mind he turned toward the group of prostitutes and repeated his elaborate bow. "Welcome to Cheyenne, ladies," he said with his old confidence. To Jerrod, he said in a low voice, "Let's get these fillies settled in as quick as possible. I have plans for tonight."

"But I thought you and me had—"

"Not tonight, boy," the handsome saloon owner interrupted with a sly grin. "I have a dinner date, remember?"

Chapter Two

"I still cannot believe the nerve of that man!" In a display of anger, the statuesque blonde flung her velvet cape down on the parlor sofa, then paused as a guilty expression overcame her face. "Oh, I *am* sorry, Mrs. Crowly. I hate to keep carrying on about that embarrassing incident, especially since you told me that man is a friend of your husband's. But the idea of what he insinuated is just so humiliating."

Mrs. Crowly retrieved the discarded cape from the sofa and carefully hung the elegant wrap on a nearby coat rack. When she turned around to face the other woman she couldn't help but feel a pang of jealousy. Abigail had expected a woman of at least thirty years of age, but Jubilee Hart could not be over twenty-four or twenty-five. Her pale blonde hair was worn in an abundance of long loose curls, and her style of dress was ornate and flashy. Abigail was amazed that this young woman was such a success with the suffrage movement, but she could only pretend to be shocked by the saloon keeper's mistake. She almost had to agree with Chance Steele, because Jubilee Hart did appear to be more the type of woman he had implied, than a staunch suffrage leader from Washington, D.C.

"Whiskey is the poison of our society, you know," Jubilee said with an agitated nod of her head. She unfastened the row of dainty buttons which ran down the front of the short red jacket that topped her ensemble.

20

The fitted jacket fell open, revealing the tailored white satin shirtwaist she wore beneath. A pang of envy struck through Mrs. Crowly when she observed the younger woman's voluptuous curves. Instinctively she glanced down at her own flat chest, and inwardly gave a disgusted sigh. Mr. Crowly had an endless supply of rude jokes concerning her skinny unattractive shape, and he unabashedly eyed women who were more endowed than his wife. His attitude toward other women was a constant source of pain for Abigail, especially since the years had taken away the tiny bit of fragile beauty she had once possessed. To Abigail, it almost seemed to be a cruel twist of fate the way her husband had managed to grow older with such dignity. At fifty-six he was in excellent physical condition. His hair had almost completed the transition from brown to gray, but unlike the brittle yellow tinged gray hair that thinly covered Abigail's head, Howard's hair was turning a gentle shade of white. When involved with business, Howard was a no-nonsense banker, but with the ladies he was a charmer of unequalled magnitude. Abigail wondered what effect Jubilee Hart's presence would have on the old fool, especially since the beautiful young woman would be staying right under their own roof.

Jubilee opened her mouth to continue her verbal assault on the evils of drink, but the stricken look on Abigail Crowly's face stopped her. She silently cursed at herself for being so selfish and rude. She was a visitor in this woman's home and here she was ranting and raving about an issue that was her own private crusade and did not concern this poor woman in any way. "I am so sorry," she said in a meek voice. "You must think I'm an awful person for carrying on like this when I just arrived at your lovely home." She took a deep breath and crossed her arms over her bosom, since the woman's odd stare made her unusually self-conscious.

Mrs. Crowly quickly shifted her gaze to Jubilee's face. "And you must think the same of me for being so

21

thoughtless and inhospitable. Would you like some tea to warm you? Then I can tell you about the preparations for the upcoming rally before we meet my husband for dinner tonight."

Jubilee's spirits brightened. The cold Wyoming wind had left her chilled to the bone, and she was worried her stay at the Crowlys' would be strained and awkward—thanks to that infuriating man at the train depot! "Yes to the tea, and to the conversation about the rally," she answered with real gratitude. Things may have started badly, but Jubilee was sure they would improve. She felt a growing comfort in the tastefully decorated home, and her confidence and energy returned. She smoothed back her hair and followed her hostess eagerly. Now that her anger and embarrassment had subsided, she realized that it had been many hours since she had taken nourishment. Dinner would be most welcome.

The Railroad Inn could boast of serving the best food in Cheyenne. Its comfortable but expensive surroundings made it a popular place for Cheyenne's upper class to spend an evening of relaxation and social conversation. The atmosphere of the inn was a bit too refined for most of the local cowboys and roughnecks, who preferred a less formal atmosphere. Jubilee and her hostess were seated at a large, linen covered table. The women continued an animated discussion about the suffrage rally while they waited for the arrival of Abigail's husband.

The rally was to be held in a large room here at the inn, which was used for various groups and organizations whenever they held conferences or meetings. Since Cheyenne's female population was very sparse, Abigail made sure the rally was well advertised throughout the newly formed territory of Wyoming. She hoped that within the next couple of days the town would start filling up with enough women who supported their cause to make the men of the territory sit up and take notice. In less than a week the legislators were scheduled to meet, and on their agenda was the

22

issue of granting women the vote. The bill was being presented to the legislature with very little fanfare, other than the upcoming rally at which Jubilee was to speak.

When Howard Crowly and his guest entered the restaurant, the two women were engaged in a lively exchange of ideas for the rally. From across the room Chance Steele noted that the lovely blonde had changed into another suit of elegant velvet. But this outfit was a vibrant shade of royal blue, which matched the color of her flashing eyes. The soft tendrils of her light blonde hair were woven into an array of curls atop her head, with the exception of one long curl, which was left to dangle in a teasing manner over one shoulder. An intriguing smile hovered on the gambler's lips as he accompanied Howard Crowly through the crowded restaurant. He decided that coming here tonight might turn out to be better than having an ace up his sleeve.

Neither woman was aware of the approaching men until they stopped at the table. But when they did look up, both Abigail and Jubilee were stunned into silence. Knowing that he had precious little time to talk his way into their good graces, Chance Steele swept off his top hat and bowed toward Mrs. Crowly.

"I hope your kind offer to join you and your lovely guest for dinner is still open?" He then focused his most humble expression upon the younger woman, adding, "And I did not want to miss on another chance to apologize to Miss Hart for my unforgivable mistake. It was horrible beyond all imagining. But—" beneath his dark mustache, his lips trembled slightly, making him appear even more vulnerable. "—I pray that I will be forgiven." He dropped his gaze to the floor, ebony lashes covering his dark eyes. He slowly raised them to the unmoving face of Jubilee Hart. When she did not look away, Chance was confident that the stakes were in his favor.

Though his attention was directed solely toward Jubilee Hart, it was Abigail Crowly who first fell prey to his contrite performance. "Oh, of course you're forgiven. And the invitation for dinner is always open for *you* Mr. Steele."

At the other woman's announcement Jubilee Hart's eyes were diverted away from the handsome face of Chance Steele. Her reeling senses attempted to organize themselves into some sort of normal pattern as she listened to Abigail Crowly not only accept this man's apology, but forgive him for his horrid mistake as well. It was not Abigail's place to do either, and Jubilee felt a slow anger begin to burn inside her breast. The object of her fury, however, was none other than Chance Steele. He might be able to deceive the older woman, but his performance was all too familiar to Jubilee, though it had been a while since she had witnessed such an accomplished act. Because he possessed such a handsome exterior, she had almost permitted herself to be taken in by his appeal for forgiveness when he had first approached the table. That is, until she caught the glint of victory lurking within his eyes. She had seen that look a hundred times in her father's eyes. They, too, had been the eyes of a gambler.

Jubilee's thoughts were torn in opposing directions as she pondered her next move. She could try to expose Chance Steele for the underhanded sneak which she knew he was, but that would also reduce Abigail Crowly to the position of his fool. Besides, it was obvious that in the elderly Mrs. Crowly's eyes, this man could do little wrong. Jubilee reminded herself that she was the Crowly's house guest, and in just a few days she would be gone from Cheyenne, and from the likes of a man like Chance Steele. Until then, she decided, it would be wise to be diplomatic and play the hand exactly as the slick-talking Mr. Steele had dealt it to her.

"Mrs. Crowly speaks for me as well. Please *do* join us." Jubilee said with the imitation of a smile and a tilt of her perfectly-coiffed blonde head. Her eyes remained on Chance Steele's face for a moment; long enough to leave him wondering what unspoken thoughts were concealed behind the cold glint contained within her steady gaze. She then shifted her eyes toward Howard Crowly and extended her hand in a dainty fashion, while she continued, "And you, of course, must be Mr. Crowly."

At the mention of his name, Howard Crowly snapped from the trance he had been in since his arrival at the restaurant. His image of the Eastern suffragette had been much the same as Chance Steele's proposed version of a dried-up old maid. He was dreading the idea of having to play host to some manhating female for even a few days, yet he had agreed to let her stay at their home to pacify his wife. At times, Howard felt a bit of sympathy toward his mousey little wife, and since the issue of womens' equality had been the first thing she had shown any interest in for years, he indulged her in this temporary diversion from her wifely duties. When he had given his permission for the suffragist to be their house guest, he'd never imagined that their home would be host to a woman as lovely, as *desirable* as Miss Jubilee Hart. In just the few moments since he had first glimpsed this beauty, Howard's mind had conjured up a dozen different ways in which he could seduce his enchanting visitor during her brief stay. The eager expression upon his face did little to hide his lascivious thoughts as he responded to Jubilee's introduction with a lingering handshake that was more of a caress than a greeting. Jubilee practically had to pry her hand away from his grasp, and when she glanced up at him in bewilderment, his intense stare made her look away at once.

An odd twinge of uneasiness alerted Chance Steele as he noticed the other man's outlandish behavior although he too, had been entertaining those same thoughts when he first saw the lovely blonde departing from the train earlier today. Even Chance's appearance here at the inn had been spurred onward by thoughts of a sexual nature. Now, however, Chance had discovered something else in those flashing blue eyes . . . determined challenge, which appealed to his gaming nature and left him with a desire to conquer this beauty in more ways than one.

When Jubilee's spinning thoughts began to function properly, her first concern was for Abigail Crowly. What must the poor woman think about her husband's blatant display? Abigail's expression, however, appeared as unmarred as a statue of stone. It took Jubilee only a few minutes to realize that the woman was not surprised by her husband's behavior. Jubilee's heart went out to the elderly woman who sat silently across the table from her. Though Abagail was obviously used to enduring the public humiliation she received from her no-good husband, the pain contained within her guarded gaze was not so easy to disguise.

As the men seated themselves between the two women, Jubilee considered her treacherous situation. She had to be careful not to be overly friendly to Howard Crowly, or he would think she was encouraging his attentions. But at the same time, she reminded herself, she was a guest in his home and could not risk making him angry, either. An instant disdain for Howard Crowly filled Jubilee—and she had only met him a few moments ago! But then, she reminded herself silently, a person's first impression is usually correct. With this thought settled in her mind she glanced at the fancy-dressed gambler who sat at her side and reaffirmed her belief in this theory.

"Where do you hail from, Mr. Steele?" she asked, careful not to sound too enthusiastic. Acting kindly toward this man was completely against Jubilee's principles, yet she felt that even a gambler was a safer bet than the over-zealous Howard Crowly.

"Mississippi," he said with a surprised rise of his dark brows. He had not expected her to be this cordial toward him, and he had prepared himself to spend the better part of the evening receiving the cold shoulder from the lovely blonde. At least, until his unyielding

26

charm had dispelled the bad feelings from their first encounter at the train station.

"Of course," she replied, unable to prevent her pale pink lips from curving with a knowing smirk.

"It seems that you are not surprised that I am from Mississippi, Miss Hart. Do I have a telltale look about me that all Mississippians bear?"

A sweet smile replaced Jubilee's smirk, but the gesture did not remove the cool glimmer from her vibrantly hued eyes. "Not all Mississippians, Mr. Steele. You do, however, possess the telltale look of a polished backguard and rogue the likes of which I have observed only in the gamblers on large Mississippi river boats."

Her contemptuous attitude toward his profession set the smooth-talking man aback, especially since he was not accustomed to being treated by women in such a degrading manner. When he had regained his composure, he gave his shoulders a nonchalant shrug. "Well, everyone is entitled to misjudge someone once in a while. The fact that I mistook you for a lady of the evening earlier today is proof of that, wouldn't you say?"

His retort left Jubilee infuriated to the core, but she did not have the chance to reply. Howard Crowly's loud guffaw intervened instead. "I must have missed something." He leaned as far toward Jubilee as the table would permit and winked, "But maybe you can fill me in . . . later?" The pause in his question made it evident that he hoped to have some private time with his houseguest.

Without a moment's hesitation, Jubilee responded as though she had missed his insinuation. "Of course, Mr. Crowly. Your wife and I will be glad to tell you about Mr. Steele's enormous error in judgement when we return to your home. Because," she forced a weak chuckle and a quick glance at Chance Steele before continuing, "it really is not worth talking about at this time, is it, Mrs. Crowly?"

Abigail snapped her head up, startled by the reference to her name. When they were in the presence of other women, it was her practice to fill her head with thoughts that would distract her from her husband's disgusting remarks and gestures. She usually tried to think about the early days of her marriage, times when Howard was content to be with no one else but her. Lately, though, Abigail was having a harder time recalling those days. Sometimes, she wondered if there had ever been a time when her husband's wandering eye had not roved to every woman with whom he had made contact. A wan smile touched the corners of her thin mouth as she shook her head in agreement with Jubilee Hart, even though she had no idea what the girl had just said to her.

Abigail's small gesture seemed to pave the way to turn the strained conversation in a different direction, and Chance Steele was perceptive enough to take advantage of the situation. "I would love to hear about your work, Miss Hart—or may I call you Jubilee?"

Though she hated the idea of being so familiar with this saloon keeper, she could think of no graceful way to refuse his request. She did, however, make a mental note never to refer to him by his first name. *'Chance' ha!* She laughed inwardly at his name, which she was sure was derived from his gaming lifestyle. In spite of herself, Jubilee began to wonder what his real name might be. When she cast a questioning look in his direction, she discovered that he was also studying her with an intent expression upon his handsome face. She was sure his inquiry about her work was just a polite question, because it surely wasn't possible that he would be interested in something besides cards and prostitutes. Still, the guarded look began to fade from Jubilee's lovely face when she started talking about the campaigns to which she had devoted her entire adult life.

Jubilee captivated her audience of three as she told them of her brief but successful career as a speaker for the womens' suffrage movement. In an effort to give the conversation a friendly tone, she purposely avoided the mention of her involvement with temperance, although she had spent a great deal of energy helping to close down several notorious saloons and houses of ill repute in Washington, D.C. By the end of the evening Abigail Crowly understood why this young woman was such a prominent speaker for the cause. If Jubilee Hart could fire all the women of Wyoming with as much inspiration as she had instilled within Abigail with no more than her dinner conversation, then the success of the rally was well assured.

The two men were also inspired by the beautiful woman. Howard was fascinated by the way her bosom rose and fell as she spoke. He tried to imagine what it would be like to release her soft curls from their pins and to have a cascade of blonde hair fall loosely over her bare shoulders. While he watched Jubilee speak about her mission in Cheyenne, he calculated the limited amount of time he had in which to accomplish the task of adding this lovely to his list of conquests. Once, he even glanced briefly at his wife and was amazed to see a rosy glow of excitement flowering her pasty complexion. No doubt, Jubilee Hart was a true leader, and she had led Howard Crowly into a frenzy of wanton cravings from which he would not emerge until his fantasies became a reality.

The wind whipped around Chance Steele's six-foot frame as he stood outside the Railroad Inn and watched his dinner companions depart for the Crowlys' luxurious home on Carey Avenue. Jubilee Hart had left him inspired, too, but in a way that was as disturbing as it was pleasant. He had come to the inn with the hope of tantalizing her into a sweet soiree, if for no other reason than to boost his male pride. Though it was apparent that Howard Crowly shared his interests, Chance was appalled by the other man's obvious intent to seduce his house guest. Chance had the wild urge to run after the old man, grab him by the collar and warn him to keep his filthy hands off Jubilee Hart. He shook his head with aggravation. What craziness had invaded him that would cause such ridiculous ideas to circulate through his head? Howard Crowly's thoughts were no different than his own—except that Howard Crowly possessed something of a much greater value . . . respectability.

Chance Steele pulled his wool coat together tightly in an effort to shield himself from the cold wind and began to walk toward his saloon on 17th street. He reminded himself that he should be grateful that people like the Crowlys' even took the time to speak to him, let alone to socialize, with a man in his position. The last thing Chance needed right before the opening of his new saloon was to anger someone as prominent in Cheyenne as Howard Crowly, and especially over a woman! With sagging spirits, Chance let himself into the back entry of the saloon, which led to his private quarters. Depression was an unusual state of mind for the gambler, and he began to grow angry with himself—and at the woman who had brought about the strange emotions that were invading his mind and heart.

Why did the appearance of this blue-eyed beauty suddenly throw his world into a spin? Until today, Chance felt that he had climbed to the top of the fortune heap. In a few days, his saloon would open its ornately carved wooden doors to the citizens of Cheyenne. By that time, Jubilee Hart would be gone, and he would probably never set eyes on her again. He walked through the dark rooms of his private quarters, carefully, so as not to wake Jerrod. Chance paused and observed the sleeping teenager for a few minutes, while trying to ignore the guilt he felt whenever he glanced at the boy. There were worse places than the back of a saloon for a sixteen year old boy to live, Chance decided as he forced himself to move away from Jerrod's cot. Anyway, how could he have known that his brother and sister-in-law would get themselves killed by a tornado out in Kansas, and that he would end up with the boy?

With a heavy sigh, Chance quietly opened the door that led to the main room of the saloon. In the shadows, the elaborate crystal chandeliers and brocaded walls of blue and gold looked foreboding and garish. The gambler slumped against the smooth wood of the curved bar, and reprimanded himself for being in this low state of mind. At thirty-six years of age, and as the sole owner of this classy establishment, he was about to embark on a lucrative adventure. Until now, he had never owned anything besides the clothes on his back and a dog-eared deck of cards. With the exception of a small loan from Howard Crowly's bank, Chance had built most of the saloon with his own money. In an impulsive gesture, he slammed his hand against the polished bartop. Money was money! It didn't matter that a portion of his resources had been earned in card games that were less than fair. Money was power, and power was all that mattered — in any business!

He glanced up at the sober-faced nude woman who stared down at him from the huge painting that hung on the wall behind the bar. The sound of giggling coming from somewhere upstairs reminded him of the troop of prostitutes he had imported from St. Louis. They were not just ordinary hookers, either. Just as he had told Jerrod at the train station earlier today, these 'ladies' were the best money could buy. Everything in The Second Chance Saloon was of top quality — from the gaming tables to the employees. Chance had personally chosen furniture which was crafted from the finest wood, and all the card tables were covered with a rich green felt. Brass urns and statues decorated every corner, their shining opulence reflected in large mirrors that adorned the brocaded walls. Plush carpets covered every inch of flooring, upstairs and down, with a rich shade of blue — almost the same shade as Jubilee Hart's eyes, Chance thought with another bout of intense ag-

31

gravation.

He sipped a shot of brandy as he walked among the rows of tables and contemplated his tempestuous past and the hopes he had for a prosperous future. He had finally made it, hadn't he? So what if he had come to Wyoming with plans of buying land and cattle, and instead had used his hard-earned money to build a saloon and whorehouse? He drained the last of the brandy into his mouth, then forced the liquor down his throat. It left a sour taste in his mouth, or maybe it was just the return of the strange sense of defeat that had come over him in the past few hours. He could still buy that land someday, he told himself, and then Jerrod would have a proper home again. This thought made Chance feel somewhat better, because providing the best for his nephew was becoming more and more important to the gambler with each passing day. Perhaps it was because he never had a real chance to get to know the boy until the untimely death of his parents had sent the child in search of his only known relative. Before that, Chance's brother and his wife had asked Chance not to interfere with the boy's upbringing. And at that time, Chance had been too indebted to them to do otherwise.

Chance hung his head and forced the recollections of the past from his mind. There were things—and people—he did not want to remember; memories that were still too painful to dwell upon. The giggling from upstairs quieted, leaving the whole saloon in an eerie silence. Chance walked slowly back toward his private quarters. Tomorrow he planned to get better acquainted with his 'girls', and he wanted to speak to the trio of professional gamblers he had hired to keep the card games enticing. There was an endless amount of work to do in the next couple of days, but tonight he just wanted to go to bed and forget about everything . . . everything except his thoughts of the beautiful Miss Jubilee Hart.

Chapter Three

Chance Steele watched Ina Devine from across the room with mild interest. This morning he had placed her in charge of the other ladies. Close observation of the way she handled herself convinced him that he had made the right choice. The addition of the ladies was vital to the success of his new establishment, but he did not wish to be bothered with the petty problems of the women. By promoting Ina to position of Madame, she would be the person to whom the rest of the women would turn when there was a detail that did not need to concern the boss. Chance felt Miss Devine was the epitome of her chosen profession in appearance, and she appeared to have a mind as well — a combination not always found among these women.

When she noticed the direction of her employer's intent gaze, she returned his stare with a sultry look which exposed her innermost thoughts. When a bold smile parted her red lips, Chance noted how her orange-red hair clashed with the gaudy shade of red face paint she wore upon her mouth and across her pale cheeks. Though he was used to being in the company of women who frequently altered their natural assets, he could not help but wonder why they went to such elaborate lengths to set themselves apart from women who led more conventional lives. The shapely prostitute approached his table, and Chance did not allow his eyes to waver from her face. The expression she wore was an inviting one for a woman of her caliber, and normally Chance would not have hesitated to join her for a few hours of unrestrained passion. Yet, even with the grand opening of his saloon just a couple of days away, Chance's thoughts kept drifting away from the business at hand.

By the time Ina had paused before his table, Chance was furious with himself. He was allowing himself to be distracted by memories of that blonde hell-raiser again. Ever since he had spent the evening in the company of Jubilee Hart he had thought of nothing else. He kept envisioning the way her blue eyes lit up like flickering candles when she talked about her dedication to her work. And though he tried to resist it, his mind continuously painted detailed pictures of himself holding her in his arms, and of kissing those tempting pink lips. No paint on that soft mouth, he told himself.

He gave a rueful chuckle. Was he really foolish enough to think he could lure a woman like Jubilee Hart into his arms? Although he usually fulfilled his manly desires with women who worked as prostitutes and barmaids, he had also made love to a score of wealthy upper class ladies while he was employed on the riverboat. But they had been bored wives with little or no morals, and rich socialites who were either too homely or too insufferable to attract a man of their own station. Back in those days Chance had not been too particular in his choice of women. Even an ugly woman could be a valuable companion during a riverboat journey if she supplied him with an endless supply of spending money with which to indulge his immense passion for playing cards. Until a few days ago, Chance Steele had been confident there was not a woman alive whom he could not entice with his good looks and charm — regardless of her social status. His alliance with women like Abigail Crowly was proof of that belief, wasn't it?

Thinking about it now, however, Chance realized that women as intelligent and ambitious as Jubilee

Hart seldom crossed his path. Abigail Crowly was just another neglected wife, even more so than most wives, if Howard Crowly's behavior at the Railroad Inn the other night was any indication of the extent of his devotion to the poor woman. Almost everyone in Cheyenne was aware of Howard Crowly's lust for any woman other than his own wife. It was no surprise that the elderly lady responded with such enthusiasm to Chance's attention, even if he was just a saloon keeper and a gambler. Chance decided that he must be a real fool if he thought a successful woman like Jubilee Hart would ever consider seeing him again. She had only tolerated his presence at the inn because she was too much of a lady to do otherwise.

In the time it took Ina Devine to cross the expanse of the large saloon, Chance felt like he had just aged ten years. Why should he care if the haughty Miss Hart ever spoke to him or not, when there was a beautiful woman within his grasp, who could fulfill any man's deepest desires?

"A penny for your thoughts, Boss Man?" she asked in a deep southern drawl, which contained more than a hint of seduction. The satin of her low cut green dress dipped open, revealing her well-endowed bosom as she leaned down and placed her hands on the round tabletop.

Though the vision was not displeasing, Chance tore his gaze away from the heaving bosom which had been presented for his approval, and forced himself to look back up at Ina's face. Beneath the black layer of makeup which coated her lashes he noticed that she also had blue eyes. In desperation he searched their depths for any further similarities to the other eyes which had captivated him with their flashing blue radiance. But Ina's large eyes lacked the luster and fire of the royal blue eyes belonging to Jubilee Hart. In Ina's gaze he saw only a hungry longing, a look not unfamiliar for a woman in her profession. Ina Devine, like all her peers, was always surrounded by members of the

35

opposite sex who lavished her with attention, money and gifts. Yet they were the loneliest women upon the face of the earth. The men they associated with usually belonged to someone else, so there was seldom a chance for these 'ladies' to get to know anyone beyond the hour or two they spent in lustful intimacy.

Chance understood these women so well because in many ways he was their exact counterpart. Women of all ages constantly told him that he was a handsome man and he was as vain as any woman when it came to his appearance. Rarely was there a time when he went out in public wearing anything less than his Sunday best. His closet was filled with expensive suits, silk shirts and boots shined to perfection. Whenever he passed a mirror he always took time to check to see if his mustache was trimmed evenly or to make sure his wavy raven hair was not tousled and disorderly. Chance did not think these little vanities were inappropriate or prissy. His good looks were his major asset, and he knew it. His years on the riverboat had also instilled in him a keen insight which made him cunning enough to use his great asset to its fullest extent.

At this moment he knew that Ina would believe anything he told her, and an hour from now, she would do the same with the next man she met. The pretty redhead would pretend there had never been another man as important as the one she was with at that moment. And she would appear to be immune to the future, acting as though it didn't matter that this man's attention would cease to exist outside the bedroom door. Chance knew all of these things because he reacted with the same false pretenses whenever he was involved with a woman. He did not think Ina Devine was a stupid woman, so no doubt she understood all this, too. But Chance knew that even people like he and Ina Devine had feelings, and the last thing Ina would want to hear was that though he was looking at her, he was thinking about another woman.

"I was thinking about you, of course," he lied. Yet

even as the deceitful statement escaped from his mouth, Chance's thoughts were diverted by the fleeting image of Jubilee Hart's angelic face. He reminded himself of how ridiculous it was to hope that she would associate with him the next time they met. Since Chance's thoughts were more than just friendly toward Jubilee Hart, it was outlandish for him to think about her at all!

Ina's red lips smiled; her laugh was throaty and low. "Well then, we were thinking along the same lines. I was thinking about me too . . . about me and you, that is." Her brows raised in a suggestive arch and she leaned farther over the table, making the top of her dress fall open with an explicit view of her ample bosom.

Her pose left nothing for the mind to imagine. Even a strong-willed man would find it impossible to look away or divert his attention elsewhere, and where the opposite sex was concerned, Chance Steele had always been too weak for his own good. A defeated sigh was his only reply as he pushed back his chair and began to rise to his feet. Maybe Ina Devine could help take his mind off of that infuriating Jubilee Hart, at least for a short time. This was Chance's feverish hope as he took ahold of Ina's hand. "Haven't I shown you my private quarters yet?" he said in a quiet, husky tone.

"Not yet." She noticed the raspy sound of his voice, then became aware of the profuse heat of his palm as he began to escort her toward the doorway which led to his office and living area. Although she had never doubted that eventually they would rendezvous between the sheets, she had not expected such an anxious reception from her handsome new boss. A victorious feeling overcame her, since she was the first one of his 'girls' to be singled out by the debonair Mr. Steele. For one impulsive moment she even entertained the idea of becoming the sole property of her boss. Of course, she had been in the sporting business long enough to know that it was a rare occurrence for a man like Chance Steele to be content with one woman for any length of time.

"Nice, very nice," Ina said as she looked around the luxurious sitting room of her employer's private quarters. With few exceptions the room was decorated exactly like the rest of the saloon. The room was void of any personal effects—only a sofa and a couple of overstuffed chairs designated it as a living area. Although his previous activities were of no consequence to her, Ina still thought it was strange that a man who would have enough wealth to build this elaborate establishment would not display any mementos from his past. She shrugged her bare shoulders, reminding herself that she was not one to pry into anyone's private life. She had a few skeletons in her closet, too.

"Where's your boy?" she inquired as Chance held a glass of brandy out toward her.

"Nephew," he corrected, sharply. He turned away from the woman and grabbed the glass of brandy he had poured for himself. In one gulp he drained the dark liquid into his mouth, then poured another glass full before he pivoted back around. His mouth curled with a smile that almost seemed to be a snarl as he repeated, "He's not my boy. Jerrod is only my nephew."

Ina shrugged again. Son or nephew, it hardly mattered as long as he wasn't anywhere near. "Well, does he go to school, or what?" she asked, intent to learn the boy's whereabouts before they proceeded any farther. Though the young man was almost as handsome as his uncle, and Ina was not above introducing boys his age to the sweeter pleasures in life, she wanted to make sure there would be no interruptions when Chance Steele made love to her for the first time.

"He's running some errands for me," he replied, then polished off his second glass of brandy. A wave of ebony hair had fallen down on his forehead, and he pushed it back with his hand as he focused his dark gaze on the woman. A reckless smile teased about the corners of his mouth when he added, "And he probably won't be back for some time."

Ina did not need more of an invitation. She moved forward and took the empty glass from his hand. When she placed the glass upon the table behind him, she purposely pressed her body against Chance's lean frame in an intimate manner. She was much shorter than the gambler and had to toss her head back in order to look up at him. Her position placed her within kissable distance from Chance's mouth, so when she closed her eyes and pursed her bright red lips, it was evident that she expected him to take advantage of the situation.

Kissing her seemed to be the natural thing to do, yet Chance hesitated. He had kissed dozens of mouths like hers, and the unexpected memories came crashing through his mind like a avalanche. Only two conclusions were possible when a man continued to kiss this type of woman — one pair of red lips was indistinguishable from another and each kiss was no different from the last, or the next. Ina Devine's kiss would blend into the kaleidoscope of lips smeared with red paint, and the memory of making love to her would soon disappear into the sea of bodies Chance's tortured memory had collected through the years. But worst of all, Chance realized with a startling revelation, kissing Ina Devine would not take away his intense yearning to kiss the sweet lips of Jubilee Hart. Nor would making love to this flame-haired prostitute dispel any of the ache he felt in his heart whenever he thought about the blonde beauty.

"I — I can't," he said. His voice was strained and hoarse, and a heavy layer of perspiration blanketed his brow. Though his mind was going in a dozen different directions at once, he was coherent enough to know that he must have an explanation for his irrational behavior. "I forgot . . . I — I have an important meeting." In an attempt to put a safe distance between Ina Devine and himself, he took a staggering step backward. "I'm already late."

The rejected woman was too stunned to do anything

39

other than watch as her boss stalked through the door and left her standing alone in his sitting room. As the shock began to wear thin, fury began to cloud her thoughts. Just who did Chance Steele think he was dealing with? Maybe he did have to be somewhere else, but Ina Devine had been expecting much more from her boss than a tour of his living quarters. And perhaps—just perhaps—he was lying about his important meeting. Ina stomped back into the main area of the saloon and hurried up to her own room on the second floor. This morning Chance Steele had promoted her to a position of authority, and she surmised that she could not do her job to its full extent if she did not trust her employer.

Hastily, she rummaged through her armoire and yanked out a heavy woolen cloak. Chance Steele had asked the ladies to remain anonymous until the grand opening so they could be presented to the men of Cheyenne at the same time as the unveiling of the saloon. Abiding by his request, she had not stepped outside since her arrival, but now she would. The sound of the wind howling beyond the walls of the saloon told her of the frigid December temperature. There had not been time to organize all of her belongings either, and in the disarray of her room she could not locate her muffler and scarf. Time was wasting, however, and Chance Steele was already gone from the saloon. She told herself that she would have to go without the warmth of her muffler, and since the hood of her cloak did not provide much protection against the wind, her ears would just have to suffer.

When Ina rushed through the doorway of the saloon she was struck by a gust of wind that nearly drew the breath from her lungs. She had only been here a couple of days and already she despised the foul Wyoming weather. Luckily, her job did not require that she venture out into the elements unless absolutely necessary. Finding out if Chance Steele was lying to her *made* this exertion a great necessity. In an aggravated gesture,

Ina pulled the hood tight around her head and kept ahold of the loose head-covering as she made her way along the icy walkway. Her hands were freezing, but if she let go of her hood, the wind would reach her ears. She cursed at the weather under her breath while her eyes searched for some sign of her tall employer. Finding him among the townsfolk should not be difficult, she decided. His six-foot frame made him stand above many men, and his fancy attire definitely separated him from the hordes of cowhands and ordinary businessmen who walked the streets of Cheyenne.

Ina paused and raised up onto the toes of her pointed kid-skin slippers, scanning the crowd for a dark gray bowler hat. The cold from the icy street took a hard grip on the soles of her dainty shoes and worked its way up through Ina's whole body. A blinding shiver accompanied the chill and made her teeth bang together. She gritted her teeth until they stopped their wild chattering as another rush of anger overcame her. She knew without a doubt that before too long her boss would expect to continue with the liaison they had started today—men like him always came crawling back to the security of their own kind. But if he was lying to her about his important meeting, he would not find her such a willing partner the next time.

With another shiver and a huff of annoyance, Ina lowered her cold feet back to the ground. Where in this town would a man go for a business meeting? With all the businesses that lined this one street alone, Ina knew she would never find Chance Steele now that he had disappeared from her view. She started to head back toward the saloon when she happened to glance in the direction of the railroad tracks. The woman could not believe her good fortune when she caught a fleeting glimpse of her employer entering the front door of the Railroad Inn. *"What kind of meeting would be held at an inn?"* she wondered as she began to head in the direction of the tracks.

When she reached the Inn, her pace slowed as she

entered the busy establishment. She kept her hood secured around her face in an attempt to hide her identity in case she should happen to come upon her boss unexpectedly. Since there was no logical explanation for her to be here, he would know that she was following him. Using extreme caution, she stood to the side of the entrance which led to the restaurant and peered into the large dining area. At least half of the tables in the room were occupied by patrons who were being served a late lunch or had stopped by for a cup of coffee to warm themselves from the cold. The discovery that Chance Steele was nowhere in sight caused her ire to reach a new height. If he was not in the dining area, where was he? She swung around and stared at the second floor of the large inn. Was it possible that his meeting was with one of the guests who was staying at the hotel? But who? Were they male or female? Her mode of thought could only think of one reason why he would be in one of those rooms on the upper story of this structure, and she did not relish the idea that Chance Steele had rejected her for the company of another woman.

Fury drove her common sense away as she allowed her hood to drop away from her face, then twirled around and headed towards the front door. She was convinced he was in one of the upstairs rooms, and she was too angry to care if anybody else here at the inn noticed her presence. The same uncanny luck which had afforded her a glimpse of Chance Steele earlier, occurred a second time when she glanced in the direction of the conference room. The double doors leading into the large room were open and Ina could see the tall saloon owner standing in the middle of the room. She crept up to the entrance and repeated her careful observation from the side of the doorway. The room was filled with rows of chairs for the upcoming rally on equality. Chance Steele stood alone in the center aisle. His back was to Ina and it appeared he was staring at something toward the front of the room. Ina leaned a little farther out into the opening with the hope of see-

42

ing what, or whom, he was observing with such intensity.

Her inquiring gaze settled upon the large poster, which hung above the podium at the far end of the room. In bold black letters was the announcement about the suffrage meeting scheduled to take place tomorrow afternoon. But most important was the image in the center of the poster depicting the woman who was to be the guest speaker for the rally. Ina's heavily coated lashes narrowed with fury as she glared at the detailed print of the face. It was the woman from the train—that snooty blonde who thought she was so much better than everybody else. Ina and the rest of the girls were still laughing about their new employer's mistake at the train station the other day. They felt to be mistaken for a prostitute was a fitting fate for a woman who acted so high and mighty. But Ina's contempt for the uppity female did not explain what Chance Steele was doing here now.

Ina pondered several reasons as to why her boss would leave her at such an inappropriate time to come here and stare at a picture of Jubilee Hart. Was he waiting for someone to meet him here at the conference room? Surely he would not be meeting that woman! Ina threw a disgusted glance back up at the poster. The sound of Chance Steele's heavy sigh sent Ina into a panic—she was sure he had caught her spying on him. But he was still facing the picture and almost appeared to be in some sort of trance. Relief flooded through Ina when she was confident that he had not noticed anyone was watching his odd behavior. Curiosity was eating Ina alive, and made her even bolder. She leaned further into the room with the hope of seeing the expression the man wore upon his face. Without being discovered, Ina could only inch forward enough to observe Chance Steele's countenance from the side. His slumping shoulders and the melancholy tilt of his dark head provided her with enough of the clues she sought. She could only surmise that he had rejected her because he was pining for that blonde snob!

She backed away from the doorway and swung around. A fierce fire raged through her and only revenge would quench it. Chance Steele was obviously not the intelligent man Ina had thought him to be if he had fallen under the spell of a woman like that blonde do-gooder. If he was stupid enough to think that he could toy with Ina's affections when he was dreaming about another woman, he had a lot to learn. Though Ina decided his education should start without delay, she first intended to repay Jubilee Hart for a couple of things — such as the way she had treated Ina and the other girls during the train ride from St. Louis, for instance. But especially for the way her mere presence in Cheyenne had managed to interfere with Ina's passionate interlude with Chance Steele today.

By the time Ina had stomped back to the saloon she was not even aware of the cold that clung to her quaking limbs. Her anger toward Chance Steele and the blonde suffrage leader had her too upset to care about anything other than her hurt pride . . . and the retaliation that would make her feel much better.

Chapter Four

Jubilee was overcome by a great sense of satisfaction and excitement as she walked around the conference room. Abigail Crowly's committee had done a fine job of decorating the entire room with banners and posters depicting the suffrage issue. A podium stood at the front of the large room and was adorned with the patriotic colors of the American flag. Jubilee smiled up at her own likeness on the large poster behind the wooden structure and took a deep breath. She turned around and her gaze wandered out over the rows of empty chairs. In a couple of hours she hoped those chairs would be filled with women who had taken a precious bit of time from their homes and families to come here to listen to her speech. With the meeting of the territorial legislature just days away, Jubilee was amazed at how the women of Wyoming had not created more of a stir over the issue of equality. Only two other female speakers had preceded Jubilee to the Wyoming territory to talk about the suffrage issue. In the booming gold camp of South Pass City, northwest of Cheyenne, a woman named Esther Morris was a strong advocate of suffrage and devoted much of her time to promoting sympathizers for their cause. Regrettably, Mrs. Morris had wired Abigail Crowly to decline the invitation to be an honored guest at the Cheyenne rally, due to an illness in her family.

In Washington the impending bill had created a

great deal of gossip and joking, especially since the territorial governor of Wyoming was a bachelor. The ratio of males to females in the Wyoming territory was an overwhelming six to one. If women were granted the right to vote, the publicity the enfranchisement would attract might also interest more families, and hopefully, unmarried women to settle in the new territory. At least this was the fervent hope of the men who had taken the initiative to propose the bill. Jubilee had a feeling that today would be a memorable occasion for the women who assembled here, because she had a trembling in the pit of her stomach which suggested that something extraordinary was about to happen.

"Is everything satisfactory?"

Jubilee looked toward the doorway where Abigail had just entered and nodded her blonde head. "It looks very nice. I just hope enough women show up to make it worth all your hard work."

Abigail shrugged. "Well, the cold weather has certainly made a hardship for many of the women who planned to attend, but I think enough women will show up to make a difference. It *is* a shame that Mrs. Morris could not come, however." Her gaze wandered over Jubilee Hart's impeccable outfit, which was fashioned from a woolen material of pale pink. Without a doubt, the color of her attire was a perfect shade to compliment the young woman's rosy complexion. She had fixed her hair in a style which Abigail considered to be more respectable, with all of her long tresses woven into soft curls atop her head. The combination of Jubilee's pale blonde hair, flashing royal blue eyes and pink attire was breathtaking. Abigail Crowly had never felt so homely and old as she did when she foolishly compared her own appearance to that of the lovely speaker.

Jubilee sensed Abigail's sagging spirits, and she also noticed how the elderly woman had taken special care with her grooming today. Not only was she dressed in a fashionable gown of lovely green, but her faded gray hair was adorned with a beautiful comb of green and gold. Jubilee felt the woman deserved a note of recognition, especially since she was sure Howard Crowly never paid her any compliments. The thought of Howard made Jubilee fill with annoyance again. Her stay at the Crowlys' was a living nightmare as she constantly tried to avoid the old man's forward advances. He had no shame in his unyielding attempts to lure Jubilee into his unscrupulous clutches. During her short stay at the Crowly's, she had discovered her only escape was behind the locked door of the guest bedroom where she slept. Even then, on several occasions, she was certain she had heard someone — presumably Howard Crowly — trying the doorknob to see if it was open.

She had planned to remain in Cheyenne until after the meeting of the legislature, but staying any longer in the same house with that lecherous man was intolerable. Moving to a hotel, however, would undoubtedly hurt Abigail's feelings. While holed up in her room until Howard had left for his bank this morning, Jubilee had made the decision to cut short her stay in Wyoming and depart for Washington on tomorrow's eastward bound train. Howard Crowly, as well as Chance Steele, would be nothing more than unpleasant memories by tomorrow afternoon. Now why, she wondered with aggravation, did she even have to think about that low-down gambler again? She had been forced to be cordial to him at dinner the other night, but she had been fortunate enough not to see him again. If she had extended her stay in Cheyenne, she had planned to distribute her flyers about the evils of Bawdy houses upon a decent society all over town on the day of his saloon's grand opening. She was still fuming over the gambler's inexcusable mistake concerning her identity, and she thought she deserved some sort of retaliation. But now she only wanted to get away from the tension of staying at the Crowly home as soon as possible. With any luck, Chance Steele would not cross

47

her path before she left tomorrow. Yet she was surprised once again when his handsome visage flitted without an invitation through her mind once again.

"You look lovely today, Abigail," Jubilee said in earnest, while hoping to distract her thoughts from the raven-eyed gambler.

A flush of red colored Abigail's pale cheeks. She was not accustomed to receiving compliments from anyone — except Chance Steele, of course. She smiled gratefully at the younger woman. In spite of her husband's offensive behavior during Jubilee's brief stay in their home, Abigail had grown fond of the other woman. Not only did Abigail admire Jubilee for her unselfish work for women's rights, but she was also very grateful to her for the tactful way she dealt with Howard. She was not the least bit surprised when the young woman told her earlier today that she had decided to cut short her stay in Wyoming and leave as soon as possible. But she was disappointed that they had not had more time to become closer friends. As things were now, however, Jubilee's intended departure tomorrow would be the best thing for all of them.

"Do we have time to eat lunch before the guests begin to arrive?" Jubilee asked, remembering that she had not taken time to have breakfast this morning. Whenever she was preparing to give a speech she was usually too keyed up with excitement to remember simple things like eating until it was almost time to speak. Then, her stomach would begin to demand food with obtrusive noises, which not only distracted Jubilee from her speech, but also reminded her of her unhappy childhood and the times that she had gone without eating because her father had lost all their money in a card game. Now that she was responsible for caring for herself, she never denied herself food. She ate whenever she felt the slightest pang of hunger. Fortunately, she could eat all the rich delicacies she wanted and never add bulk to her slender form. On more than one occasion she had joked with friends that she would rather eat than have a beau. However, if the right man came along, Jubilee reasoned that she might forego a few meals once in awhile.

But as the years began to roll by, even Jubilee was growing doubtful that she would ever encounter the man of her dreams. She was twenty-five years old, a virtual old maid by the standards of her society. Her work for women's causes kept her too busy to look for a husband. Through the years Jubilee had grown far too critical of men, anyway. She hardly met a man whom she did not begin to compare to her no-good father. It seemed nearly all men had at least one of Ben Hart's worthless traits; they were either lazy and selfish, or too slick and polished. In some cases, they contained all of these bad afflictions — such as Chance Steele.

"If I ate a meal like you just did, I would burst my seams," Abigail joked as they exited from the dining room at the inn. She had picked at her fried chicken and mashed potatoes, while the slender blonde had polished off an entire plate of roast beef, carrots, and potatoes in a thick brown gravy. Jubilee had managed to find room for dessert as well.

Jubilee chuckled, but did not bother to make excuses for her hearty appetite. Instead, she began to go over her speech in her head once again as she and Abigail walked back toward the conference room. Waitresses were carrying platters of finger foods into the room for the guests, which were being placed on a long table that ran along the side wall. Inside the entrance Jubilee had arranged another long table with stacks of pamphlets concerning the suffrage movement. She had also left a pile of information regarding temperance among the leaflets. Even though she did not plan to speak on the subject of alcohol today, she never ignored the opportunity to promote the issue of abolishing the widespread use of whiskey.

"Those were just delivered by a young boy," one lady

guest said the moment Jubilee and Abigail entered the room. A hush immediately followed as the two women turned to see the focus of the women's attention. In the center of the table, which was covered with the leaflets and pamphlets, sat the most beautiful array of dark red roses that Jubilee had ever seen. At least two dozen sweet scented blossoms fanned out from an elaborate, footed crystal vase accented with feathery ferns of dark green.

"Are they for me?" she asked in a tone of uncertainty. All the women in the room nodded their head in reply, while their scrutinizing gazes watched her every move. When she spoke in front of large gatherings, Jubilee was accustomed to being on the center stage. But now, knowing that everyone's attention was focused solely on her and the elaborate bouquet of roses, Jubilee blushed like a child who had been caught in the middle of some mischievous deed.

"Is there a card?" Abigail Crowly inquired with dread. Would Howard be so hideously blatant as to send roses to Jubilee Hart, even when he knew that half the population of Wyoming would be here today?

Astonished by the huge bouquet, Jubilee did not realize Abigail's fears, nor did she think about how strange her next action would seem to the worried banker's wife. Jubilee snatched up the tiny white card, which was lying amongst the roses, and quickly unfolded the paper. A rush of heat inflamed her cheeks as she read the simple message scrawled across the paper. 'Good Luck today.' It was signed simply, and with only one name . . . 'Chance'. Jubilee's thoughts were not rational for a minute as her mind filled with half a dozen humiliating examples of what the other women would think if they knew who had sent her such an exorbitant, and intimate, gift.

"It's—it's unsigned." Her tiny discretion was a vain attempt to protect her own reputation, but her lie crushed Abigail Crowly.

The elderly female had no doubt that her womanizing husband had sent the roses as part of his latest ploy to overcome Jubilee's resistance. Thank God, the suffrage speaker was sensitive enough to conceal who was the sender of the flowers in front of the other women. But as the room began to fill with the women of Cheyenne, and with those who had braved the cold temperatures from the outlying communities, Abigail's thoughts began to turn from gratitude toward Jubilee Hart into a gnawing feeling of contempt for her scandalous husband. She lived in one of the nicest homes in Cheyenne, but she would gladly exchange it for a shack if her husband would give her just a fraction of the attention he lavished upon other women. Why, in their entire marriage of thirty-six years he had never given her a *single* rose!

Jubilee did not have a chance to converse with Abigail again once the rally began to get underway. She told herself that she would not allow thoughts of Chance Steele to distract her. After she had given her speech, she would return his gift without delay. But when she looked up and saw his tall frame saunter casually through the doorway of the conference room, she was overwhelmed by sight of him. The attire in which he was clothed, of dark brown trousers, brown and beige dinner-length coat and velvet vest of light tan, was subdued in contrast to his usual costume. His dark head was unadorned by the little round hat he normally wore, and his wavy ebony hair was combed neatly to the side of his forehead. A slight grin barely turned up the thin line of his black mustache, and his eyes twinkled with an air of amusement as he glanced around the room full of females. He was, Jubilee realized, the most handsome man she had ever known, even if he was one of the most despicable. As her gaze unwillingly moved over the entire length of his muscular body, she also noticed that a shiny gold watch-fob chain hung from his vest pocket. Images of her father once again

51

invaded her thoughts with faded recollections of the past. Ben Hart had worn a shiny chain from his vest pocket, too. But a time piece did not rest within the lining of his vest pocket. Instead, his pocket concealed a tiny derringer attached to the end of the chain. When accused of cheating in a card game, the gambler could rely on his hidden weapon to help him escape from the bloodthirsty opponent he had just cheated. What was lurking at the end of the gold chain that disappeared into the velvet pocket of Chance Steele's vest? Jubilee felt a growing curiosity to learn more about this man, whose appearance had caused her pulse to explode with wild anticipation.

With this unsettling thought, Jubilee tore her eyes away from the man, but not until she glanced at his face again. For a brief, wordless moment their gazes seemed to reach out across the room like a pair of fiery fingers, leaving Jubilee's whole being ablaze with a strange sense of affinity that she could not shake, not even after she forced herself to turn away from the man. When she extended her arm to welcome another suffragette, her hand trembled visibly. She could still feel his dark eyes watching her, but she was afraid to turn in his direction again — afraid that if she met his gaze she would not be able to look away a second time.

By the time Jubilee had made her way to the podium at the front of the room, the trembling in her hands had worked its way through her entire body. The pit of her stomach knotted with the contents of her large lunch and her knees quaked so violently her limbs felt as though they could not support her. Only the podium kept Jubilee from falling as she hung onto the wooden structure. She took a deep breath, while trying to clear her spinning senses. Was it just that Chance Steele reminded her so much of her dead father that made her feel so odd? Or was it something else . . . something Jubilee's tortured mind could not yet conceive?

With another breath from deep within her trembling

breast, Jubilee raised her eyes to the group who sat before her. She would not allow that gambler's presence to interfere with her speech today. Abigail's assumption that the cold weather would prevent many women from attending had been grossly incorrect. The large room was packed to capacity, filling every seat and leaving standing room only, with an abundance of male listeners in attendance, too. Yet, in this huge sea of faces floating out before her, the first person Jubilee's wandering gaze settled upon was the grinning countenance of Chance Steele. He was leaning against the table where the huge bouquet of roses sat. How appropriate! The lurking beast and his bait, Jubilee thought, hoping to draw upon the anger she felt because of his showy gift. In spite of her desperate attempt to summon up a tiny bit of the fury she had experienced when she first received the flowers, she was once again overcome by the fleeting sensation that the events of today would somehow influence the rest of her life.

Only the sound of the exuberant applause that filled the room snapped Jubilee Hart from her floundering trance. She pushed herself up to her full height and focused her attention on the reason she was standing in this prestigious position. These people were here to listen to her speak about an important issue that affected all of them. They had not fought the freezing temperatures just so they could watch her fall apart because some handsome, good-for-nothing gambler had sent her a vase of flowers, and was now staring at her from the back of the room with a teasing come-hither gaze.

Renewed with dedication to her cause, Jubilee began her carefully arranged speech. The words she spoke began with the various roles that women had played since the beginning of time. Women were—as quoted by an editor of the Montana Post in the mid-1860's—"The salt of the earth." But as the lovely speaker pointed out, as equals of mankind, women were not to be tolerated. A woman's place was in the home, but women such as

53

Jubilee Hart were determined to prove that a woman's place was anywhere she darned well pleased!

To help the audience understand all that women had sacrificed for their men, Jubilee told heart-wrenching accounts of the thousands of pioneer women who crossed the rugged mountains and lonely plains, leaving behind all traces of their civilized lives so that they could be at their men's sides. Not a dry eye remained in the room as Jubilee called upon her dramatic nature to emphasize the true meaning of the term, 'women's suffrage.'

A radiant smile parted Jubilee's pink lips as she waited for the applause to die down. She was always overcome with emotion, not only because of the admiration she received, but most of all, because of the immense meaning in the words she spoke. "Yes, we truly *are* the salt of the earth," she said when the room had grown silent again. "And without both men and women, there would not be mankind. Together, we are the bearers of life. But alone, women are expected to be the unselfish givers of our own youthful dreams. Our quest today is not to replace the men who run our country and make our cities safe. Indeed, our plight is not that complicated. For men can grant us the recognition we deserve and we would still yearn to cradle their sons against our breasts. We would not desert our homes in an attempt to overrule their businesses. We are considered to be the weaker gender—but we are weak only in the size of our stature, not in our intelligence and common sense. Our strength has evolved over thousands of generations, through perseverance, patience, and above all, suffering.

Jubilee accented the importance of her next words by slamming her clenched fist down upon the podium as she added, "We deserve the right to help decide the future of our great country by casting our votes in public elections. We no longer want to be merely the suffering counterparts of our mates! We are, and we demand to be their equals!"

Her last statement brought the seated guests to their feet. Applause and loud cheers signaled that Jubilee Hart had once again left her audience with a sense of spirit and pride for the women's cause. For several minutes the bravos and shouts continued as Jubilee clenched her hands together tightly and sighed with relief. It appeared she had been a success with this audience — but then, that was not an unusual occurrence. Nearly every group she was asked to address reacted with the same thunderous approval, and each time, Jubilee's confidence in herself increased. She tossed back her blonde head and laughed when several women in the audience held up brightly colored signs with various slogans about women's rights to vote such as, "Slaves to our men no more, give us the right to be equal!" and "If men want us to cook and clean for them, they'd better give us the vote!" The humor was lost to Jubilee when she remembered that even ex-slaves who were of the male gender had been granted the right to vote several years earlier.

After a few moments of enthusiastic applause the occupants of the large room began to settle down, reducing their shouts and cheers to excited chatter among their neighbors. Chance Steele began to inch his way toward the front of the room with the hopes of being the first to congratulate the beautiful speaker when she stepped out from behind the podium. In his effort to reach Jubilee Hart before she was lost among the crowd of swarming women, Chance did not notice the new arrivals who were now standing at the far side of the room beside the long table, which was laden with food. He too was caught up in the pulsing ebullience which vibrated throughout the entire room. His interest in the blonde suffragist was rapidly expanding from a nagging distraction to the height of indescribable longing. He yearned to know everything about her past, about the life she led back East, and most of all, about her dreams for her future. The gambler realized with a stunning revelation that he also wanted to be a part of her future, regardless of the differences in their social status. It *was* possible for complete opposites to fall in love, wasn't it? By the time he had maneuvered his way through most of the female bodies who blocked his path, he had determined that it was definitely possible, because his interest in Jubilee Hart involved much more that just the lustful cravings she had first aroused within him. Even though it had been many long years ago since he had experienced this foreign feeling, he still remembered what it felt like to fall in love.

The people who were standing near the food table were the first to notice the troupe of prostitutes who had positioned themselves along one side of the room. The surprising appearance of the women threw half of the crowd into a stunned silence. When the rest of the occupants in the room became aware that something was awry, the entire crowd reduced their loud chatter to a low murmur of hushed voices. Jubilee Hart was in the midst of the throng along with Chance Steele, who had managed to come within a few feet of her. They were among the last to realize that there was sudden change in the atmosphere of the crowd. It was not until Ina Devine spoke, however, that everyone was made aware that these uninvited women were here to cause trouble.

"What are y'all staring at," she demanded as she positioned her hands upon her rounded hips. Her purposeful gesture parted the woolen cloak she wore over her shoulders. She had chosen to garb herself in her most revealing gown, so that the swell of her bosom pushed brazenly through the front opening of the long cape. The distinct slur of her words was the result of the strong whiskey she and the other courtesans had chugged down in the hope that the bitter brew would add to the courage they needed for this appearance today. She giggled in a drunken manner, then took a step forward, still holding her hands on her hips and leaving

56

her exposed bosom open to the gaping eyes who swarmed before her blurry vision. When she moved ahead, the entire population of the room took a step backwards. Gamblers and saloon keepers such as Chance Steele and his fellow businessmen were accepted among most circles of society, but women who had been led down this same pathway of self-destruction were complete outcasts.

"Ain't we welcome here?" Ina continued as she tossed her head back and gestured toward the handful of prostitutes who stood behind her. "After all, we're women too, and we deserve a few rights of our own, don't we girls?"

Her comrades all shook their heads in agreement, but it was apparent that the other 'girls' were not too sure as to why they were there. After a few drinks Ina had bullied them into accompanying her to this meeting to confront Jubilee Hart. She had baited them with the information that the uppity blonde was invading their territory by trying to seduce their handsome boss. These hussies thought nothing about having decent women's husbands in their rooms for an hour or two, but they were selfish when it came to sharing the gamblers and saloon keepers who were their own peers. When they had agreed to come to the inn with Ina to have a public showdown with that woman from the train, however, they had not anticipated encountering such a large group. Nor had they realized that they might face a confrontation with their new boss, either. But before Ina had another opportunity to make a greater spectacle of herself, Chance Steele had worked his way through the crowd, and was at her side.

Ina, incapacitated by liquor, giggled when the tall man grasped ahold of her arm. She slumped against his hard body, then threw her head back to look up at him. "Hello, Boss Man." Her smile began to fade when she met the unyielding glare contained within his raven gaze.

"You're making a fool of yourself, and you are making me look bad as well," Chance said between tightly gritted teeth. With the grand opening of his saloon only one day away, he could not afford to be an enemy to the entire female population of Wyoming. He knew at once what had initiated Ina's behavior. Apparently she thought this charade would repay him for running out on her the day before, but to air her anger in public was not something Chance Steele would tolerate, especially by one of his own employees. "It's time to go," he added in a tone so saturated with ice that his words sent a shiver down Ina's spine. Still, she permitted the liquor to reduce her rationality to a state of nonexistence.

"Consortin' with the likes of that phoney Jubilee Hart will make you look alot worse, Boss Man."

Her statement cut into Chance like a saber, and caused his raven eyes to narrow with deadly intent. Ina had already overstepped her bounds by coming here to spew out her anger at him, but for her to include Jubilee Hart in her retaliation ploy was completely inexcusable. His hold on Ina's arm tightened, slowly, until he saw her eyes widen with surprise. He had never even considered striking a woman before now, so it was only her gender which kept her from receiving the slap that Chance felt she deserved. Ina Devine, however, was not worth more public humiliation. He leaned close to her and spoke in a quiet tone. Though his lips barely moved, Ina could not miss the unspoken threat flashing from within his piercing gaze. "We'll discuss this in private because all of us are leaving now. But, I can assure you that your association with my establishment will be on the line if you say one more word."

His declaration caused Ina to sober up as quickly as if he had tossed a bucket of ice water in her face. She had wanted to put a damper on Jubilee Hart's big hullabaloo for two reasons; she did not like the uppity blonde suffragist, and because she hoped that her daring ploy would impress upon Chance Steele how deeply she had been affected by his rejection yesterday. Most of the gamblers Ina had known throughout the years were sneaky and secretive, but they also welcomed a display of public recognition. To have more than one or two women vying for their attention at the same time was usually a welcome event for these devil-may-care men. She had underestimated Chance Steele's degree of competitiveness, however. He was the most dangerous type of gambler, she realized, searching his dark eyes for a hint of the excitement she had hoped to stir up within his gaming nature. Instead, she saw the fury collect in his unwavering gaze like black storm clouds, and it was too late to undo her mistake. She was wrong to have assumed *anything* about her new boss. This man was not a gambler simply because he enjoyed taking chances — whenever Chance Steele played, he intended to win.

When Ina felt him let go of her arm it was almost as painful as if he had slapped her in the face. She threw a quick glance at Jubilee Hart, and was filled with regret over her rash action to come here today. Since her drunken escapade had backfired, Ina was expecting to see a victorious look upon the blonde woman's face; instead, she saw an expression of pity. Nothing had turned out as she had planned — Chance Steele was not flattered by her performance, and Jubilee Hart's reaction was even more baffling. But worst of all was that Ina was the one who was humiliated even though she had not thought it was possible for anything — or anyone — to ever lower her self-esteem again. For years she had believed there was nothing left in this world that could shock or embarrass her. But Chance Steele and Jubilee Hart had just proven her wrong.

Ina bowed her head and turned around toward the rest of the prostitutes who were still standing in front of the food table. Their feeling toward the woman who had convinced them to come here was evident in the accusing glares that were directed at her from their heavily painted eyes. The whiskey Ina had consumed earlier was now causing her head to feel as though it was spinning out of control. The angry faces of her co-workers were nothing more than a conglomeration of blurry red lips and cheeks swimming before her blue eyes. She tried to force her gaze to settle upon the platters of carefully arranged vegetables and cold meats and little plates with wedges of pie sitting on them. Once she was able to sort out a fraction of her drunken thoughts, she began to believe that as soon as they returned to The Second Chance Saloon, Chance Steele would probably tell her to pack her bags and head back to St. Louis. Well, she didn't like Cheyenne anyway. And she still did not like Jubilee Hart. To hell with leaving here with dignity, Ina's foggy mind decided. She reached for the nearest slice of pie.

Chapter Five

Jubilee exhaled the suffocating breath she had been unconsciously holding while she tried to anticipate Ina Devine's next move. The woman had just insinuated that she was having an affair with the saloon owner, but her accusation had not yet sunk into Jubilee's turbulent thoughts. At this time she was consumed only by her vast concern for the people who had come to hear her speak. Relief flooded through Jubilee when the red haired prostitute backed down from her employer and turned away. The rally had been an overwhelming success until now, so Jubilee was praying the entire event would not be ruined by this group of hussies. If they left without any further disruption, the effect of Jubilee's speech would not be spoiled.

With Ina Devine's apparent withdrawal, Chance turned to face Jubilee again. The blonde speaker did not wish to meet his gaze, but she was helpless to stop her eyes from seeking out his face. As they stared at one another the innuendo Ina had just made about Jubilee's involvement with the gambler began to wash over her. Her relief over Ina's retreat became a confused mixture of anger and embarrassment as the prostitute's words echoed through her mind over and over again. She did not want all these good people who had come here to listen to her words of wisdom to leave with the belief that she was a fraud who only pretended to be proper and respectable. After Ina Devine's false declaration, they would think she was nothing more than a frivolous trollop who consorted with the likes of Chance Steele.

While the mismatched couple continued to gaze at one another from across the crowded room, Jubilee could not retain her rage against Chance Steele. Ina Devine had corralled all of her fury, but Jubilee's amorous feelings for Chance Steele were growing more powerful with each passing second. During the short span of time while their eyes were in contact, Jubilee forgot that this man was a gambler and a saloon keeper. Nor did she care. Perhaps this wondrous new feeling of affinity she was experiencing toward this man would have extended past this moment — and beyond this room — if it were not for the piece of pumpkin pie which was targeted at Jubilee's unsuspecting face.

Jubilee stood frozen to the spot for what seemed like a very long time before the shock wore off and she was able to realize what had smacked her face with such malice. However, it did not take her long to figure out who had thrown the gooey confection at her. By the time Jubilee finally reached up and wiped the pumpkin away from her eyes, a major battle had erupted around her. She was still too stunned to move, but she watched the pillars of Cheyenne's society charge towards the food table where the uninvited group of prostitutes still huddled. As the chaos raged around her, an array of thoughts were going through Jubilee's mind, but not one of them made any sense. She couldn't believe what a good aim Ina Devine possessed. Why, she had thrown that slice of pumpkin pie for at least twenty feet, and she had still managed to hit a bullseye! Could pumpkin pie make a person blind? Jubilee's mind was floundering. As another piece of pie whizzed past her head, Jubilee also worried that the russet colored pie would discolor her pale blonde hair. The crazy image of herself with hair as orange as Ina's fake tresses made her snap out of her shocked trance.

In disbelief, Jubilee looked at the fiasco ensuing around her. The room had become a war zone of flying pie, ham, and turkey, along with pellets of corn, beans and potatoes. The prostitutes numbered only a dozen, and the room contained well over a hundred people who were attending the rally, so Jubilee could only assume that the good folks of Wyoming had gone to battle for her after Ina Devine had thrown the pie. Yet now it was impossible to determine who was aiming at whom as the food fight became a free-for-all, and everyone was slinging handfuls of food at anyone who stepped into their way. A sick feeling came over Jubilee and she moaned in agony. How could something so terrible have happened?

Her heart took a violent plunge in her chest as Abigail Crowly grabbed onto her arm. "Let's get out of here," the elderly woman said in a panicked tone, while she tugged ferociously on the suffragette to follow her.

Jubilee's startled eyes flew up to Abigail's head, where the elderly woman's gray hair was coated with the remains of a piece of juicy apple pie. The sticky stuff was hanging in straggly strands around her pale face. The anger which had failed to surface while she was still engulfed by shock intensified as Jubilee stared at the frail-looking woman. How dare those trollops come in here and disrupt the lives of these decent people! Her flashing blue gaze burned with fury as she glanced around the room. The men who had been attending the speech were doing their gallant best to calm the enraged females, but an aura of hostility reined over the entire room.

Jubilee did not see Chance Steele—nor his troupe of troublemaking prostitutes—anywhere among the soiled crowd. She clenched her hands into tight fists as she decided it would be just like their cowardly hides to start a fight, then turn tail and run once the damage was done. In dismay, Jubilee continued to look around at the mess as her anger increased. The food was completely gone from the table, and was now splattered in grotesque decorations against the walls, and in slippery globs across the shiny planks of the floor. Traces of the bounty were blotched upon the fine dresses the women wore, leaving permanent stains to remind them all of this horrible day. When they remembered this day, Jubilee thought, they would also recall Ina Devine's devastating accusation.

"Come on, Jubilee," Abigail pleaded. The older woman feared that if she did not distance herself from this place immediately, she was sure to have an attack of some sort. Still, she would not desert her obligation to look after her houseguest. What would Howard think when he heard about this at the bank? Abigail had thanked God when Howard told her this morning that he might not be able to attend the rally because of a business meeting he had scheduled for today. She was grateful not to have to contend with her unfaithful mate in the midst of all these females, but now she was equally thankful that he had not been here to witness the awful conclusion of this meeting. Howard thought females to be mindless and only useful for pleasing a man, anyway. She knew his placid attitude toward her interest with the suffrage issue would be short lived and before long he would forbid her to pursue any further involvement with voting rights. After hearing an account of today's events, he would undoubtedly reaffirm his notions about women's limited roles in a world he considered to belong solely to men.

Jubilee's wrath continued to cloud her thoughts as she allowed Abigail to drag her toward the back entrance of the conference room. She felt as if she should try to salvage what remained of the day, but she did not know what to do or say to make up for the calamity caused by Ina Devine. Besides, now that the heat of the battle had begun to cool down, most of the women were rushing out of the front entrance of the room in mortification over their loss of dignity and control. The uncivilized actions of that prostitute had provoked them into acting like a bunch of savages, and this was not a pleasant thought for these respectable females, who considered themselves to be among the most elite citizens of their new territory. Although Jubilee Hart had not tossed one morsel of food, she too felt as lowly as if she had single-handedly destroyed everything in sight. Casting one more sorrowful glance back over her shoulder as she followed Abigail Crowly from the room Jubilee noticed—ironically—that someone had knocked over the huge bouquet of roses Chance Steele had sent to her before the rally. The beautiful crystal vase was lying on its side on the table where the pamphlets and leaflets were now a soggy mass of paper from the spilt water. Delicate red blossoms were scattered across the grimy floor, lending a forlorn epitaph to the day's events. By the time the two women had grabbed their cloaks and fled out the back door of the inn, Jubilee was certain her career was as dead as those trampled roses.

"I'll never be able to show my face in public," she cried, emphasizing her statement by throwing her hands over her face.

Abigail Crowly was more concerned with getting them to the warmth of her home, rather than standing behind the inn in the freezing cold while Jubilee Hart wallowed in self-pity. But how could she blame the woman? Today would not be beneficial for Jubilee Hart, or for the pertinent issues concerning all of the women in the country. Men who thought as Howard did would use today as an example of how temperamental and unrestrained females could be in tense situations. Abigail shivered with cold, and also with a sense of defeat. Rather than impressing upon the men of Wyoming how women were their intelligent equals, today's disastrous event just might set women's rights back a hundred years or more!

"This will not seem so bleak when we are away from here," Abigail lied in an attempt to hurry the blonde toward Carey Avenue. "We'll have some tea and pie— oh dear!" the woman gasped without thinking. She glanced out of the side of her eye at the strands of her gray hair, which the chilling air had rapidly frozen into brittle strands of apple pie remnants.

"I'll never be able to eat pie again," Jubilee vowed, hastening her steps. "I'll never eat again, period!" The two women continued to quicken their steps until they were practically running through the frozen streets. The Crowly house was one of the most welcome sights either of them had ever seen as they rushed inside and slammed the door on the rest of Cheyenne.

"I'm ruined — my work is finished, washed up, all because of that horrible, disgusting woman." Jubilee collapsed against the wall, and crossed her arms across her bosom. Her next thought was of Chance Steele. She reminded herself that he was not innocent of blame, either. Ina was in his employ, and that made her actions partly his responsibility.

Jubilee squeezed her lids together, hoping to wipe away the handsome image of that infuriating man. For a few moments back there in the conference room, Jubilee had found herself hypnotized by his mischievous ebony gaze. Now, she convinced herself it had meant nothing. Chance Steele was a master at seducing people with his cool and well-rehearsed mannerisms. How could she have been stupid enough to imagine that she had observed something more meaningful in his eyes when they had stared at one another for those few foolish moments? Jubilee felt the swell of tears pushing against her lids. She needed to cry to rid herself of the tremendous sorrow she felt over today's events, but she also wanted to be certain that her tears were not because of that horrible Chance Steele!

"You have every right to cry," Abigail said in a sympathetic voice as she patted the other woman's shoulder gently. Her own eyes were filled with a film of tears too, so it was easy to understand Jubilee's torment.

Jubilee's eyes flew open, and her chin protruded with anger when she forced her mind to function more sensibly. She could not, however, prevent the hot tears from rolling down her smooth cheeks. "It's just that I'm so humiliated over everything that happened today. All the work I've done for my sister suffragettes was lost because of that awful woman. But that's not the worst of it!" She rubbed at the aggravating tears with a furious swipe of her hand, adding, "Everyone is going to believe that I've been consorting with that low-down gambler while I've been here in Cheyenne."

Abigail continued to pat the woman's shoulder, though her simple gesture was of little consequence. The older woman hated to agree with Jubilee, but her assumption was probably correct. Ina Devine's brief remark, linking her boss with the blonde suffragist, would certainly have tongues wagging throughout the town. "Well, gossip is not important when you know the truth," Abigail said. But once the words had left her mouth she realized how comfortless her statement must sound to Jubilee Hart. She was planning to leave Cheyenne tomorrow, but her departure would also leave behind many questions and speculations about what had happened between her and the raven haired gambler.

The same thoughts were going through Jubilee's tortured mind. How could she prove that Ina was wrong when she was two thousand miles away? There had to be a way for Jubilee to combat Ina Devine's accusation, while at the same time, regaining the respect of her peers. She did not have a chance to consider her dilemma any longer though, because Howard Crowly burst through the front door, along with an icy blast of wind from the storm that was brewing outside.

"Good God!" he said while he slammed the door shut behind him. He shook off his long coat and tossed it at his startled wife. "I came as soon as I heard what happened." Howard pushed past the two women, who still stood in the front entry, and walked into the adjoining parlor. He turned impatiently. "Well, I've heard several different accounts of what happened. Now, I want to hear your side of the story. And I do hope your version is not as outlandish as what I've already encountered." After a disgusted look at the food that was still caked all over the faces of his wife and houseguest, Howard leveled his sights on Jubilee with an accusing glare.

His patronizing attitude enraged Jubilee to new heights of anger. He did not have to voice his position about today's calamity. The expression on his face was proof enough that he had already drawn his own conclusions from the gossip he had heard before coming home. With her face layered in streaks of pumpkin pie it was hard to project a dignified presence, but Jubilee mustered up a shred of pride as she tossed her head up and met Howard Crowly's unwavering eyes. "Your wife and I can relate to you a truthful account of what occurred today. Or, you can believe whatever you choose to believe. Because," Jubilee pointed her slender finger in his direction before continuing to speak. "I will not waste my breath trying to explain it to you if you have already chosen to listen to wild tales and vicious gossip."

Howard was left speechless by Jubilee's firm declaration. He knew she possessed a fiery nature, but he had not imagined that she would challenge him while in the presence of his wife. Ever since her arrival he had noticed that she went to great lengths to avoid hurting Abigail's feelings. She resorted to even more drastic measures to avoid him. Howard grew infuriated every time he saw their guest dogging Abigail like a devoted puppy in an attempt to avoid being alone with him. He grew even more furious at night when she barricaded herself in her room until she heard Abigail's voice in the morning. Howard had almost given up his merciless quest to overcome Jubilee Hart's resistance. Now, however, he was once again enticed by her display of anger and he renewed his vow to conquer this beauty before her departure from his home.

"Please accept my apology for my rash behavior," he said to the surprise of both women. "I'm sure the gossips of Cheyenne are having a heyday, but I honestly wish to hear the true account of what happened at the rally." Howard hoped to convince the ladies he was sincere by converting the hard, angry expression he had previously worn upon his face into one of repentence. When Jubilee weakly nodded her head in gratitude,

Howard was certain his ploy was working. His rigid frustration began to soften as he envisioned all the lustful possibilities the impending nightfall might bring.

Both women were anxious to explain their identical versions of what had actually taken place at the rally — with the exception of one minor detail. Neither of them mentioned the bouquet of roses that had been delivered to the conference room shortly before the event. Jubilee omitted this bit of information for fear that Howard would think Ina Devine's accusation had some ring of truth to it. And since Jubilee hadn't confided in her about who had sent the roses, Abigail did not mention the flowers because she was still convinced they had been sent by her faithless husband.

When they were finished with their detailed accounts, Howard was more intrigued by the spirited blonde than ever before. Even without the mention of the roses, he was also wondering if there was some basis to Ina Devine's appearance at the rally. Chance Steele was no different from himself. Perhaps the prostitute had overheard some suggestive remark her boss made about the blonde suffrage speaker. Or maybe — just maybe — there was something more to Ina Devine's story. He had no idea what his house guest did when he was away at work, but he could not imagine that a woman as lively as Jubilee Hart would just sit around all day and watch his wife conduct her boring daytime routines. Had Jubilee Hart found a more exciting way to spend her days while she was visiting Wyoming?

Howard Crowly nodded his head and cleared his throat, hoping to disguise the wayward direction of his thoughts. He had not heard the last of the women's interpretation of Ina Devine's actions, but then, he was not paying much attention any longer. "Well, it was unfortunate, I agree. But you know how jealous and frivolous you females can be at times."

His nonchalant dismissal of the incident made both women aware that their explanation had been wasted on Howard. He merely wanted to pacify them by listening to what they had to say, and now he was ready to move on to another issue, which he considered to be of far greater importance.

"What's for dinner?" he asked, leaning forward and sniffing at Jubilee's pumpkin-hued complexion. "Smells luscious," he added with a sly wink.

Jubilee stepped back, while glaring at him through narrowed lashes. "I'll be in my room," she announced, making way for a quick exit from the parlor. As she rushed past Abigail, she said in a low voice, "Please excuse me from dinner tonight. I don't feel up to eating." She did not need to elaborate, because Abigail did not have an appetite either.

Alone in the guest bedroom Jubilee crossed her arms over her bosom and shivered in spite of the heat from the fireplace. She had heard the Crowlys retire to their own bedroom some time ago, but she did not feel as though she would be able to sleep at all tonight. A disintegrating log in the fireplace popped sharply and caused her to jump with alarm. Outside, the wind howled like a savage beast, and the gusts made the whole house shake. The heavy black clouds which had filled the sky shortly before nightfall had forewarned that another snow storm was moving across the Wyoming plains and would undoubtedly hit the town sometime during the night. Jubilee was frightened again by another gust of wind that rattled the walls of the two story house. The Wyoming weather was atrocious, she decided as she walked to the window and peeked out through the center of the lace curtains. A heavy veil of snow made visibility impossible, and because of the violent wind, the snow appeared to be falling sideways rather than from the sky overhead.

Jubilee shook her head and shivered again. Although it snowed in Washington D.C. during the winter months, she had never witnessed as fierce a storm as this Wyoming blizzard. Her thoughts of her home in the East made her feel more depressed than ever. Compared to the Crowlys' large house, the place where Jubilee resided was not much of a home, but she had determined long ago that she did not need to occupy a big empty house to remind herself that she was alone. Dreams of having a home and a family had a way of sneaking into her thoughts every so often. But to rid herself of the emptiness the dreams evoked, Jubilee usually tried to replace her musing with memories of her own horrible childhood. As the years began to roll along, and Jubilee immersed herself in her work, the daydreams were becoming easier to dismiss.

In her travels, she occasionally encountered other women who, for one reason or another, had never married. Unfortunately, many of these women were embittered by their loneliness, giving a substantial meaning to the term 'Old Maid'. Jubilee constantly told herself that she would not allow herself to become ruled by a sense of defeat because of the nontraditional role she lived as an unmarried woman. Besides, there was still a possibility that somewhere in this big world there was a man who was capable of overcoming her resistance. He would have to be the exact opposite of her worthless father, however!

Jubilee stretched her weary body out upon the crotcheted covering on the bed and placed her hands behind her head. Sometimes she wondered why she felt such a relentless urge to prove to herself and to everyone else how strong and independent she could be. Maybe everything would be easier if she had a man to take care of her and to share her life. A disgusted expression scrunched up Jubilee's pretty face with this unexpected thought. She never wanted to be at a man's beck and call as her mother had been, or like the poor woman down the hall. Abigail Crowly might have a lovely home, but living with a man like Howard Crowly made Jubilee's crowded room at the boarding house seem much more appealing. Jubilee was amazed that the selfish man even allowed Abigail to have any involvement with the women's movement at all. Affording his wife one interest outside of caring for him must be his way of easing his own guilt, Jubilee decided. Her contempt for the banker increased and her affection towards Abigail expanded.

In some ways, Abigail Crowly reminded Jubilee of Miss Gurdy who ran the boarding house where she resided in Washington D.C. They were both sweet, gray-haired women who were kind to everyone they met, but—a frown drew Jubilee's freshly-scrubbed face into an expression of aggravation—Miss Gurdy was drastically different from Abigail Crowly in other aspects. No man would ever treat Miss Gurdy the way Howard Crowly treated his wife. Jubilee rose from the bed to stoke the waning fire. While she stirred the disappearing embers, and added a couple of extra logs to the flames, she thought about the spirited Miss Gurdy again. During the five years that Jubilee had resided at the boarding house, the two of them had become the best of friends. There was not another woman alive whom Jubilee admired more than Miss Gurdy, and on this cold, wintry night, Jubilee missed her terribly. She smiled to herself as she recalled the old woman's constant predictions. . . . "Someday, Jubilee, you mind my words!" Miss Gurdy always said. "Some handsome man is going to come along and marry you so fast that you won't have time to compare him to your father. And it won't matter anyway, because no two men are alike." Of course, Jubilee always disagreed with her, then changed the subject by reminding Miss Gurdy of her unmarried status. To which Miss Gurdy would retaliate by reminding Jubilee that Almighty God had determined her fate over forty years ago by taking away her only true love in a tragic accident two days before their wedding. Their bantering over this issue had become a favorite pastime as they sat in the parlor and shared a late night snack.

The thought of food, combined with the hollow feeling in Jubilee's stomach, reminded her that she had skipped dinner. The idea of eating had not been appealing for a while after observing the rambunctious food fight at the inn. But now the idea of suffering through the long cold night without a bite of food seemed unthinkable. Surely the Crowlys were sound asleep, and no one would be the wiser if she made a quick raid of the cupboards. She smiled with amusement when she recalled how Abigail's mention of pie had horrified the two of them earlier. Pie of any flavor sounded scrumptious now, Jubilee decided, as she unlocked her bedroom door and peeked out into the quiet hallway. Sneaking past Howard Crowly's bedroom door even sounded tempting, and her smile widened at the challenge. Being the daughter of a devoted gambler was not something Jubilee was proud of, but she could not deny that she was Ben Hart's offspring when she was overcome by the wild urge to throw caution to the wind, and place all her bets, at one time, down upon the table.

Chapter Six

In her anxious desire to satisfy her gnawing hunger, Jubilee did not think to grab her dressing gown or don her slippers. She regretted this omission the instant she reached the bottom of the stairway. The rooms downstairs were noticeably cooler than the upper story, even though the fireplaces had been well stoked for the long cold night. Jubilee wondered if the wind ever stopped blowing in Wyoming as she heard the unrelenting gales beat against the house. A shiver shook her body, which was clad only in a white flannel gown. She hesitated at the bottom of the stairway and debated whether or not to go back up to her bedroom to grab her robe and slippers.

The upper floor was silent and dark, so Jubilee decided she would rather not take the chance of making any unnecessary noises that might wake Howard Crowly. She planned to find herself something to eat, then head right back up to her room. Surely, she would not freeze to death in that short a time. As she tiptoed toward the kitchen, a sense of loss filled Jubilee. As a child she had dreamed of living in a big house like this, but when she was growing up she had never resided in anything other than rented houses that had barely accommodated her family. At times, the Hart family had been forced to rent a room in a hotel, and on occasion they even stayed in the back room of the saloon where her father was working for their keep. It was these unhappy memories that Jubilee despised the most about her youth. Laying in bed late at night, her young ears used to listen to the sounds of the saloon rowdies as they caroused, drank and played cards. Every so often the roar of a gunshot or two would explode above the rest of the loud noises, which usually signaled that someone had been caught cheating at a game of cards. With the outburst of gunfire, Jubilee would be paralyzed with fear that her father was the one who was at the receiving end of the bullet.

But Ben Hart was not so fortunate—a quick and sudden death was not to claim his life. Years of abusing his body with the vile alcohol he consumed each day would cause him to die a slow and painful death as the poison ate steadily away at his innards, destroying his health and finally, his reason.

Once in the kitchen, Jubilee wasted no time in hurrying to the pot-bellied stove that stood in the center of the room. She stood as close to the heat emitting contraption as possible, and tried to erase the painful recollections of her younger years as she attempted to warm her chilled body. A sound from somewhere behind her nearly sent her through the roof and choked her with terror as she quickly turned around and glanced at the doorway which led into the kitchen. She drew in a deep breath of relief when only emptiness greeted her fearful eyes. It must have been the wind again, she told herself, while trying to calm the rapid pounding of her frightened heart. Still, the thought of Howard Crowly sneaking up on her through the darkened house overcame her with a sense of panic. She felt a grave urgency to return to the sanctuary behind her locked bedroom door as she scurried toward the cupboards. The first thing that came into her mind was the apple pie she had helped Abigail bake the day before. Oh, it didn't matter that just a short time ago she had thought she would never be able to even look at a piece of pie again. Now in the grip of her hunger, Jubilee decided she could manage to force down at least one tiny sliver of pie.

The appetizing smell of baked apples and cinnamon alerted her to the pie's whereabouts as soon as she began rummaging through the cupboards in the dim light of the wood-burning stove. She raised up on her toes again and carefully lifted the pie tin from its hiding place. As she turned around with her bounty she heard another noise from the doorway. She was frightened so badly by the sudden disturbance that the pie plate fell from her shaking hands and crashed to the floor at her bare feet. In a numb stupor she stared at the glob of apples and crust for an instant before her dread filled gaze raised up to seek the source of her terror.

"Howard! You startled me!" she gasped in a high pitched voice, which exposed the horror she felt at his unwelcome appearance. Inwardly, she cursed at her stupidity for presenting him with the opportunity to get her alone, knowing he had been waiting for this ever since she arrived at his home.

With a lecherous swagger, Howard entered the kitchen and chortled, "You sure are having a rough time with pie today." He stopped several feet in front of the unmoving woman as his devouring eyes traveled over her modest attire. Clad only in the white gown, and with her pale hair floating loose around her shoulders, she looked like an angel, and the sight of her aroused an ache of devilish proportions within Howard's loins. He licked his lips in a most vulgar manner, then smiled with a wicked sense of satisfaction as he felt his manhood swell within the confines of his pajama bottoms. His patience had prevailed, and Jubilee Hart had definitely been worth the wait. He yearned to run his anxious fingers through the golden tresses that cascaded down her back, and to touch her in places that would make her ache for him as desperately as he craved her touch.

He took another step forward as Jubilee jumped back. The kitchen counter halted her retreat as her backside pressed against the barrier and caused her terror to envelope her in a blanket of doom. There was no

76

escape other than to try to reason with him, but the strange glint reflected in his eyes told Jubilee that his lustful thoughts had stolen away any sense of decency or reason Howard Crowly might have possessed. "I— I'd better clean up my mess. Bu—but there is no need for you to stay—you can go back to bed," she said. Her voice was still weak from fright, but she knew that words were her only hope of stopping him.

A sly chuckle escaped Howard's curled lips as he dismissed the woman's suggestion for him to leave. The curve of his evil grin remained fixed upon his lips, while he unconsciously toyed with the belt that tied around the waist of his finely tailored silk robe and pajamas. He had met with resistance from women before, but he was not easily deterred once he had his mind set on something. Usually, he was content to limit his endless cravings to extreme bouts of flirtations, which served to sooth his aging ego. On occasion, though, he did encounter a woman who fueled him with more than just a mild case of ego-altering desires. To entice and conquer a female who resisted his advances, Howard had learned to effectively use his position of power and his well-endowed pocketbook. There was always something these deprived women of the rugged prairie yearned to possess, whether it was a bolt of material for a new dress, or an extension on the mortgage note the bank held on their land and homes. Howard did not think he was an evil man for using the assets within his control to obtain the few pleasures that life afforded him. Besides, he knew women did the same thing when they used their feminine wiles to better themselves. In the case of Jubilee Hart, Howard could think of only one tidbit which he could use to overcome her resistance. But he would only use his degrading piece of verbal ammunition if she forced him to resort to such drastic measures.

"I'd rather stay down here with you," he said in a husky voice. His eyes focused on the exciting way her bosom rose and fell in rapid succession beneath the soft material of her white gown. He sighed with annoyance when she drew her arms over her chest in defiance of his gawking gaze.

Jubilee's fear began to make way for the anger that his appalling behavior caused to surface within her trembling being. "I don't like the way you're staring at me, Mr. Crowly. And I don't think I like *you* very much either." She tossed her long mane of hair over her shoulder with a defiant flip of her head. It no longer mattered to her if she was a guest in his home; she would not tolerate his behavior under any circumstances.

A resigned sigh escaped from Howard's smirking mouth. He hated to resort to blackmail, but this stubborn woman did not leave him any choice. "So you've been consorting with that low-life gambler while you were staying here under my roof, if that is my understanding of Ina Devine's insinuation at the rally today?"

In an indignant gesture of unrestrained abhorrence, Jubilee dropped her arms from her bosom and angrily placed her hands on the curve of her hips. "That is a vicious lie, and you know it." His grin widened as his eager gaze swept over her breasts again, now that they were no longer hidden from his view. At once, Jubilee became aware of his ploy to force her into submitting to his repugnant advances. She was surprised that she was capable of feeling so much disdain toward another person and felt her hatred for Howard Crowly overwhelm her entirely. "What a sad specimen of a man you are," she said. "I don't have to stand here and listen to your ignorant threats," she added as she took a step forward. Her plan was to push past him and make a hasty, but quiet, retreat to the upstairs before Abigail was alerted to her husband's absence from the bedroom. Besides getting away from this insufferable man, Jubilee's second greatest desire was to spare Abigail the pain of knowing just what a truly dreadful man she had married.

At the same instant Jubilee moved forward, Howard took another step to block her from rushing past him.

He was not ready to give up on his acute need to make this lovely blonde his latest victory. But in the heat of the moment neither of them remembered the spilt pie that was still splattered across the smooth planks of the floor. When his foot came into contact with the slippery mess Howard felt the loss of his footing. Instinctively, he reached out to grab ahold of something to prevent him from falling. His groping hands clutched onto the nearest support, which happened to be the startled form of Jubilee Hart. She did not realize that he was trying to balance himself when he reached out for her. Certain that Howard had intended to make a forceful lunge at her, Jubilee's only instinct was to fight him off as she doubled up her fist and swung her arm wildly through the air. A searing pain shot up the entire length of her arm when her hand made contact with the man's unsuspecting face. In her terrified attempt to flee from this madman, she forced herself to ignore the pain in her hand and arm and she tried once again to get past Howard's lurching body. She stepped into the smashed pie, and gasped with fear when the cold, gooey substance touched her skin and caused her to stumble against Howard. Her sudden gesture forced both of them to plunge toward the hardwood floor.

Howard Crowly crashed down upon her. Jubilee felt the air being knocked from her lungs as every inch of her body exploded in agony. But her pain was nothing compared to her fear. The fall had enabled Howard Crowly to pin her beneath him, and if it was his actual plan to force himself upon her, then his dominant position was to his advantage. She opened her mouth to scream, but nothing other than a weak cry escaped her lips. Jubilee had been convinced that the earlier fiasco at the rally had destroyed her life, but she realized that nothing could compare to the indescribable horror of what was happening to her now. She squeezed her eyes shut, praying she would discover she was asleep and that when she awoke she would learn this had all been a terrible nightmare.

A blinding light penetrated through Jubilee's tightly closed lids, and for a short period of confusion she thought her prayers had been answered. Maybe she had awoken, and her nightmare was about to end. When her eyes opened, however, it was the bright glow of a kerosene light which lit up the kitchen. She cringed visibly as she tried to imagine the vile sight which had greeted Abigail's eyes when she had lit the lamp.

"Get up, Howard," the gray-haired woman commanded in a flat, but powerful tone of voice. Abigail felt sick to her stomach, but she was not going to allow her shock and dismay to detour her from doing what she should have done years ago. "And then get out!"

Howard rolled from the unmoving form of Jubilee Hart and jumped to his feet. He was not certain what had happened to cause the chain of events which led to his collapse on top of the blonde suffrage speaker, but he *was* certain that there was no logical way of explaining to his wife the reason he was lying on the floor, with a woman underneath him, in the middle of their kitchen. He opened his mouth to respond to her blunt command, but her unexpected show of spirit had left him speechless. In all the years of their marriage she had never talked back to him. But, he told himself, this defiant change in his wife was his own fault. If he had not allowed her to become involved with the suffrage movement, and with pushy women like Jubilee Hart, she would still be the docile, obedient doormat he had married.

As the husband and wife stared at one another through an uneasy silence, Jubilee raised her pain-racked body to a sitting position. Despite the fact that Howard had attacked her unmercifully, she did not want to be the reason for the Crowly's disastrous marriage to fall apart. She was filled with her own sense of guilt over what had happened when she said in a meek voice, "Howard does not have to go. I'll leave so the two of you can work this out."

Howard's tousled white head nodded fiercely in

agreement, but Abigail's determined mind was not swayed. "No, Howard goes," she said. The tone of her voice was resolute and clear. She was a tiny woman who barely cleared five feet, but the unyielding way she squared her shoulders and gritted her teeth made her appear to be a figure of powerful dimensions on this fateful night. From Jubilee's speech today she had learned a lot about the issue of suffrage, but she had been educated in the subject of suffering long ago. She had suffered through Howard's belittling treatment of her, along with his endless score of infidelities, for far longer than any woman should have to endure. But the sight of him sprawled upon the defenseless young woman, who had become her new friend in the past few days, was more than even Abigail Crowly could tolerate. She'd had no idea that her husband would resort to such a disgraceful form of violence in order to fulfill his craven lust. She hated him as much as she pitied him. At this time, nothing could change her mind when she repeated, "Howard goes!"

The man stumbled forward in blind shock. He could not believe that this was the spineless woman with whom he had lived for thirty-six years. "I'm your husband, for God's sake! If anybody should leave this house, it should be that hussy who tried to seduce me right here under your nose."

A disbelieving cry flew from Jubilee's mouth as she heard Howard Crowly's lies. Abigail did not give her time to answer in her own defense. The elderly women spat at her deceitful husband. "I know what happened tonight. I have ears and I have eyes. And, believe it or not, Howard, I have feelings, too. Although it's been so long since you've noticed *anything* about me I'm sure you've forgotten that I'm even a real person."

Howard continued to stare at his wife, stunned by the startling transformation he had just witnessed. His mind fought to find some way for him to rationalize with her. He'd be damned if he was going to leave his own home in the middle of the night, especially because of some woman! "Why don't you just calm down, Abigail. You're too distraught to think clearly. We'll go back to bed and I'll explain to you what really happened here tonight." His voice had a deeply patronizing tone, which suggested that he did not think his wife was capable of understanding his explanation. His obvious attitude only served to fuel Abigail's fury.

"If you don't leave immediately, I am going to send for Marshal Elliot."

"The marshal?" Howard's face grew red with anger. "You're sending for the marshal? What for?"

Abigail's eyes became two slits of unspoken rage as she glared at her unfaithful husband. She noticed that one side of his face looked strangely out of proportion. It began to swell with a purplish tinge along the top of his cheekbone and beneath his left eye. "I'll tell him how you tried to violate my houseguest against her will," she answered without further hesitation. For the first time since she had appeared in the doorway of the kitchen, Abigail glanced down at Jubilee Hart. Her heart was filled with sympathy for the woman whom her husband had shamelessly been pursuing.

Howard's gaze also fell to the floor where the blonde beauty still sat in the middle of the splattered apple pie. Her long hair was hanging in a tangled mass around her pale face, and her soiled white gown was hiked up in an enticing manner about her knees. He sighed heavily with disappointment. Even in her disheveled state, and in the heat of this unfortunate incident, he still ached for her with an insatiable yearning. But he quickly reminded himself that if it wasn't for that woman, he would not be in this uncomfortable predicament now. He mulled over his wife's threat for a moment. In Abigail's irrational state of mind, she just might be crazy enough to go for Simon Elliot. The newly-appointed Territorial Marshal had not yet approached Howard's bank for a loan, and to make matters worse, he was also a bachelor. In despair, Howard realized he had nothing to bargain with when dealing with the lawman. His eyes flitted back and forth between his wife and Jubilee Hart as he pondered this aggravating situation.

"All right," he said in mock defeat. "I'll leave . . . for now." Spending one night at his bank would not be the end of the world, he determined. Anyway, Abigail had told him over dinner tonight that their guest was planning to leave sooner than they had expected. By tomorrow afternoon, Jubilee Hart would be on the eastbound train, and everything would resume its normal pace again. The first thing Howard planned to do was to forbid Abigail from any future participation with the equality movement. He could not leave without one final threat, however. As he exited from the kitchen, he paused in the doorway and turned toward the unmoving woman who still sat upon the floor. "If you think your reputation was endangered by Ina Devine's insinuation, just wait until I finish telling my version of your scandalous liaison with that gambler while you were staying under my roof!"

Jubilee could only stare at him in silence as his vicious words cut her down even lower than she already felt. If Howard began spouting additional lies about her and Chance Steele, there would be no way to salvage what was left of her damaged reputation. Oh, how many times in the past few days had she wished that she had never come to this awful prairie town of Cheyenne, Wyoming.

"He's bluffing," Abigail said when she approached Jubilee and extended her hand. "Are you hurt?" she asked. She strained to listen to the noises coming from her husband. In the distance, they could hear Howard cursing, his heavy footsteps stomping up the stairs.

With Abigail's question, Jubilee's thoughts snapped back to her immediate pain. She took the woman's hand and struggled to stand on her shaking limbs. There was not one inch of her body that did not hurt from Howard's heavy body crashing down on top of her. But her greatest agony was in the hand that she had used to slug Howard's face. "I might have broken my hand," she said meekly. She winced with pain as she held out the swollen member for Abigail's inspection. The woman cradled the injured hand in her own palm as she gently moved every one of Jubilee's fingers, which made the younger female gasp with each movement of her hand.

"It's broken," Abigail stated. She put her arm around Jubilee's waist and guided her toward the door. "I'm so sorry, my dear. I never thought . . ." Her words died as Howard's loud footsteps were heard stomping back down the stairs. They remained rooted to the spot where they stood until they heard the sound of the front door open, and then slam shut. Abigail glanced back down at Jubilee's injured hand and added, "I just hope your well-deserving target received the worst end of the damage!"

Chapter Seven

"I'm glad you've decided to stay an extra day in Cheyenne, but I still think you need to rest. Are you sure you're feeling up to this?"

Jubilee's weak smile served as her reply since she was not sure she was up to anything after yesterday's series of disasters. Abigail had been fretting over her all morning, and in numerous attempts to make her feel better, the elderly lady repeatedly told her that none of the previous day's events were her fault. She even confided to Jubilee about her knowledge of Howard's past affairs, a revelation that only increased Jubilee's contempt for the awful man.

Because the woman was going to such great lengths to ensure the continuation of their friendship, Jubilee decided not to tell her how terrible she really felt. Her nose throbbed from the pie plate that had smacked her in the face at the inn, and her back was bruised from the fall onto the kitchen floor, her ribs hurt from Howard's heavy body landing on her, and sharp pains shot through her broken hand almost constantly. But worst of all was her damaged pride. She was still humiliated by the outcome of the rally yesterday, and Howard's attack last night almost made her feel like the unscrupulous person Ina Devine had insinuated her to be. It was the thought of Howard Crowly, spewing more ugly lies about her, that had strengthened her resolve to stay in Cheyenne for an extra day. If she went through with her plan to leave today, she would never have a chance to defend her own honor. Instead, she would be two thousand miles away while her reputation was being stripped away shred by shred, by malicious lies repeated so often, and by so many, that they would acquire a patina of truth.

"Do you think it's fair to Mr. Steele to do this on the day of his grand opening? He's such a nice man, and what happened at the rally was not really his fault." Abigail's high regard for the gambler was obvious in her pathetic expression. The old woman understood how Jubilee's concern over Howard's hateful threat had compounded the fears she already felt. In a small town, Ina Devine's untruthful innuendo could do untold damage. Still, she thought it was a shame that Chance Steele had to receive the blunt end of Jubilee's retaliation.

Jubilee huffed with indignation. "Nice! He's nothing more than a scheming gambler! How can you think he's nice?"

"Just because Howard is a respectable banker, does that make him a nicer man than Chance Steele?"

Abigail looked fully into Jubilee's blue eyes. Her smile was tender, but her voice held a note of challenge for the young woman, and Jubilee was taken aback. In her wildest imaginings she could not conceive that Chance Steele would attempt something as despicable as what Howard Crowly had tried to do last night. But she would not say that he was nice, either. With a stubborn tilt of her head, Jubilee retorted, "If he were not opening a saloon and a bordello, women like Ina Devine would not be in Cheyenne. Do you want your new city filled with prostitutes and drunks?"

A frown fell over Abigail's thin face while she mulled over Jubilee's question. A part of her agreed with the younger female, but she still hated the idea of picking on Chance Steele! To even think of holding a protest rally at the Second Chance Saloon! On opening day! Still, perhaps it would be best to pacify the young woman's pride, she thought. When the injured female felt she had sought her revenge then perhaps she would be able to put yesterday's terrible experiences behind her.

"All right. What can I do to help?"

Jubilee's scowling countenance brightened into a look of excitement as she leaned toward Abigail. "I'll need you to talk to as many women as possible. I hate to make you go out alone, especially in this terrible weather, but I'm afraid most of the decent women of Cheyenne would slam their doors in my face. If you could just speak with them, tell them that Ina Devine was lying or crazy, or something. Tell them she was drunk. Then, ask them if they would help us to picket the saloon this afternoon. Go first to the wives of men who frequent the saloons, since I'm certain they will be the ones most likely to help us."

Abigail sighed as her thoughts drifted off to how Howard had fared through the night. He would not be happy to learn about Jubilee's protest against the grand opening of The Second Chance Saloon, especially since his bank had helped to finance the business. "Will you rest while I'm gone?" Abigail asked with concern. Once again Jubilee insisted she was fine, but the pained look in her glazed eyes told Abigail otherwise.

"If you'll help me to gather up the supplies before you leave, I'll make up some signs for us to carry." When she noticed Abigail glancing down at her bandaged hand, she quickly added, "I can manage with one hand. I'll be fine—please don't worry."

After much fussing over Jubilee, Abigail left the determined suffragist to work on the posters, while she headed out into the deep snow to fulfill the woman's request. It was a weekday morning and all the women Abigail knew would be busy with their chores. She had no hope of finding any recruits for Jubilee's proposed protest of the saloon. Still, Abigail figured the least she could do for Jubilee was to talk to a few of the women she knew and try to convince them that Miss Hart's character was respectable and good. Two hours later

Abigail returned to her house burdened with home-made goodies, and an abundance of praise and good wishes for her houseguest.

"They'll all be there," she gushed with rare enthusiasm. She scattered the jars of preserves, candied yams, pickles and other assorted gifts upon the table where Jubilee diligently worked over the posters.

Jubilee laughed while she stared at the bounty of food. "What — what is all this?"

"It's for you! Everyone sends their regrets about the fiasco at the inn yesterday." A more solemn expression came over her flushed face as she added, "But I'm afraid I had to tell another little lie concerning you."

"Lie?" Jubilee repeated the word with a sense of dread. Enough lies had already been told about her in the past couple of days to last an entire lifetime. "What sort of lie?"

"Well, I knew we could *never* tell the truth about how you had injured your hand, since that would only cause more gossip." She hesitated, then took a deep breath. "So, I told them you were so angry at that prostitute for trying to spread rumors about you that you . . . accidentally slammed your hand in a door . . . in a fit of rage. Whenever I told one of the ladies that story, they offered their condolences, and then they would insist on sending you a little something to convey their sympathy for the terrible things that woman has put you through ever since you first arrived in Cheyenne." Abigail's eyes widened with excitement as she rushed on. "And they said your plan to protest the grand opening of the saloon was proof that Ina Devine was lying about your involvement with Chance Steele. Oh, and they'll all be at the saloon when the doors open at two o'clock this afternoon."

Jubilee glanced at the clock which ticked away on the mantel. "That's less than an hour from now!" She started to run up to her room to ready herself for the protest, but she stopped abruptly and turned back to the smiling elderly woman. "Thank you," she said quietly. Only the two of them knew how close she had come to absolute ruin. "I can't tell you how much your kindness means to me." She smiled warmly at Abigail, then hurried upstairs to get ready for the protest.

The older woman smiled as she watched the beautiful blonde race up the stairs. *I should be thanking you,* she thought. A few hours ago she had been worrying about whether or not Howard had a good night's sleep. The task Jubilee had found for her to do had taken her mind off her servitude to a worthless husband and had put her to thinking about more important things, such as the issue of temperance. Strange, but that was something she had never even thought about before today. Howard was always stopping at some saloon for at least one drink before he headed home at night, and sometimes he never made it home at all. Abigail had never given it a second thought—in fact, it was more pleasant around their home when he was gone. But after Abigail had spent the morning talking to other women about the subject, she realized some families were suffering a great deal because their menfolk spent so much of their time drinking and carousing at the local saloons. Perhaps if a temperance order were to go into effect while Cheyenne was still such a young city, it would be better for all the occupants, Abigail decided.

In vain, Jubilee attempted to ignore the throbbing pain in her hand as she and Abigail headed toward 17th Street. The freezing cold seemed to make the pain more intense, but she kept telling herself that it would go away once her mind was occupied with the protest. In her good hand she carried several posters proclaiming the evils of alcohol, while Abigail also toted several of the hand printed announcements. The storm from the previous night had given way to an ugly day of low-hanging gray clouds, and the temperature had barely risen above freezing all day. When the women spoke to one another, the vapors from their breath billowed out in front of their faces and hung suspended in the icy air.

"I have to warn you," Abigail said in a worried voice.

"Howard will come to the protest as soon as he hears about it. He might even take advantage of the opportunity to start following through with his threats."

Jubilee drew in a wary breath. Knowing what a contemptible man Howard Crowly was, Jubilee knew Abigail was probably correct in her assumption. "Well, Chance Steele will be there, and surely he will dispute Howard's claim." She glanced at Abigail's strained expression and her fears increased. "Won't he? You did say he was a nice man?" Her brows drew together in agitation.

"We're not exactly doing him any favors by protesting his business on the day he opens up for customers, my dear. And besides, Howard holds a banknote on The Second Chance Saloon, so Chance will be hesitant to anger Howard."

"Oh no," Jubilee sighed with a sense of impending catastrophe. It was just her luck to be accused of being involved with a 'nice' man who was also indebted to one of her accusers. Was there no end to this revolting affair? Who would have expected such a mess in this cold, forlorn territory? Off in the distance the wail of the train's mournful whistle sounded, reminding Jubilee that she had planned to be on that very train when it pulled out of Cheyenne today. How she wished she was headed out of this terrible place, and would soon be back in the safety and comfort of her own room at Miss Gurdy's. But she could not go until she was satisfied that her good reputation was restored when she did depart.

Jubilee was astounded when they rounded the corner of 17th Street and glimpsed the crowd of women who were already gathered in front of The Second Chance Saloon. Undaunted by the severe weather conditions, they were decked out in their heaviest layers of clothing as they waited anxiously for Jubilee Hart to arrive with further instructions for the intended protest. Any worthwhile diversion from their dreary lives was welcome among these hard-working women, but combating the types of establishments where their menfolk found solace in bottles and with prostitutes was a challenge to which they rallied without any amount of coaxing.

When the crowd spotted Jubilee Hart and Abigail Crowly, a rousing round of cheers rang out, alerting the occupants inside the saloon to the increase of activity outside their front door. Chance Steele and his employees were busy with last minute preparations for their opening night, which Chance hoped would be an overwhelming success. Ina Devine's outburst at the rally had dampened his enthusiasm somewhat, but he had been too involved with the business of his grand opening to dwell upon the events of the previous day. Every so often, throughout the busy day, he had toyed with the idea of going to the Crowlys' to apologize to Miss Hart. But, he had put it off until, finally, he had run out of time. Then he considered meeting her at the train station before she left for Washington, D.C. Yet he had continued to putter around the saloon until he had heard the train whistle blow, signaling the departure of the locomotive. He had no doubt that she would be furious about Ina's accusations at the rally, and he also knew she would be placing a portion of the blame on him. If he thought she would accept his regrets and apologies, he would have tried to see her one more time. But he did not want to take the chance that their last parting would be filled with anger and contempt. A powerful attraction had drawn their gazes to one another at the rally, but once she was thousands of miles away, it would no longer matter. It was for the best that they didn't see one another again, he told himself over and over throughout the long day.

"You'd better take a look outside, Boss Man," Ina Devine suggested as she stared out the front window.

Chance glanced at her with aggravation. As far as he was concerned, her behavior yesterday was unforgivable. Even as a saloon owner, he wanted to have the respect of his fellow citizens. Ina's drunken display yesterday could easily destroy all that he had worked to achieve in the past two years. Although she had promised him that she would never overstep her position again, he was still tempted to send her back to St. Louis. He prided himself on being a good judge of character, and when he had chosen Ina Devine to be in charge of the other girls, he had done so with confidence. His deduction that she was as smart as she was pretty had been wrong, and now his intuition told him that her presence only meant more trouble. A gambler had to rely on his intuition, yet he needed Ina at The Second Chance Saloon tonight. Besides, the last thing Jubilee Hart needed when she boarded the train was to encounter the woman who had thrown a piece of pie in her face.

"What is it?" he asked with obvious annoyance. He turned from the table where he had carefully been stacking poker chips and moved toward Ina's direction. In spite of his anger toward her, he couldn't help but notice how perfect she looked for today's grand opening. Her bright red tresses were adorned with a large black bow, which was made from the same black satin as her elegant gown. The rich look of her shimmering ebony attire gave her the appearance of a high class courtesan, which was of course, the image Chance wanted his ladies to convey. If only Ina could conduct herself like a woman of dignity, too!

As the tall gambler sauntered toward the window where Ina waited, he noticed the gloating look upon her painted face. He began to wish that he did not *have* to look out that window, but curiosity pulled him forward. At first glance, Chance thought a crowd was gathering in anticipation of the moment when he would open the doors for his first day of business. A bolt of excitement shot through him, but just as quickly he became aware that only women were standing outside his establishment. Confusion overcame his elated feeling as he stared at the group of women and tried to imagine why they had suddenly appeared at his front doorstep.

He planned to allow women entrance to his saloon on rare occasions, but it was not his intention to regularly allow them to frequent his place of business. A saloon was a man's escape from his womenfolk; it was his place to tell rude jokes, smoke cigars, and forget about the pressures of his ordinary life. The women who were provided for the clientele of these establishments were not like their wives and sweethearts. Saloon girls were only here for the patrons' enjoyment, and when the men made their exits, no obligations followed them out the door.

Chance continued to stare out the window in amazement. He recognized these women as the wives of Cheyenne's leading businessmen. It was not until he saw the blonde suffrage speaker move into the center of the crowd that his confused thoughts began to focus on the women's intent. Chance inched Ina Devine aside, leaning forward for a closer observation of the outside activities. He watched in stunned silence while Jubilee Hart climbed atop the highest pile of snow that banked the walkway, then began to speak to the women as Abigail Crowly started passing signs out amongst the crowd. When the first homemade poster was hoisted into the air, Chance's confusion was cleared up at once. 'Soldiers of God . . . Women against drink!'

An agonized moan was the only sound that escaped from Chance Steele when he headed toward the front door. He pushed past Ina Devine without saying a word, but his raven gaze screamed with unspoken profanities. She longed to accompany her boss out into the street so she could tell that haughty blonde, and her bunch of biddy friends, what she thought of the whole lot of them. Instead, she repositioned herself at the window. Her pride was still stinging over the way her boss had minced no words when he said that her job was now on a trial basis, and would continue to be so until he was certain that she was worthy of her employment at The Second Chance Saloon.

Chance didn't take the time to grab his heavy coat as

he rushed out of the saloon, and he regretted this oversight the moment the cold air hit his unprotected body
and face. He was wearing his most dapper suit of gray
and black plaid, and on his feet were shiny black boots,
whose smooth, new soles made walking on the frozen
ground next to impossible. His exit from the saloon was
a comical sight, as onlookers watched him slipping and
sliding across the walkway, desperately trying to control
his floundering feet. When he was able to grasp onto
the hitching post at the edge of the street to balance
himself, the giggling and snickering which reached his
ears did not improve his frame of mind. His plan was to
walk outside calmly, then try to talk to the women in a
sensible and business-like manner, with the hopes of
ridding himself of their presence before they scared
away his first customers. The women's obvious mirth at
his exit from the saloon galled him greatly, and when he
focused his dark brooding glare at the crowd, his eyes
fell first to the woman who stood above the others.

There was no smirk upon the blonde's face when she
met his unfriendly gaze. She was too tired, and in too
much misery to see any humor in his clumsy performance. But, under any circumstances, it was hard to
ignore how handsome the dark-haired saloon owner
was. With his indignant pose against the post and the
stubborn squaring of his chin, his scowling countenance made him look more like a naughty little boy
than a polished gambler. Jubilee pulled her eyes away
from his face at once. She could not risk a repeat of
yesterday's strange occurence when their gazes met this
time. Her mission here today did not include fantasizing over the hidden meaning in Chance Steele's midnight gaze.

In an effort to retain a small amount of his dignity,
Chance also looked away from the beautiful young
woman and cleared his throat. He had not prepared
himself to see her again, and the strange way she affected him made him a man without a mind of his own.
Sometimes, he almost felt that she knew him better

than he knew himself. But that was ridiculous! Although she had made a reference to riverboat gamblers the other night over dinner, Chance was willing to bet her knowledge of gamblers and their cohorts was derived strictly from distant observation. How often would a woman like Jubilee Hart be in the company of anyone other than her own high class of people? Chance could only imagine the type of life the beautiful blonde must lead in Washington, D.C. Just by her appearance, he could guess that she was from a long line of wealth and breeding, and undoubtedly resided with her arrogant relatives in a mansion in the finest section of town. Once again, Chance prided himself on being able to perceive a person's background. *Right now, standing on this snowbank in the middle of the prairie town of Cheyenne must make this pampered wench feel like she was stranded in hell,* he thought. Chance Steele felt a growing sense of anger toward the woman who was trying to initiate a protest against the only thing Chance had ever owned in his entire life. Perhaps it was about time Miss Hart felt his real wrath!

Shaking off the cold with a surge of hell-bent fury, Chance Steele straightened his slouching form and threw back his broad shoulders. "Lovely ladies of Cheyenne," he began in a tone that belied his inner anger. Without looking at Jubilee Hart, he was able to control his true feelings to some degree as he continued his deception. "I am honored to have you attend the grand opening of my humble establishment." He did not let the blonde's loud huff from the top of the snowbank distract him, although he found it extremely difficult not to look up at her when he spoke. "However, I'm sure you all have better things to do on this cold afternoon than to be standing out here in the street." To underscore his meaning, he glanced at one of the women and added, "Why, Mrs. Horton, who's tending for your brand-new baby daughter while you're here? And," a sympathetic expression hovered on his face as he looked at another woman. "Is that you, Roberta? Does this

95

mean Arnold is feeling well enough to be left alone now?"

Rage flooded through Jubilee as she listened to his insinuations that the women were neglecting their duties as wives and mothers to be here with her today. By the expressions on the women's faces, his words had set them all to wondering if they had indeed made a mistake by agreeing to partake in this demonstration against The Second Chance Saloon.

"Mr. Steele!" Jubilee called out before the women had more time to mull over their indecision. "We are not here to escape the responsibilities of our homes and families. Indeed, these women are here today for the purpose of making Cheyenne into a decent place in which to raise their families. Bawdy houses, such as the one you are introducing into this town today, are the devil's aid to mankind's destruction."

Chance was unable to dismiss the suffragist now that she had publicly confronted him, and when he did take a good look at her face, he was startled by the sickly pallor of her complexion. His gaze dropped to the bandaged hand, which she held tightly against her midriff. Had she been hurt in yesterday's scrimmage at the inn? If he was not so angry at her for gathering these women here in front of his saloon at such a crucial time, he would have shown her more consideration. But he was a proud man, and her words cut away at him like the blade of a razor. His entire life's work, along with Jerrod's future, would be determined by the success of his saloon. Anytime she desired, the haughty Miss Hart could run back to her fancy house and wealthy family and friends in Washington D.C. Then she could also wipe out the memory of the lowly people she had trampled over in the forgotten territory of Wyoming.

A snide smile curled his lips beneath his thin mustache as he fixed his glare on the blonde's frowning face. "You, Miss Hart, are womankind's destruction." He did not give her an opportunity to speak when he saw her mouth open in readiness to combat his denouncement of her character. "Yesterday, you had all of Wyoming in the palm of your hand with your rousing speech on women's suffrage. By the time you were finished with your speech, every *man* in attendance," he accented the reference to gender forcefully before rushing on, "carried with them the burdens from centuries of grave injustice that has been directed toward the women of our country." Chance took a step towards the silent group of females, being careful not to slip again upon the slick ground. He no longer felt the sting of the cold, because he was too enraged by the fire in his soul.

"In just a few days the territorial legislature will convene to determine the issue of women being granted the right to vote. But tonight those same men plan to meet at this saloon, where they'll unwind, share a few drinks, play a game or two of cards and then, discuss the introduction of the enfranchising bill." Chance gave a quick nod of his head toward the structure which stood behind him. He pointed a well manicured hand at the blonde suffragist when he added, "Do you think your protest here today will endear them to your efforts to obtain equality?"

"But that tart who works here already ruined it for us," Abigail Crowly snapped. Everyone was surprised by the woman's unusual outburst, but no one was as shocked as Abigail herself. Her sudden decision to take a stand against the evil abodes that harbored acts of indecency was the result of her recent insight to the silent suffering of her friends and neighbors. She was deeply disturbed by all the stories the women had related to her today about their men's devotion to the bottle, and to the prostitutes who were made readily available to them at exactly the type of establishment Chance Steele was about to introduce to Cheyenne. For years she had felt as though she was the only woman who had to endure an unhappy marriage. Now that she realized she was not alone with this terrible affliction, she was more determined than ever to help to make a change in the lives of her sister suffragettes.

97

Chance was taken aback for an instant when the tiny woman spoke up so unexpectedly. Abigail Crowly was the one woman whom he never would have thought would speak out against him. But then, Jubilee Hart had a way of firing people up with all sorts of enthusiasm. If Chance had discovered that trait in the lovely lady by his own submission to her tempting wiles, it was no wonder that the weaker Abigail Crowly had fallen victim to Jubilee's influence. The poor woman obviously allowed other people to rule her thoughts, which was apparent by the way her own husband treated her. Still, she was the wife of the banker who held the note on The Second Chance Saloon, and Chance did not wish to make a rude retort to her remark about Ina Devine.

"I admit that my employee made a fool of herself yesterday. She did not, however, ruin your chances of equality," he said in a confident tone, which once again suggested that he had an insight to the legislature's impending decision. "But ladies," the gambler turned away from Abigail Crowly and ran his dark gaze over the entire assembly of females, who were now joined by a large gathering of men who had seen the commotion and wandered into the crowd. ". . . A protest against my saloon at this delicate time will only serve to make all of you look as foolish as Ina Devine."

The men who stood in the street began to nod their heads and voice their agreement with the saloon owner, leaving the protesters with no recourse other than to back down . . . for now, anyway. With pathetic guilty glances at Jubilee Hart and Abigail Crowly, the rest of the woman began to murmur among themselves about the truth in Chance Steele's words. With the meeting of the legislature only a few days away, now was not the time to anger any of the Wyoming men, but especially not the men who served in the legislature. The crowd took on a note of panic as they decided to disperse before any of those men showed up for the grand opening of the saloon and discovered them standing here with signs of protest still in their hands.

Hurried words of apology followed as the women handed the posters back to Jubilee and Abigail. They wasted no time in heading back toward the security of their homes. Jubilee only half listened to the women's parting remarks because she was too angry with Chance Steele to concentrate on anything other than slapping that smug look off his face. But the throbbing in her bandaged hand reminded her that she would have to resort to less violent battle tactics if she ever hoped to conquer the smooth-talking gambler.

"We'd better get you out of this cold," Abigail suggested with a worried glance in the direction of Howard's banking establishment. She felt fortunate that they had not encountered him as of yet, and she did not want to press their luck.

With a resigned nod, Jubilee climbed down from the pile of snow. She hated this feeling of defeat, and she despised herself for allowing it to happen. As she followed Abigail away from the saloon, Jubilee glanced back at the man who still stood beside the hitching post and watched her with his piercing black eyes. His look was no longer taunting or victorious. Instead, his solemn expression almost seemed regretful. Jubilee told herself she was stupid if she thought he would feel badly about making her idea to protest his saloon appear foolish and impulsive. He was only playing more games. Well, he was not the first gambler she had dealt with, and she had learned a few tricks of the trade from her father. Perhaps it was time that she fought fire with fire, but the next time, she would make sure Chance Steele was the one who got burned.

Chapter Eight

Chance did not wait for the two women to walk out of his sight before he swung around and hurried back into the protection of his saloon. All at once, he had became aware of the way the chill of the late afternoon had begun to grind its way through his body. Even after he was behind the closed doors of the saloon, he could not seem to regain a sense of warmth. He had bullied those women into retreating today, and Jubilee Hart knew it. Those dark blue eyes of hers had screamed accusations at him. What she didn't know was that he was not proud of manipulating any of those decent woman into thinking they were not good wives and mothers. Chance shivered and crossed his arms over his chest, but nothing seemed to help. Inwardly, he laughed at himself when a fleeting thought passed through his mind. Maybe he was not cold . . . maybe he was just plain scared.

"Y'all took care of them old bit—"

"I used a tactful approach to a delicate situation," Chance interrupted. His brooding glare immediately brought Ina's discussion of the episode to a halt. "Are all the girls ready for tonight?" he quizzed, with yet another wasted attempt to wipe the vision of the blonde Easterner out of his mind.

Ina gave her bare shoulders a nonchalant shrug. "I'll go see," she said in a patronizing voice, which was laced with the drawl of her deep southern accent. With a defiant toss of her red head, she scooted past Chance. Since she knew he was watching her departure, she made certain to swing her satin-draped hips in the most provocative manner she could manage. He might have rejected her once, but it would not be long before he grew bored of mooning over a face on a poster and felt the urge to succumb to his manly needs. Ina knew her upstairs room would be the first place he would come when that happened, and when he did, she planned to reject him as coldly as he had denied her the other day.

Chance shivered again, though he still did not wish to acknowledge the strange sensations that were surging through his numb body. Just a few days ago, Ina Devine would not have had to do anything other than be available to entice him into her bed. But then, it had only been a few days ago that he had first glimpsed Jubilee Hart walking down the train plank. Another visible tremor shot through Chance as his face became drenched in sweat. He was not just afraid of this foreign feeling, he was downright terrified. It had taken him sixteen years to get over the first woman he had fallen in love with when he was still a very young man. Leaving Mississippi and throwing himself into the building of his own business were the only things that had finally eased Faith Barnett's memory from his tormented thoughts. But now Jerrod had reentered his life, and so had another woman who affected him in the same manner as Faith had all those years ago. It just didn't seem fair.

"Uncle Chance, are you all right?"

Chance took a deep breath, hoping to clear his mind of things that could be detrimental to both his and Jerrod's future. He forced a wane smile and nodded his head at the dark-eyed youth. "Just a case of nerves, boy," he said as he gave his nephew a playful slug in the arm. "Have you got some good books to read tonight?"

The boy's worried expression turned into a look of disappointment as he nodded his dark head and shoved his hands deeper into the pockets of his faded overalls. "Do I really have to study tonight?"

"You know how I feel. A sixteen year old has no busi-

101

ness hanging out in a gaming house at night. You study hard and learn all you can about raising cattle, so when I make enough money to buy us a chunk of land, you can be in charge of running the ranch."

With his uncle's proposal, Jerrod's pouting expression faded and he asked, "You mean it? I'd be like a foreman or something?"

Chance laughed and his mood began to ease into a more comfortable mode. Until Jerrod had shown up on his doorstep a month ago, he'd had no idea how much he enjoyed having a youngster around. If only Jerrod's arrival could have been under happier circumstances, rather than as the result of two tragic deaths. The only thing Chance regretted now was missing out on all of Jerrod's younger years. But Frank and Emily had done a fine job of raising the boy. They sure didn't need a gambler's influence on Jerrod while he was growing up. At least, this was what Chance constantly told himself for the past sixteen years to ease some of his own guilt over the situation.

"Well, flip that sign over, boy, and let's start pretending like this is a real business," Chance said with a wave of his hand towards the 'open' and 'closed' sign which hung in the front window.

Jerrod wasted no time in doing the small task his uncle had asked of him. Even if he did have to stay in their private quarters at night, living in the back of this lavish saloon was still more exciting than anything he had ever experienced in Kansas. He felt guilty when thoughts like this passed through his mind, because his parent's death had left him with a void that would never go away. But his Uncle Chance provided him with an adventure far different than that of a Kansas farm boy, and Jerrod was loving every minute of his new lifestyle. His only complaint was that his uncle seemed to think of him as a child. But heck, sixteen was practically a grown man, and he had the same needs as any other normal red-blooded man. Jerrod glanced toward the second floor of the large establishment, where the closed doors

102

of the upstairs rooms only fueled his young imagination with thoughts far more tempting than reading a book about livestock management on this chilly winter night.

Chance had to chuckle outloud when the first customer who pushed through the carved doors on opening day happened to be Howard Crowly. His mirth was short-lived, however, when he saw the banker's swollen cheek and the smudge of black that encased the lower edge of his eye. The image of Jubilee Hart's bandaged hand was the first thing that came into the saloon owner's mind, since a broken hand and a black eye usually accompanied one another. Knowing Howard as he did, Chance was certain Jubilee's injury was closely related to Howard's.

"Run into an irate client at the bank today?" Chance joked, hoping to gain some insight to the events that had led to Howard's swollen face. He motioned to the bartender to give the businessman a drink, then told the man behind the bar the shot of whiskey was on the house.

Howard nodded his head in gratitude for the free drink and quickly raised the shot glass to his lips, although he did not offer a reply to the saloon owner's question. All morning long he had been asked repeatedly about his black eye and bruised face. Each time someone inquired about them, his fury over losing his chance to seduce Jubilee Hart increased. He felt like a fool because of the way he had allowed his desire for the lovely blonde to overcome his sensibility. If he had approached her with more tact, he was certain she would have given into him without too much resistance — they always did. He was still amazed that his mousy little wife had ordered him out of the house, and after sleeping all night on the uncomfortable sofa in his office, the prying questions of his employees and clientele had only caused his already foul mood to deepen. To escape, he had taken the afternoon off and had ridden over to Laramie. The next stop on the Union Pacific Railroad line was also the home of a rowdy dance hall called 'Belle of the

103

West.' Howard had quenched his thirst for alcohol as well as his hunger for a woman during the afternoon hours that he had spend at the 'Belle.' When he returned to Cheyenne a few minutes ago, he was delighted to see the 'open' sign being placed in the front window of the city's newest house of pleasure so he could continue onward with his voyage of self-indulgence.

"Where's those St. Louis whores I've been hearing so much about?" he asked. His obvious attempt to change the subject did not go unnoticed by Chance Steele, who restrained his urge to demand an answer from the other man. He eyed the banker in close scrutiny, while Howard glanced around the large room, which was still empty at this early hour, and frowned. "I still haven't got a glimpse of any of them sweet things," Howard continued. "They'd better be real special if they're going compete with those luscious creatures over in Laramie."

Chance had never been fond of Howard Crowly, but his indifference toward the man was beginning to develop into a seething contempt. He ignored Howard's reference to the dance hall in Laramie since he had never considered that sleazy saloon to be any real competition for his new business. He still had not dismissed his urgent need to learn the truth about Howard's damaged face, however. "Is that where you encountered the black eye?" he asked. "It looks awfully sore."

Howard waved at the bartender for another drink, then shrugged and said, "What the hell, just set that whole bottle over here. I'm in no hurry to go home tonight. That luscious vixen has already headed back East by now, and I'm not too anxious to look at that homely wife of mine."

The saloon keeper mulled over Howard Crowly's confusing statements for a moment before coming to the conclusion that the banker was not aware that Jubilee Hart was still in town. An inner voice told Chance that it was best to allow Howard to continue to believe that the suffrage leader was gone. He was certain that the longer Howard Crowly stayed here at The Second Chance Saloon, the better it would be for the two women who were undoubtedly sitting at his home. He did not bother to ask the man again about his face, because Chance no longer had any doubts as to what had happened. He just hoped that Jubilee had been able to escape from his lecherous clutches with nothing more than a damaged hand.

As the night progressed, Chance's dream of a successful opening night was realized time and time again. Cheyenne's leading businessmen and politicians sat around the polished oak tables, as well as every cowboy, farmer and railroad worker for miles around. Ina and the rest of the ladies from St. Louis were not a disappointment to any of the men who had anticipated their arrival. While the men who desired private time upstairs waited for their turns with the ladies, they could busy themselves at the gaming tables. The trio of professional gamblers Chance had hired made sure the games never lacked excitement. As the piano player banged away at the ivory keys with one rousing tune after another and whiskey flowed like water, Chance mentally counted his profits from the first night of his new endeavor. He was enough of a businessman to know that he could only expect to have such a large crowd on rare occasions, but once word got around that his establishment was the best in the territory, he knew he would never lack for business. What he did lack, however, was the ecstatic feeling of success which he had been expecting to feel tonight.

After witnessing Howard Crowly's third trip up to the second floor, Chance decided that he needed a breath of fresh air. He donned his knee-length sheepskin coat and slipped out the back entrance of the saloon into the freezing dark night. The music and laughter from the interior of his saloon floated out from the walls and filled the empty alley with an array of mingled conversations and sounds. Chance tried to shake off the detached feeling he was experiencing toward the activities that were taking place on the other side of the wall. He had thought this would be his greatest moment — finally opening the doors for business. His entire life was bound up inside this huge building, along with everything he had always loved: whiskey, women, and most of all, enough card tables to engage any gambler's wildest desires. Tonight he did not even feel like playing cards, and this was a grave concern to him.

His gaze kept being drawn toward the direction of Carey Avenue. What was she doing tonight? The gambler entertained no fantasies that she was thinking about him in the same manner that he was thinking about her on this lonely December night. If she thought about him at all, her thoughts would not be very pleasant, but he couldn't help but worry about her welfare. She had looked so pale and fragile earlier today that Chance wished he could have scooped her into his arms and protected her from all the bad things — and bad people — in the world. He was sure he would have met with her other fist if he had tried to approach her at all. Still, what would it hurt if he was to call on her and Abigail . . . just for the purpose of wishing her a speedy recovery from her injury? With an anxious stride he began to make his way down the dark streets. He harbored no expectation of being received by Jubilee Hart with open arms, but he planned to make every effort possible to repair the damage that had occurred, caused by the unfortunate events of their first meetings. No matter how hard he tried, he would never forget the way their eyes had met across the crowded length of the conference room at the inn yesterday, nor could he ignore the way he felt about her, in spite of everything that happened since then.

There was only one light burning downstairs when Chance reached the Crowly residence on Carey Avenue. Though the hour was late for a visitor, he did not reconsider his rash decision to come here. He wanted — no ,needed — to see Jubilee Hart. For his own sanity he had to understand why meeting her had affected him so deeply, especially after he had spent years of conditioning himself to reject his heart's yearning for love again.

106

Maybe he could even walk away from here tonight a free man once more . . . free of the torment that falling in love always brought to evasive men such as himself. He knocked on the door, unconsciously holding his breath as he waited for someone to answer. The sight which greeted him when the door swung open did not dispel his longing for freedom. Instead, his heart felt as though it had just been taken away from him for all eternity!

Jubilee had not been able to sleep for a multitude of reasons, but her fear of Howard Crowly was the main reason that she had positioned herself by the window to keep watch throughout the long night that still loomed ahead. She was terrified that he would return home tonight and find that she was still there, and that there would be an even worse episode than they had already endured. She was equally concerned for Abigail's safety when the hateful man returned home. There was no telling what Howard's mood would be after last night's outrage.

At first glance at the man who was walking up the dark street, Jubilee had panicked, thinking he was Howard Crowly. On second glance, though, she had recognized the man as the handsome gambler. As she watched him approach the house from her guard post beside the window, her curiosity increased with each step he took. Although she thought it was improper of him to call on them at this late hour, she did not waste any time in getting to the door to receive him. When she was not fretting over Howard's return, she had also been mulling over the attraction she felt towards the enigmatic Chance Steele. He was a worthless gambler and the owner of a bordello. Jubilee knew she should hate him for these two traits alone, but she could not hate him at all. All her hatred at this time was directed toward Howard Crowly, along with the lingering contempt she retained for Ina Devine. Maybe that was why she was so relieved to see Chance Steele sauntering up the street. At least, this was what she told herself in a desperate attempt to dismiss the excitement his arrival had stirred within her trembling being.

"This is—is a surprise, Mr. Steele. I would have thought you'd have your hands full with your grand opening tonight."

Chance's gaze quickly assessed every inch of the beautiful woman who stood before him. He was certain he was glimpsing a bit of heaven through the front doorway of the Crowlys' home. Even his cherished memories of the lovely auburn-haired Faith Barnett could not compare to the sight of Jubilee Hart tonight. She was wearing a gown of white flannel and lace, which was topped by a teal-colored dressing gown of a heavy velvet material. The exquisite material suited her so well. *Did she always wear velvet?*, Chance wondered. He longed to run his hand over the soft folds of her long robe. "I was worried about you."

A look of surprise crossed Jubilee's face. "Worried about me?" She clutched her bandaged hand against her body in an unknowing gesture. "Whatever for?"

With a nervous chuckle, Chance motioned towards her injury. "I noticed your hand when you were down by the saloon today. I . . . I . . . ." He remembered that he had not removed his hat when she had opened the door. He grabbed the little bowler from his head and glanced down at the ground as if he were embarrassed by his lack of manners.

Jubilee was taken aback by his humble display. She couldn't help but wonder if this silver-tongued man had ever been at a loss for words before now. Despite her feelings toward cardsharks and their cohorts, she inwardly prayed that he was sincere in his reasons for coming here at this hour of night. "It's very late, but I'm sure Abigail would not mind if you came in for a minute or two," she said as she became aware of the cold air that was rushing into the house. As for herself, she was overcome by a sudden surprising rush of warmth, which soared through her body like a heatwave.

"Thank you," Chance mumbled as he stepped past her. He clutched his hat in both his hands, while inwardly cursing at himself for acting like a foolish young boy who had never been in a woman's presence. *Why, Jerrod would probably act with more sophistication!* the debonair gambler said to himself. He turned to face the woman again, and had to swallow back the lump in his throat before he could speak. Her pale blonde hair was hanging loose and unencumbered about her shoulders, and against the dark teal of her dressing gown, the gentle curls looked almost ethereal. It was no wonder Howard Crowly found her so irresistible that he had lost all of his self-control. If he had not been so terrified of his feelings for her, Chance would also have had a difficult time corralling his own urge to take her into his arms.

"Would you care to join me in the parlor?" she said with a quick glance towards the stairway. It was terribly improper for her to be alone with a man this late at night, but Abigail was only a short distance away if she needed her. Still, she felt very safe. All of her previous fears had disappeared the moment she had opened the door and gazed into the handsome face of Chance Steele.

Chance did not miss the unspoken meaning of Jubilee's uncertainty in allowing him to enter the house at this unorthodox hour. In fact, he was surprised she had opened the door to him at all. He made a mental note not to say or do anything that would make her regret her decision to permit him to stay. He did not wait for her to ask him if he wished to remove his coat, and he hung the heavy garment, along with his little gray bowler hat, upon the coat rack which stood at the parlor entrance. When she motioned for him to sit down on a nearby chair, he did so without delay, while she scurried to the chair furthest from the one she appointed for him.

"Howard's face doesn't look much better," he blurted out as he noticed the swollen fingers which extended past her bandage. He silently cursed his tactlessness when he raised his eyes to her face.

Several different shades of red colored Jubilee's pale complexion. She wanted to deny what had happened between her and Howard, but she could not speak because of the huge lump that had formed in her throat. All the torment and humiliation of everything that had happened in the past few days began to wash over her in a crushing avalanche of unbearable pain. Jubilee was not accustomed to allowing her personal feelings to surface in front of others, but then, she had not been prepared to come to this desolate territory to have her entire life crumble down around her either. She tried in vain to hold back the well of tears which sprung into her blue eyes without warning. The agony she felt inside made her powerless to control her emotions as hot tears began to roll down the hollows of her soft cheeks. The strong and independent nature that she was so proud of possessing, was now pitifully gone, and in its place was a breaking heart. She longed for a pair of muscled arms to surround her with their strong security.

Chance was at her side in less time than it took her aching heart to complete a single beat. When Jubilee felt his arms encircle her quaking body, she did not even try to resist. There had never been a time before now when she had needed to feel the strength of a man's embrace with such desperation. She couldn't help but wonder — when she had grown tired of trying to be so strong? And why hadn't she noticed how lonely she had become in her quest for independence? Perhaps it was just an accumulation of the disasters that had happened while she was here in the Wyoming territory which had disillusioned her for the moment . . . or maybe it just took meeting Chance Steele for these longings to finally surface.

Chapter Nine

Chance did not understand the reasons behind Jubilee's sudden outburst, but when he took her in his arms the strange sensations he had been feeling since their destined meeting engulfed him with the truth he had come to this house hoping to escape. All the sorrow he had carried through the years after the tragic loss of his first love was erased from his mind as he realized that he had fallen in love again. But just as quickly, he became aware of the similarities between his two loves that would make them both equally tragic. When he was a young man he had clung to the foolish dream that someday Faith Barnett would return the great love he harbored for her. Now, he was older and wiser. Faith had been cut from the same cloth as Chance, and even then she had not been capable of loving him. How could he ever hope that Jubilee Hart would respond to his desperate love, when she was the complete opposite of him?

"I'm so sorry," she sobbed into the rich floral silk of his brocaded vest. She noticed that he smelled faintly of cigars and whiskey. They were disturbing odors that Jubilee always associated with saloons. But tonight they didn't seem to bother her as she added, "I never cry in public."

Chance gloried in the feel of her long gossamer hair against his cheek, while he tried to uplift her spirits along with his own darkening mood. "Well then, should

I have bought tickets for this private showing?" He felt her pull away slightly from his close embrace, and when he glanced down to study her somber face, he was grateful to see that her tears were beginning to fade. Only traces of the burning rivulets marred the smooth skin of her face. His heart wrenched inside his chest when their eyes met again, and he glimpsed the depth of her inner pain. Could she be this distraught over the outcome of the rally and the protest? Or did her torment have something to do with Howard Crowly?

"How did you injure your hand?" Chance asked, without caring if he was being too forward and personal. Jubilee's dark blue eyes grew wide, revealing her answer without her saying a word. Rage ripped through Chance as he drew his own conclusions from the fear he could see contained within her red-rimmed eyes. "Did Howard—did he—" Chance was so angry he could not say the words outloud. He would kill the bastard if Jubilee confirmed what he already knew to be true.

The fury that collected in the handsome features of the gambler's countenance surprised Jubilee. She would not have expected him to care one way or the other if Howard Crowly had already had his way with her. It had been her belief that the opportunity to lure her into his bed was also what Chance Steele was after when he had showed up for dinner at the inn, and then again when he had sent her the elaborate bouquet of roses. Because she could not tear her eyes away from his face, Jubilee continued to stare at the multitude of emotions that flashed from within his dark gaze. Outwardly, he appeared to be no different than the scores of other gambling rogues whom she had encountered during the years that she and her mother had followed her father from one hell-hole to another. Yet, at the same time, there was something so very different about this strange, dark-eyed man. Jubilee found herself being torn apart by her own conflicting sentiments.

"Howard tried, but he didn't succeed," she said in a

voice choked with emotion. A visible change overcame Chance's face as he was flooded with relief. When his midnight gaze remained locked with her eyes of deep azure, it was inevitable that they would kiss. Jubilee felt the pull of desire draw them toward one another at the same time she felt the tug of her heart strings within her breast. All her years of common sense blew out the window with the wild Wyoming wind that whipped ferociously around the house. Her mind screamed inwardly that kissing this man was not proper, but her heart whispered that nothing had ever been more right. It was the hushed voice of her defiant heart which drowned out the last of her protests as their lips gently molded together in intimate contact. The brief and shy kisses she had shared with one or two suitors in the past could not even begin to compare with the engulfing tenderness of Chance Steele's lingering kiss. To the surprise of both of them, it was Jubilee's lips which grew more daring as she leaned forward in a bold attempt to prolong this wondrous contact. Although this man represented all the things she vehemently fought against, it did not matter in these few moments of new passion. In the short interval between the time their lips first touched, and the instant when they were forced to draw apart, the chains that had once imprisoned Jubilee's well-guarded heart broke free and crumbled to dust. *How could fate have dealt me such an unfair hand?* she wondered, as the realization of what had just happened filled her with sadness. Even as she felt Chance's mouth slowly pull away from her aching lips, she knew that she had fallen in love. But she would resist this unexpected discovery until her dying day . . . or until her heart would no longer allow her to deny it.

"I—ah—I guess that shouldn't have happened," Chance said. He worried that she would naturally assume he had come here for no other purpose. The kiss had happened as easily as though tonight had been set aside just for this one spectacular event, and he did not think either of them could place the blame. His entire body was enraptured by her sweet-tasting lips, and his mind was reeling with the delirium caused by her touch. If he had felt this elated when he had kissed Faith Barnett for the first time, he could not remember. But, even if he never had another opportunity to hold Jubilee Hart in his arms again, he knew that he would remember this one overpowering kiss for all eternity.

Jubilee ran her tongue over her lips as if they were already thirsty and impatient for another kiss. She had regained a small portion of her lost senses, so she merely nodded her blonde head weakly and moved behind the back of the chair, as far away from Chance Steele as possible. "It was just another one of those unfortunate mishaps, which we always seem to encounter whenever we're in one another's presence." If only she could believe the hoarse-sounding words that came from her own mouth . . . the same mouth that yearned unmercifully for his second kiss.

"You'd better leave," she whispered in a voice that was barely articulate. He was still too near, and far too dangerous. The beating of her heart sounded deafening and she was amazed that he didn't seem to notice the loud pounding coming from within her breast. She cleared her throat and traced the outline of her dry lips with a swipe of her tongue once more. "You'd better—" she began again, since she was certain that he had not heard her over the thudding of her wild heartbeat.

"Ah, yes. I should go," Chance interrupted. Because of his own turbulent frame of mind, her strange behavior did not seem unusual to him. He rose to his feet on weak and trembling limbs, then looked around in confusion for his hat and coat. When his misty gaze located the articles of clothing, he stumbled towards the coat rack.

Jubilee did not make any effort to move from the chair. She was sure that she was shaking too severely to even make an attempt to walk. If nothing more than this man's kiss could affect her in such a drastic manner, how would she ever survive if anything more passionate was to happen between them? Well, that was not possible anyway, she quickly told herself. Tomorrow, she would definitely be on the next train headed East. The pounding of her untamed heart beat increased with this thought, although Jubilee fought to calm herself before her heart crashed from within her breast. *Was it possible to crave someone's touch so badly that one's heart could burst at the seams?* she wondered in a moment of panic. Leaving Cheyenne was the best thing — the only sensible thing — Jubilee could do, especially after this latest, and most puzzling, incident. Yet, as she watched Chance Steele don his long coat and little round bowler hat, she knew that leaving him would also be the most difficult thing she had ever had to do.

Chance paused at the parlor doorway and turned to gaze upon the beautiful woman who observed him silently from the chair across the room. He wanted to memorize everything about her before he left, so that he could file the picture away in his mind along with the memory of her kiss . . . just in case his eyes never gazed upon the sight of her again. Sadly, he traced the gentle contours of her lovely face; his frenzied mind painted a mental image of the way her eyes shimmered like royal blue gems in the dim light of the kerosene lamp. He felt his mouth burn with renewed longing as his gaze passed over the slight upward tilt of her nose, then lingered for an instant on the pale pink lips that had just kissed him with such passion. He tried to immortalize her entire visage in his mind's deepest passages for a few seconds longer. Then his mouth curved beneath his thin mustache as a poignant smile settled upon his handsome face. He was a professional at the card tables, a champion diplomat, and a charmer of unequalled talent. Yet when it came to losing at love, he would never learn how to walk away with any amount of dignity.

With his sad expression still intact, Chance turned around on the heels of his shiny boots and exited from the house, leaving Jubilee alone with only the sound of the lonesome wind to comfort her. A crazy urge to run after him, out into the snow and wind, played with Jubilee's unstable mind when she heard the sound of the front door close softly behind him. But she could not make herself move from the chair. She had waited twenty-five years to experience the glorious feeling that his one kiss had evoked in only a few seconds. Still, she could not allow herself to forget who she was, and more importantly, who he was.

After her father died from the liquid poison he gulped down daily, and her mother had already worked herself into an early grave trying to make a living for her daughter and worthless husband, Jubilee made a determined vow. She would never again associate with gamblers, and drunks, or anyone else whose lives were determined by the outcome of a card game and a flask of whiskey. With this ancient vow reverberating violently through the passages of her mind, Jubilee realized that she could not run after Chance Steele—not tonight, or tomorrow. Not ever!

Chapter Ten

The opening night of The Second Chance Saloon exceeded all of Chance's expectations. But at the same time, it had also proven to be one of the most disappointing nights of his entire life. If it was within his power to hold back the approach of the new day, he would have grasped onto the darkness forever, so that he could have remained within the realm of Jubilee Hart's captivating kiss. But the harsh light of the dawn fell without mercy on Chance Steele's aching heart, which was almost as severe as the pain in his head. With the last drop drained from his whiskey bottle, he slumped against the back wall behind the corner table where he had brooded and drank away the night. Morning had found him a great deal wealthier, but in areas of a more personal measure, he was as destitute as he had always been.

His inability to drink himself into a state of oblivion had increased his mood of self-pity. The blurry vision that greeted the opening of his blood-shot eyes told him that he was drunk to a degree, but the fact that he was still awake and reasonably coherent infuriated him. The remnants of the previous night's celebration were scattered about the large establishment, but Walker — Chance's live-in bartender and cleaning man — was already hard at work. Walker avoided the area where his brooding boss sat as he feverishly worked to clear a pathway through the litter of strewn beer glasses and whiskey bottles. At another corner table, one of the professional gamblers was lost to a drunken slumber, face down, at the place of his last card game of the night. Ah, the pleasures of the trade, Chance thought in a sardonic vein. He could not count the number of times he had awakened in a similar position with a head that felt as though it was split in two, a mouth to which cotton could stick, and most times, an empty pocketbook.

"Boss?" Walker said apprehensively as he approached the corner table and held out a tin box. "This is last night's profits." A proud twinkle glistened from the bartender's eyes as he waited for the other man to count the proceeds.

The hint of a smile hovered on Chance's mouth when he finished with the tally. He had made more money in one night as a saloon owner than most men made in an entire year. "A good night's work. Wouldn't you say so, Walker?"

"And that don't include what they took in," Walker said as he motioned towards the second floor.

A crude snicker greeted this statement. "Ah, yes. They should have raked in a tidy sum as well." He recalled the numerous trips Howard Crowly had made to the upper story. A renewed bout of anger flooded through the dark-eyed gambler when he thought of Jubilee's bandaged hand, but he reminded himself that Jubilee Hart was not his concern. His heart begrudgingly understood that they had each reached an unspoken agreement when they parted last night, and they would probably never see one another again. Ah well, that was for the best . . . her best, anyway. He motioned for Walker to take the money bag, then grabbed for the whiskey bottle again. After taking another large swallow of the brew, which emptied the remains of the bottle, Chance smashed the bottle down on the table. He was better off without love, too!

With this firm resolution, Chance attempted to stand up. He realized, as he rose up on his wobbly legs, that the alcohol had definitely taken its toll on his weary body and senses. Until the room stopped spinning like a top across his drunken mind Chance clutched onto the edge of the table for support. He drew in a heavy breath when he was finally able to focus his gaze long enough to let go of the table and attempt to walk across the floor. His only goal was to reach his private quarters, where he planned to pass out the instant his weary body found the comfort of his bed. The trip across the large main room of the saloon was pure torture, and by the time he staggered into his living area, he was seriously considering doing away with his miserable hide. *What makes a man put himself through such agony?* he wondered, as her blonde image flashed through his reeling thoughts.

When his bed was in sight, he was overcome by an odd sense of parental conscience. He had not even bothered to check in on Jerrod all night, although at sixteen, the boy hardly needed strict supervision. Still, something kept nagging at Chance, despite the fact that his bed was almost within reach. It would only take a minute or two, perhaps a bit longer in his slow moving mode, to look in on the boy. With a moan, Chance turned slowly around and dragged his leaden feet to opposite side of the sitting room. Jerrod's cot was concealed behind a heavy curtain, which provided the boy some privacy. He reached out his shaking hand and pulled back the curtain, expecting to encounter the sleeping teenager.

"Je—Jerrod?" he managed to croak out through his whiskey-thick tongue. Where in tarnation was that boy? Chance pulled the watch fob out from his vest pocket and carefully separated the time piece from the tiny derringer, which also dangled from the end of the chain. Eight o'clock—straight up. Jerrod must have gone to school already, but didn't school start at eight-thirty? Chance replaced his watch, along with his miniature weapon, back into his vest pocket and ran his hand down the front of his vest in an unconscious gesture. Jerrod couldn't be too far away, and Chance's head was pounding too hard to dwell on the boy's whereabouts. He stumbled back across the room with an urgent need to find his mattress once again. Just as he was about to fulfill his quest and flop face down upon his bed, a loud knock sounded at his door.

"Boss?"

Chance snarled in response. "What is it, Walker?"

The bartender cringed at the angry tone of his boss, but he had no choice but to disturb him. "It's Brandy. She needs help gettin' rid of a customer who's reluctant to go. Keeps sayin' he's a friend of yours, and he doesn't have to leave until he's good and ready."

The saloon owner growled. Every man in Cheyenne had suddenly become his bosom buddy last night—for a drink on the house, or a free hour or two upstairs, and even for a loan on a bad hand of cards. With his new plenitude of friends, Chance figured he would never lack for companionship. Once again, he dragged his aching body across the room and opened the door. Even the simple gesture of turning the knob took a huge effort as the large quantity of liquor he had consumed during the night began to wear itself thin.

"Shoot the bastard," Chance grumbled as he glared at Walker from the painful side of his swollen eyes.

A knowing grin moved across the bartender's mouth as he stepped back to allow his boss to pass through the doorway. He had been a cohort of Chance's back in their riverboat days, and he was used to seeing the gambler in this frame of mind after a night of wild abandonment. However Chance Steele had not been in very wild form last night, and as far as the bartender knew, his boss had not abandoned too much, either. From Walker's observation, Chance had spent most of the night at the corner table. Perhaps that was his problem? If he had ventured upstairs during the wee hours of the night, his outlook this morning might be a bit more jolly.

"Where is he?" Chance said as he staggered toward the stairs. He hoped the man would leave peaceably, because he knew that in his disabled state, he would never be able to use any amount of force. He was almost tempted to crawl up the curved stairway, rather than walk to the second floor, which seemed to hover above him like a impassable mountain summit. But he decided he should salvage at least a portion of his dignity. He nodded his tousled dark head as Walker pointed toward the room that housed the reluctant customer. The fellow must have had a darn good time at the grand opening if he refused to leave, Chance mused to himself. Still, The Second Chance Saloon was not a boarding house.

"Brandy?" Chance called out hoarsely as he swayed before the closed door. He just wanted to go back downstairs to his bed. Whoever this freeloader was, he'd better be prepared to take his worthless presence elsewhere without delay.

The pretty prostitute known as Brandy swung open the door almost before Chance had finished saying her name. "He says he's not goin' home," she volunteered, while she motioned toward the bed. When she stepped back to reveal the stubborn man who reclined amongst the sheets, Chance Steele moaned with frustration.

"Ah, Howard Crowly," he said without a note of surprise in his voice. The proprietor of the saloon moved into the room using the support of the door frame. If the whiskey had not killed him by now, the hangover surely would. In a fleeting moment of reform, he silently vowed to never take another drink for as long as he lived. The way he felt, though, he might not have to go without a drink for too long. He forced himself to straighten up in an effort to convey a small amount of authority. "What's this I hear about you refusing to leave?" Chance tried to imitate a smile and to sound as if he was amused by the man's obstinate behavior, but inwardly, he was still seething with contempt for the man.

It was apparent the older man had spent the better portion of the night engaged in the same activity as Chance, because when he glared at the intruders, his red puffy eyes had a difficult time remaining in focus. An empty whiskey flask on the bedside table confirmed this suspicion. "That's right! I paid a tidy sum into this establishment since yesterday afternoon, and I think I'm entitled to stay as long as I please."

Chance started to dispute him, to explain to him that the ladies deserved their fair share of privacy once morning came around, but he didn't have the energy to go into a detailed explanation about common courtesies that any decent man should understand without being told. He reminded himself that Howard Crowly was not a decent man. With a defeated sigh, Chance turned toward Brandy. "He'll have to go to the bank before too long. Later today, Ina Devine and I will discuss what sort of rules we should set up to prevent this sort of thing from happening in the future." He could only hope he was correct in his assumption that Howard Crowly would leave on his own before too long. He turned to go back to the bed that was urgently calling out to him, when Brandy's next statement stopped him in his tracks.

"Ina ain't going care, cause she let the boy spend the whole night in her room too."

Her words seared through Chance like a fiery bolt of lightning. Jerrod had not been in his cot this morning, and now this woman was telling him that some boy was sleeping in Ina Devine's room. Impossible! Chance's pounding head was introduced to a new level of pain as the agonizing thought passed through his mind. Surely Ina would have more scruples than to seduce a boy who was barely more than a child? It couldn't be Jerrod to whom Brandy was referring anyway, Chance feverishly told himself, because Jerrod had not yet begun to think about women in such a manner.

"What boy?" he finally managed to choke out in a raspy voice. He leveled the glare of his raven eyes upon the prostitute, while his ears waited to hear the youth's identity.

Brandy gave a nonchalant shrug and flung her long

brown hair over her shoulder. "That boy of yours, who else?" she answered casually.

Sharp, violent shock penetrated into the whiskey-clogged brain of the saloon owner. He should have followed his revised intuition about Ina Devine and sent her packing back to St. Louis yesterday, before she had the chance to destroy the mind and body of an innocent young boy. Chance felt sick as vile thoughts concerning the ruination of his nephew rolled through his anguished mind. That flame-haired hussy had definitely over-stepped her boundaries this time, and Chance intended to see that her insolence did not go unpunished.

"Now Boss, give yourself a chance to cool down before you go chargin' into Ina's room," Walker said when he saw the dark rage collect upon the other man's countenance. Through the years he had observed Chance a countless number of times while the gambler was engrossed in a card game. Walker had always marveled at the uncanny patience the card shark seemed to possess. He never pushed for an opponent to hurry with a bet, or for himself to make a rash move. Even in the event that he would find himself in a touchy situation with an opponent who accused him of cheating, Chance always managed to remain in control. Like a coiled snake, the gambler would remain calm and poised until the other man made the first move. Then he would whip out his little .22-caliber derringer and drop his accuser swiftly just as a poisonous rattler strikes his prey. Patience was just one of the many traits that made Chance Steele so good at his chosen profession.

This morning though, Walker saw a deadly side of the man he had never been a witness to before, and he also realized the depth of Chance's affection toward his nephew. The bartender was surprised at the way Chance had taken on his new responsibility toward the boy with such a devotion, especially since he had always had the impression that the gambler never allowed himself to become too close to anyone. Although during their association on the Mississippi over the past decade, Walker and the gambler had become friends. Walker figured he knew the other man as well as it was possible for anybody to know a private man like Chance Steele. But he did not like the violent side of Chance Steele, which the information about the boy's whereabouts had just brought to the surface. In an effort to avoid another unpleasant episode between Ina and the boss, Walker decided he would try to talk some sense into his boss one more time.

"I don't know who you're placin' at fault, but if you'd stop to think about it, this might not seem so bad." Walker hurried on in spite of the cold black gaze that was settled upon him. "All boys Jerrod's age need a little schoolin', and who better but a woman like Ina Devine to give him a proper education?" Walker's rationalization was persuasive, but Chance did not alter his attitude.

"He could have gotten all the lessons he needed to know at this point in his life from a school book!," the gambler spat back. He realized this must be Ina's way of paying him back for the other day when he had run out on her. But she had cut her own throat this time. Chance glanced back into Brandy's room, where Howard Crowly was still stretched out beneath the bed coverings, wearing nothing more than a sodden, gloating smirk upon his aging face. He still was not ready to deal with the old coot, because Howard reminded him of Jubilee, and he just spent the whole night trying to drink her out of his mind. But he *was* prepared to deal with Ina Devine!

Walker motioned for Brandy to return to her room when he became aware of his boss' determined intent. A pouting expression came over the woman's face as she was forced to return to the clutches of the selfish old banker. She had gladly accepted her turn to accompany him up to her room last night, thinking that a man of his position and wealth would be generous with his money, as well as with his attentions. He was neither, she found out in the interval between last night and this

124

morning. Women in her line of work could not usually be choosy about their clientele, but Brandy made a solemn vow never again to allow Howard Crowly to step foot in her room at The Second Chance Saloon—that is, if she was ever fortunate enough to get him out of it!

As Chance marched down the carpeted hallway toward Ina Devine's room, he tried to clear his foggy mind of the crazy thoughts that raged through it. Jerrod's youthful romp with the prostitute had summoned up a flurry of memories that did not settle easily in Chance's suffering mind. He had not been much older than the boy was when he had begun the perilous journey that led him into the shameless life he lived upon the riverboat. Chance's first encounter with a woman had been with Faith Barnett in a back room of the large boat where he had taken a job as a deck boy. He too, had been an eager student, while she had been a dedicated instructor who did not fail to teach him the lessons he would carry with him for the rest of his life.

"Boss, are you sure you want to do this? You could wait until the boy comes out on his own?" Walker said in a pleading tone of voice, which was lost on the man to whom he spoke.

Chance raised his arm up into the air with the intention of banging on the door before he entered. He drew in a raspy breath and he hesitated, wondering if he should just burst in without a forewarning. Had Ina Devine been as gentle with Jerrod last night as Faith Barnett had been with him the first time? Chance wondered as his mind continued to travel back through the years—it was not so difficult to recall those long ago events. Until Jubilee Hart had replaced them with a new source of grief, Chance had carried the memories of his youthful escapades close to his heart . . . the beautiful afternoons spent making love to the easy sway of the boat, and the nights of wretched repine when Faith was working, and Chance was left alone to wonder what kind of man she was with this time. Surely Jerrod would not be foolish enough to fall in love with a

125

prostitute, too? But then, history seemed to have a way of making a repeat performance every so often. Hadn't Chance just confirmed that belief by falling in love for a second time with a woman who was as unattainable as his first love?

Slowly, Chance drew his arm away from the door, then ran one sweating hand down the front of his silk vest, before dropping his arms to his sides with clenched fists. He heard Walker heave a sigh of relief when he took a step backward. Jerrod had been disobedient, but he was only an impressionable young man. The realization that Jerrod was no longer a child hit Chance square in the center of his unprepared being. Through the years, he had never readjusted his thinking where Jerrod was concerned. To him, the boy was still the red-faced infant he had turned his back on over sixteen years ago.

"You can go back to your cleaning now," Chance said to Walker as he dropped his chin down upon his chest. His sins from the past were rapidly catching up with him, and he was not sure if he was ready to deal with any of them. "I'm going to bed."

He trudged back down the stairs without another word. After he slept for a while he would think about all the things that had drastically altered his life in the past few weeks, beginning with Jerrod's arrival and accelerating with the disastrous events of the past couple of days. When he reached his private living quarters, Chance did not allow himself the opportunity to dwell upon his disintegrating world as he crumpled face down onto his bed. The blackness which engulfed him was welcomed by his overloaded mind and exhausted body. Yet the unpleasant dreams that ensued were not so inviting. In slumber, Chance's unwilling thoughts were subdued and guided back to the years of his young manhood. The demons of time drew upon his most painful recollections and filled his head with visions of the beautiful Faith Barnett and the way she had looked on the last day he had seen her on the river-

126

boat sixteen years ago. He tried to cling to the image of the breath-taking beauty, but she kept fading farther from view until she was only a blur against the dark hollows of his unconscious mind. In her place another image of a woman even more beautiful began to emerge in the form of Jubilee Hart, but this time it was Chance who felt his essence diminishing in strength until nothing of him remained but a pile of fancy clothes at the blonde's dainty feet. And throughout all of the disturbing dream, Jerrod's image remained steadfast in the background—constantly growing and changing—from a frightened dark-eyed babe, whose auburn-haired mother had deserted him on the banks of the mighty Mississippi, to a strong young man of integrity and wisdom.

Chance bolted from his world of tangled dreams in a cold sweat. A sound from somewhere in the room had managed to break through his deadened senses. For a moment, he did not move from his face-down position on the bed, hoping the disturbance would go away and that he could fall back into a deep, dreamless, sleep. The noise occurred again though, and as Chance's hazy mind began to clear he was reminded of the educational endeavor Jerrod had embarked on during the previous night. He raised himself up to a sitting position while trying to ignore the agony of his hangover. His blurry vision settled upon the sight of the dark-eyed young man attempting to sneak out the back door.

"Going somewhere, boy?" Chance asked in a hoarse voice.

Jerrod's footsteps froze to the spot. Without turning around to face his uncle, he replied, "To school. I—I overslept a bit—too much studying last night, I guess."

"That's an understatement, I'd guess," Chance retorted in a snide tone. He thought about trying to stand up, but quickly decided he was doing well just to be sitting up at this point. He did not say another word as he waited to see if Jerrod would attempt to lie about his recent activities. He wondered if the boy possessed any of the integrity that his strange dream had portrayed, and if he would admit to where he had spent the night. Jerrod's decision was etched deep into his regretful expression when he turned around to face the man he believed to be his uncle. Chance was struck hard by the irony of his desire for Jerrod be truthful with him today, when he himself had deceived the boy for sixteen years. A crushing sadness enveloped Chance with a longing to somehow recapture everything he had lost during those years when he had spent all his time wallowing in whiskey bottles and trying to escape from no one other than his own spineless self.

His plan to berate and punish the boy for his misdeeds, then to lay down a rash of new rules about Jerrod's boundaries in the saloon, disappeared from Chance's mind. He stared across the room wordlessly, while he became acutely aware of the person who stared back at him. *"How could I have been so blind?"* Chance wondered. He looked at Jerrod as if he was seeing him for the first time. A swell of pride arose in Chance—not for the boy's one night of lascivious behavior—but for the strong, intelligent young man who had developed from the seed of his own loins. Chance could not take any credit for the boy's upbringing; his brother and sister-in-law deserved that honor. But he could have a hand in helping the boy adapt to his new role as a man.

What Jerrod had done last night was not right, and it was evident by the young man's expression that he was suffering the agony of his mistake. But his bad judgement did not have to mean that Jerrod's entire life was destined to go astray. For once, history did not have to repeat mistake after mistake. Jerrod had received some eye-opening schooling in the past few hours, but it was not too late for him to learn a valuable lesson from his romp on the second floor . . . and to the surprise of Chance Steele, his realized that it was not too late for him, either.

Chapter Eleven

Ina Devine lagged several yards behind the man who sauntered ahead of her as they made their way down the icy street. She would not speak to her ex-employer, and she even refused to allow him to carry her luggage. The two heavy bags she toted kept dragging on the ground, making each step she took a struggle. With a burst of profanity, she hoisted the bags up and continued with her slow pace until the bags would once again scrape against the frozen ground and she would mumble another round of obscenities. Someday, she promised herself, Chance Steele would regret the way he had treated her. The first thing she planned to do when she returned to St. Louis was to tell everyone who would listen that The Second Chance Saloon was a Pandora's box, which was run by an unscrupulous proprietor who housed cheaters, liars, and other assorted hooligans. If Chance Steele wanted his establishment to gain world-wide fame, then Ina Devine was determined to see to it that he received his wish!

Both Ina and Chance knew that her night of abandonment with Jerrod was the main reason behind her dismissal, but since he did not care to elaborate, Chance merely told her that he did not think their arrangement was going to work out. Under the circumstances, he felt it was best for her to return to St. Louis before any more hard feelings developed. Of course, he knew that she already harbored enough animosity toward him to last her for a long time to come, and her hostile attitude this afternoon was proof.

"Here is your ticket," he said in an aloof tone as he extended his hand out to her once they had reached the depot. His outward composure was a facade, because it took all of his control to remain calm and sensible where this malicious female was concerned. Ina grabbed the train ticket from his hand and turned away from him without a word. A shrug of indifference accompanied the dark frown upon Chance's face as he unintentionally turned toward the direction of Carey Avenue.

The pace of his heart suddenly increased like the ticking of a clock that had gone berserk when he glimpsed the two women who were walking toward the depot. For an instant his entire being was thrilled by Jubilee's approach, but then his thoughts moved past the first jolt of ecstasy that he felt for the opportunity to see her again. He became aware of the baggage she and Abigail Crowly carried. Ah yes, *she* would be leaving today, too. With all the recent distractions involving Ina and Jerrod, Chance had not thought of this possibility. Since he had convinced himself that they would never see each other again, the joy he felt at their fated meeting today rapidly turned into a crushing despair.

"I ain't riding all the way back to St. Louis on the same train as that goody-goody," Ina Devine declared the instant she noticed the new arrivals.

Chance ignored her snide remark, because Jubilee Hart had just spotted him too. As the women drew nearer, he could sense the conflicting emotions Jubilee was also feeling about seeing him again. She acknowledged his presence with a restrained smile and a polite nod of her head, but when she briefly allowed herself to look up into his eyes, the sparkle contained within her royal blue gaze, suggested that she was stirred by an inner excitement. His earlier resolution — that it was never too late to learn from one's mistakes — came rushing back to him with an urgent demand. Could there be a reason for their coincidental meeting here today, and also for all the other strange and ironic events of late?

"Oh dear," Abigail Crowly said as they approached the roundhouse and she became aware of the tall saloon owner and his consort. Her worried gaze was focused solely on the prostitute who was glaring at them with deadly intent. "Perhaps you should wait until tomorrow to leave."

Jubilee did not attempt to reply to Abigail's suggestion. Oh, how she wished she didn't have to leave him at all. Yet, how could she even allow such a foolish thought to pass through her mind? There was absolutely no way she could stay in Cheyenne. She was still too worried about another encounter with Howard Crowly, and she was even more terrified of giving into the intense feelings she had acquired for the raven-haired gambler in the short time that she had been in this rough territory. Jubilee could not control her urge to throw the painted trollop her most withering look. She and Abigail were forced to halt beside Ina Devine and Chance Steele while they waited for the train to begin loading passengers. Ina returned the blonde's gesture with her own contemptuous glare, but as she opened her red-stained lips to hurl an insult to match, Chance Steele stepped between the two females.

"Ah, Abigail, how nice to see you again," he gushed with sincerity, while hoping to prevent a cat fight between Ina Devine and Jubilee Hart. He had never witnessed such a deadly exchange of looks between two women, and he had no doubt that either of the fiery-tempered ladies would tolerate one word of abuse from the other one. "You're looking as lovely as the weather today," he said as he gestured towards the clear azure sky that had abruptly replaced the black storm clouds, and had allowed the absent sun to shine down upon the prairie town for a spell.

Abigail blushed in her usual shade of red at the handsome gambler's fib. Little did it matter that his

131

compliments were the meaningless chatter of a smooth-talker; Abigail would gladly accept any little bit of recognition from this charming man. She was relieved that he was not angry at her for her outburst in front of his saloon yesterday, and she did not mind when he turned his attention away from her and focused his ebony gaze upon the beautiful woman who accompanied her.

For a moment, Chance was at a loss for words. It seemed that Jubilee Hart caused this strange affliction to occur each time he was in her presence. "I see you're leaving," he finally said as their eyes met in silent understanding. He noticed she was wearing the same red velvet suit that she had worn on the day of her arrival, and Chance was unexpectedly reminded of the holidays which were coming up in a few weeks. Why would such a strange thought pass through his mind? It must have something to do with Jubilee's red attire, he decided, because he had not bothered to celebrate Christmas since he had become an adult. As he stared at Jubilee Hart, he became overwhelmed by a sense of expectation for the approaching New Year.

Jubilee glanced down at the ground as a nervous flutter settled in the pit of her stomach. This man had a way of making her feel as if they were the only two people in existence every time their eyes touched upon one another. When she looked up again, she willfully avoided his direct gaze. "Abigail has had to tolerate my presence long enough," she replied in a light-hearted tone. The smile upon her lips, though, was not as bright as she had planned, and she wondered if Chance Steele could see the sadness her smile belied. "I'm anxious to return to my — my home before the holidays," she stammered, attempting to convince him — as well as herself — that she was glad to be leaving Cheyenne.

"Of course," Chance responded. He was surprised to learn that she was also thinking about the impending festivities. Once again he tried to imagine the elegant home in Washington, D.C. in which she undoubtedly resided. But he did not want to dwell on drastic differ-

132

ences of their lifestyles, so he tried to think of something else to say that would sound half way intelligent. His mind was a complete blank, however.

"I said, I ain't sharin' no train with that blonde goody-goody!"

Once Ina's heavily accented voice cut through the silence, Chance's mind snapped back into a functioning mode. He had completely forgotten she was standing behind him, and once he put her on the train, he intended to wipe her out of his mind all together. In aggravation, he swung around and opened his mouth to retort to her interference. But before he could utter a word, Jubilee answered in her own defense.

"Well, that's quite all right with me. I have no desire to share a ride with an orange-haired, painted up harlot who—"

"I think you've both made your positions clear," Chance interrupted in a forceful tone. He remained as a barrier between the two hostile females, but he had to keep inching back and forth as each of them tried to get around him to face each other in a confrontation. After several sways to each side that caused him to grow dizzy, Chance finally blurted out, "Enough! This is ridiculous."

When he noticed how his firm command had halted the fiesty women, he straightened his tall form to its full height and squared his jaw in a fierce expression. "It's obvious you two have nothing nice to say to each other, and I am one who believes that when you can't say something nice, then you shouldn't say anything at all." He paused as his eyes flitted towards Jubilee and then to Ina. Although his ominous expression and tone of voice had distracted the women momentarily, the hostile glares they directed toward one another told Chance he was treading upon dangerous territory. A touch of diplomacy was required in a situation such as this, he told himself. He ran his hand over the front of his vest, an unconscious gesture which hinted at the insecurities he hid from everyone—including himself. He cleared

133

his throat and continued.

"The problem, as I see it, is that you both need to get somewhere else, at the same time and in the same train coach." He shrugged, and with a heavy sigh dropped his arms to his sides. "A definite problem since there is only one train departing for the East today." A devilish grin appeared beneath his thin mustache, in spite of his attempt to contain the rush of excitement he felt over the possibility this dilemma created. "I guess one of you will have to wait until tomorrow to leave, and—" in a purposeful gesture he leaned toward Jubilee, who had opened her mouth to voice her opinion, and added, "Ina's departure can *not* be detained another day."

Jubilee clamped her mouth shut in angry silence as she threw the prostitute one more look of contempt, which was returned without hesitation by the smirking redhead. She then turned her flashing blue gaze towards Chance Steele as she pondered over her limited options. Riding to St. Louis with that foul-mouthed trollop was not nearly as repugnant as the thought of returning to the Crowly house for one more night. Her departure from Cheyenne today was essential, because where Howard Crowly was concerned, Jubilee already felt she had pressed her luck far beyond its normal boundaries. Yet the longer she stared at the handsome man who stood before her, the more her strange affinity for him increased. All her caution began to evaporate into the crisp winter air, along with the bad feelings of the past few days. A tingling in her being filled her with an odd sense of fulfilling her own destiny. She slowly became aware of the fact that she could not leave Cheyenne, nor could she desert the way she felt about Chance Steele. Her uncertainty disappeared as if a strong Wyoming wind had just blown through her heart, and her developing love for this gambler seemed as endless as the clear blue sky overhead.

The enraptured couple hardly blinked an eye when Ina Devine huffed with fury and stomped toward the waiting locomotive with her bags dragging along beside her. Nor did they care when Abigail Crowly stepped back to allow them a moment of privacy when she became aware of what was happening between the gambler and the suffrage leader. If they had taken a second to glance at the elderly woman, they would have noticed the elated smile she wore upon her thin face as she hauled Jubilee's bags away from the pathway of the passengers who were loading onto the train.

The loud bellowing of the departing train whistle brought their soaring souls back to earth. An easy grin fell upon Chance's lips, which made his dark gaze sparkle like stars in a midnight sky. His grin was contagious as Jubilee's solemn expression began to change to a look of teasing opposition. "Well, looks like I'm staying."

"I don't think you were ever meant to leave," he said with a roguish tilt of his dark head.

"I'll have to go eventually."

Chance's heart quickened in his breast as he noticed the slight narrowing of her royal blue eyes. He recalled the hidden challenge he thought he glimpsed in her blue gaze ever since the first night he had met her. Their social stations in life might be as opposite as fire and ice, but he sensed that deep inside she was a gambler by nature. With this deduction, Chance took the greatest gamble of his life.

"Not if you marry me," he said with a nonchalant shrug of his broad shoulders.

Chapter Twelve

Jubilee swung around and stared at the man who had just proposed marriage to her. The illuminating glimmer in her blue gaze hinted at a multitude of emotions. Chance wished he could read her thoughts as he waited for a reply to his impulsive solution to her departure. Though he would never allow his flustered state to surface, he was just as surprised as Jubilee by his suggestion of marriage. He was a man who assumed all things happened for a purpose, so he concluded that the idea of marrying this lovely lady had occurred to his unsuspecting mind for a very good reason. He only hoped it wasn't because someone up above felt he needed another lesson in rejection and humility. Unconsciously, his dark eyes glanced up towards the heavens . . . *no dark clouds up there today.* His optimism increased as he looked back down at the woman in red velvet.

"M-Ma-Ma—" Jubilee finally attempted. The words kept tripping over her tongue. "You?" she managed to spit out at last. He was standing so close she had to tilt her head back to stare up into his face. The fur trimmed hood of her cloak slipped gracefully from her head. Soft tresses that had been held within its loose confines tumbled softly down her back along with the velvety hood as she glazed up at the handsome gambler. Marriage to this man was out of the question! So why couldn't she just say no to his preposterous proposal?

If he lived to be a hundred years old, Chance knew, he would never allow himself to forget the way Jubilee Hart looked at this moment. With her pale blonde hair unbound in the sunlight, and her royal blue eyes shimmering she was without a doubt the most tempting female he had ever known. But best of all was his elated joy over her indecision. If she had refused him, or had even laughed in his face the moment the suggestion of marriage popped out of his mouth, he would have understood. But her obvious confusion gave him more hope than he had ever thought possible. He had not underestimated her gaming nature, nor had he been wrong about the overpowering affinity which had drawn them both together from the first moment they had looked at one another. His sly smile widened as he nodded his dark head in response to her jumbled reply.

"Marry you?" Jubilee repeated with some semblance of a normal tone. She would die an old maid rather than consider such an outlandish proposal. And, she would tell him so just as soon as she could rediscover her lost senses.

When her pale pink lips parted, then closed one more time, Chance knew he had to help with her indecision. "I realize we have not known one another long, and it's obvious we have very little in common." When she nodded her head in rapid agreement, Chance rushed on before he talked her into making the wrong choice. "We do, however, share an attraction towards one another that neither of us can deny. If you leave Cheyenne before we have an opportunity to discover the depth of these new feelings, it would be the biggest mistake you've ever made."

A deep frown crossed Jubilee's flawless countenance. She did not like the way he managed to place the full responsibility of their unexplainable attraction upon her shoulders. Although it was possible she would regret running away from the strange emotions their meeting had aroused in both of them, she was more concerned about what would happen if she discovered

137

that staying in Cheyenne turned out to be an even greater mistake. Because it was impossible to think coherently when she was looking into his teasing black gaze, she tore her eyes away from him and glanced down towards the frozen ground. Finding a solution to his proposal and an explanation for her conflicting emotions, could be as elusive as finding warmth in the winter sunshine.

"Ah," Chance sighed as he ran his gloved hand down the front of his woolen coat. "Why don't you throw caution away for once, and take a chance," he chuckled at the irony of his words. When he noticed she had not caught the humor in his remark, and how the intensity of her frown began to increase, he quickly added, "If you'll stay in Cheyenne for a while longer, I will make you a wager."

"What sort of a wager?" Jubilee queried at once, while her willful eyes sought his mischievous countenance again. Inwardly, she cursed at herself for sounding so eager to learn of his intended venture. When his twinkling eyes narrowed slightly, she became even more agitated with herself for allowing him to think she would even consider making a deal with him about any issue, but especially about something as important as marriage.

His thin mustache curled above his smiling lips when he spoke again. "The legislature convenes day after tomorrow. We could make a bet on the outcome of their decision concerning the equal rights issue."

A snide-sounding huff emitted from Jubilee. "A bet? I hardly think that would be a fair wager for my side. Women in this country have been campaigning for equality for half a century, and it has gotten us nowhere."

Chance rolled his eyes upward as though he was contemplating her statements to great lengths. "Well, I think the men of Wyoming are about to change the course of our country's future, and I'm willing to place all my cards on the table in favor of the vote being passed. I say that before the week is out, the women of our great territory will be as equal as any man. And the rest of the country will be in awe of Wyoming women, as well as of the generous and considerate menfolk who reside here."

His certainty about this issue eluded Jubilee. Her thoughts were still too unsettled to consider his confidence over the outcome of the impending vote, but she couldn't resist the temptation to meet his challenge. "And how would this outcome affect our wager?"

"Ah, yes, our *marriage*." Chance was struck by the realization of how she was even more beautiful when her face carried a childish pout like the one she now wore. "If women are denied the right to vote, then you are free to leave as soon as possible. I'll give you my word that I will not make any attempts to see you again. However, if the enfranchising bill passes, then you will stay and we'll become better acquainted with one another, while you consider the possibility of becoming my wife."

A tingling sensation began to work itself through Jubilee's being as his words spun through her disoriented mind. Visions of living in a real home and of having a cluster of dark-haired children at her feet flashed before her eyes. But the beautiful reverie was quickly replaced by remembrances of her own tragic childhood. How could she even think of marrying a saloon owner who was exactly the type of man from whom she had been trying to escape for most of her life? Chance Steele's home was in the back of a saloon and she had already lived in the backroom of too many gaming houses in her lifetime. She squeezed her eyelids together in an effort to wipe away the image of her worthless father, and when she opened her eyes again, she focused on the tall gambler. Was she allowing his handsome, teasing exterior to make her blind to the man he was inside? Or did his outward appearance conceal the deep sensitivity hiding in the shimmering pools of his ebony gaze, which Jubilee was certain she glimpsed every so often?

"I will stay until after the legislature convenes," Jubilee said before she gave herself time to ponder a future she was certain would be doomed if she allowed herself to pretend that Chance Steele was any different from every other gambler she had ever known. "But marriage is out of the question." She did not intend to sound haughty or superior, but when she tossed her head back and glared up him, this was exactly how she appeared. "I could never marry a man who makes his living by poisoning the minds and bodies of his fellow men with alcohol, and by cheating them out of their hard-earned money at a card table." While she watched his joyful, teasing expression alter into a guarded look of contained anger, she realized how harsh her words must have sounded. Telling him about her turbulent childhood, and why she felt she was qualified to judge men of his caliber, occurred to her in a fleeting thought. Before she had a chance to explain or to rephrase the meaning of her previous denouncement, he retorted.

"Ah, and I suppose it would be out of the question for you to give up your pampered lifestyle in Washington, too? Why, I'm surprised you were able to lower yourself down from your pedestal long enough to associate with all us heathens out here in this uncivilized territory."

The cold glint, which replaced the teasing shine in his eyes, caused an unexpected chill to race through Jubilee's veins. His assumption of her character and way of life enraged her. "You know nothing about my life in Washington!" she replied in defense.

A cruel grin touched the corners of his lips as he raised his dark eyebrows in speculation. "Judging by your expensive attire, and your snooty attitude, I would assume you have never known a hint of poverty or despair. It's easy for someone like you to preach to others about the evils of the world, when you have no idea what it's like to be in their position."

His words sliced through Jubilee like a razor as thoughts of the miserable life she had lived as a child flooded through her mind. This man did not deserve an

140

account of her life, she determined in a moment of fury, while she raised her blonde head higher. "You *presume* to know everything about me, and you place your presumptions on the style of my *clothes?*" A rueful laugh rang through the crisp winter air as she raked her fiery blue eyes over his flashy ensemble. "I had always thought there was more to a person than just their outward appearance. But if one judges another strictly by this type of shallow observation, then my first impression of you has not been altered in the least."

"Are you saying it's possible that there's more to a person than meets the eye?" Chance asked. The twinkle returned to his black gaze as he realized he had struck upon a strong bargaining ground.

"Of course!" Jubilee spat back at him. "It's rather narrow-minded to reduce a person's worth to the style of her dress."

Chance shrugged his broad shoulders. "You determined what type of man I was by the way I dress."

"I know what kind of a man you are by your choice of *occupation*. It takes a rare breed, Mr. Steele, to make a living from other men's weaknesses."

Rage flared through the gambler, but he forced himself to remain outwardly calm as he reassessed this situation in his mind. When it came to narrow-mindedness, she won hands down. He had already determined that she rallied to a challenge, though, so he figured his best option was to return to his original plan of seducing her into a bet. "You are obviously convinced your judgement of me is accurate, but I'd be willing to bet that I can prove you wrong by the time the legislature has granted the women of Wyoming the right to vote."

"I doubt it," Jubilee huffed with indignation. Since he was just too self-assured for his own good, she decided it was time for someone to put this low-down hustler back into the pit where he belonged. "You've got a bet, Mr. Steele. By the week's end, I'll depart from this God-forsaken place, free of any fear that I will ever have to see you again."

A grin of victory washed over Chance's face. He had the rest of the week to win this beauty—more than enough time for a man like himself to overcome a stubborn female's heart. In a bold gesture, he leaned down until their faces were only inches apart. "This type of bet should be sealed by a kiss."

"I will not kiss you in public!" Jubilee gasped. She felt the flame of embarrassment color her cheeks, while the warmth of his breath touched upon her face. Her eyes flitted from side to side as she prayed inwardly that no one was watching them. He was standing so close it was impossible for her to see anyone, or anything, beyond his towering form. She took a step backward, but the slick ground beneath her smooth-soled boots made it difficult for her to move more than a few inches. His handsome face was still too close for her to think in a rational manner, and her jumbled thoughts were rushing through her mind at a breakneck speed. A deal was not a deal until it was sealed, and under no circumstances would she permit him to kiss her with all of Cheyenne as a witness. Before she could repeat this determined vow out loud, however, he clasped ahold of her uninjured hand.

"A handshake will suffice, for now," Chance said as he gave her limp arm a vigorous shake. All traces of their previous insults toward one another were wiped from his mind as he anxiously plotted his strategy for the next few days . . . as well as for their future as Mr. and Mrs. Chance Steele. "May I call on you at the Crowlys' home this evening?" he asked in an excited tone, while he regrettably released her trembling hand. A kiss from those sweet-tasting lips would have been much better, he told himself, but even the brief contact with her unresponsive hand had left him shaky and weak in his knees.

Jubilee's unsettled thoughts finally began to put themselves back into focus until she realized how staying in Cheyenne also meant dealing with Howard

142

Crowly again. Her wide-eyed gaze flew in the direction of Abigail Crowly, who was pretending to stare at something down the street as she patiently waited to learn the outcome of Jubilee and Chance's intense conversation. "I — I will be staying . . . here at the inn," Jubilee said in a hesitant voice. She motioned toward the large building beside the tracks. In an unconscious gesture, she clutched her bandaged hand against her body.

"Of course," Chance said when he noticed her protective motion. He still had to settle that score with Howard Crowly. First though, he had to prove to Jubilee that he was not the hooligan whom she had determined him to be because of his rowdy profession. "Would you have dinner with me at the restaurant, then?"

A weak nod of her head was Jubilee's only reply. Since this smooth-talking gambler seemed to have a way of enticing her into situations from which she could not escape, she was almost afraid to say anything. If she could avoid Howard Crowly, then perhaps a few more days in Cheyenne would be tolerable. However, considering all that had happened in the short time since she had arrived, even a few more days might have a tremendous affect on the rest of her life.

Chapter Thirteen

Jubilee sat in a chair in the corner of her hotel room, and stared at the huge bouquet of roses which had been delivered a short time ago. *Where did Chance Steele find such extraordinary fresh flowers in the dead of winter?* she wondered. *How did he ever manage to connive me into staying in Cheyenne until after the meeting of the territorial legislature?* She sighed heavily and contemplated the most recent upheaval in her life. Chance was correct when he had told her she could not deny the attraction she felt toward him, but she still did not wish to succumb to the feelings she had developed for the gambler.

She eased herself up from the chair, being careful not to use her broken hand. The dull ache in the injured limb reminded her once again of how she was still in the dangerous vicinity of Howard Crowly. She was overcome with dread when she recalled his vile threat on the night of their last encounter. Once she was seen in the company of Chance Steele by the local citizens, everyone would assume Ina Devine's accusation about her relationship with the gambler was correct. Howard's vicious lies would only add to the speculations. Jubilee began to feel ill as she realized there was no way to protect her fragile reputation after she dined alone — and in public — with the saloon owner. *Oh, why did I ever come to this terrible place?* she asked herself for the hundredth time.

The nervous churning in the pit of her stomach

144

made her feel that perhaps she really would be sick. She could then excuse herself from her dinner date tonight. She flopped down on the bed in defeat. Chance Steele would never believe she had become seriously ill in the short time which had passed since they parted at the train station. Besides, she had agreed to stay here for several more days, and she could not hope to convince him that she was incapacitated for the rest of the week. Her hand still ached terribly, though. Would that do for a legitimate excuse? Probably not—not with a pesky man like Chance Steele, she decided. She had made a deal, and she wasn't about to let him think she was the type of person who backed out of a bet.

Besides, Jubilee thought as she unpacked her clothes, once the legislature convened she would have nothing more to worry about, anyway. She was certain the equality bill would not pass the first time it came up for discussion. Her obligation to this ridiculous bet would then be fulfilled. Unfortunately, until that time, she was forced to pretend she was interested in getting to know Chance Steele better, even though everything about this entire bet would be in vain. She would never consider the possibility of marrying him!

She sorted through the pile of clothes strewn across her bed, while considering what to wear to this dreaded rendezvous. For the sake of respectability, she decided her attire had to be the most prim and proper garment she had in her wardrobe. However, the problem was that since moving to the progressive city of Washington D.C., she had acquired a flare for the dramatic fashion, and none of her ensembles were as staid as she wished. Her modest income as a speaker for the suffrage league provided her with a comfortable room at Miss Gurdy's, and paid for the extensive traveling which her position required. Still, to supplement her wages, Jubilee occasionally accepted temporary employment as a clerk, and also wrote speeches for the numerous politicians in the vicinity of the White House. This extra income provided her with cash to spend at her favorite D.C. dress shop, which specialized in the latest European fashions.

"This one will have to do," she muttered to herself as she held up a heavy silk gown of a deep turquoise hue. The gown's high neckline created an elegant and formal look; however, the fitted bodice accented her curvaceous bosom and made her waist appear minute in size. As she stood before the full-length mirror to check her appearance, Jubilee imagined Chance Steele's hands encircling her tiny waist as he drew her up against his muscular body for a passionate kiss.

"Stop it!" she said aloud, furious with herself and her wild, undisciplined thoughts. It wasn't that she had never allowed herself to daydream of such sensuous activities with the opposite gender—it was just that she had always imagined the man in her reverie to be someone with political interests; perhaps someone with high ambitions in the field of law, such as a lawyer or judge. Whoever the man of her dreams turned out to be, he had to be above reproach . . . and the complete opposite of Chance Steele. So why was she unable to escape from his relentless dark eyes, and from the feel of his tender kiss, which still made her entire body grow weak from the memory?

Jubilee gritted her teeth and made another firm vow as she searched through the pile of clothes upon her bed for a shawl that would cover her volptuous form. She would never permit herself such intimate musings about Chance Steele again. But even while she repeated this promise to herself, her mind was engaged in a detailed recollection of the feel of his hands upon her trembling body. Jubilee had to pause at the doorway of her room for a moment in an attempt to calm the excited fluttering of her stomach. Once again, she reprimanded herself for these outlandish desires. Scandalous thoughts of this nature had to be the work of the devil! Thank God tomorrow was Sunday, and she had made plans to meet Abigail at church in the morning. Although the thought of encountering the woman's unsavory husband was not too appealing, surely even Howard Crowly would respect the Sabbath enough not to cause an embarrassing scene at church.

As she made her way toward the restaurant on the lower floor of the inn, Jubilee attempted to convince herself that the next few days would not be as horrible as she feared. The legislators would meet on Monday and she would be gone by Tuesday . . . what more could possibly happen? By the time she had walked to the entrance of the restaurant, her imaginative mind had created at least a dozen possible catastrophes. Yet when she entered the large dining area and spotted the handsome gambler sitting at a corner table, her previous worries seemed to settle somewhere at the back of her mind. She was overcome with anticipation. Much to her surprise, he was not alone. Though she had not paid much attention at the time, she remembered Abigail mentioning that Chance's nephew lived with him. Their physical resemblance was unmistakeable. Even if she hadn't been told who the boy was, Jubilee would have known at once he was related to the saloon owner. The dark-haired youth was the spitting image of his uncle, and as Jubilee observed the two of them conversing and laughing like two mischievous boys, she also became aware of the close bond that existed between the two of them.

When Chance glanced up and noticed Jubilee standing in the doorway, his smile grew even wider, and seemed to light his entire being with a visible glow. He rose to his feet to greet her, and as he did so, Jubilee noticed how he ran his hand down the front of his brocade vest. Several times she had witnessed this unconscious habit of his, and each time she had found herself wondering about the gold watch-fob chain which dangled from his vest pocket. She did not have time to dwell on the contents of his pocket, however, because before she had taken more than a few steps, Chance was standing before her. He bowed from the waist — another irritating habit he possessed, Jubilee noted. Her eyes met his twinkling dark gaze.

"Mr. Steele," she said in a formal tone, with barely a nod of her head when he reached out to take her hand. She still had no intention of allowing him to touch her in public.

When he realized she was not going to greet him with a handshake, Chance knew she would never permit him to hold her hand while he escorted her to their table. He dropped his arm to his side, although the smile upon his face never wavered. "Ah, please call me Chance. Mr. Steele is much too formal."

"We are still on a formal basis, sir."

The gambler cocked his dark head to the side in contemplation for an instant, then quipped, "I would have thought our intimacy in the Crowlys' parlor last night dispensed with all formalities."

Jubilee felt her cheeks flame with embarassment and quickly glanced around to see if anyone was close enough to have overheard his obnoxious remark. A frowning couple at a nearby table, whose complexions were as red as her own, provided the confirmation Jubilee dreaded. She groaned inwardly, while cursing herself again for agreeing to meet this awful man in public—or any place else for that matter!

Chance's gloating quickly ceased when he noticed the enraged dart of her royal blue eyes. He had promised himself not to intentionally anger her tonight, and he had managed to infuriate her the moment she had entered the room. He reminded himself of how his goal was to win this woman's love, not to make her into a life-long enemy. With a glance toward the neighboring couple, who were listening intently, he shrugged and added, "I—I only meant that we should be on a more friendly basis after the other night."

Another rush of color consumed Jubilee's cheeks. Why did he insist on rambling on about that episode? He was only making matters worse, and by the time he was through, all of Cheyenne would probably think they had used the Crowlys' parlor for the scene of their sordid affair. Still, she was sensible enough to realize that the sooner she steered herself—and the babbling Chance Steele—away from the center of attention, the better it would be for both of them. She forced herself to remain as dignified as possible when she assumed a sweet smile and said, "Shall we be seated now?"

With a nod of his head and an undeniable smirk upon his face, Chance turned without offering her his hand and began to lead the way toward the corner table. It was his habit to always pick a table where he was able to freely observe the rest of the room. When engaged in a card game, a gambler had to be aware of everything going on around him; Chance carried this habit over into his personal life, as well. He paused at the table and gestured toward Jerrod as he made the customary introductions.

Jerrod tugged awkwardly at the starched collar of his dress shirt with one hand as he rose to his feet and gave the blonde suffrage speaker a quick nod of his dark head. Accompanying his uncle on this date tonight was not his idea. But after he had been caught in Ina Devine's room this morning, the boy was not about to cross his uncle on any matter. Actually, his uncle seemed to be handling the situation better than Jerrod would have thought. Uncle Chance had hardly said a word about the incident since he had hauled Ina Devine to the train depot and sent her back to St. Louis. When he had returned from the depot, his entire outlook had improved. While Jerrod was expecting a severe punishment for the previous night's escapade, his uncle had told him that their lives were about to take a dramatic turn for the better.

The only thing about his uncle's attitude which did not please Jerrod was the way his uncle had also decided it was time for him to dispose of his comfortable farm duds. The stiff new suit he was wearing tonight was only one of the many outfits Uncle Chance had bought for him during their buying spree that very afternoon. Jerrod was still reeling from his uncle's odd enthusiasm, but it wasn't until the beautiful blonde woman entered the restaurant that Jerrod understood the reason behind the change in his Uncle Chance.

"I thought you might feel more comfortable if Jerrod joined us tonight," Chance said, much to Jubilee's surprise. The young man's presence did make her feel better about being seen in public with the gambler. She nodded gratefully, although words eluded her. The nagging fear of saying something that would land her in the middle of another bet with this quick-witted man reminded her to think about every word that fell from her lips.

"What do you think of Jerrod's suit? I thought it was time he began to dress with a bit more dignity." Chance smiled at the boy and added, "After all, he is a man now."

"It's very nice," Jubilee responded, noticing the young man's embarrassment and the high color which enflamed his face. She wondered if the scarlet shade of her own cheeks matched Jerrod's bright coloring.

"Jerrod is my brother's son," Chance offered. His face grew solemn when he added, "He recently came to live with me after the death of his parents."

The blush faded from Jubilee's face as she met with Chance's sorrowful gaze. "I'm sorry," she answered with earnest sympathy. She glanced at the younger man, whose dark eyes were downcast. He looked up briefly, and when he noticed the direction of Jubilee's gaze, a sad smile curved his lips. Her opinion of Chance Steele began to soften slightly. It took a sensitive man to accept the responsibility for a boy Jerrod's age. Most gamblers whom she had known in the past were too absorbed in their own welfare to care about anyone else . . . and her own father was included in that tally. When Jubilee was Jerrod's age her father hoped and expected that she would be long gone from his life. Once she was living on her own, she was one less unwanted responsibility. He died shortly after she had moved out of the shack they had called home since her mother's death a few months earlier. As a result, Ben Hart had precious little time to be free from the burdens of his family. He died a lonely death, yet Jubilee could not find it in her heart to grieve for him.

"We're goin' buy us a cattle ranch," Jerrod blurted out, unexpectedly. He straightened up in his chair and gave his head a firm nod. "And I'm going to be Uncle Chance's foreman."

"A ranch?" Jubilee asked in surprise as she glanced at Chance Steele. "Are you planning on changing careers, or will the ranch merely be a diversion from your gambling career?"

Chance did not miss the snide undertone of her voice, but he ignored it as he replied, "Eventually, I do plan to turn in my deck of cards for a rope and a pair of spurs. Until I'm ready to do so, however, I intend to profit as much as possible from the success of my new saloon."

"A rancher is a far cry from a saloon owner, Mr. Steele. And raising cattle is a great deal harder than shuffling cards."

Chance ground his teeth together tightly, while he reminded himself that he was not going to engage in a sparring match with this sharp-tongued woman tonight — no matter what she said to provoke him. "Jerrod needs a home. The back of a saloon is not a suitable place for my s—" Chance paused for an instant as his raven gaze leveled at the woman who sat across the table from him. "For my brother's son to live. Nor is it the place where I wish to spend the rest of *my* life."

Jubilee did not attempt to look away from him this time. Instead, she tried to study the conflicting emotions she continually sensed were behind his outward facade. At one time or another every gambler she had ever known had said they were not going to touch one more drink or that they would never play another hand of cards, for as long as they lived. Jubilee supposed all men, regardless of who they were, longed for some sense of respectability. But in Chance Steele, she felt a discipline and strength to achieve this goal that most gamblers lacked. Maybe Miss Gurdy was right; perhaps no two men were alike?

The conversation throughout dinner remained in a lighter vein as Jerrod related tales of his youthful exploits in Kansas. Jubilee thought he was a delightful young man, and she loved to watch the proud expression upon Chance Steele's handsome face when he listened to his nephew speak. What a shame he had never had children of his own, Jubilee thought, then quickly erased that image from her mind. No child deserved to be raised by a gambler. It was lucky for Jerrod that he was nearly grown by the time he had sought refuge with his uncle. Still, by the end of dinner, and over a lingering cup of coffee afterward, Jubilee was more convinced than ever that Chance Steele was not a heartless cheat, the characteristic which she felt dominated the personality of most gamblers.

"Would you excuse me for a few moments while I escort Jubilee up to the second floor?" Chance said to his nephew. He hoped Jubilee would note how careful he was not to assume that she would want him to accompany her all the way to her room. When she did not offer any resistance to his suggestion, he stood up quickly and guided her chair away from the table. As naturally as if they had always been on such friendly terms, she permitted him to take her hand as she rose to her feet. Chance felt as if he had just grown wings and was slowly ascending towards heaven. He winked at Jerrod, a careless gesture which had no basis, but it did not go unnoticed by the scrutinizing eyes of Jubilee Hart.

Without a word to the tall gambler, she allowed him to drape her shawl over her turquoise dress while she said goodnight to Jerrod Steele. Chance's wink had renewed her irritation, and she had no desire to do anything that might invite familiarity. She busied her uninjured hand by cradling her broken one in a protective hold as she walked out of the busy restaurant, thereby preventing Steele from offering to escort her on his arm. Several of the occupants in the large dining room were women she had met during her stay in Cheyenne, and Jubilee felt obliged to acknowledge them. The women returned her greetings with quick waves and mumbled words of hello. The question on the face of each of them was apparent: what was the suffrage leader doing in the company of a gambler whose business she had tried to shut down the very day before? Undoubtedly, all were assuming that Ina Devine's insinuation was true. There was absolutely nothing Jubilee could do to repudiate this accusation now that she had entered into this ridiculous bet with Chance Steele, so she merely departed from the room as hastily as possible.

"May we meet again tomorrow?" Chance asked as he lengthened his stride to catch up to the blonde.

As she bolted up the stairway Jubilee answered, "I've made plans to attend church services with Abigail tomorrow." She prayed that he would return to the restaurant before anyone who had seen them leave together would begin to think he was escorting her into her room. The instant they reached the second floor, Jubilee turned and said, "Goodnight, Mr. Steele. Thank you for dinner."

Chance stared, completely dumbfounded, at the woman as she rushed down the hallway toward her room. What had happened to change her attitude so suddenly? All through dinner she was jovial and friendly, but now she was as cold as a Wyoming blizzard. "How about after church?" he implored in vain. Jubilee did not even pause until she had reached the locked door of her hotel room. As she fumbled with the key, Chance reached her side.

"Jerrod is waiting for you," she reminded him. Just as she was about to turn the key in the lock, Chance's hand closed over her trembling fingers. She didn't even look at his face as he spoke.

"It was a wonderful evening. Please, don't spoil it

153

now." He felt the shaking of her hand beneath his palm, while he grew more confused by her strange behavior. If only he could understand her complex nature, but she had never offered any facts about herself. Was she as frightened of all men as she seemed to be of him?

Jubilee gave up her futile attempt to turn the key as her hand went limp within his grasp. "It—it was a very nice evening. It's just that I don't want everyone to think I allowed you to enter my room. If too much time passes they—"

"Ah, of course, respectability again." A sigh escaped from Chance as he pulled his warm hand away from her icy one. Ever since he had left Mississippi he had been chasing after the elusive sense of respectability, which he felt he had lost seventeen years ago. How could he blame Jubilee Hart for wanting to retain an unblemished reputation? "I understand," he said in apology as he ran the palm of his hand down the front of his silk vest.

Once again, Jubilee was taken aback by this man's unusual sensitivity. But she was even more stunned when he leaned down and kissed her upon the mouth without warning. It was only a brief contact of their lips; she did not even have time to respond before he pulled away. As she stared at him wordlessly, he reached out and turned the key. When the door swung open, he bowed deeply from the waist and motioned into the dark room. "Sweet dreams, Jubilee."

Jubilee's feet stumbled forward, but her disappointed soul remained behind. "Good—Goodnight, Mr. Steele," she said as she slammed the door shut. She leaned against the heavy door and was grateful for the solid feel of wood. The barrier between them did not dispel the yearning in her heart, though. The trembling, which had been only in her hand earlier, was now consuming her entire body. The feel of his lips lingered like hot coals upon her mouth, and the urge to open the door and beg him to kiss her again grew stronger with each passing second. Instead, she leaned forward and pressed the side of her face against the wooden barrier which prevented her from rushing out into the hallway like a woman possessed by a maddening desire. She could not deny this feeling forever . . . not as long as she was so near to this man who caused such desperate longings to surface within her. To be in his presence was an even greater danger, Jubilee decided and she vowed to avoid him until after the meeting of the legislature. Then, she would leave Cheyenne — and him — before she had grown too weak to resist these growing feelings of love and passion.

On the other side of the doorway, Chance Steele also leaned against the rough wooden barricade. A cold sweat had broken out upon his face and his breathing was hard and irregular. He struggled for so long he had believed he could never love another woman as much as he had loved Faith Barnett. Now, he wondered if he had ever known love before he had met Jubilee Hart. He could never allow her to leave him; he would follow her to the ends of time, and he would do anything to win her devoted love in return. He backed away from the door and retraced his steps down the dimly lit hallway, while his mind began to formulate another plan. He had not been to church since he had left his parents' home years ago, but it was high time he and Jerrod started to attend services on a regular basis, and tomorrow was as good a time as any to start.

Chapter Fourteen

Sunday morning the sun was shining down gloriously upon "The Magic City of the Plains." From her hotel window Jubilee looked out across the vast prairie which sprawled out beyond the boundaries of the town for as far as she could see. Snow deeply blanketed the ground. It reflected the morning light with a blinding brilliance, and the young woman was forced to turn her eyes away from the scene that lay before her. After the sleepless night she had just spent, her eyes were weary and sensitive. Even cold compresses had not disposed of the dark and puffy circles beneath her eyes. And it was all Chance Steele's fault!

Jubilee grabbed her cloak from the coat rack and rushed from the room in a useless attempt to flee from the haunting image of the dark-eyed gambler. The moment she was standing in the hallway, however, she was reminded of their impromptu kiss the previous night. How could such a brief encounter affect her so drastically? She paused to catch her breath, and much to her relief, Abigail Crowly appeared at the top of the stairway.

"I see you're all ready to go," Abigail said in a joyful voice. Her pale complexion seemed to have a glow of rapture which Jubilee had not seen in the elderly woman's face before today. She was even dressed a bit more gaily than usual. Although she wore the same long dark purple cloak which she had worn on the first day she met Jubilee at the depot, the hat she now wore was a floppy-brimmed hat of black velvet that boasted a long purple plume. For a prim woman like Abigail Crowly, the hat seemed an extravagance of great proportions.

Jubilee tossed her own black velvet cloak over her shoulders and proceeded to meet the older woman. "You're absolutely glowing, Abigail!" she said warmly. Jubilee harbored a faint hope that the other woman's happiness reflected greater stability in her marriage and home life. Howard would not be tempted by her presence any longer, she thought, since she was no longer staying at their home.

"That's because Howard has not come home yet!" Abigail gushed, then giggled like a school girl. "My life is so peaceful when he's gone. I hope he *never* comes back."

"You don't really mean that, do you?" Jubilee asked in a shocked tone. She would never forgive herself if it turned out Howard Crowly deserted his wife because of what had happened the other night.

Abigail shrugged in a carefree gesture, before turning to descend the stairs. "Why yes, I *do* mean it," she said. She paused and glanced at the younger woman who walked beside her, adding, "And I have you to thank for granting me these past few days of happiness. It's given me time to think about the changes I intend to make in my life."

"Changes?" Jubilee asked fearfully, hoping that none of them were related to the incidents which had led up to Howard's departure.

"The first thing I intend to do when I see that no-good womanizer again is to kick him out of my house for good!"

A groan escaped from Jubilee. Howard Crowly was not going to receive that bit of news with good grace. He would be looking for someone to hold at fault for his wife's sudden change, and Jubilee knew exactly where he would look. She only hoped she would be

157

back in Maryland by then, although judging from the luck she seemed to have these days, she suspected that this was probably hoping for too much. As they headed towards the Methodist Church, one of many denominations which had sprung up throughout the new community, Jubilee fought inwardly with herself. She had a notion to forget about the stupid bet she had made with Chance Steele, and hop on the next train headed East. Her desire to escape intensified when she and Abigail entered the church, where they were confronted by the scowling face of Howard Crowly on one side of the pews, and by Chance Steele's sly grin on the opposite side of the aisle.

"Oh dear, there's Howard!" Abigail said in a tone which did not appear to be nearly as self-assured as she had sounded when she had spouted off about her plans at the inn a short time ago. She drew in a deep breath, "I should have known he'd be here. He always has to repent on Sunday morning for the things he did on Saturday night."

Another agonized groan came from Jubilee, although she was not certain whose presence — Howard's or Chance's — was causing her the greatest distress. She avoided looking at Howard Crowly as she followed Abigail down the aisle, but it was impossible to keep her gaze away from the handsome gambler. As if they had a mind of their own, her eyes purposely sought out his smiling countenance, and they refused to look away until she had passed by the pew where he and Jerrod sat. Jubilee noticed they were dressed in almost identical suits of impeccable taste. Jerrod, however, looked as though he was suffering terribly as he tugged on the collar of the stiff white shirt he wore beneath his neatly tailored black suit. When the two women walked through the row of pews, both the older and the younger Steeles nodded their dark heads. Jubilee could not help but compare the strong similarities between the boy and his uncle. A fleeting thought of how Chance could easily pass for the young man's father flitted through her mind, along with the repeated idea that Chance Steele might have made a good father if he had chosen a different line of work for his livelihood.

As she situated herself beside Abigail Crowly, a heavy sense of defeat settled over Jubilee. She could almost feel Howard Crowly's deadly eyes drilling into the back of her head. After the initial shock at seeing her walk into the church with his wife, and realizing she was still in town, his expression had turned to one of smouldering rage. Jubilee was terrified he was going to make trouble, in spite of the fact that they were in the house of the Lord. On the other hand, she could also sense the teasing gaze of Chance Steele upon her. The emotions this thought aroused were just as worrisome, although in a completely different way. Since she was in the perfect place to ask for a small favor from God, she took this opportunity to pray that He help her find a solution to the terrible situations she kept encountering in this prairie town.

Throughout the entire sermon Jubilee tried to focus her wandering mind on the words the minister spoke, but it was a useless task. She was certain the entire congregation was whispering and gossiping behind her back. By now, the women who had seen her dining with Chance Steele had probably told everyone else in town about her date last night. No doubt all of them were assuming that Ina Devine's accusation was the truth. Jubilee wished a hole would appear beneath her feet and swallow her up within its depths. When the minister was finished with his sermon and everyone rose to their feet to leave, Jubilee felt as though she was weighted down and could not move. She knew when she turned around, the first person she would see would be Chance Steele, but knowing that Howard Crowly was also lurking nearby was almost as bad.

Jubilee glanced up at the beautiful wooden cross which hung serenely above the pulpit and closed her eyes for one more silent prayer. *Help me, please . . . I am in desperate trouble.* If only she and Abigail could escape from both of those men without another public display, she vowed that nothing would keep her from boarding the eastbound train this afternoon.

"I guess we'd better go," Abigail whispered in Jubilee's ear. She had also been delaying their departure for as long as possible. Although she was determined to go through with her plan to separate from Howard, his presence here today had left her unnerved and shaky. Since they had not acknowledged one another's presence, Abigail could only imagine the yarns that were already circulating about them. She was also beginning to understand Jubilee's desperation to avoid being the source of vicious gossip. In an attempt to distract her thoughts from her own despair, Abigail leaned close to Jubilee again. "Did you notice that Chance Steele and his nephew were in attendance today?"

Jubilee rose to her feet and straightened her velvet cape around her shoulders. "Yes, I did. Is that unusual?"

"It's the first time they've ever come to Sunday morning services as far as I know."

"Oh really?" Jubilee retorted as she began to grow suspicious of the gambler's motives for being here today. She had assumed he and Jerrod attended church on a regular basis. But apparently Chance Steele had brought his nephew here today with the hope of impressing her. "Well, it won't work!" Jubilee hissed aloud as she turned around to give that sneaky gambler her most abasing look.

"What's that, dear?" Abigail asked in confusion. When she noticed the younger woman's strange expression, she also turned around. But they had dallied for so long in their seats that the entire church was empty. A flood of relief washed over both women. "Well, we have to leave sometime," Abigail said in a tone of voice which suggested she would rather stay

160

within the sanctuary of the church walls.

Jubilee gave her head a brave nod and began to follow the other woman down the center aisle of the church. The large double doors at the front of the newly built church were both flung wide open, and Jubilee could see the black-clad minister standing on the front stoop basking in the brilliant glow of the midday winter sunshine. With each step she took, Jubilee felt as if she was headed straight into hell.

"Abigail, Miss Hart, how nice to see you on this glorious day," the young minister said as the two ladies reached his side. He held out his hand to Jubilee, adding, "We haven't been formally introduced, but I attended your speech at the inn the other day."

The shame she still felt over the disastrous conclusion of the rally stung Jubilee with a renewed sense of humiliation as Abigail quickly made the polite introductions. With proper courtesy, Jubilee shook the minister's hand, but her mind was in a turmoil as she vividly recalled Ina Devine's words, and the horrid food fight which had followed. Oh, what must this man think of her?

The Reverend Mahan seemed to be unaffected by the outcome of the rally, however. He clasped Jubilee's uninjured hand with both of his own and continued to hold her hand long after the initial handshake had ceased. "Meeting you is an honor, Miss Hart. I had hoped to get a chance to meet you after your speech but," he gave his shoulders a unconcerned shrug, "I'm thankful for this opportunity to make your acquaintance now." His smile seemed to echo throughout his entire countenance, and his hazel eyes focused directly upon Jubilee's stunned face.

She had not been sure of what to expect from this man, but his exuberant attitude left her at a complete loss for words. She returned his glowing smile with a feeble one as she looked up toward his face. He was a young man, perhaps even younger than herself, and within the sphere of his friendly golden-brown gaze,

Jubilee experienced the first sense of security she had felt since her arrival in Cheyenne. He allowed his eyes to settle upon her face for only a second longer, then he gently released his grip upon her hand and looked toward Abigail.

"So, where are you ladies off to now?" he asked with an even broader smile. Since a round of invitations always followed the services, the minister was accustomed to eating his Sunday meal at the home of one of his congregants. Today, he declined every offer he had received in the hopes that he would be invited to spend the afternoon in the presence of the beautiful and articulate suffragette.

Abigail gave her companion a befuddled look. She was afraid to invite anyone to her house, since she had no way of knowing when Howard would decide to come home. Whenever he did show up again, she did not want anyone else around when she made her position about their marriage clear to him. "Well, Jubilee, would you care to have dinner at the inn?"

Jubilee struggled with indecision as she sorted out her latest plan. She could eat first, and still have time to catch the afternoon train. "Yes, that would be nice," she answered, then glanced back toward the minister. "Would you like to join us?" She asked the question out of kindness, so she was not expecting him to receive her invitation with such an enthusiastic response.

"Yes! Yes, I would love to join you," he exclaimed as he clapped his hands together. Without a moment's hesitation, he turned around and swung both of the church doors shut behind him. Then, with a tilt of his head, he motioned toward the walkway. "Shall we, ladies?"

As the two women began to descend the few stairs leading to the snow-packed walkway, they both became aware of the audience they had attracted. Among the church folk, who stood in scattered groups, were the two men the women wanted to avoid. It was obvious all eyes were on the trio as Jubilee, Abigail, and the minister walked past. Whispered voices and sideways glances bespoke everyone's conversation, and though the minister strode through the crowd as if nothing was unusual, both Jubilee and Abigail were certain they would surely die from the humiliation of once again being made the objects of everyone's attention.

The smile never faded from the preacher's face as they made their way down the street. When they had rounded the nearest corner and were out of earshot, he shrugged. "Gossip is the next issue you should wage a war against, Miss Hart. Like bigotry and alcohol, words of malice can also destroy humanity."

Jubilee was shocked by the young minister's pronouncement, but her sense of security began to expand. She felt as though she had met a true ally in the person of Reverend Mahan. Not only did the curly-haired preacher exude an aura of serenity, which made him easy to relate to, but he also had a wonderful personality. He kept the two women entertained non-stop with his quick wit. She watched him from the side of her eye once they were seated at a table in the center of the dining room at the inn, and Jubilee also noted that he was rather handsome—in a boyish sort of way. When the ruggedly handsome face of Chance Steele stole into her thoughts, however, the young minister's appeal faded in comparison. Aggravated, Jubilee grabbed her water glass and took a drink, while attempting to ignore the rapid increase of her pulse. It took only a fleeting image of that dark-eyed rogue to throw her entire being into a feverish pitch. When she took the glass away from her lips and glanced toward the doorway, the actual sight of the tall gambler sent her senses spinning into a deeper turmoil.

Since he was not wearing a hat, Chance Steele gave her a salute, along with a suggestive grin which hinted at the same type of thoughts that Jubilee was trying to force from her mind, In return, she batted her long lashes flirtatiously and turned her full attention toward the minister. "Where do you hail from, Reverend Mahan?" Oh, why did she have to ask that question just as Chance Steele and his nephew passed by their table? The knowing smirk upon the gambler's face told Jubilee he was remembering how she had asked him that same question the first time they had conversed over dinner. But now it was different; she was truly interested in learning more about the minister. The happy expression which overcame his countenance was proof that he was equally anxious to tell the beautiful young woman all about himself.

"I'm originally from Virginia, although I have spent the past few years out here in the West," he began. He continued to tell the women all about his travels through the Western territories, but Jubilee only caught bits and pieces of his story. It took every ounce of her willpower to keep from turning around to look toward the corner where she knew Chance Steele was sitting. She also knew he was watching her every move, because she could feel his dark gaze upon her as strongly as if his eyes had fingers that were reaching out to her from across the room.

"And now it's your turn to tell me all about yourself, Miss Hart," the minister said when he was finished with his own life story. He placed his arms upon the tabletop and leaned toward her, granting her his full attention.

A rapid rise of color washed through Jubilee's complexion when she became aware that the preacher was addressing her. She had been so wrapped up in her enamored thoughts of that infuriating saloon keeper that now she had no idea what the minister had just said to her. In startled confusion she stared blankly at the minister until Abigail Crowly came to her rescue.

"The poor dear has had *such* a rough time of it ever since she arrived in Cheyenne, but back in Washington, she has led a very exciting life. Tell Reverend

Mahan about some of your campaigns for the suffrage."

Jubilee gave the elderly woman a grateful smile. Like a dutiful child, she began to relate some of her past experiences. However, the enthusiasm she usually had when she talked about the suffrage issue was sorely lacking today, as she hurried through a brief rundown of her work. Fortunately, their dinner arrived and the conversation was directed toward the cuisine of the day. But, unfortunately, Chance and Jerrod Steele were first to finish their meal. Since the saloon owner and his nephew had not stopped to visit on their way in, it was only common courtesy for them to pause at the minister's table on their way out.

"Good day, ladies," Chance said as his dark gaze floated over Jubilee with a ravishing twinkle. "I enjoyed the sermon today," he said to the minister in a friendly tone of voice.

"I enjoyed seeing the two of you in church today. I hope it will become a common occurrence?" The minister's friendly expression remained intact, but his eyes traveled back and forth between the tall gambler and the beautiful woman as if he was watching for a signal of some sort to pass between them. "But then," he added as he looked at the lovely blonde who dined with him, "today has been full of surprises."

Chance's smile took on a patronizing look when he followed the preacher's gaze. "It's just been one revelation after another," he replied with a sly wink at the blushing Jubilee Hart. His devilish smirk grew bolder when he noticed another wave of crimson spread over her cheeks. If she was hoping to make him jealous by spending time with another man, it was definitely working. Chance had nearly choked on every bite of food he forced into his mouth, while he watched her converse and laugh with the minister. Even worse was the adoring look upon the young preacher's face whenever he glanced in her direction. Jealous was not the word to describe the rage that consumed the gambler as he was forced to observe the pair from across the room, However, he would never give Jubilee Hart the satisfaction of knowing how much her childish ploy agitated him.

Abigail Crowly and Reverend Mahan were both witness to the gambler's indiscreet wink, and each of them watched with eager anticipation for Jubilee's reaction. But, Jubilee could be as cunning as the debonair saloon keeper. Though she could not control the heat from flaming through her cheeks, she was able to convey an aura of detachment which belied her inner embarrassment. Her royal gaze narrowed slightly as she leveled her eyes upon the grinning male who stood beside their table. "Perhaps if you attended church on a regular basis, Mr. Steele, you would also discover a few revelations about the evils of liquor that might prove to be useful to a man in your profession."

Chance Steele shrugged nonchalantly as he ran his hand down the front of his dark vest. "Ah, yes, that reminds me," he glanced at his nephew, "We'd better get the saloon opened up for business." With his smile still intact, he looked down at the minister and added, "You of all people should know how busy the local saloons get on Sunday afternoons." He casually saluted the ladies as a parting gesture, then reached out and playfully slapped the clergyman on the back. "I won't say goodbye to you Reverend, because I know I'll be seeing you again real soon."

With Jerrod following closely on his heels, Chance departed from the dining room. He longed to turn around and take another look at the trio he had just left behind, but he hated to gloat and there was no way he could wipe the smirk from his face. The young preacher was a kind and wonderful man, whose generous devotion to his congregation was appreciated by all who knew him. However, the Methodist minister had one minor weakness . . . he enjoyed an occasional glass of rye whiskey, and every Sunday evening was the occasion he chose to indulge himself. Chance also knew his insinuation about the preacher's habit would not aid in the preacher's quest to win Jubilee Hart's admiration. As he and Jerrod exited from the inn, Chance noticed that a large dark cloud had moved into the sky overhead. He shivered with dread and repeated his habit of tracing his hand down the front of his vest as a guilty feeling overcame him. Undoubtedly the preacher had more clout with the Lord, Chance realized, as he glanced upward again and wondered if he had over-stepped his boundaries this time.

Neither Jubilee or Abigail said a word as Chance Steele strode out of the room. But when he had disappeared from their view, their eyes immediately settled upon the red-faced minister who chuckled and raised his hands above the table in a defeated gesture. "Sometimes, after the week has come to an end, I like to indulge in a sip or two of whiskey."

"On the Sabbath?" Abigail asked in a shocked tone of voice.

The minister gave his shoulders a helpless shrug. "Well, it's the only time I do it."

"On the Sabbath?" Abigail repeated. She found it hard to believe that the minister of their church was also a man who frequented the local saloons after he delivered the Sunday sermon on the evils of the world. Her determination to support temperance expanded with this new discovery.

"Well, I think it's shocking!" Jubilee said in a huff as she threw her napkin down upon the table in a display of disgust.

"It's the only day of the week I take a drink," Mahan said in a panicked voice.

Jubilee gave him a look of annoyance, then glanced back at the empty doorway where Chance Steele had just exited. "Oh, I don't *care* about your drinking habits," she said more harshly than she had intended. "I mean, I think it's shocking that the saloons are even allowed to be open for business on the Sabbath. And, it's even more appalling to know Chance Steele's young nephew is forced to be an accomplice to this sacrilege."

"You're right, Jubilee! Something needs to be done about it," Abigail chimed in enthusiastically. "There should be a law that prevents the saloons from opening up on Sundays."

"A law?" Jubilee said with a thoughtful frown, drawing her brows together. Now, that was something to think about; something which just might be attainable if by some remote chance the legislature granted women the right to vote tomorrow. A multitude of mixed emotions filled Jubilee with confusion. If the enfranchising bill passed, it would mean a great victory for women all over the country. She had worked too hard for herself and her sister suffragettes to turn tail and run now. Her plan to flee from Cheyenne on the afternoon train was pushed to the back of her mind and she was overcome with the excitement of tomorrow's meeting of the legislature. Just to have the bill introduced to the legislature was a great achievement, and Jubilee realized she did not want to miss out on any of the impending events. Besides, on the slim chance that the bill might happen to pass, she also wanted to be in on the upheaval that would follow—such as the idea of proposing a law that would close saloons on Sunday. Jubilee's mind overflowed with a dozen different ideas which would help to promote temperance if the vote was given to women. Although she had vowed to be gone on the afternoon train, she realized now she could not even *think* of leaving when there was so much work for her to do here. Surely, God would understand why she had to postpone her departure for a day or two.

When the memory of her bet passed through her mind, along with the taunting image of Chance Steele's smiling face, Jubilee firmly told herself she would not allow that gambler to distract her from her true purpose for coming to the Wyoming Territory again. Since their wager concerning the outcome of the equality bill was absolute nonsense, she determined that she would never again permit herself to dwell on the few moments of sweet bliss she had experienced during his kisses. But, since she intended to keep this vow, she allowed herself to recall those sensuous occasions just one more time.

Chapter Fifteen

Jubilee fidgeted nervously with her muffler as she stood in the doorway of the Railroad Inn and waited for Abigail Crowly. While attempting to keep her self-imposed vow to wipe away all immodest thoughts of Chance Steele, she had spent another long, sleepless night. With every hour that passed since he had kissed her so passionately — first in the Crowlys' parlor, then outside her room here at the inn — the more she yearned to have him kiss her again. How could she ever hope to dismiss this man from her life, when all she could think about was the feel of his gentle lips against her own hungry mouth?

"Well, it looks as though I've finally caught you without your guardian angel," Howard Crowly said with a hateful curl of his lips as he approached her. He glanced around, then asked, "Where is that homely wife of mine, anyway?"

Jubilee's initial shock at seeing the man she dreaded more than anyone else was quickly transformed into loathing. Abigail was her friend, and she did not take kindly to anyone belittling her, especially this man. "How can you be so cruel to your own wife?" Jubilee asked, hoping the trembling in her breast was not conveyed in her voice when she spoke.

A wicked laugh escaped from deep down in Howard's throat as his gaze raked over Jubilee like a razor-sharp knife. "Because she is my *wife*. I can be anyway I want toward her." He glanced around as if he was hesitant to be seen by anyone. "Just don't forget that you and I have a score to settle. It's all your fault Abigail kicked me out of my own home." He pointed an accusing finger at her face as he continued. "You owe me!"

"I owe you nothing! I'm not to blame, and you know it," Jubilee retorted, clutching her injured hand close to her bosom. Her hand still throbbed without mercy, but she noticed his face was almost completely healed from their confrontation in the kitchen. "I'm not even staying at your home anymore, so why haven't you bothered to go back to your wife?"

A surprised expression shadowed Howard's icy glare. He had not known the blonde beauty was no longer staying with his wife. His reason for not wanting to go home was because he was still too engrossed with the tantalizing whores at The Second Chance Saloon. He had spent the past couple of nights at the bordello, despite Chance Steele's new rule that no one could spend the entire night upstairs. The gambler drew into a reluctant retreat when Howard reminded the saloon keeper who was holding the mortgage note on the premises. His new interests had kept his mind off Jubilee Hart, and until yesterday morning he had thought the blonde speaker was already gone. Still, when he saw her in church with his wife, he had decided the haughty Easterner was not worth a repeated effort if it also meant another encounter with his wife. The discovery that she was no longer a guest in his home altered his decision. Since he was certain she was staying here at the inn, Howard started to invite himself up to her room, when they were interrupted by the arrival of Reverend Mahan.

After a brief greeting to the older man, the minister turned his full attention toward the beautiful woman at his side, "Miss Hart, you are truly a vision to behold in this bleak Wyoming prairie town." His hazel gaze traveled appreciatively over her entire visage. Jubilee noticed how his boyish smile almost seemed out of place above his tall, starched collar. She forced a small smile in reply to his compliment. Although she was grateful for the minister's sudden appearance, she was still too upset by Howard's presence to talk in a rational manner.

The minister cleared his throat. "I hope you won't mind if I join you while you're waiting to hear the decision of the legislators?" he asked.

Jubilee shrugged her shoulder's beneath her velvet cloak. "Abigail will be joining me too. If she doesn't mind, then I certainly don't." She avoided looking at Howard Crowly, even though she found it difficult to ignore him since he was breathing heavily at her side.

Not wishing to make his intentions toward Jubilee Hart public knowledge in front of the minister, Howard decided to make a hasty departure before his wife arrived. He quickly mumbled his goodbyes to the pair, but as he walked away, he glanced back over his shoulder. The chilling look upon his aging face caused Jubilee to feel a renewed sense of foreboding. She knew, without a doubt, that as long as she was in Cheyenne she would never be safe from Howard Crowly. A visible tremor shot threw her body, which was followed at once by the concerned voice of the young minister.

"Are you all right?" Reverend Mahan asked when he noticed the pallor of her skin and the violent manner in which her whole body shook. He had not missed the look of malice upon Howard Crowly's face, either. But before he could began to speculate on the reasons behind the strange behavior of the two people, Abigail Crowly called out to them as she rounded the street corner.

Jubilee sighed with relief when she saw that Howard Crowly had already disappeared around the opposite corner of the building. She did not think she could tolerate a confrontation between the banker and his wife at this time. A wan smile curved her lips when she waved in response to Abigail's greeting. She avoided meeting the minister's inquisitive stare. Her personal life was already a subject of endless prattle in this town, so Jubilee had no desire to tell the young minister anything about her ongoing battle with the unscrupulous banker. Still, she knew if he decided to ask her what was going on, she could not bring herself to lie. She felt enough guilt about the way she had sat silently at the table during lunch yesterday, while Abigail Crowly had related the fabricated tale of how she had broken her hand by punching the wall in a fit of rage over the issue concerning Ina Devine.

"The legislators met over a half an hour ago, but nobody has heard a thing yet," Abigail said as she rushed up to the waiting couple. In her excitement she did not notice their subdued attitude, but her announcement turned Jubilee's despair into eager anticipation to learn the outcome of the important meeting which was convening at that very moment.

"Esther Morris arrived this morning," Abigail continued. "It will be wonderful for the two of you to meet." She clasped onto Jubilee's arm in an affectionate gesture, which once again made Jubilee grateful that Howard Crowly was out of sight.

"Yes, tha—that would be wonderful," Jubilee stuttered as she envisioned herself standing beside the prominent figure of Mrs. Morris when they received the news of the important decision they were all waiting to hear. Today could be the highlight of her entire career, Jubilee realized with a sense of pride. Could it be possible that all her hard work, and that of her sister suffragettes, would finally pay off? She hoped fervently that it would. The idea that this desolate prairie town would change the course of history for all womankind, however, still seemed a bit too far-fetched to believe.

"Is this a private party, or can anyone join?" Chance Steele's deep voice invaded Jubilee's thoughts of glory and fame, and replaced them with the feelings of the confusion she always felt whenever he was near.

The tall gambler smiled at Abigail and tipped the brim of his small gray hat. "You look younger and lovelier every time I see you," he said.

A red blush raced through Abigail's cheeks at the handsome man's teasing words, but for once she did not giggle like a silly girl. She merely greeted him with a

173

dignified nod of her gray head. In the past few days, her awareness of alcohol had increased, and because of this, her opinion of saloon owners and gamblers had been greatly altered. Even Chance Steele's words of flattery could not deter her from her new-found cause.

At once, Chance noted the difference in the elderly lady. He also reminded himself of her recent interest in temperance. She had been suppressed for a very long time, and now that she was experiencing the birth of her new-found independence, she could prove to be a dangerous foe. He was not overly concerned, however, especially since he was sure that eventually she could be won over with a few well-phrased compliments. He turned his attention toward the young minister, even though he was aggravated to no end to find the grinning man already at Jubilee's side. "I missed not seeing you last night, Mahan," he said with a narrowing of his dark lashes. "After all, you've become a regular at the local saloons on Sunday nights."

An angry expression flashed over the minister's smiling countenance for a moment. He was not blind to the gambler's jealousy, but he was not about to back down from his interest in the beautiful Easterner, either. The minister had decided that a fine lady like Jubilee Hart deserved someone better than a saloon owner, and he felt it was his personal duty to look after her welfare. "I've decided to give up whiskey for good," he answered as his frown was replaced by another broad smile. With a quick glance toward Jubilee, he added, "There are things far more important than an occasional drink of rye whiskey."

The aggravation that filled Chance Steele was not evident upon his face and he reserved his comments about the young preacher's sudden change of character. It seemed Jubilee Hart had the power to make everyone around her want to readjust their entire lives just to suit her. Well, there were a few things Chance wanted to change about his life, too. But, he sure wasn't going to do it just to please Jubilee Hart!

"How commendable!" Jubilee exclaimed in an excited voice. She graced the minister with a proud smile. "Whiskey is the evil of our society, don't you agree?" She turned her blue gaze in Chance's direction, then said, "And even worse is the destruction of our young and innocent by these poisonous influences."

Chance knew her barb was meant to demoralize him, but he was not certain how. His face lost its mirth, and he leveled a steady stare at her. "Are you accusing me of destroying the youth of our country?" he asked.

"Why yes, Mr. Steele, I do believe I am." Her jaw was tilted at him, and it was clear that she believed a battle line had been drawn.

The gambler straightened his tall form to its full height, which towered over the two women and topped the minister's curly head as well. With an indignant huff he stepped closer to the blonde. "I refuse to accept the blame for that monumental claim, Miss Hart!" He emphasized her name with a loud hiss.

Straightening her shoulders, Jubilee glared back up at him. "Do you *deny* that your young nephew takes part in all the activities that go on in your gambling hall? Do you expect any of us to believe that!?"

"Yes, I do deny that charge," he retorted instantly. "I do not allow Jerrod to partake in any of the card games, nor do I permit him to drink at all. As for what you believe, well . . . I suggest the truth, but the choice is yours."

Jubilee's blonde head jerked to the side in a gesture of fury as she continued to stare up at the gambler. "And what of the *other* activities, Mr. Steele?"

Chance's hand instinctively ran down the front of his vest. The bulge of his tiny derringer caused his hand to rise up slightly as his palm passed over the hidden weapon. He noticed the flashing eyes of Jubilee Hart glance down toward the gold watch-fob chain which hung from his vest pocket, but he ignored the icy shadow that moved across her face.

"I-I don't know what you're talking about," he stammered.

"The *bordello*, upstairs," she retorted, impatiently. "Is your young ward subjected to the temptations of the flesh as well as to the evils of alcohol, Mr. Steele?"

Left speechless by her question, Chance could only return her unyielding stare. He had come here today with the hope of endearing himself to Jubilee by offering her support while they waited to hear the outcome of the meeting of the legislators. The last thing he was expecting today, was to be accused of destroying Jerrod's life. The intensity of Chance's fury made him unable to think coherently for a moment. He wanted to shout at this snooty woman that he would never hurt Jerrod, because Jerrod was his own son! But armed with that much ammunition, Jubilee would never consider him to be a suitable mate. The fact that Jerrod was conceived in a floating bordello on the Mississippi, and deserted by his prostitute mother, would only be another piece of dirty evidence to be used against him.

"I love my dead brother's son," he finally said in a low, controlled voice. "And I want only what's best for him." He avoided a straight answer to her question. Even as he stated his elusive reply, his mind was filled with recollections of finding Jerrod in Ina Devine's upstairs room. He wanted to direct all his anger toward Jubilee Hart for attempting to reveal something evil about the personal life he and Jerrod lived behind the closed doors of The Second Chance Saloon. Yet, her challenge had summoned up all the deep feelings of guilt he had lived with for the past sixteen years; ever since he had adopted the same cowardly path that Faith Barnett had chosen when she had deserted their infant son.

As she watched their discussion convert Chance's face into a multitude of tempestuous emotions, Jubilee felt once again the sensation that there was something behind this man's outward facade of silk and smooth-spoken words which made him different from all the other gamblers she had known. She wished she could learn everything about his past and why he had chosen the gambling profession, when it was obvious he had a compassion that most men in his business lacked. But now was not the time for her to discover any of these things. The sound of Reverend Mahan clearing his throat loudly interrupted Jubilee's troubled thoughts and reminded her of the reason they were all gathered here this morning. She struggled to regain her composure.

"Why don't we all go back into the inn and have something warm to drink while we await the decision of the legislators?" she suggested. Her voice quivered when she spoke, and she hoped they would all assume she was chilled by the cold morning air. But even Jubilee was not sure why her entire body had began to tremble like a willow in a wind storm. Perhaps, she thought, it was because Chance was so near again, and each time she looked into his raven eyes, she experienced such a longing to have him take her into his strong arms and smother her entire body with tender kisses and . . . *No!* Stop it! she told herself firmly as they all marched towards the dining room in a grim silence.

Jubilee and Chance's confrontation in front of the inn left an obvious damper upon the atmosphere of the group while they sat around the table and sipped coffee and tea. When the renowned Esther Morris entered the dining room, Jubilee sighed with relief to have a diversion which would draw her thoughts to something besides the memory of Chance Steele's kisses. Mrs. Morris was a fascinating woman in her mid-fifties, who weighed almost two hundred pounds and was nearly as tall as the six-foot Chance Steele. Abigail was already acquainted with the woman, but Jubilee Hart struck up an immediate rapport with the other suffrage leader. The gentlemen in attendance, which including Esther Morris' own husband who had traveled from South Pass City with her to hear the outcome of the legislature's decision, listened intently to the women's exchange of ideas and future plans for the suffrage movement.

When Abigail Crowly mentioned the idea of passing a law which would force all saloons and brothels to close down on the Sabbath, Chance Steele nearly choked on the sip of coffee he had just taken. His humiliation over the round of coughing which followed was accelerated when the young minister reached over and gave him several hard whacks upon his back. "Th-Thank you," Chance gasped in a high-pitched voice. He took a deep breath, then added in a sarcastic tone, "I needed that." With a grunt of annoyance he turned away from the grinning preacher and stared across the table toward Abigail Crowly. He was aghast by the devastating words that had just come from the little gray-haired woman. But just as he started to dispute her suggestion, the territorial marshal burst into the restaurant.

"The meeting of the legislators just broke up," Marshal Elliot said to the anxious occupants of the room. His announcement brought everyone to their feet with eager shouts to hear the news of their decision. The lawman shook his head and raised his hands high into the air. "Simmer down. There ain't been no definite decision yet." His last words brought about an even louder round of disgruntled voices. He waved his arms through the air again in an effort to get the crowd to quiet down long enough for him to relate the rest of his news. When the room was finally silent, he lowered his arms and spoke. "Governor Campbell wants to mull it over for a day or two before he signs the bill, but the legislators already voted for it to pass."

Since everyone was certain the governor would not refuse to sign the petition once the legislators had agreed to pass the enfranchising bill, a rousing cheer rang out from the occupants of the restaurant. Around her, Jubilee listened to the excited commotion in a numb silence. She had dreamed of this day for such a long time, and now that it had finally arrived, she was void of any emotion. When her mind began to function in a rational manner, her first thought was of Chance Steele; he had known all along that the bill would pass! Instinctively, she sought out his dark, handsome face again. She was not surprised to find that he was watching her too. Since

178

she was becoming accustomed to meeting his gaze from across a crowded room, she did not even attempt to look away. When he motioned with his head for her to follow him, she was helpless to resist.

Jubilee moved past Abigail Crowly, Reverend Mahan, and everyone else in the room as though no one else was present. She did not even take the time to congratulate Esther Morris, or wait to receive the praise which would surely come her way with this latest victory for women. Something in that ebony gaze mesmerized her senses; she was too weak, and too filled with a desperate yearning to resist. When she reached the waiting man she allowed him to take her hand while he led her from the dining area. Only one fleeting thought crossed through her mind about the gossip their departure would arouse among the onlookers. Yet, that worry disappeared with the feel of Chance Steele's warm grip encircling her hand.

"Where are we going?" she asked when they were standing alone in the hotel foyer.

Chance shrugged, "I just felt the need to be alone with you for a moment, and since the preacher has elected himself your constant companion, there are few opportunities for us to share one another's company."

"You're not jealous of him, are you?" Jubilee asked in a coy voice, which was accompanied by an innocent smile. His reply, however, wiped the smile from her lips.

"You can bet your emancipated petticoat that I'm jealous of him, and any other man who spends time with my fiancée!"

For a moment Jubilee thought he was only joking, but his odd expression told her he was dead serious. "Surely you — you are not going to *hold* me to that ridiculous bet?"

"It was a fair wager, and we shook on it," he replied quickly, with a firm nod of his head. A wave of hair fell down upon his forehead. He shoved the stray locks back with an impatient push and replaced the little gray bowler, which he carried in his hand, to its designated position upon his head.

"Marriage can not be determined by a bet, Mr. Steele."

"Don't you think it's time you called me by my first name?" he asked in exasperation.

"Don't try to change the subject," she retorted. "I don't know you well enough to consider marrying you, and even if I did, you are not the type of man I would choose."

Chance was determined she would not make him angry — no matter what she said. Still, he could not shake off the intense jealousy he felt toward the young minister, especially since he imagined the grinning clergyman was exactly the type of man she would chose for a husband. "A part of our agreement was that you would get to know me better while we waited to learn the outcome of the legislator's decision. And you would know me better if you had spent more time with *me*, instead of with the preacher."

Jubilee shook her head in disbelief. She found it inconceivable a dandy like Chance Steele could be jealous of anyone, but especially of a nice man like Reverend Mahan. This entire situation was getting out of hand, and she was growing tired of these ridiculous games. "I'm not going to stand here and bicker with you, and I'm not going to continue with this stupid bet, either."

"Are you folding?" he asked with a sly rise of his dark eyebrows. His reference to gambling terms was a language he was certain she would not understand, so when she fired back a rapid reply, he was left speechless.

With a smug expression upon her pretty face, Jubilee smiled and said, "No, I'm calling your bluff, and I'll raise your bet, Mr. Steele."

"Wh-What are you saying?" Chance stammered as his palm retraced the buttons along the front of his vest.

The long lashes that framed her royal blue eyes dropped coquettishly as she continued to grace him with a smile. "You say you want to marry me? But I'd be willing to bet you don't want to marry me badly enough to give up your gambling den, or your gaming lifestyle."

Chance did not have to ask her want she meant, because he understood her ploy at once. Her only goal was to close down his saloon. Once his livelihood was wiped out for good, she could carve another notch in her victory belt. Her attempt to trick him placed her on thin ice, because Chance was not used to being outmaneuvered by his opponent. But, he reminded himself, it took two to play this game, and he still had the means to meet her challenge, as well as to add to the bet she had already placed. Calling upon his proficient skill in cunning and trickery, he sized up his opposing player with a sweep of his dark gaze. He noted how her breathing increased when he allowed his eyes to linger carelessly upon her voluptuous curves, and he rejoiced when he noticed the thin film of perspiration that formed upon her silken complexion when their eyes locked. Her outward resistance was only a flimsy barricade, because it was easy to see she wanted him as badly as he yearned for her.

Patience was a virtue Chance was grateful to possess at this moment. As he stared down at the stubborn blonde hellcat who stood before him, he realized he could allow her all the time she needed to exhaust her meager resources. Then, like the professional he was, he would calmly lay down his cards and scoop up all the winnings.

His frowning countenance turned into a taunting expression of satisfaction and confidence. A true gambler never entered into a bet unless he was certain the stakes were in his favor . . . and Chance Steele always kept an ace up his sleeve for emergencies which might require a bit of extra assistance.

Chapter Sixteen

From the narrow crack in her doorway, Jubilee peeked out into the dimly lit hallway. The walls of this room felt as if they were closing in around her, and she was certain she would go insane if the territorial governor did not sign the equality bill soon. Four long days had gone by since the legislators had voted to pass the bill. The entire country was waiting for the final signature which would seal the political fate of the women of Wyoming. Jubilee had feigned an illness for the first couple of days, which allowed her to remain in her room. By yesterday, though, she was nearly crazy with boredom from being cooped up in a small space with nothing to do, except to grow more eager to obtain her freedom. Her imaginary sickness received a swift recovery as the minutes stretched into hours and days, and she realized it might be several more days until the governor decided to sign the impending bill. Still, the fear of seeing Howard Crowly again made her extremely cautious when she braved the world beyond the safety of her hotel room.

On her first excursion out of the hotel yesterday, she had paid Abigail Crowly a visit. The elderly woman's amazing transformation from a shy brow-beaten wife to a woman who was ready to fight for her newly formed beliefs, was even more startling when Jubilee observed Abigail in her home on Carey Avenue. Abigail's revelation that Howard recently rented a room at the Railroad Inn had wrapped Jubilee in a blanket of panic and sent her rushing back to the sparse security behind her locked door. It had been early in the afternoon when she had returned to the hotel from the Crowly home, but as she ascended the stairs she caught a glimpse of someone lurking at the end of the hallway. She was certain it was Howard, but the man remained hidden in the dark shadows while she hesitated at the top of the stairway. Jubilee's panic subsided slightly when another hotel guest exited from his room. While the stranger stopped to lock his door, she took the opportunity to make a hasty entrance into her own room. Now, she feared she might not be able to escape from Crowly a second time if he was still determined to fulfill his vile threats. Knowing he had chosen to take a room here at the inn, rather than to go back home, only served to fuel her distrust of the man.

In an outbreak of cold sweat, Jubilee slammed the door shut and relocked it, then leaned against the wooden barricade until the shaking in her limps subsided. To be stuck here in this room like a captive animal was a living nightmare! But then, everything that had happened to her in the past week was unbelievable. Frustration overcame Jubilee and she banged her head against the door like an angry child. Oh, how she hated Wyoming—and when she *did* finally get away from this freezing wasteland, she was never going to come back! The sound of her head knocking against the door was echoed by a loud thudding on the other side of the barrier. Her heart felt as though it had stopped beating as her fear of Howard Crowly reached a new height. She held her breath and remained unmoving against the door as she listened for another sound.

"Jubilee? Are you all right in there?"

She squeezed her eyes shut and sighed with relief at the sound of Chance Steele's deep voice. He had stopped by everyday, but she had never permitted him entrance into her room. "I'm still not feeling too well," she shouted back at him through the closed door, just as she had done for the past few days.

"This is preposterous," he retaliated in an irritated tone of voice. "I know you're not sick, and I'm not leaving here today until you let me in."

As she growled with aggravation, Jubilee checked to make sure the lock was secure. She had no intention of allowing this man, or any other man, entrance into her room, Even the minister had met with a closed door when he had called upon her on the second day of her self-imposed illness and confinement. But, at least *he* had been kind enough not to keep pestering her everyday. "I'm *not* opening the door, so you might as well leave."

"I'm not leaving, and I have good news," he shouted in a loud voice.

Jubilee cringed at the booming sound of his voice on the other side of her door. She hated the idea of him standing out in the hallway, while announcing to the entire inn what he wanted her to hear. "If I open the door, will you promise to leave right away?"

"I'll leave as soon as I tell you the news,"

Jubilee shook her head at her own stupidity and began to unlock the dead bolt on the door. There was always the chance he had come to tell her the governor had finally signed the enfranchising bill. Then she would be able to leave Cheyenne with a clear conscience since she felt she would have fulfilled her part of the bet by staying here until the decision was final. When she swung open the door and gazed upon his smiling face though, she began to wonder if she would ever be free from this man again.

"May I come in?" he asked as he swept his hat from his head, and took a step forward so that he was standing just inside the doorway. If she suddenly changed her mind about speaking to him, his quick maneuver prevented Jubilee from denying him entry into her room, or from slamming the door in his face.

She stumbled backward a few steps to avoid close contact with him, then shrugged her shoulders in a manner which suggested she did not care what he did. "Do you have news about the bill?" she demanded. She jumped slightly when he slammed the door shut behind him. They were alone—truly alone—for the first time since they had met. But the worst thing about having him here was that she did not trust her own actions any farther than she trusted him. "W-What is it?" she said in a voice that cracked when she spoke.

Chance could not contain the low chuckle that escaped while he observed her skittish performance. His experience with the opposite gender told him a woman only acted like this when she was nervous about her own emotions. Since he also knew Jubilee Hart was too darned stubborn to give into her feelings without resistance, he could only begin to imagine the battle she was waging within herself at this moment. He wanted to sweep her into his arms and offer her a cure to her acute turmoil. But that was an area where Chance had to rely on his patience again. He had to keep reminding himself of this, over and over, when he entered the room and beheld the blonde beauty who caused his blood to boil, leaving him a man with very little control, or patience. He cleared his throat, but could not clear his mind of the urge to reach out and pull her into his embrace.

His strange silence, along with the burning desire which blatantly emitted from his ebony gaze, made the ache in Jubilee's quaking body increase. Her feet stumbled backward again, until the edge of the bed stopped her escape. After an instant of trying to regain her balance, she straightened up and faced him with an embarrassed blush upon her smooth complexion. "I hope you've come to tell me that the governor has finally signed the bill," she said in a rush of words.

The grin upon the handsome gambler's face widened beneath his dark mustache. "I've come to tell you that I'm taking you to the party which is being held tonight in celebration of Wyoming being the first legislature to pass a full bill of equality for the women of our great territory."

As the impact of his announcement began to settle in Jubilee's spinning thoughts, she rushed forward. Without thinking about her actions, she threw her arms around his neck in an exuberant hug. "I can't believe it has finally happened!" she squealed in joy as their bodies drew together like two magnets. Her dream of women obtaining equality was finally a reality, but the excitement of that fact was suddenly lost to the strange mania of emotions that came over her when she realized she was holding onto Chance Steele in a very intimate manner. All at once, she became aware of the way he had wrapped his arms around her waist and of the manner in which their bodies were molded tightly together, as if they were made to fit against one another for all eternity. Every inch of her being had become a tingling mass of boundless yearnings; an awaking which she sensed only this man's touch could satisfy. She felt her breathing intensify, until she feared her lungs would explode.

An even greater battle raged within the heart of the reckless gambler as he fought against his urge to take advantage of the beautiful woman whom he held within his grasp. He had not expected his announcement to reduce her to a woman of abandon, yet, there was no denying the look of longing he could see upon her radiant face at this moment. He had no doubt that he could seduce her right this very instant if he so desired. He also knew that when she regained her senses, she would hate him for the rest of her life. He wanted this woman, but he wanted to have her forever. It took every ounce of his strength to release his shaking grip from around her narrow waist.

"I—ah—I knew you'd be thrilled to hear the news," he choked out in breathless gasps. He wondered if the heat in his cheeks had colored his face in a shade as crimson as Jubilee's complexion was at that moment. With a deep inhale of cleansing air, he tried to regain his normal keel of breathing. But it was too no avail.

Until he knew this woman was truly his, he would never be normal again.

Jubilee attempted to speak, but only a rasp of stammering fell from her trembling lips. She paused, then tried to retrace a few backward steps, although no amount of distance could take away the shame she felt because of her own impetuous conduct. She had convinced herself that Chance Steele would use any excuse to have his way with her. Yet, she had just presented him with the perfect opportunity to obtain his quest, and he had reacted in the most respectful way a gentleman could behave. *What must he think of me,* Jubilee wondered. A mortified feeling was working its way through her being. Without thinking about her next approach, she relied on the only defense she could think of in this moment of harried confusion.

"Now I can finally leave this awful place," she blurted out, forcing herself to turn away from the dangerously handsome man, whose nearness threatened to steal away her common sense again.

Chance remained unmoving as he mulled over her heartless words. She had never intended to fulfill her share of the wager, he realized. He stared at the back of her blonde head. By doing everything within her power to avoid all contact with him, she had also reneged on their bet. The only thing she cared about was escaping from him . . . and from her own feelings, too. He wanted to rush forward, grab her up into his arms again, and force her to admit to the overwhelming attraction they shared for one another. However, he was too proud — and just as stubborn — as she was about facing up their star-crossed destinies.

He glanced down at the little gray bowler hat he clutched in his hand, then raised his sorrowful gaze back up to the beautiful woman, whose face was still turned away from him. "Yes, you're finally free to go. So . . . I guess this is goodbye." His softly spoken words seemed to fill the entire room with a deafening echo, and for a few seconds Jubilee's heart felt as through it was tightening into a heavy ball of anguish. She was free. She twirled around with the intent of saying goodbye to him while she was still brave enough to speak the words out loud. Yet, the moment their starving gazes met, the thought — along with the words — was stolen from her lips and erased from her mind. What was it about this gambler, she wondered, that made her forget all the solemn vows she had diligently rehearsed throughout her whole life?

She attempted to disguise her indecision with a hoarse cough. "Didn't you say there was going to be a celebration tonight?"

A bolt of optimism flashed through Chance's weak limbs and settled smack in the center of his breaking heart. Since he was not sure he could speak because of the suffocating lump in his throat, he nodded his dark head in reply.

With her uninjured hand, Jubilee waved her arm through the air in a frivolous gesture. "I should at least stay long enough to attend the party."

Without wanting to sound too encouraged, Chance tilted his head to the side and rolled his eyes upward in an exaggerated gesture. "I would think it would be the *least* you could do." Because she was overcome with excitement about the idea of attending the celebration tonight, Jubilee ignored his snide remark. She also tried to dismiss the joy she felt at the prospect of being with him again, but the tides of anxious expectation that washed over her made her grow even more eager.

"I'll call for you at 7 o'clock this evening," Chance stated as he replaced his hat upon his head and ran his hand down the front of his vest.

"Why don't I meet you there," she retorted in a tone of uncertainty.

Chance stopped in his tracks and reminded himself of his patience virtue. But, damn it! She was definitely trying the small amount of that trait which he was trying to retain. He had no doubt she was worrying about her precious reputation again. But didn't she realize it was too late to care about what the people of Cheyenne thought of her? The folks who lived in this harsh land also lived by their own set of rules; the decision to grant women the right to vote was proof to that fact. For a while, they might gossip and speculate about the lives of the other people who were around them, but their own lives were too hard and demanding for them to dwell on idle talk for any length of time. Survival was the main object of these hardy people, and the way this one woman chose to live her life was of little concern to them. The sooner she became aware of this, and got over her prudish fears, the better off they would all be, Chance decided sternly.

"I will call for you at 7 o'clock," he repeated as he twirled around on the heels of his shiny black boots and exited from her room without another word.

Jubilee stared at the closed door for a few seconds while she tried to calm her soaring heart. The reality of the equality bill passing was wonderful, but not nearly as thrilling as the idea of being with him again. While Jubilee yanked her heart back down to earth, she also tried to convince herself that her elated feeling was due only to the great victory the women of this territory had obtained on this historic day. After tonight, she could begin to concentrate on other important causes which needed her attention, such as the temperance issue . . . and the touch of Chance Steele's strong arms around her waist again and . . . "stop it!" she told herself one more time.

sacked yet?" he asked, hoping to ease the boy's discomfort.

as he gave her ...a quick glance from the side of his eye. "No Ma'am, but to obey without analysis is ..."

Chapter Seventeen

"Can't I go home and change into somthin' different? A party ain't no fun if you're miserable, and I ain't never been more uncomfortable in my whole life!" To emphasize his meaning, Jerrod bent down and tugged unmercifully at the tight-fitting legs of his suit trousers.

"No," Chance grumbled in a tone which defied argument. The boy remained silent, but his intense pout was enough to make Jubilee stifle a chuckle as the three of them made their way toward the conference room. She could not help but feel grateful to Chance for bringing his nephew. With Jerrod as chaperon, Jubilee did not feel quite so conspicuous in the gambler's presence.

"You look very handsome," she said in an effort to ease the boy's discomfort. "In fact, I'll be willing to bet you will have to fight the young ladies off with a club tonight."

A faint blush of red streaked through Jerrod's cheeks as he looked up with an embarrassed smile, but before he could say anything, his uncle interrupted. "Ah, another bet? I knew deep inside you were a true gambler."

Jubilee did not bother to reply to Chance's remark, Instead, she gave the man a look which suggested he was treading on dangerous ground. Her annoyed expression intensified when she noticed how his mirth seemed to increase with her discomfort. She returned her attention to Jerrod, purposely ignoring the smirking man who walked beside her, "Do you have a girlfriend yet?" she asked, hoping to make polite conversation.

The scarlet flush upon the young man's face darkened as he gave his uncle a quick glance from the side of his eye. "No Ma'am! I-I'm too busy with my studyin' to think about those things. Why, my Uncle Chance makes darn sure that I don't have nothin' to do with any of those women at the saloon and he makes sure that—"

"I'm sure Jubilee gets the idea," Chance cut in with a patronizing tone. He had talked to the boy about the importance of keeping up a respectable image, especially since Jubilee had already questioned the influence of the saloon on a young man Jerrod's age. He had hoped Jerrod would use a little tact, however, when he was questioned on this matter.

Jubilee drew in an indignant breath and returned her narrowed gaze towards Chance Steele. It was obvious the man had rehearsed his nephew on what he should and should not say on this particular subject. If they hadn't reached the entrance of the conference room, she would have given Chance her opinion of his deceptive maneuver. But the moment they arrived at the scene of the party, she was overcome by the dreadful recollections of the food fight, which had occurred on the last occasion she had been in this room, As a reminder, Jubilee noticed that a long table of food stood in the same location. She cringed visibly as she fought within herself to wipe away the vivid memories of that awful day.

The area was already filled with the elite of Cheyenne's society, who had turned out for the celebration of the passing of the equality bill. Jubilee was sure every pair of eyes in the room was focused directly upon her and her escort. But as the guests began to notice their arrival, she was surprised at the reception she received. The women she had met at the rally, and who had participated in the unsuccessful protest of the grand opening of Chance's saloon, overwhelmed her with words of congratulations and praise. Even a reporter from the

Wyoming *Tribune,* the territorial newspaper, approached Jubilee and asked if he could write quotes from her last speech in the article he was preparing about the historic event. Jubilee felt as though a thousand pounds of disgrace had been lifted from her shoulders, since it appeared that all the horrid events of the past week had been forgotten.

"I see one of my friends from school," Jerrod mumbled to his uncle in a relieved tone when the crowd which had surrounded them finally began to move on, "Can I go over there with him?" The attention they were receiving was not the boy's idea of a good time.

A knowing grin curved the gambler's mouth and he gave his dark head a nod. "Ah, to be sixteen again," he sighed. Leaning close to Jubilee, he added, "Before Jerrod came to live with me, I could barely remember what it was like to be young."

In a voice that sounded more cynical than she had intended, Jubilee retorted, "I never knew what it was like to be young, and I try to forget everything I do remember about my childhood,"

Her strange comment filled Chance with confusion for a moment, while his image of her perfect lifestyle in Washington recreated itself in his mind. Ah, but that was usually the way it was the rich and pampered, he reminded himself. He had not encountered one wealthy lady on the riverboats who did not feel sorry for herself in one way or another. He quickly decided that Jubilee Hart's statement was undoubtedly a ploy for sympathy, but she would not receive any from him just because she had been a poor little rich girl. "Would you care for a glass of punch?" he inquired as though he had not heard her last remark.

She glanced toward the long table again and gave a sharp nod of her head. The one long spiral curl, which dangled teasingly over her shoulder, swung to and fro for an instant. Chance's eyes caught the slight movement, and his mind immediately envisioned his nimble fingers twisting themselves in those long silken strands.

He felt a familiar ache working its way through his loins, and it took all his willpower to contain his erratic senses within an outwardly calm facade. He cleared his throat and ran his palm down the front of his black velvet vest. To compliment the velvet attire Jubilee usually wore, Chance had chosen his garments for tonight with great care. He hoped she would notice his tailored suit of heather gray, which was accompanied by a white shirt and the black vest, but so far she had not bothered to comment on his new apparel. He had complimented her on her beautiful royal blue suit, Chance thought with aggravation, even though it was the same ensemble she had worn on the first night they had dined here at the inn with the Crowlys'.

As he walked away to fetch their drinks, however, Jubilee's willful gaze traveled the entire length of his tall form. Not only did she notice the way his elegant suit fit perfectly along the lines of his well-defined muscles, but she also noted how the the mere sight of him affected every one of her awakening senses. She took a deep breath in an attempt to regain a normal rhythm of breathing, but it was not worth the effort. Telling herself in a firm inner voice she did not care for Chance Steele was just as useless. The lustful sensations he aroused in her body were undeniable, she decided as she wiped her hot brow with the back of her shaking hand . . . but did she *love* him? Until she could answer that question without any doubts, she could not even begin to overcome the resistance her staunch mind demanded from her irrational heart.

"What are you boys up to?" Chance asked as he approached the table where the huge punch bowl sat amongst the array of party food.

With a suppressed chuckle, Jerrod gave an innocent shrug. "Nothing, Uncle Chance." His raven eyes flashed with a guilty glimmer as he glanced at his cohort. When the two boys caught each other's eye, they both burst into a fit of giddy laughter. Their mirth seemed contagious and Chance could not stop the chuckle

193

which escaped from his lips. But before he had an opportunity to ask them what the joke was, the pair made a quick exit into the crowd. Chance shook his head and chuckled again to himself at the boys' mischievous behavior. When he turned around and glanced toward the area where he had left Jubilee, his humor quickly faded. Jubilee was no longer standing alone, and the man who stood beside her was not a welcome addition. An annoyed growl echoed from deep in Chance's throat as he glared at the way Reverend Mahan was boldly touching Jubilee's arm as he spoke to her. When the two of them burst into a round of laughter at the same time, Chance nearly spilled the drinks he held in his hand. With a louder grunt, he carefully sat the two punch glasses down and grabbed a napkin to clean the sticky substance from his hands. It was difficult to concentrate on his task, however, because his flashing black gaze kept being drawn to the opposite side of the room.

As he started to pick up the glasses again, Chance recalled the little flask of whiskey he had slipped into one of the inner pockets of his suit. When he had placed the container in his pocket before leaving the saloon that night, he had not intended to take a sip of the liquor until later in the evening. But as he observed the minister with Jubilee, he decided he needed that sip sooner than he had planned. With a discreet glance around to assure himself no one was paying him any mind, Chance quickly poured some of the liquor into one of the glasses, then replaced the flask back within the confines of his suit pocket. While he walked towards his date and the minister, he made a mental note to be careful which glass he handed to Jubilee. The last thing he wanted was for her to get tipsy and accuse him of trying to get her drunk. The sound of Jerrod and his friend laughing caught his attention again, and Chance gave the boys a serious frown as he passed them. They had to be up to no good, he decided, since Jerrod's sulking mood had changed dramatically in the past few minutes. Boys will be boys, he reminded himself and he

recalled some of the pranks he and his brother had con-
cocted when they were Jerrod's age.

"Good evening, Mahan," Chance said curtly, as he
pushed himself in between the smiling couple. His
forceful gesture lacked both politeness and tack, so he
was not surprised to see the icy glare Jubilee focused in
his direction when he handed her a glass of the punch.
"Shall we find a table where we could have some privacy?" he asked with a smile as innocently as if he did
not understand the meaning behind his rude actions.

Jubilee returned his smile with her own look of false
sweetness. "A table for four would do." Before he had a
chance to ask the question she could see hovering upon
his lips, she rushed on. "You, me, Jerrod, and, I've
asked Reverend Mahan to join us. So that makes four."

"Jerrod has joined his own friends and—" Chance
leveled his dark gaze on the minister, while he added in
a flat voice, "I think Reverend Mahan would probably
like to do the same."

The young minister gave his curly brown head a firm
shake, while he also shook off the other man's exaggerated act of jealousy. "No, actually, I would love to join
Miss Hart." Not mentioning Chance's presence was an
intentional oversight, but the minister's smile remained
in a fixed position as he added, "I'll just grab myself a
glass of that punch and say hello to a few people, then I
will find your table." The men each gave one another a
silent glare, which seemed to dare either of them to say
another word on the touchy subject. After a couple of
uncomfortable seconds, the minister turned his smiling
countenance towards Jubilee again, then took his
leave—for the time being, anyway.

"Shall we?" Chance said in a light tone of voice, completely different from the way he had spoken to the
minister. He bowed slightly, careful not to spill his
drink, and held out his arm for Jubilee. She hesitated
for a time, then decided taking his arm as he escorted
her across the room would not damage her reputation
any worse than all the other events of the past week.

Expecting to see a victorious smirk upon his lips, Jubilee directed a guarded glance up toward his face. Instead, she was surprised—and touched—by the proud expression he carried upon his handsome countenance as she allowed him to lead her to a corner table.

"What is that nephew of yours up to?" she asked when she was seated at the table. "I just saw him and another boy over by the punch bowl, and they were giggling like a pair of imps."

Chance gave an exasperated glance in the direction Jubilee had just mentioned, as his expression took on a shade of annoyance. Those boys were sure acting suspiciously, and the way they took off like a bolt of lightning when they noticed Chance and Jubilee's interest in their activities made them appear all the more conspicuous. But Chance could not imagine any real harm that the boys could induce with so many witnesses around, so he merely shrugged and said, "Jerrod is just stretching his wings. He was used to living a mighty quiet life on his parents' farm, and his new life with me is quite a contrast." A strange expression crossed Chance's face as he added, "But he's a good boy, and he's got my brother and his wife to thank for his upbringing."

"You must have been very close to your brother and sister-in-law," Jubilee said in response. There had been a time when she had wished she had siblings, but as she grew older, she realized even one child had been too much of a burden for her suffering mother to look after.

"He did something for me that most people would never even consider doing, so in at least one way, I guess you could say we were close. But, I wish now that we could have been much closer."

In a rare show of public affection, Jubilee reached across the table and lightly squeezed Chance's arm. "But now you're doing something for him that is very commendable, and you should be proud of yourself for being so kind to Jerrod."

Because her words and actions contained so much

196

emotion, Chance could not bring himself to reply. He could never repay his dead brother for the responsibility he had placed upon him sixteen years ago, and he would never be proud of the way he had deserted his own son. Yet, he still feared that if he attempted to explain any of these anguished feelings of guilt to Jubilee, she would only see the disgrace he had brought upon himself and his family all those years ago. But sometimes — like now — Chance yearned to confide in someone about his painful past. He found himself imagining what it would be like to admit to the whole world that Jerrod was his son. Admission of his immoral past was impossible, Chance reminded himself firmly, and as he snatched up his punch glass and drained the whiskey-laced liquid into his dry mouth.

"I still can't believe this is really happening," Jubilee said as she looked around the crowded room in amazement. "Who would have thought the entire future of our country would be determined here in this sparsely populated frontier?" A tingling of excitement rushed through her body as she daintily picked up her glass and took a deep drink of her punch. When she sat her glass back down, a curious thought passed through her mind. "You never doubted for one moment that the enfranchising bill would pass. Why was that, Mr. Steele?"

With an exasperated upward roll of his dark eyes, Chance leaned forward and asked, "Why do you insist on calling me Mr. Steele?"

"Because I assume that is your last name, and I'd be willing to bet that your first name is not Chance."

A stunned expression clouded Chance's dark features, but when he responded to her insinuation that he was using a false name, his voice had its usual taunting tone. "I have a lot to teach you about betting. A gambler should never make a wager without having something substantial to back it up."

"You still didn't answer my question."

"Ah, yes, the suffrage bill?" He picked up his empty punch glass and frowned as if he was in dire need of another drink. "It was a simple deduction," he answered with a careless shrug. "Wyoming is a new territory, a vast land of windblown prairies and rugged snow-capped mountains. To a daring adventurer, it is an uncharted paradise, but it also represents a life of hardship and challenge. We've got our share of transients and low-lifes, but Wyoming lacks the romantic lure that entices most homesteaders to the West. After today, women all over the country will want to settle in the Wyoming Territory, because now we can offer them something which no other territory can."

A thoughtful scowl tugged at the corners of Jubilee's lips as she mulled over Chance's last words, "Giving the women of Wyoming the right to vote was only a ploy to attract more families to settle here, wasn't it?" Her head jerked back in an indignant toss as she quickly continued before Chance had an opportunity to answer her question. "Passing the equality bill was planned all along, but not because the men of Wyoming thought women were their true equals. It was destined to pass so that more men would settle here once their wives heard about the heroic decision of the legislature." Her voice began to crescendo into a pitch of rage as Jubilee zeroed in on the real intent behind today's historic judgement. "And those men would be good, decent family men a more respectable class of men than the low-lifes that are already here!"

Chance was at a loss for a reply when he realized how angry she was becoming, especially since he could see no probable cause for her attitude. The women of Wyoming had achieved a status that no other women in the rest of the country had acquired; what difference did it make why the men had been so generous to the weaker gender?

"Would you like another glass of punch?" he asked in a helpless tone as she gulped down the last of her drink. He felt he needed another drink as well—only this one would be a great deal stiffer than the last one.

Jubilee gave her head an angry nod, but she did not

bother to answer. Although, as she watched him walk away, she did have the urge to jump up and announce to the entire room the real reason as to why the Wyoming men had been so kind to their womenfolk. She glanced around the circumference of the conference room at the jovial faces and her rage expanded. Was it only her imagination, or where the men standing around as if they were noble gods, while the females clamored around them in humble gratitude? No, she determined as she studied the crowd more closely; the men were in their highest glory tonight as they accepted the women's words of praise for their generosity in granting the women the right to cast votes.

"Isn't it wonderful!" Abigail said as she interrupted Jubilee's silent fury. "Our men have finally recognized us as their equals," she paused for a moment and took a drink from the glass of punch she carried in her hand, then added, "Well, Howard will never feel that I'm his equal, but who cares?" She giggled and tossed her head back to drain the last of her drink into her mouth.

Jubilee stared up at the elderly woman in silent wonder. Every time she saw Abigail there was more of a change in her appearance and attitude. Tonight, however, was the most drastic change Jubilee had noticed so far. Not only was Abigail dressed in a gown of bright pink, but she was acting as giddy as Jerrod and his friend were behaving. "Hasn't Howard come home yet?" Jubilee asked, permitting her astonishment to edge into the tone of her voice.

"No. Isn't that wonderful, too?" Another high-pitched giggle sprang from her mouth as she turned and noticed the approach of Chance Steele. "Oh, Jubilee, if I were only twenty years younger, I think I'd give you some competition."

A gasp flew from Jubilee lips at Abigail's insinuation. "He's not my — I mean — there is nothing going —" her stammering was cut off when Chance reached the table and greeted Abigail Crowly with his most dashing smile.

"Have you found the fountain of youth, Abigail?" he said with a sly wink. "You're more lovely every time I see you." His teasing smile widened when he noticed the woman was blushing profusely in the same manner she used to whenever he greeted her with exaggerated words of flattery. "Are you going to join us?" he asked as a polite gesture, but he sighed with relief when the older woman turned him down.

"Thank you, but no." She shrugged her thin shoulders and glanced around the room. "I'm not ready to sit down yet, but I do think I will head back toward the punch bowl." With a glance at Jubilee, she asked, "Isn't that just the most wonderful punch you've ever tasted? Why, I've probably drunk three or four glasses already."

Jubilee replied with a slight nod of her head. She was still trying to figure out what had happened to Abigail Crowly in the past few days, and especially, what had brought about her uninhibited behavior tonight. As she watched the woman practically skip away from their table, she turned her questioning look toward her companion. "It's almost frightening the way she has changed."

"No, I think it's wonderful," he teased in an imitation of Abigail Crowly. When his remark brought a smile to Jubilee's lips, his heart soared within the confines of his chest. He raised his punch glass into the air, "Let's make a pact."

The guarded look filtered back into Jubilee's expression. "About what?"

"That we both agree to take Abigail's example and have a good time tonight."

For a moment, Jubilee hesitated to answer him. There were many things that she still wanted to discuss about the deceptive reasons the suffrage bill had passed today. But, as she looked at the handsome gambler, all the things she had wanted to talk about seemed to erase themselves from her mind, almost as though they were not worth remembering. Instead, she became aware of the magic that seemed to engulf the room in its binding spell; the lights were dim, and soft music floated from the violins and guitars. The excitement of the crowd was pulsing through the air like the rhythm of a frantic drumbeat. The beautiful blonde's expression began to soften as she stared into the hypnotizing eyes of the man who held his glass up into the air in anticipation of their toast. She reached out and picked up her own drink and raised it up until it clinked lightly against his glass. Abigail was right; the punch was wonderful . . . and so was everything else.

Chapter Eighteen

"I thought they'd figure it out long before now," Jerrod whispered to his partner in crime. He wrapped his arms around his aching stomach, and forced himself not to laugh again. His whole body hurt from the non-stop laughter, which was induced by the knowledge that he and Tommy had pulled off a caper of enormous proportions without being caught.

"Well, I say we quit watching everyone else makin' a fool of themselves and start drinkin' some more of that punch before it's all gone," the other teenager replied with a firm nod of his head.

"Are you two boys still hanging around the grub table?" Chance said with a noticeable slur as he approached them again. He did not bother to wait for them to answer him, because he was too engrossed in serving up two more glasses of punch. As he flipped open his gray suit jacket and removed the near-empty flask, he cast the boys a sly grin. "Just a little something to liven up the punch." He poured the last of the liquor into his glass, then snickered as he leaned towards the boys. "But don't tell anybody. All these old tea-toddlers would be shocked right down to their liberated underdrawers." He carefully scooped up the two glasses of punch and swaggered away, leaving the two boys stunned. It was only a few seconds, however, before they were forced to give into the stifled laughter that was about to choke them.

"He's spikin' the spiked punch," Tommy gasped out through his uncontrollable mirth. When he had suggested this escapade to Jerrod, he had no idea how much fun it would turn out to be. Observing the entire population of Cheyenne's most prominent citizens fall victim to their harmless joke of keeping the punch bowl laced with liquor was hilarious to the mischievous pair. Jerrod's only worry was that after this celebration was over, his Uncle Chance might discover he was the one who had supplied the added ingredient from the liquor supply at The Second Chance Saloon.

Reverend Mahan's mouth drew into a distinct pout when the other man returned to the table with only two full glasses of the sweet-tasting brew. Several times the minister had asked the saloon owner to replenish his glass. Steele had consistently ignored the minister's requests. "I suppose I'll have to get my own drink again," Mahan sighed as he rose on his unsteady legs. Sometime between his last glass of punch and now, the effect of the alcohol had began to take its toll on his weakening senses. He realized he was drunk, but his mind did not comprehend how this phenomenon had occurred. Besides, he was having too much fun antagonizing Chance Steele to care. And even more important, he was still in the company of the beautiful Jubilee Hart.

"I hope he gets lost," Chance spouted like a spoiled child as he watched the preacher stagger across the room. The gambler was unaware of the odd behavior of everyone around him since he had toted down every last drop of the liquor he had hidden away in his coat pocket. In his drunken state, he was still a bit surprised that such a meager amount of alcohol had inebriated him to such a degree. He was even more amazed that his temperance-minded date did not seem to notice his unstable condition.

The silken contours of Jubilee's face scrunched up as she watched the minister walk across the room on his wobbly legs. "I like him," she said, much to Chance's annoyance. Since she knew her comment would not please her escort, she graced him with a challenging smile. Her long lashes blinked several times in an attempt to clear her wavering vision. When she was able to focus on Chance's face, she pushed away the nagging thought that something was drastically wrong with the way she felt. Alcohol, of any sort, had never touched her lips, so she had no idea she had succumbed to a state of total inebriation. With each sip of punch, her inhibitions had slowly deserted her, leaving her with a sense of awareness that she had never possessed when she was sober. She had never laughed so much in her life, nor had she ever wanted something — or someone — as much as she wanted Chance Steele to hold her again.

Chance was not coherent enough to understand what it was about the odd look upon Jubilee's radiant face that enticed him to blurt out his next question. Even in his drunken state, he knew nothing was more right. "Let's get married tonight?"

His unexpected suggestion bolted through Jubilee's disoriented mind like a flaming arrow. Her first reaction was to refuse him, to tell him all the multitude of reasons as to why she could never marry a man like him. Yet, her liquor-tainted mind could only conceive one reason for her to give in to his outlandish proposal. If they were married there would be nothing to prevent him from holding her in his arms again. Still, somewhere deep down inside of her, where the liquor could not dominate, she continued to fight with her own desires. She couldn't consent to marry a man just because she yearned for his kisses. There had to be a deep element of love involved before she could make such a tremendous decision. Her foggy eyesight sought Chance's gaze again as a visible tremor shot through the entire length of her being. The way she felt about this dashing gambler had to be more than just a passing fancy that would fade once he had held her again. Something told her these feelings would never go away. Could it be that all these strange emotions were the unselfish, eternal love she had been seeking her whole life?

Her long hesitation did not influence Chance's determination to fulfill his quest before the night was over. From the first moment he had seen the beautiful blonde walking down the wooden plank at the train station, he had sensed his life would never be the same again. And he knew they had to make their desires a reality before the vast differences in their lives pulled them apart. "Marry me," he repeated, falling to his knees in an unexpected gesture of gallantry. He clasped ahold of her unbandaged hand and gazed up into her startled face. "I love you, Jubilee Hart. Please say you'll marry me — right here — tonight?

"Before Jubilee's alcohol-weary mind could respond, a round of applause and cheers rang out from those who were within earshot and witness to Chance's flamboyant proposal. Since all who had attended the celebration from its beginning were now in the same inebriated state as Jubilee and her ardent date, the idea of an added attraction sounded like great way to highlight the evening. The fleeting realization of how her entire life had become a public spectacle since she had arrived in Cheyenne passed through Jubilee's mind as she listened to the enthusiastic shouts around her. *Marry a gambler?* But, Chance Steele was not just a gambler — he was the man who caused her deepest desires to consume her.

Jubilee's hesitation seemed like an eternity to Chance. To the woman whose life was about to take a drastic turn, the few moments' interval appeared to whisk past with vivid recollections of her unhappy childhood, intertwined with the dreams she harbored for her perfect future. She was not sure if the cheers and words of encouragement grew louder, or if it was the frantic pounding of her heart that drowned out all her usual logic. She was used to taking chances, but marry Chance Steele? *Well, why not?* she decided with a shrug of her velvet-clad shoulders.

She had not looked away from his ebony eyes ever since he had knelt before her, but something in her own expression must have given him the signal he was waiting to receive. Jubilee's hazy gaze saw the light of victory illuminate his face, and she wondered if she had said yes without even being aware of it.

"Yes, yes!" Chance laughed as he jumped up to his feet, pulling her up with him. At once they were surrounded by well-wishers, although to Jubilee's spinning vision, not one face was recognizable until Father Mahan's unhappy face loomed before her.

"You're not serious, are you?" he shouted as he swayed towards her. "Are you?" he demanded a second time.

Again, Jubilee shrugged, oblivious to any form of reasoning beyond the excitement of this moment. When she felt the strong arm of Chance Steele slip around her waist, drawing her close to him, she did not care about anything else, either. Marriage to him meant being close to him, feeling the warmth of his touch for all time. There were only two stipulations, but she would inform him of these minor details when her thoughts were running along more coherent lines; he would have to sell The Second Chance Saloon and swear off gambling for the rest of his life. This discussion could wait, she told herself as her trembling form melted up against the hard body of the handsome gambler.

"You can perform the ceremony right now, preacher," Chance informed the distraught minister. "And all these wonderful people of Cheyenne can be our witnesses." Another round of drunken cheers echoed through the crowd. As if he had just committed a heroic deed, Chance bowed and flashed the large gathering of guests a brilliant smile.

His elaborate display had a sobering effect on the young minister. With his senses beginning to clear somewhat, he leveled his sights on Jubilee. "If you can tell me this is what you really want, then I will marry you to that man. But if you have doubts, any at all, then under no circumstances will I proceed."

The seriousness of his tone penetrated Jubilee's whiskey-filled mind, but it could not distract her from the marvelous effect of being held within Chance's embrace. Almost as if Chance sensed her desperate need to have him near, he tightened his enslaving hold around her waist. "I—I have no doubts," Jubilee replied in a manner which was as positive as her unstable condition could permit.

The minister studied her for a moment longer. He so hoped he would see something in her countenance which would discourage him from fulfilling this mission. Yet, her radiant expression told the minister more than he wanted to know. In defeat, he sighed and looked away. He was a man of the cloth, a servant of God and of mankind. How could he refuse this simple request without just cause? When he pulled the small bible he always carried from his pocket, the entire room fell silent, while the anticipation of the impending event hung heavy in the air.

"Is there anyone present who has an objection? If so, speak now or forever hold your peace."

The minister's words were merely a standard preliminary, but for the woman whose mind struggled to regain a semblance of normality, his question held a tremendous amount of meaning. Her worried gaze filtered around the room at the group of fuzzy faces who stood before her. There must be a dozen reasons as to why this marriage should not take place. Still, no one could decipher one of them. Her eyes settled on the tiny figure of Abigail Crowly, who was blushing as if she were the soon-to-be bride. How Jubilee wished her dear friend, Miss Gurdy, could be here to advise her. Briefly, Jubilee thought of her career and of her life in Washington. But she still could not concentrate for any length of time on any one subject, so her unsteady mind quickly reverted back to the idea of kissing the handsome gambler again. When the minister began to speak, Jubilee could not even command her mind to retain the important words he spoke; something about love and honor, obeying and death. She even answered "I do," when he asked her to repeat the words at the appropriate moment, but when the minister paused, Jubilee was only vaguely aware of reason.

"What do you want to do about a ring?"he asked of Chance Steele. Before the saloon owner could think of a solution, Abigail Crowly moved forward.

"Here, take mine," she said defiantly. "I don't want it anymore." The entire room gasped with shock at the woman's sudden admission, as all eyes searched the crowd for Howard Crowly's reaction. But the banker was conspicuously absent. The men who frequented The Second Chance Saloon, however, whispered to one another about the man's whereabouts. Within a matter of seconds everyone in the area knew the man had recently taken himself a room at the inn, but spent all of his evening hours in the company of the St. Louis whores who worked at the new establishment.

Abigail ignored the whispered comments about her husband. The hateful man with whom she had shared her bed for so many years no longer affected her with any feelings other than relief that he was gone. As the gray-haired woman wiggled the tight-fitting gold band from her finger, barely a breath was taken by the occupants of the room.

"Here," she said as she placed the ring in Jubilee's shaking hand. "I hope it brings you more luck than it brought me."

For the first time since this charade had began, Jubilee's whirling senses started to snap back to a state of rationality. She stared down at the weathered gold band that rested in her numb palm. But before she could begin to sort out the mixture of fears and emotions that rushed through her, Chance reached out and picked up the ring. Tenderly, he turned over her hand and slipped the ring on her third finger.

"You may kiss the bride," Reverend Mahan announced in a grim voice when the ceremony was completed. He did not look at the couple — instead he stared down at the open bible he held in his own shaking hands. The liquor had worn thin enough to leave him with a feeling of loss and sadness, along with the new emotions he was still discovering for the blonde suffragette. But after tonight, after this instant, he could no longer acknowledge those feelings. A wave of guilt washed over him for his involvement in this wedding obscenity, which induced him to make a silent vow. If he ever suspected Jubilee regretted her rash decision to marry this man, somehow, he would personally see to it that she was set free.

Jubilee was not granted the time to wonder about her impromptu marriage, because just as her cloudy mind tried to function in a sensible manner, the ravenous hunger which had seduced her into this proceeding was satisfied at last. The kiss for which she had been yearning descended upon her unsuspecting mouth, wiping away the small amount of common sense she had just reclaimed. The shouting and cheering of the on-lookers resumed as they all crowded close to the couple, but Jubilee was only aware of the rapid pounding of her heart when she became lost in the sweet reverie of her new husband's kiss. A repeat of the sensations which had soared through her the first time they had kissed swept over her with a new intensity. But the poignancy of their first kiss, which they had also believed to be their last, was replaced by the overwhelming feeling that this was the beginning of a new world of enchantment that neither of them had ever known before now.

When, at last, they were forced to pull apart the first thing each of them was presented with was a fresh glass of punch. The beat of the music resumed and the magical feeling seemed to prevail over the entire room again as Chance held his glass up into the air. "To our marriage," he said with a broad smile curving up the edges of his dark mustache.

His words reached into Jubilee's very soul while she

began to come to terms with the enormity of what had just taken place. As her trembling hand rose slowly into the air, she caught a glimpse of the tarnished wedding band upon her left hand. By the time the punch glasses clicked together in a toast, nearly all of the sweet liquid had splashed over the sides of her glass. Someone close by quickly provided her with another full glass, which Jubilee wasted no time in draining down her parched throat. The blurred face of her handsome husband loomed before her as a dozen questions mingled with the alcohol in her brain. *Is this really happening? Why won't my vision remain steady? And what is causing my head to spin so ferociously? When is he going to kiss me again?*

"Congratulations, Uncle Chance," Jerrod said as he finally made his way through the closely-knit crowd. He held out his hand to the older Steele, which caused Chance a moment of confusion. He kept expecting the boy to act like a child, so when Jerrod presented himself like a man, Chance was repeatedly caught off guard. As if he was moving in slow motion, Chance's arm raised until his hand came into contact with the young man's. An avalanche of emotions hit the gambler as he took hold of his son's hand. He had an overpowering urge to make this a night of new beginnings in every way. But even the excessive amount of alcohol he had consumed could not fill him with the bravado he needed to tell Jerrod of his true parentage. Tomorrow though, Chance vowed inwardly, tomorrow he would have that long overdue talk with his son. The thought of a new day also made Chance think of the impending night as he returned his attention to his bride. He was beginning to understand that the strange feelings which came over him every time he gazed at the beautiful woman were brought about by his abounding love and desire for her. He found it almost inconceivable that she had agreed to become his wife, and before the sun rose in the sky, he would make her his woman in every way.

His anticipation to complete this intention made him gulp down the next glass of punch he was handed, then turn to Jubilee and implore her to do the same. "When you're finished with that," he said, motioning to her glass, "Let's get out of here."

Jubilee gave her head an obedient nod. The last two glasses of the nectar, which she had gulped down without hesitation, had sent her back into a world of oblivion. She would do anything this man asked of her.

The instant she polished off the last of her drink, Chance pried the glass from her fingers and handed it to Abigail Crowly. "We're leaving," he announced to the elderly woman, who was too drunk to care, before clasping onto his wife and dragging her through the unruly crowd. The guests had quickly lost interest in the couple now that the music had taken on a faster tempo. Amongst the stomping of feet and loud yah-hoos, Chance and Jubilee were able to make their exit without much notice, pausing only long enough for Chance to grab his heavy coat from the coat rack which hung along the wall. He draped the garment over Jubilee's shoulders, although the cold air barely affected either of the intoxicated newlyweds as they stumbled towards 17th Street.

Jubilee vaguely wondered where he was taking her, but her thick-feeling tongue would not allow her to ask. Besides, it didn't matter. All that seemed important was that he was still holding onto her.

For a reason Chance could not comprehend, he felt an urgent need to hurry as he led his bride into the back entrance of his private quarters at the saloon. Propping her against the nearest wall, he quickly lit the wick of the closest lantern. Then, after a second of reconsideration, he flicked another match and lit a fat candle that stood next to the lantern. When he doused the light from the lamp, he glanced around the room with satisfaction. The candle light provided the area with the romantic atmosphere he wanted for their wedding night. He also noticed, as he approached her, how its flickering shadows cast the most enticing glow upon the face of his beautiful wife.

Jubilee jumped with surprise when she felt the coat being pulled from her shoulders. The short time she had been left to lean against the wall had left her in a state of lethargy. Now, all she craved was a warm bed in which to lay her limp body, so that her tired mind could take a rest. When she was lifted up from the floor and cradled within the comforting arms of her husband, she was aware only of the relief she felt at no longer having to support herself.

Chance Steele, however, had much more sensuous thoughts on his mind. He planned to make love to this woman until neither of them had enough strength to move, and then he would make love to her again. Never had he wanted a woman as badly as he wanted the tempting blonde who had just become his bride. So when he gently placed her down upon his bed, his disappointment had never known such depths. Unaccustomed to alcohol, Jubilee's groggy senses were easily overtaken by unconsciousness the moment she was no longer responsible for remaining in an upright position. With a heavy sigh, the gambler stared down at the sleeping angel who was sprawled out upon the mattress where he had so wished to ravish her with love.

"Ah, Jubilee," he said in a choked whisper as he sat down beside her and began to stroke her silken hair. I suppose we'll have a lifetime to consummate our marriage, he thought to himself. But, he really had his heart set on fulfilling that quest tonight. Still, even in his befuddled frame of mind, he was a man of honor . . . and patience. In defeat, he resigned himself to a wedding night of abstinence. Since there was nothing left to do but to give into his own weariness, Chance decided to make himself and his new wife as comfortable as possible. He rose to his feet on wobbly legs and began to undress himself. As was his habit, he carefully folded each garment as he removed it, then placed the pile of clothes on the arm of the chair which stood close to the bed. He preferred to sleep without the encumberment of any clothing, and he assumed his bride would also be comfortable in this state.

As a last minute thought, before he began to undress his lovely wife, he remembered to pull the privacy curtain around his bed. When there had only been him and Jerrod living here, he had no need to worry about his own privacy. Now things were different. Not only did he have Jerrod to think of, but he also had the responsibility of a wife. He could not expect them to live in the back of a saloon indefinitely. Ah, but he would think about those things when his head was not pounding so violently from the liquor, and when his heart didn't feel as though it had risen to his throat from the inviting sight of his bride.

Restraint took on a much more intense meaning for the man as he started to unbutton the front of Jubilee's blue velvet suit jacket. When the jacket was unfastened, the material slowly fell to the side of her bosom, revealing the ruffled white shirtwaist she wore beneath. Perspiration broke out across Chance's forehead at the sight of her gently rising and falling breasts. The thin cotton allowed him to see the outline of her lacy camisole, and as if he were not tortured enough, he could also make out the outline of the pert nipples, which seemed to beckon to his trembling hands through the cotton barrier. He groaned with agony, then took a deep breath and began to unbutton the tiny row of pearl buttons. With this task completed, he carefully lifted her shoulders up from the bed and pulled the clothing away from her limp body. He eased her back down to the mattress, then folded the two garments and placed them beside his own pile of clothes.

"Have mercy!" he muttered when he returned his attention to the slumbering female. The restricting stays of her camisole held her bosom in tight restraint, and above the ridge of the undergarment, the swell of her creamy white breasts almost appeared to cry out for release. The long curl of golden hair, which had always tempted him, was now resting in a coy manner in the deep crevice between the two sweet mounds of flesh.

213

Chance closed his eyes, but the image only grew more vivid. No mortal man should have to take this punishment! He told himself he would remain calm as he pried his lids open and feasted upon her exquisite beauty. However, the boiling of the blood in his veins told him that it was impossible for a man to retain a tranquil mood when encountering such bewitchery. He could just toss a blanket over her, then retreat into the main room of the saloon so that he would not have to endure any more suffering. But that would mean leaving her, and that would cause him even more pain.

It was no trouble at all to relieve her of her high-topped shoes, and he willed himself to concentrate on the act of making her more comfortable as he began to unfasten her skirt, then slid the heavy round of velvet material down over the curve of her hips. He sighed with satisfaction when the bothersome garment was folded and placed on top of her other clothing. Confronted with her lithe form, clad only in lacy undergarments, the patient man was nearly undone. He smacked the side of his face with his sweating palm, unaware of the profuse amount of perspiration that cloaked the entire length of his nude form. Perhaps he should leave her to sleep with the remainder of her clothes on, he told himself. But he had already danced with the devil ever since he had unbuttoned that first button, so why stop now?

He cursed out loud as his shaking hands fumbled with the miniature clasps and ribbons that kept the front of her camisole together. He had to pause to wipe the beads of perspiration away from his eyes while he inched her pantaloons down past the silken contours of her shapely legs. When all the tedious work was done and Chance Steele allowed his eager gaze to travel along each and every perfect curve of his luscious bride, he was overcome by a fierce rush of guilt, and he had to look away. The throbbing in his loins shouted at him to take what was now his, to fulfill his deepest desires and needs, but his grave sense of honor told him that he was lower than the most venomous reptile that slinked through the bowls of the earth. As he reined his thrashing emotions and attempted to corral his unleashed male urges, he reminded himself of how wonderful it would be to make love to Jubilee when she was conscious. With this thought planted firmly in his mind, he gently eased the covers back from beneath her limp body, then covered her satiny form with the blankets. Now that her lush curves were concealed beneath the covers, Chance took his first complete breath since this whole ritual had begun.

A sense of pride accompanied him as he stretched out his stiff frame on top of the bedcovering. He had no intention of allowing their skin to touch, or else all his restraint would flee. On the contrary, he was going to prove to his bride what an honorable man he was by sleeping next to her all night and not laying a hand upon her succulent flesh.

With a proud sense of achievement, he leaned over, careful not to touch her when he whispered, "I love you, Jubilee." He wasn't sure if he imagined the tender smile that touched her lips for an instant, or if it was just the flickering shadows the soft candle light cast upon her lovely countenance.

Chapter Nineteen

Jubilee tried to open her eyelids, but they felt as though they were made of lead and molded shut. If the pain in her head was any indication of the way she would feel once she was fully awake, she did not think she wanted to open her eyes anyway. What had happened to her that could cause such an atrocious pain? The fleeting thought that she might be dead passed through her mind, but she quickly determined that death would be more merciful than this. By the time she managed to pry her eyes open again, she wished she *could* die. The ceiling was spinning like a top and she had to squeeze her eyes shut again to control the frantic motion. Though she was aware she was lying in bed, she could not remember coming upstairs to her room at the inn. In fact, she realized she could not recall anything of the previous night. The ferocious pounding in her head was not aiding in her desperate search to recall the latter half of last night's celebration.

When, at last, Jubilee felt as if she could prevent the room from spinning, she once again permitted her eyes to open. The unfamiliar pattern of the elaborate blue and gold ceiling was the first thing to throw her thoughts back into turmoil. The ceiling at the inn was a plain, unadorned white stucco. An engulfing sense of dread overcame her as she started to bolt up from the bed. A weight across her midsection prevented her hasty movement as her reluctant gaze moved down in horror. In confusion she stared at the limb, covered with dark hair, until she realized it was a man's arm. Her next reaction was to scream, but before the sound could escape her dry throat, her disbelieving eyes flew to the form of the naked man who still slept on top of the covers, face-down beside her. A choked cry finally escaped, but it was void of almost all velocity.

In a useless attempt to hide the sight of Chance Steele's nude body, Jubilee threw her hand over her eyes. She tried to tell herself that this couldn't be happening! When she reopened her eyes, she would discover this was all a bad dream, a nightmare of outlandish proportions. Fate had something else in mind for Jubilee when her trembling lids opened again, however — and it was worse than any nightmare she could have ever conjured up in her slumbering mind.

"Oh, it's not possible," she sobbed in a whispered cry as her gaze slowly turned back toward the sleeping gambler. With sinking despair, she became aware of her own unclothed state as reality painted a horrible picture of what must have happened during the night.

An agonized groan hovered on her lips as she fought to recall the events which had led to this morning of black disgrace. The last thing she could remember was sitting at a corner table with Chance and Reverend Mahan, and laughing hysterically at their endless wit and humor. She also remembered thinking that she was having the best time she had ever had, as the two men tried to outdo one another for her undivided attention. Nothing else came to mind that could even begin to explain the shameful position she found herself in now. Since she would rather die than to face up to her guilt, a crazy notion entered her head to somehow do away with herself before the truth of what happened became one more tidbit for the gossips of Cheyenne. She was ruined for life after her night of unabashed lust with the owner of this sinful brothel. How could she hold her head up high enough to walk the streets with decent people again?

Engrossed by her own self-pity, Jubilee gasped with fright when her bed-mate suddenly rolled over in his sleep. His movement drug his enslaving arm from her midsection, but it also granted her with a full view of the front of his naked body. She gasped again as her curious eyes immediately sought out the area of his maleness. In horror, she grabbed the blanket and pulled it up over her face. Did she really allow him to—to—with that—oh, it was not possible! Why didn't the gates of hell just open up and swallow her?

As the seconds began to merge into minutes, Jubilee knew she had to do something other than lie here and imagine all the unthinkable things she had most likely been a partner to while in this bed of sin. The *last* thing she wanted to do, however, was to face the man whom had done these awful things to her.

Summoning up all her courage, she lowered the blanket from her face, careful not to glance in the direction of Chance Steele again. Her energy was exhausted by the time she had forced herself to raise up to a sitting position. Her head felt as if someone were sitting on top of it and pounding on the sides with a sledgehammer. From her neck up, there was not one area which did not vibrate with indescribable pain. From her neck down, her entire body throbbed with shame. After several movements that induced incredible suffering, Jubilee managed to slide her legs over the edge of the bed and rise to her feet. Her limbs felt as though they had been stripped of their bones. She had to grasp onto the bedside table for support, and remain unmoving for several minutes until her knees stopped their terrible shaking. She wanted to look over her shoulder to see if her movements had aroused Chance Steele, but she was too afraid she would discover that he was awake and staring at her naked body. This thought made her entire being break out in a fevered blush that colored her pale skin in deep shades of scarlet.

In spite of her anxiety, she drew in a raspy breath and turned around. Thank God, he was still lost in deep slumber. In the dim glow of the gray morning light which filtered through the curtain that was drawn around the bed area, Jubilee spotted her clothes, stacked and neatly folded beside the gray suit Chance had worn on the previous evening. She shuddered at the idea of how those two stacks of clothing represented the loss of her innocence and respectability. Again, she pleaded with her mind to grant her some memory of last night. As she tried to swallow back the heavy lump which had formed in her dry throat, her first clue was revealed. She needed something to drink, to soothe her constricted throat and fuzzy tongue. The punch she had consumed at the party was the first thing to pop into her head. She must have consumed gallons of the sweet brew. And Chance had fetched every single glass for her.

The long lashes surrounding her eyes narrowed with rage as the dawn of recognition joined in with the dawn of this dreadful day. She had witnessed her father on many occasions after the eve of one of his excessive drinking binges. He would hold his aching head and groan in agony every time he tried to focus his reddened eyes on the fearful forms of his wife and daughter. If, by accident, they made a small noise, he would shout at them to keep quiet because his spinning head could not stand any sort of sound. She knew what a hangover was capable of doing to someone, but she had never imagined she would become a victim to something so despicable. The only consolation was that she was an innocent victim, but this act of defilement seemed too low even for a knave like Chance Steele. She did not dare look at him again, for she was certain she would not be able to control her fury much longer.

The need to get away from him was her most desperate wish as she grabbed her clothes and clutched them against her breast. Without thought to what waited on the other side of the curtain, Jubilee pushed through the cloth barrier. She was greeted by the quiet expanse of Chance's living quarters. One window, which was encased by the back door, permitted the hazy light to enter the area, and also gave Jubilee a glimpse of the uncluttered, impersonal place that Chance Steele called home. With a nervous glance toward the window, she began to inch across the room until she was as far from the glass opening as possible. Her location placed her at the opposite side of the room, and a good distance from the curtained seclusion of the gambler's bed. In her frantic turmoil, Jubilee did not remember that there was another person who also occupied this small apartment. She didn't notice the sleeping youth because his bed was concealed behind another curtain, which was only an arm's length away from where she stopped to dress.

She bent down and placed the pile of clothing on the floor with the intention of dressing as quickly as possible. When she straightened up, she was overcome by a bout of dizziness, which caused her to grasp the nearest object for support. Unfortunately, the thin curtain she grabbed did not offer much support. It came loose from its meager frame and collapsed at the startled woman's bare feet. When her eyes raised up from the crumpled heap of material that lay on the floor, a gasping cry of horror rang out from her mouth. The commotion made the sleeping boy stir slightly beneath his bedcoverings. It did not wake him though, since he too was deep in a liquor-induced slumber. Another muffled sound came from behind the curtain where Chance Steele slept, which made a chill race down Jubilee's exposed spine. Her reeling mind could only conceive the image of her standing here in this evil-infested abode, buck naked, for all of Cheyenne to see.

She bent down and grabbed her clothes again, then spun around in a wild circle. When she stopped, her head felt as if it continued to pivot upon her shoulders for several seconds longer. There were two avenues of escape visible through the dim light; one led to the alley behind the saloon, and the other doorway held an unknown retreat. To reach the alley she would have to pass by the curtained area surrounding Chance's bed. The thought of being close enough for him to jump out at her left her aghast with horror. Her first priority, before she did anything else, was to get herself dressed.

"Jubilee? Where are you?"

The hoarse voice from behind the curtain did not allow Jubilee the time to consider a rational decision. Like an escaping prisoner, she could only think of fleeing. The back doorway appeared to be out of reach, especially now that she knew he was awake. The sound of Jerrod stirring in the bed beside her made her next move one of desperation. She clutched her pile of clothes against her thudding breast and charged for the nearest doorway. Effortlessly, the knob turned in her shaking hand and she was granted release as her feet raced through the opening. In her crazy state of mind she even took the time to close the door behind her before she allowed herself to glimpse her new surroundings.

Her shock at being in the private quarters of Chance Steele's saloon was nothing compared to the plunging feeling of helplessness which overcame her when she realized she was now in the main room of the large gambling den. A dozen thoughts rushed through her mind at once, but the thought of her nakedness prevailed. The picture of the nude nymph, hanging above the bar, stared down at her with accusing eyes. As Jubilee stared back at her, she told herself she could not take another step until she was decent. Fighting against her immense panic, Jubilee dropped the pile of clothes at her feet once more, and grabbed her undergarments. With her one good hand, which was rendered nearly useless by its intense shaking, she took the time to hook the center eyelet on her camisole. Her ruffled pantaloons were easier to slip on since she only had to step into the top opening and yank them up over her hips. A vague hope began to surface; perhaps she was really going to escape. Once she was out of this corrupt palace, and away from that unsavory gambler, nothing would prevent her from leaving Cheyenne either! But as she leaned down to scoop up her velvet skirt, however, a chilling voice cut through the silence of the large saloon.

"Well, would you look at what we have here?" Howard Crowly's voice seemed to boom, then echo across the room. A crude snicker followed as he walked down the curved stairway that led from the upper floor. When he awoke this morning, he had vaguely regretted missing the celebration at the inn last night. Now, he was eternally grateful he had decided to spend another night at The Second Chance Saloon. To have missed out on seeing the uppity Eastern miss in this precarious position would have been a crime. This was a sight he would carry with him for all time. The idle threats he had tossed at her in attempts to overcome her resistance were nothing compared to the evidence he now had to use as a weapon.

Jubilee's fear rendered her paralyzed. She had spent every day since she had arrived in Cheyenne trying to avoid this man, but to confront him now was the worst horror she could imagine. Her mouth opened, but not one sound found its way past her heavy tongue. She knew the reason she was standing in the doorway of Chance Steele's living quarters in her undergarments spoke for itself, so it would be useless to try to defend herself.

Howard approached her like an vicious animal moving in for the kill on a defenseless prey. This minx had caused him more trouble than he thought humanly possible. But, the look upon her face told him her gravest fear was his knowledge of her recent activities. His evil smile converted his aging features into demonic creases as his eyes traveled over her disheveled state. Her pale blonde tresses were in wild disarray, almost savage, about her bare shoulders. And she might as well have been wearing nothing at all with the way her breasts were hanging out over the top of the unfastened ridges of her thin camisole. The blonde beauty presented the eyes with a feast that could convert any man into an uncontrollable beast.

At last, Jubilee's strangled voice found an escape as a loud, terrified scream flew from her mouth. Crowly's approach had summoned up the vivid recollections of their struggle at his home on Carey Avenue. Even her hand started to throb relentlessly with the remembrance of the blow that had been the cause of its injury. She stepped back, but the doorway of the private quarters blocked her retreat—just as the kitchen counter had done during his last attack. Unlike the fateful night when Howard had attempted his first assault, this time Jubilee's mind and body were weak and lacked the fight she had possessed before. She slumped against the door in defeat and was unprepared when it swung open and she was shoved out of the way by the gambler. Like a limp rag doll, she floundered to the side of the doorway, then fell against the wall and slid to the floor. She watched the unfolding scenario before her with a feeling of detachment because it seemed too far-fetched to be happening.

"What did you do to her, Crowly?" Chance demanded when his towering presence filled the doorway.

Howard was undaunted by the other man's appearance. His rude laugh once again filled the silence of the early morning. "I haven't had a chance to do anything to her—yet. But I keep trying."

The anger which clouded Chance's vision had been simmering long before today, and he had been aching for the opportunity to confront the old man about Jubilee's broken hand. The accumulation of that fury, added to by his certainty that Howard had just made another attempt to attack Jubilee, made the saloon owner's rage course through his tense body. He had no qualms about avenging his wife's pain, even if his own future was at stake.

Howard laughed again when he became aware of the gambler's exaggerated anger. That the snooty Jubilee Hart was no more than a common whore was not a sufficient reason to entice two sensible men into a duel; even a low-life like Chance Steele should be wise enough to know this. Yet, as his eyes flitted back and forth between the gambler and the woman, Howard began to sense there was more to their relationship than just a casual romp in the back room of this saloon. The intensity of the emotions that hung heavy in the air was almost suffocating, and this realization made Howard all the more determined to claim another victory. Perhaps this woman would be more receptive if he presented her with another form of blackmail. His leering eyes settled on the nearly nude Jubilee as he gave her a lecherous wink.

"Don't worry dearie—I won't carry through with my previous threat to tell everyone that you've been consorting with that gambler." His attention diverted to the man, adding, "That is, if your boyfriend is willing to cooperate."

Before Howard had an opportunity to announce his evil scheme, Chance retorted with a threat of his own. "The only cooperation you'll get from me is the feel of my fist when it rams down your throat." He stepped forward, his hand running down the front of his unbuttoned vest; the only garment—except for his pants, he had taken the time to throw on when he had heard Jubilee scream.

A unconcerned chortle emitted from Howard. How often had he heard those types of threats? "Have you forgotten who holds the bank note on this place? Touch me, and I'll foreclose on your house of pleasure faster than you can blink your bloodshot eyes."

He hadn't forgotten, but the banker's insinuation added to the building fury that already flowed through Chance's veins. In his anger he took another step forward, bringing himself within a couple of feet of the other man. His fists yearned to wipe away Crowly's sinister smirk, while a minute sense of rationality told him to hold his temper in stock before they both reached a point of no return. "Get out!" he commanded through clenched teeth.

The other man's unyielding order reminded Howard of the night his homely little wife had made the same demand. This time, however, he did not plan to slink away without a fight. He had money, prestige, and everything else other men desired—everything—except Jubilee Hart. An instant of insanity overtook him when he charged at the younger man with deadly intent.

Chance had no time to contemplate his next action. Instinctively, he sensed a threat on his life, and reached for the hidden weapon in his inner vest pocket. His only thought was to pull the derringer on Crowly long enough to scare the older man into retreat. He did not expect the banker to make a wild lunge at him. When Howard's body slammed against Chance, the gambler attempted to divert the barrel of the gun away from the man. His gesture was useless, because in the struggle which ensued, the gun became lodged between the two of them. Chance felt Crowly's hand clamp down around his own, but he had no idea who actually caused the bullet to fly from the end of the short barrel. Neither man moved as the explosion ricocheted through the hollow interior of the large saloon. The permeating silence which settled over the room afterward was even more deafening.

At the sound of the gunshot, Jubilee bolted back through time. All the brawls she had witnessed as a child resurfaced and somehow became confused with events occurring at the saloon in which she now huddled. For a fleeting instant, she almost thought she heard her mother scream, but then she realized it had been her own anguished cry that ripped from her throat. She saw the flash of the shiny gun emerge from Chance's vest, its barrel glistened like polished silver in the hazy morning light. A fevered prayer for Chance hovered on her lips as she waited to see who would fall and who would remain standing. When neither man fell immediately, she closed her aching eyes and said another silent prayer of thanks. But God did not feel so gracious today. And when, after a long deceptive pause, Howard Crowly slowly began to sink down to his knees, then tumble back onto the carpeted floor, Jubilee felt the guilt of last night devour her soul.

The gunshot woke Walker, whose room was at the back of the bar. He arrived at Chance's side in a matter of seconds, and was followed closely by the sparsely clad prostitutes who inhabited the second story of the saloon. As they all began to rush to the source of the commotion, Jubilee's eyes remained fixed on the crumpled form of Howard Crowly. He looked as if he was enveloped in a peaceful sleep, but a small jagged hole in his shirt, surrounded by a wet red circle in the center of his stomach, told her he was not sleeping. She still felt as though she was removed from her own body and was observing a fictitious enactment. But this was really happening, and if Crowly was dead, she was the one to blame.

"You'd better go for the doctor," Chance said to Walker. "Then, fetch Marshal Elliot," he added. His dark gaze sought solace from his bride, but when he looked down at her he could tell she in a state of deep shock. He took a step toward her, but something told him that she was not the only person who needed him at this time. Twirling around on the soles of his bare feet, Chance met the frightened face of his son. He was torn in two different directions as he attempted to decide who needed him the most. As his indecision halted his steps, he glimpsed the expression on Jerrod's young face. When their eyes locked, Chance knew he did not have to worry about his son. An unspoken understanding passed between them in the next few seconds and as Chance turned away he was confident he had not lost the boy's devotion.

The look upon his wife's face, though, was not so easy to decipher as he knelt down beside her. Her body shook in visible spasms, which Chance hoped to soothe her by taking her into his arms. Yet, when he reached out to her, she cringed and inched back against the wall. Chance was not deterred. Despite her resistance, he moved closer and wrapped her in his arms. Her first reaction was to try to pull away, but he tightened his hold until he felt her stiff body begin to relax within his embrace. He could not expect her to witness this brutal episode without an extreme amount of fear and disbelief. But he would just hold her until her shock subsided, then he would tell her how much he loved her, and of the wonderful life they would have, in spite of what had just happened on the morning of their first day as man and wife.

Chapter Twenty

"He's a lucky man," Marshal Elliot said to no one in particular as he watched Howard Crowly being carried away on a travois to the hospital which had recently been set up on the second story of a building at the corner of Dodge Street and 23rd. "A couple inches higher would have put that bullet smack in the center of his heart, and he'd be a dead man."

"He's lucky, all right," Chance agreed when he felt another shiver shake through the fragile body of his wife. *The next time he threatens my wife,* Chance thought to himself, *the old coot won't be so fortunate!*

The deadly tone of the gambler's voice captured the Marshal's full interest. "Why don't you tell me what happened here this morning?" His inquisitive gaze moved back and forth between the saloon owner and the disheveled blonde at his side. He did not wonder why she was here, since along with most of Cheyenne's citizens, he vaguely remembered being a witness to their unorthodox wedding the night before. "Perhaps Mrs. Steele would like to tell me her side of the story?" he inquired as he leaned toward Jubilee.

She stared up at him, although she had no idea whom he was addressing. His mention of a "Mrs. Steele", however, drew her full attention. Her head swiveled to the side as she glared up at the man who held her tightly against him. She had ceased to resist his embrace because it seemed his arms were the only thing that could comfort her. But she had not forgotten he had tricked her in the worst manner imaginable by getting her drunk just so he could lure her to his back room and seduce her when she was too intoxicated to resist. *He was worse than Howard Crowly!* she realized as hell-bent anger replaced her shock.

"Mrs. Steele!" she hissed as she pushed against the gambler with her uninjured hand. Her sudden movement freed her from Chance's side, and she took advantage of her release to step away from him. His stunned expression did not faze her as she conjured up an imaginary wife, whom he kept locked somewhere within the brocaded walls of this lust-filled bordello. With a gesture of indignant rage, she threw her hand over her breast, which was now covered by her velvet jacket. At least Chance had been decent enough to help her into her skirt and jacket before the Marshal and the doctor had arrived. But Walker and all the prostitutes, as well as Howard Crowly, had already observed her previous state of indecency.

Marshal Elliot gave a defeated shrug when Jubilee ignored his request for her to relate her version of the shooting. He then glanced at the saloon owner for an answer. "I reckon you can give me your account first. But I'm still goin' need a statement from your wife."

Jubilee was sure someone just kicked her in the stomach when the lawman confirmed the fact that there really was a "Mrs. Steele." Her narrowed eyes flew toward the group of prostitutes who stood at the bottom of the stairway. She almost expected one of them to charge at her in a fit of jealousy. But when they only stared at her through the dark smudges of their thick face paint, she decided that whomever it was who was unfortunate enough to be Mrs. Steele obviously did not think the gambler was worth fighting over. She turned away from the sight of the reckless women, appalled by the realization that after last night, she was no better than any of them. To Jubilee, the untimely arrival of the young preacher almost seem to confirm her belief that her character was tarnished beyond repair.

"I was taking a walk when I saw the doctor's coach pulling away," Mahan said in breathless gasps as he rushed through the front door of the saloon. He was not lying about his activities. His involvement in the wedding farce last night had left him too upset to sleep. Lost to his own sense of failure and guilt, he had been wandering down by the tracks since before dawn. He was in deep thought when the sound of the gunshot had shattered the eerie silence of the winter morning. For awhile, he was not even sure if he had actually heard the shot, or if he had just imagined the noise. Yet, as he started to meander farther down the tracks, he was overpowered by the feeling that Jubilee was in trouble. As he hurried back towards town, his fear increased. What if Jubilee had taken drastic measures when she had realized the awful mistake she had made last night? By the time he reached the saloon, he was terrified of what he might discover.

"Are you unharmed?" he asked as he grabbed ahold of her arm, while presenting his back to her new husband without acknowledging his presence. "I should have put a stop to this absurdity last night."

Jubilee nodded her head and quickly looked away. She could not bring herself to face the preacher, especially now that she knew he had observed the beginning of her decline into hell on the previous night. As her tortured mind began to delve into the emptiness of her memory, she also began to wonder why there had been so many witnesses, yet, why had no one bothered to help her? If Chance had tricked her into getting so drunk that she could not remember even one detail about last night, surely someone must have noticed. Apparently, Reverend Mahan had noticed, and her fury was born again.

"You knew," she shouted when she swung around to face him. "And you still allowed him to bring me here and—and—" she could not force the words from her

230

mouth. The idea of what she must have done, the fool she must have portrayed, was too horrid to voice out loud.

The minister's head dropped down as his arms fell to his sides in defeat. He would give anything if he could redo the events of the past few hours, but he was not capable of miracles. "I'm sorry," he said in earnest, though he did not expect her to accept his meager apology.

Although confusion seemed to abound in the room, Marshal Elliot still had a crime to investigate. The saloon owner's new bride was the only witness, and he intended to carry on with his questioning, in spite of her distraught frame of mind. "Mrs. Steele?" he repeated. "About what happened?"

The lawman's reference to Chance Steele's wife, caused her to jerk back around. Her scathing glare raked across the prostitutes again as she waited to see which of them would reply to the Marshall's request. Since she was certain no decent woman would want the gambler's worthless hide, she thought nothing was more fitting than for Chance Steele to be married to one of his own trollops. Her harried mind continued to dwell on what a degrading relationship the couple must have if he was permitted to traipse about town like a man without any marital responsibilities, while his wife was forced to work as a prostitute in this gaudy prison of blue and gold brocade. A fleeting thought of her parents passed through her mind; Even her wicked father had not treated her mother with such vile disrespect.

"I realize you've had a terrible shock, and it's a shame it had to happen so soon after your weddin' and all, Mrs. Steele. But I'm afraid I must insist that you talk to me, or else I'm goin' be forced to take you down to the jail for questioning."

The manner in which the Marshall had stuck his face up next to hers only served to increase Jubilee's confusion. "Are you—are you talking to me?" she asked, incredulously.

"You *are* Mrs. Steele, aren't you?" the lawman said in an exasperated tone. It was barely sunrise, and he had a tremendous hangover. His patience with this woman was rapidly growing thin.

A hoarse gasp came from her gaping mouth, but as she started to disagree with the man, she began to understand what she still could not remember. That Chance Steele had stooped so low to claim his winnings on their bet was incorrigible, and unforgivable! Her gaze settled on the gambler in wide-eyed disbelief, and the strange expression upon his face was the confirmation she feared. Words eluded her. She felt her entire life slowly begin to crumble down around her like the brittle leaves of autumn. Fiery tears filled her eyes and raced down her cheeks in rivulets of salty rain.

The sight of her despair caused both the minister and her groom to rush to her side. They pushed the marshall away without a second thought, while each of them bent down to comfort her. When they both started to speak at the same time, they peered over her blonde head and gave one another a look that bespoke their intense jealousy and budding dislike of one another. Since he had no intention of sharing his bride with the minister, Chance narrowed his eyes with a silent threat. Mahan retaliated with his own icy glare as he inwardly repeated his vow of the previous night; if Jubilee regretted her rash marriage, he would come to her rescue without hesitation.

"Why don't you let me take you back to your room at the inn," the preacher said to Jubilee, although his eyes never left the face of Chance Steele.

"She belongs here — with me," Chance answered in a stern reply. "You married us last night, remember?"

Jubilee's teary gaze moved towards the preacher, accompanied by her staggered gasp. "You mar-married us?"

A million spears of rebuke were aimed at the young

minister when he glanced down at the troubled face of the woman. "None of us can be held responsible for our actions last night. Somebody spiked the punch," he said, although words of regret would hardly rectify his own drastic mistake. He noted the way Jubilee's accusing glare settled on Chance Steele when he mentioned the spiked punch. He didn't blame her for the thoughts that were undoubtedly filling her head, for he, too, had wondered if the saloon owner was the culprit who had altered the punch at the suffrage celebration. Since he couldn't prove his suspicions, however, he decided to not to voice his opinion without evidence.

Chance did not miss their accusing looks. "I did not spike the punch bowl!" he retorted in his own defense. The flask of whiskey he had carried for his personal consumption did not have any relationship to the inebriation of the whole population of Cheyenne. As the words of denial escaped from his mouth, everyone's thoughts began to work in unison. At once, all eyes were riveted toward young Jerrod Steele.

A sheepish expression came over the boy's face, accompanied by a helpless shrug. "We—me and Tommy—was only havin' fun. We didn't think no harm would—"

"I'll deal with you later!" Chance interrupted with clenched teeth. He was not sure if his anger was directed at the boy for his thoughtless prank, or if he was furious at himself for not realizing what was happening last night. Everyone had made reference to the mischievous behavior of Jerrod and his friend, but Chance had not been responsible enough to fulfill his parental duties.

The young man's admission eased away a bit of Jubilee's fury towards the gambler, but it did not change the fact that as a result of the misdeed, they had been united in this sham of a marriage. Nor could it bring back the memories of what must have happened behind that curtain in Chance's private quarters.

"You need to get away from here, to clear your

thoughts," the minister implored Jubilee in a determined voice as he directed his attention away from Jerrod and Chance Steele.

"Please," Chance said in a quiet tone as he reached out and rested his hand on her shoulder. "Don't go. We need to be together now more than ever." Chance's voice shook slightly as he pleaded with his bride to stay. Though he knew he could not prevent her from leaving if she so chose, he also knew that watching her go would rip his heart apart.

His softly spoken words threw Jubilee's mind into another whirl of confusion. Even if he wasn't the one who spiked the punch, she still felt as though he had taken unfair advantage of her when she was unable to fend for herself. And there were so many other things she had to sort out in her mind. Among them, the immense attraction she harbored for the gambler; the emotions she could not deny, in spite of the latest calamity to befall them. Now, however, she was too vulnerable to stay with him, because being with him would expose her to the wild cravings that had led her to this situation.

"I need to be alone," she said in a hoarse whisper, while she forced herself to look away from the troubled face of her new husband. If she allowed herself to meet his gaze again, her whirlpool of emotions would wash away her common sense once more. "Will you please escort me to the inn?" she asked the minister.

Reverend Mahan wasted no time in easing her away from the saloon owner. He had his own selfish reasons for wanting to take her away, but the pallor of her complexion made him fear for her health.

"I still have to ask you a few questions," Marshal Elliot announced, stepping in front of the departing couple.

Jubilee nodded and held her hand up toward the preacher when he started to argue with the lawman. "It's all right." She drew in a deep breath and faced the marshall. "What do you want to know?"

234

"Why did your husband shoot Crowly?"

His blunt request took Jubilee aback for an instant, but his mention of Chance Steele as her "husband" was even more startling. For the first time since this terrible episode had taken place, she became aware of Chance's precarious position. He could go to jail for shooting Howard Crowly! Angry as she was at the gambler, she could not allow him to take the blame for a crime which was not his fault. "Chance was protecting me," she snapped at the lawman.

"From old man Crowly?" the marshal said with a doubtful frown. He had not been in the Wyoming Territory very long, and though he had heard several rumors about Crowly's infamous womanizing, he still found it hard to believe that a reputable businessman such as Howard Crowly could be capable of any grave misdeeds.

His attitude enraged Jubilee, especially since she had experienced the depths of Howard's evil nature on more than one occasion. "Old man Crowly," she began through gritted teeth, "is the most despicable man I've ever met." She raised her broken hand into the air and shook it in the lawman's face. "This is a result of the first encounter I had with Howard Crowly." She did not allow the loud gasp from everyone in the saloon to halt her outrage as she continued. "If Abigail Crowly had not come to my rescue, I would have substained much more than a broken hand." She turned abruptly to glance at her husband. "Thank God, Chance was able to save me from that madman's second attack." As Chance became aware of the look of gratitude which worked through her tense face, he drew in a relieved breath.

"Are you sayin' Crowly forced himself on you on two different occasions?" Marshal Elliot demanded. A full brown beard and thick mustache adorned his round face, and the heavy growth surrounding his lips was twitching like a cat's whiskers. He had no trouble dealing with highwaymen and troublemakers, but he had no tolerance for a man who attacked a defenseless woman.

Jubilee's voice was noticeably shaken when she spoke again. "He tried to — but he never actually succeeded in —" her dramatic pause cinched the case for the marshal.

"I understand, Mrs. Steele." He turned towards the saloon owner as though he was too embarrassed to look at the woman. "Your wife is free to go." He rubbed his hand over his thick beard as a weary sigh echoed from his lips. "I'll still have to get a statement from Crowly, and I doubt his story will match up with yours, so I'll have to ask that you remain available for further questioning."

Chance shrugged with indifference, while he ran his hand down his vest again in an unconscious gesture. His fingers raked over the tiny derringer, which he had replaced in its hidden pocket. His gesture drew the lawman's attention to the gold watch-fob chain which dangled from the outer pocket.

"I think I should take that gun as evidence until the case is resolved."

With another shrug Chance pulled back his vest, revealing his bare chest, and pulled the miniature weapon out into view. The few times in the past when he had been forced to use violence to protect his own rights, he had surrendered the gun to lawmen until an investigation was conducted. He had fired with just cause during most of those bouts of gunplay — Walker could attest to that fact. But he had never had more of a justified reason to use the gun than he did on this bleak winter morning. He felt no qualms about turning the gun over to the marshal now. Yet, in the presence of his son and wife, Chance realized he also had no desire to reclaim the weapon. He did not look at the lawman when he handed over the derringer. Instead, he watched his wife, hoping that she would leave knowing of his boundless love for her.

Jubilee met her husband's loving gaze for a few seconds before she allowed Reverend Mahan to lead her from the saloon. Though she did not understand why she had faced so many difficult trials since arriving in this cold, barren, prairie town, she was aware of the reason fate had transported her all the way to Cheyenne, Wyoming; She had followed her impassioned heart and the trail had led her to Chance Steele.

Chapter Twenty-one

Chance observed Jubilee's guarded attitude, cautioning himself to chose his words carefully. He was amazed she had admitted him into her hotel room without a moment's hesitation, when only a few hours ago, he had been afraid that she would never want to see him again.

"Abigail just left. She went to see Howard at the hospital and he seems to be doing fine." Jubilee cradled her broken hand as if it were an infant, and for an instant her gaze settled on the other hand, which was now void of the gold wedding band. She had insisted the older woman take it back when she had visited earlier and they had determined how the ring had come to be on Jubilee's finger. She took a deep breath and glanced back up, noticing that Chance's gaze was also on the barren ring finger. Neither of them made reference to the missing jewelry as she continued to speak about Howard Crowly.

"He was not very pleasant to her though, and they had an ugly quarrel. Abigail was about to tell him she didn't want him to come home at all when Marshal Elliot showed up." Jubilee's worry was evident upon her face as she asked in a foreboding tone, "Did Howard make his statement, yet?"

"He did," Chance answered, while he made a promise to himself to buy her the most dazzling wedding ring money could buy. His eyes became hypnotized by the tempting sight she presented as he imagined himself slipping a beautiful diamond ring upon her finger. She was wearing her teal dressing gown again, and it was obvious she had just taken a bath because the soft odor of floral-scented bath powder still filled the air. He knew if he were to bury his face against her silken neck, she would smell of the sweet scent, too. The thought made his legs quake.

"And?" Jubilee prodded with a nervous step backwards. Being near him was never an easy task, but the idea that they had shared an intimate night together—a night of which she had no recollection—made her twice as restless.

"And what?" he whispered in an amorous voice as he took a challenging step towards her.

She tossed her uninjured hand up into the air in exasperation. "What did Howard say about the fight?"

"Ah yes, the fight." Chance felt his face flame with heat. He was glad she could not read his mind at this moment, because she would never forgive him. He was recalling the image of her lovely body stretched out upon his mattress, and the way her taut breasts had responded with anxious attention when he had unfastened her lacy camisole and . . .

He wiped the back of his hand across his perspiring brow, then ran his hand down the front of his vest. It felt odd not to have his hand pass over the tiny lump which his absent derringer had always created. "He disagreed with our version, of course," he said with a futile attempt to calm his racing pulse. When he saw the worried expression cross her face, he quickly added, "But the marshal has no doubts about our side of the story, so there's no need for us to fret."

"Where that man is concerned, I can't help but worry. What will happen when he recovers? He's made so many threats already."

Chance did not want to bother himself with Howard Crowly, he only wanted to talk about their future together. Maybe conversation was not what they needed to confirm their plans, he determined when his aching loins drew his attention to the bed at the far side of the room. His gaze did not go unnoticed by Jubilee. In spite of herself, she turned and glanced in the same direction. When she swung back around to face him, her cheeks had taken on a crimson glow.

"I still can't remember last night," she blurted out. "I keep trying, but everything is a blank." Her voice took on an accusing tone as she added, "I know Jerrod and his friend are guilty of spiking the punch, but—"

"I'm just as much to blame," he interrupted. "If I hadn't been dousing each of my own drinks from a flask of whiskey I had hidden in my coat pocket, maybe I would have been more attentive to what was going on around me. I'm sorry, Jubilee. But no matter how it came about, I'll never regret marrying you." He knew his declaration would not make up for all that had happened, but when she burst into tears again, he was sure she would never forgive him. He reached out to console her, expecting her to pull away. But she slumped against him without protest.

"It's just that I've always dreamed about my wedding day," she sobbed as she pressed her face against the woolen material of his waist coat. When she pulled away to look up at his face, a heavy pout came to rest upon her mouth. "I'll bet you remember everything about last night, don't you?"

"Ah, I—I, ah," Chance stammered, then shrugged his shoulders in a helpless manner. Her unspoken words were as clear as her insinuation. "Well, I guess I remember most of what happened. But then, I'm more accustomed to drinking than you are."

She threw her hand over her eyes and sobbed again. That he could recall the private details of their first night together was not fair! "Will you tell me what it was like?" That wasn't how she had planned to ask him if their wedding night had been a pleasant one for both of them, and the way the words had fallen from her mouth sounded just awful.

Chance felt the fire rekindle in his cheeks again as he became aware of what she was asking him. She obviously thought they had consummated their marriage last night, and now he was not sure of how he should respond. It seemed she was willing to accept their impromptu union as man and wife, and she even appeared to be able to handle the idea of them making love. But would she seek an annulment if she learned that nothing had actually happened?

"It—it was wonderful," he stated in a husky voice. He was not above cheating in a game of cards if the stakes were against him, so why did he feel as though the wrath of God was about to crush him into the depths of hell with this one little white lie?

Her hand immediately flew over her eyes again as she gasped with humiliation. She presented him with her back once more, while attempting to gather her wits. After all her years of protesting the vile evils of alcohol, it her seemed ironic that liquor had led to her own ruination. This thought conjured up vivid pictures in her mind of the wedding night she could not recall. Wonderful, he had said. And she had missed it! When she felt the warmth of his hand gently touch her shoulder, she had already begun to resign herself to the idea of being Mrs. Chance Steele. She hesitated to turn around to face him for a few seconds while she focused on all the drastic changes her life was about to take. There was no use denying the love that had developed between them in the short time they had known one another, and there was no way to undo what had happened last night.

"If only I could remember?" she said, thinking outloud as she slowly began to turn around.

"We can pretend that this is our wedding night," he whispered when their hungry eyes met. He could almost sense the thoughts that were filling her head by

241

the enraptured look upon her face. "And the memories can commence at this very instant." He did not give her a chance to voice her opinion of this suggestion. His lips descended and claimed her entire being with a kiss so demanding it left them both gasping for air.

"I remember what it's like to kiss you," she replied in a raspy voice. Her lips had never permitted the memory of their first kiss to escape from her wanton mind. The silky contours of her beautiful countenance filled with a look of submission as her head tilted back in anticipation of his next kiss.

For a moment Chance could only stare at her in awe. He wondered if he had been sent to some enchanted plateau on a special mission and had somehow encountered a goddess. Her moist lips were parted slightly, while her long lashes fanned out across the tops of her cheeks. It was late afternoon and the room was cloaked in the fading light of the winter day, but Chance was certain she was drenched with a halo of light from the heavens above. He did not want to kiss her again, he wanted to carry her to the bed and make love to her like there was no tomorrow; like he had dreamt of doing last night.

A small squeal of surprise flew from Jubilee when he scooped her up into his arms, and she did not protest his sudden action, although, she was overcome by an intense sense of embarrassment as he carried her to the bed. Since she had been spared the first episode of shyness by their drunken abandonment, she realized she had no need to feel inhibited with him now. With a fevered blush, she also realized that their love-making today would not have to be over shadowed by the pain that accompanies the loss of a woman's innocence. Even as he gently placed her down upon the mattress, she was still trying to convince herself that she had nothing to fear.

Her unspoken anxieties hovered in her thoughts as

she waited for her husband to join her. He was staring at her with such a strange expression on his handsome face that she couldn't help but feel a rush of uncertainty. It was apparent something was wrong, but Jubilee was almost afraid to learn the sudden reason for his remorseful behavior.

"I can't do it," he revealed after an intense battle with his conscience. "I lied to you about last night."

Once again, Jubilee was lost to another mass of confusion. "We're not really married?" she cried out in alarm, though she was not sure if she was feeling relieved or disappointed.

Chance shook his head in a negative gesture. "Yes, we're married. We just didn't —" his dark gaze moved over her tempting form as he repeated, "We didn't — ah — consummate our marriage. I lied because I was afraid of how you might react if you knew."

Jubilee contemplated his confession, wondering why had he bothered to tell her of his deceit when he could have pulled off his farce without her ever being the wiser? She would have submitted to him today without a moment's hesitation, and in her ignorance, she probably would not have realized it was the first time they had been together. Still, she could not overlook his honesty, a fact that only made her love for him swell within her breast.

"Why don't you show me how wonderful it could have been last night?" Her words were barely more than a whisper, yet, he heard. He was not about to give her the time to change her mind, so before their enamored hearts could complete another beat, he had her in his arms once again. His body pinned her to the mattress when he lowered himself to the bed, and his lips sought her mouth. His earlier kisses had been passionate, but restrained. Now that he knew there would be no holding back for either of them, his tongue took a bold plunge into her mouth. Jubilee's tongue was timid with this new intrusion. But, soon

243

she grew braver and allowed her own tongue to tantalize his in the same manner.

With reluctance, she felt his mouth retreat. However, her disappointment was short-lived when his tongue began to trail an enflamed path down along the curve of her throat. His delicious assault was halted by the top of her velvet dressing gown, which did not distract his attention for long as he proficiently unfastened the front enclosures and pushed the garment back away from her creamy-white shoulders. He was confronted with the lace camisole once again, inducing visions of when he had undressed her last night. This memory only fueled his eagerness to repeat this sensuous act, while his nimble fingers proceeded with the necessary work. Beneath his touch he could feel the rapid pounding of her heart as he unhooked the eyelets. The sweet scent of bath powder filled his nostrils with a heady scent, and left him senseless with desire.

In her own haste to continue with this wondrous union, Jubilee reached up and began to unbutton the vest and shirt which peeked out from between his open suit jacket. It was a simple task, but was made difficult because of the limited use of her broken hand. Still, the effort was worth the extra time when her vision was graced with the enticing expanse of his muscular chest. A mat of downy black hair beckoned for her touch as she permitted the fingers of her uninjured hand to luxuriate in the soft curls. She heard Chance sigh softly, and the sound made her yearn to touch him in other places; places she had glimpsed through the misty light of dawn when she awoke with his nude body beside her.

Chance's uncontrollable desire urged his hands to discard the rest of her clothing without further delay. Perhaps it was the advance knowledge he already possessed regarding her beautiful body that made him so anxious to gaze upon her luscious curves once again.

He pulled her up to a standing position as he reminded himself to go slowly. She was not the type of woman he was accustomed to being with, and he wanted her first memory of their love-making to be filled only with cherished thoughts. With unhurried movements, he helped her out of her clothing. He felt her tremble beneath his own shaking touch as he gently pushed her back upon the bed, while he discarded his own clothes. When his raven eyes drank in the sight of her silken body reclining upon the bed in the waning light of the December afternoon, he had to repeat his vow of patience. Since he had grown used to her prudish attitude in the past, he was amazed by her calm acceptance toward what was about to happen. He reminded himself that she was not a giggling young girl who was about to satisfy her virginal curiosity. This beautiful woman was already a great enchantress, and through her maturity, she had gained confidence in her sensuality. Still her enticing body lacked the touch of the man who would make her a woman in every way, but today, Chance intended to make her transition complete.

Her outward appearance was a deception when compared to the turmoil she was experiencing inside. Watching him undress before her eyes had made the impending event a reality, and had caused her whole body to awaken with unfulfilled cravings. Most women her age had quenched this type of desire years ago, but Jubilee's "old maid" status had left her void of these discoveries. The fact that her groom's experience in the area of ardency was more than abundant, however, only increased her uneasiness. Her worry that he would find her boring in comparison to his usual conquests prompted her to blurt out, "I've never been with a man before."

Chance gently lowered himself down to bed beside her. "I know," he answered gently. Her need to voice that information also made him aware of her intense

245

fear. "I've never been with a woman I truly loved before, either." The image of Faith Barnett flashed through his mind like the jagged edge of a broken mirror. He had thought he was in love with Jerrod's mother, but time and bitterness had made him wonder if it had been true love. When his eyes locked with the gaze of his wife, Faith's memory was gone as quickly as it had appeared. He eased his strong arms around her shaking body and pulled her close until not one inch of their heated flesh was not united. Then he gently rolled her onto her back as his own body moved with the motion and enslaved her beneath his long frame.

His mouth sought her lips again as naturally as land draws the sea to its shore. Tidal waves of desire washed over them, pulling them even closer to the impending union, which had been destined to happen ever since the moment when their eyes had first met. Chance felt the need to plunge between her satiny thighs like a man gone mad, but his sensible nature held him in restraint. With this thought corralling his eager loins, he rolled away from her again. He could see her confusion when they parted, but his actions spoke for themselves when his hand cupped her chin. His kisses reclaimed her swollen mouth once more, while his other hand slid to the downy patch of hair which blanketed the entrance to her womanly domain. Though she clasped her legs together in fearful anticipation, Chance eased his hand down into the hidden crevice. With extremely tender motions he began to work his fingers back and forth, until her whole body began to grow tense and she drew in heavy breaths, which was the signal he needed to commence with the next portion of this sensuous rendezvous.

Without warning, he rolled over on top of her again. And before she had an opportunity to clamp her limbs together, he eased himself between her legs. He heard her gasp softly when she realized his swollen manhood was pushing against the moist chasm of her most private area. He had to remind himself again to slow down, not an easy task with a woman as tempting as his bride.

With repeated kisses along the curve of her neck and across the gentle mounds of her breasts, he felt a bit of her tension begin to fade. Her taut body began to relax even more when his tongue began to tease one straining bud of her breast. At last he felt the tight restraint she had held upon her legs begin to go limp. Chance continued to tantalize her breasts until he had repositioned himself for the ultimate union of their bodies. When he heard her moan with ecstasy, his tongue trailed a fiery path up her neck again and crushed against her mouth to draw away the painful cry, which accompanied the first plunge of his hips.

Jubilee had been expecting the pain that would steal away her innocence, but she had not been prepared for the gentleness of her husband's actions. He had claimed her virginity with little more than an instant of agony, then he had permitted her enough time for her tense body to absorb the shock of his intrusion before he had moved within her again. When he did resume his movements, his actions were still slow and gentle. His consideration only fueled her own zeal to explode like kegs of dynamite throughout the entire length of her body. Never in her wildest imagining had she dreamt that making love could be so wonderful. Wonderful—that was how Chance had described it, but that was a gross understatement.

She allowed her body to follow its natural urges as her hips began to rise and fall with each plunge of his body. After awhile, their movements began to increase their rhythm, which also intensified Jubilee's pleasure and brought her to the edge of insanity. New sensations that were raging through her being. The glorious fires of passion burst through her without mercy, pulling her elated soul higher with each passing second.

Just when she was certain she would be consumed by this ecstasy, Chance took a final, dramatic plunge into her inflamed retreat. For a breathless moment, they both remained immobile while they teetered on the highest summit of this indescribable passion.

Jubilee clung to her new husband, wishing she could hold back time, so that this moment would never have to cease, yet knowing that her vast love for this man would never go away. Yesterday, the men of the Wyoming territory had granted their women equality; today, Jubilee had obtained the greatest triumph of all . . . she had been granted Chance Steele's eternal love.

Chapter Twenty-two

The sound of the howling Wyoming wind woke Jubilee from her deep sleep. The mid-morning sun was attempting to push through the dark clouds, but it appeared that another blizzard was brewing over the prairie. Jubilee's heavy eyes ached as she focused her foggy vision on the soft flakes of snow which were falling outside the window of her hotel room. She shut her eyes again, and was surprised she did not drift back off to sleep. She had spent a very vigorous night wrapped within the strong embrace of her virile husband. The memory made her body grow fevered with renewed yearnings. If only she had the energy, she would wake her slumbering husband and continue where they had left off a short time ago.

A vicious gust of wind caused a shiver to ripple through her body. Chance had stoked the fireplace with a pile of logs shortly before they had fallen asleep and the gentle flames still cloaked the room in a blanket of warmth. Although she was not the least bit cold, Jubilee snuggled up against her husband and sighed with contentment. This marriage was preposterous, and she could not imagine what the future would hold for two people as mismatched as the two of them. Still, they did love one another, and surely that was the most important factor. Jubilee realized, as she watched Chance sleeping, that outside of this bed they were virtual strangers. The night had produced boundless passion, and by the time they had lapsed into an exhausted slumber, there was not one inch of one other they had not explored. Now, in the light of day, Jubilee blushed just thinking about it. If only everything about their marriage could be so wonderful. But sadly, she knew that would not be the case.

She couldn't help but smile when something in his sleep made Chance's lips twitch slightly. With her forefinger, she gently traced the line of his thin mustache. He was too handsome for his own good, she decided. Oh, why couldn't he be a lawyer, a congressman, or anything other than a gambler and the owner of a gaming house? Her heavy sigh made him stir and the ebony lashes surrounding his eyes began to flutter. His first reaction was to grace his bride with a sly grin.

"Good morning," he said in a hoarse whisper. His brows raised with speculation. "Did you wake me for any particular reason?"

Jubilee was amazed she could still feel embarrassment after all their unabashed intimacy, but his insinuation caused a hot rush of color to flood across her pale complexion. "Good morning, Mr. Steele," she answered, then knew he would reprimand her at once.

"Please . . . call me Chance, or love, or something a little less formal."

She had to smile at his request, and also at her own foolishness. Formality had vanished the instant he had taken her into his arms yesterday afternoon. "I didn't mean to wake you, Ch—Chance."

He could see her unspoken question almost as clearly as if she was voicing it aloud. Chance said softly, "It *is* my real name." Her face scrunched up with doubt as he added, "I was the second son born to my parents. Father wanted a girl, but he said there was always a 'chance' they would produce another boy." He laughed at her perplexed expression.

Jubilee's puzzled look converted into a frown. She had no way of knowing whether he was teasing or telling her the truth. As she opened her mouth to challenge him, however, a knock on the door halted her words. "Who in the world could that be?" she asked, as she started to reach for her dressing gown.

"Mrs. Steele?"

She hesitated at the sound of the voice calling out to her from the other side of the door. "I have been Miss Hart for so long that it will take some time to get used to being Mrs. Steele," she commented. When the voice called out again, she answered that she was coming and hastily grabbed her velvet robe.

Chance concealed his amusement at the bashful way she donned the robe before she rose from the bed. He also had to hide his disappointment, since he could not think of anything more pleasing to view, first thing in the morning, than his wife's beautiful body. He felt a sigh of satisfaction whisper through his smiling lips, and he wondered if he would wear a permanent smile for the rest of his life. "What is it?" he asked after his wife had signed for the telegram and closed the door.

She shrugged as she unfolded the paper and deciphered the brief message. A strange expression clouded her previously glowing countenance. When she looked back toward the bed where her husband waited for her reply, Chance knew at once that the news would be detrimental to their marriage.

"I have to go back to Washington." She glanced back down at the paper in her hand. "They want me to give a speech at the next meeting of Congress about the Wyoming legislature's decision to grant women the vote."

From her strange look, Chance did not know whether she was glad to be going or not. He was also uncertain about how he should react, since he had always believed that once a couple became man and wife, they should never be separated. However, he and Jubilee were not an ordinary couple. "Surely someone else could do it," he said, then silently reprimanded himself for sounding so displeased when she had been appointed such a great honor.

"I have to go," she blurted out. "It's my job."

"Of course," he added in a rapid reply. Her defensive attitude told him that she wanted to go, although he hoped she would tell him that she would not leave him for any reason. "When do you have to go?"

She glanced down and read the message again. As she refolded the paper, she forced herself to remain calm as she replied, "I should leave on the next East-bound train."

Chance rose up slowly on one elbow and stared at her in stunned silence. He could not forbid her to go. But he found it inconceivable she would leave so soon after everything that had happened between them. There was so much he needed to discuss with her, but he could not say a word. He could only gaze at her as the pain of his heavy loss ripped through him like a saber.

"I suppose I should start packing," Jubilee said in a voice hinging on the verge of tears. She glanced at Chance, but quickly looked away. Why didn't he say something? Didn't he care that she had to leave? She began to make her way toward the armoire with the intent of packing her bags. It was difficult to determine what felt heavier — her feet, or her heart. Of course, she *had* to go, but couldn't he at least say that he would be sorry? As she hoisted her luggage out into the center of the room, she could feel his eyes upon her every move. Never had she known such sorrow, and it could have been prevented by just a word or two from him. Her movements became slower as her agony increased. Still, she refused to look at him; she did not want to glimpse the relief which she was sure would be written upon his ruggedly handsome face.

"I know you're going to go, but I can't let you go unless you know how much I love you."

His words were the ones she had wanted to hear, but the tone of his voice sounded so odd. Jubilee dropped the armful of clothes she held in her arms and twirled around. His expression echoed her own enormous feelings of pain, and the mist in his ebony eyes told her that

252

her fears had been in vain. As though her feet had wings, she raced across the room. She did not want him just to tell her how much he loved her, she wanted him to hold her, to show her his love.

"I love you, too," she cried as they met in one another's arms. It was the first time she had said the words out loud. How natural they sounded as they rolled from her tongue.

"Will you come back to me?" he asked. His hold around her voluptuous body tightened.

Didn't he know that after last night she could never stay away from him for long? "Come to Washington with me," she said without an instant of hesitation.

Chance pulled away and stared at her with a look of amazement. The last thing he was expecting was an invitation to return to Washington with her. His mind drew up images once again of her lavish home and upper class family, of a life into which he would never fit. "I — I have to tend to my business, and, there's Jerrod to think of," he stuttered, then pulled her close again so she could not see the agony of his decision.

"I understand." She did not resist his embrace, because she did not want him to know how deeply hurt she was by his refusal to accompany her. In a desperate attempt to avoid another bout of tears, she closed her eyes tightly. Her tendency to be over-emotional had accelerated since she had come to Cheyenne, and her heart seemed to have a mind of its own as it willed her eyes to give in to its own sorrow. The disobedient tears rolled down without regard to her inner command and mingled with the dark curls upon his broad chest.

Chance felt the warm moisture on his skin, though for a time, he did not realize what was happening. When he heard her try to hide a sniffle, he knew she was crying. Surely she was not upset because she would not be able to introduce her family to her unworthy husband? He wanted to ask her what would upset her so badly that it made her cry, but he kept quiet, for fear that she might tell him she was never coming back. Instead, he held on to her as if this embrace would have to last a lifetime.

Instinctively, his head bent down until their mouths were within kissing distance. With their lips united, it was only natural they would make this union complete. Neither of them spoke as he helped her remove her dressing gown again, and when their bodies touched once more, they each seemed to sense the desperate urgency of this intimate moment. Chance's demanding kisses intensified, while their bodies molded into one another. Each time they made love throughout the night, her body had welcomed him with eagerness. Now, however, she reacted like a woman crazed by love and passion. Taking the initiative, Jubilee rolled on top of her husband, impaling herself upon his swollen member. She heard him draw in a deep breath at her unexpected action, but she didn't care if he thought her to be a shameless creature of wanton cravings. In the past few hours, he had taught her that she was a woman of boundless sensuality, and he was the only man who would ever satisfy those desires. But now she did not know how much time would have to pass before they would be together again.

Breathless, yet frantic with the possibility of separation, they made obsessive love long past the morning hours. When Jubilee realized how much time had passed, she grew panicked that she would miss the afternoon train. "Will you help me pack?" she asked Chance as she rushed around the room gathering up her clothes and grooming supplies.

It was with reluctance that he aided her in her departure, however. As she bathed and dressed, he folded each of her velvet suits and gowns, then placed them in her two large bags. He savored the touch of each garment, drawing them close so that he could revel in the soft floral scent of them. He was certain he had never known such torture, yet he was grateful for anything that would help her memory linger with more clarity once she was gone. When she emerged from behind the privacy shade wearing the same red suit which she always seemed to wear for traveling, Chance was not sure his aching heart could let her go. He tried to imagine what it would be like if he was to go with her, but there were just too many reasons why he could not leave — Howard Crowly being the main one at this time. Chance knew the hateful old banker would not allow the shooting incident to pass without rustling up more trouble, so maybe it was best that Jubilee not be apart of it any longer.

As he stared at his beautiful wife in her red velvet attire, he had to repeat the question he had asked earlier. "Do you seriously think you will ever come back to Wyoming?" The tremendous fear he harbored was apparent on his face and in his strained tone of voice. As he waited for his wife to reply, his dread expanded like an engulfing black cloud.

Jubilee hesitated because she was surprised he felt the need to ask her a second time. "I hate this barren prairie," she began. "And my work has been my entire life." Her words snapped the flimsy thread of hope that Chance had clung to, but when she continued, his joy abounded. "But, my husband — my love — is here, so of course I will come back."

He rushed forward, taking her into his arms again. She molded against him so naturally it was obvious this was where she was destined to be. He stroked her hair, murmured words of his love and kissed her, deeply, with all of the emotion he felt within his bursting breast. Then, when there was nothing else to do, he had to let her go.

"Aren't you coming to the train station with me?" Jubilee asked in a stunned voice.

"Will you forgive me if I say goodbye now?" He believed her when she told him she would come back to him, because he could not doubt her love. Still, a nagging fear tugged at his heart, a feeling that after she returned to her plush life in Washington D.C., she would realize that marriage to him was absurd. The influence of her family, once she told them about the gambler she had impulsively married, might cast the final blow to their future as man and wife. Saying goodbye was hard enough, but watching the locomotive pull away from the Cheyenne station was more than he felt his tortured emotions could bear.

Jubilee felt a lump well up in her breast as she dropped her head down upon her chest and nodded weakly. She would forgive him, but how she wished they could somehow prolong their final moments together. "The holidays are coming up," she said when she glanced at him. "Will you and Jerrod spend them at the saloon?"

Chance shrugged in response to her unexpected question. He had no idea how he and the boy would spend the holidays. With Jerrod a part of his life now, he guessed he should do something other than his usual holiday activities, which involved a week-long drunk and and endless array of card games. He did not even know how to celebrate Christmas and the coming New Year in any other way, he realized with a crushing blow to his already unsettled senses. He shrugged again. "We have no where else to go."

His answer sent Jubilee's thoughts in a whirl of indecision as her dreams of a family and home tormented her mind. They had just become man and wife, yet they would spend their first Christmas thousands of miles apart—she in her lonely boarding house room, and he beneath the glittering chandeliers of The Second Chance Saloon. The sorrow, rage and jealousy that flowed through her was overwhelming, but she remained silent. She wanted to tell him she would not leave, if only he would close the doors of his brothel and gaming house for good. There were so many other things to consider, such as her obligation to return to Washington to fulfill her commitments to her job. And what of his obligations as a husband? He had to make a few decisions of his own, Jubilee realized as a grave sadness enveloped her.

"I guess this is goodbye for now then," she said in a whisper. Not to cry took all of her willpower, but she was determined to avoid this emotion again.

With a slow nod of his head, Chance took a step backward. He wanted to take her into his arms once more, but he could not for fear that he would become a sniveling, groveling man who would plead with her not to go. Yet, by forcing himself to remain distant from her, he was overcome by the deep sense of foreboding that seemed to hover around them at this departure. "I love you," he said, simply, before heading toward the door. He had planned to walk out without another glance in her direction, but as he stepped through the open door, he was compelled to turn around. When their eyes met again, the turmoil which was strangling their sorrowful hearts seemed to reach out from the depths of their eyes. Hers had never seemed bluer, or his more black. And all the differences in their lives had never appeared so startling.

The mournful wail of an approaching locomotive sounded far off in the distance, reminding them that it was time for them to part. Chance attempted to smile as his trembling hand moved down the front of his vest. "Good luck in Washington, Mrs. Steele." His eyes did not light up with the wane smile upon his lips as he forced himself to leave.

Jubilee did not move, nor did she say a word as she watched him exit and close the door behind him. The train whistle sounded again, only closer this time. Ever since the first instant she had set foot in the Wyoming Territory, she had wanted nothing more than to leave. At last, she was finally free to go. How ironic that now she wanted nothing more than to be able to stay.

Chapter Twenty-three

Miss Gurdy watched her young friend from the doorway of the parlor with great concern. Circumstances of fate had deprived the elderly woman of having her own children, and Jubilee was the daughter she had never had. It pained her a great deal to see her so unhappy. Miss Gurdy's gaze traveled down to the source of Jubilee's interest — an exquisite diamond ring, which had arrived shortly after her return from Wyoming. It adorned the third finger of her left hand.

"It reflects the lights of the Christmas tree," the old woman said with a cheerful smile as she entered the room and set down the tray she carried. "I thought you'd like a cup of tea before you had to go out into the cold."

A poignant smile curved the corners of Jubilee's lips. "Thank you so very much."

"It's only tea," Miss Gurdy chuckled, while filling the cups with the steaming brew.

"I mean for being such a good friend to me," Jubilee said with emphasis as she reached out and rested her hand upon the woman's arm. The diamond ring glistened like a twinkling star, catching the eye of both women. A poignant expression hovered on the beautiful blonde's face as she watched the shimmering reflection. "It's so lovely, and . . ." she exhaled a sigh burdened with the weeks of indecision she had suffered since returning to Washington. "I never imagined I would miss him so much."

Her last few words seemed to hang in the air as if they were suspended in time. Miss Gurdy did not have to hear the words to know of her young friend's heartache. Although Jubilee tried to put up a brave front ever since she had come home, the old woman had seen right through the tough exterior the young bride had erected around her emotions. She was just grateful that not too much time had passed before she had given up her resistance and acknowledged her feelings. Miss Gurdy had feared it could be months, even years, before the woman admitted how strongly she missed the dashing man she had married in Wyoming. With a shiver of excitement, Miss Gurdy's aging countenance took on a look as glowing as the sparkle from the diamond ring. Chance Steele was a smart man, she thought as she glanced down at the fabulous adornment on Jubilee's hand. Sending his bride the magnificent gift not only confirmed his devotion to their marriage, but also served to remind the hard-headed female that they should be together.

"Well, now that we've finally got that out in the open, what are you going to do about it?" Miss Gurdy asked in an impatient voice.

A frown overcame Jubilee's face, because she did not want to give Miss Gurdy the satisfaction of knowing she had been right all along. "I can't go back there yet, not until he is willing to give up that—that brothel!"

"Do you think he's consorting with his female employees?" the old woman asked with bluntly.

Jubilee gasped, while a red blush creeped through her pale cheeks. "Why—no!" She hesitated as she reaffirmed her stern resolution. "No! I don't think that at all."

Miss Gurdy tossed her gray head back and said "Well, then, his owning a brothel is no different than any other business."

An indignant cry burst from the blonde at the old woman's attitude. How could she possibly say a brothel was the same as any other business? "He's a gambler too!" she retorted, defending her own attitude.

"He's not your father," the old woman said, then fell silent. Her brief statement was the truth, and its meaning was clear. She had tried to tell the unyielding woman a number of times that no two men were alike, but Miss Gurdy decided it was time Jubilee began to realize this for herself. Though she had not met this man who had won the heart of the stalwart blonde, Miss Gurdy knew he had to be someone very special or else he would not have accomplished such a difficult feat.

Jubilee did not respond to Miss Gurdy's remark about her father, because they had engaged in similar discussions in the past. However, she was beginning to feel that Miss Gurdy might have been right all along, and she really hated to admit defeat. "I wish you'd change your mind about tonight and accompany me to the party," she said, hoping to change the subject.

Miss Gurdy stuck her nose up in the air in a snooty manner. "I have no desire to go out on this cold night and contend with the uppity wives of all those politicians. No, thank you."

A rush of affection for the old lady flowed through Jubilee as she chuckled at her performance. In honor of the New Year, she was invited to a party at the home of one of Washington's most honored Congressmen, and many important political figures from all over the country were expected to attend tonight's gala event. Since returning from Wyoming, Jubilee's life had been a whirlwind of social engagements, as well as appointments to speak on the suffrage issue. Her presence in Wyoming, and her minor contribution to the historic event which had granted the female citizens of that distant territory the right to partake in public elections, had made Jubilee an instant heroine. Normally, she would have been thrilled to be among the guests invited to the home of Congressman Wilson, but all she seemed to think about these days was the distance between herself and her handsome raven-eyed groom. Though she believed Chance would honor their marriage vows, Miss Gurdy's inquiry about his relationships with his employee's did not improve her mood. He had told her he loved her as he left her room at the inn on that snowy afternoon in Cheyenne, but she had not told him anything. If only she had said something—done something—that would have made him want to wait for her to return.

The huge, pear-shaped ring on her finger caught her attention again. Its beauty was almost indescribable and it certainly made the paisley vest she had sent to him as a Christmas gift seem paltry in comparison. She only hoped the ring was his way of telling her he was being faithful, and that his love for her had not dimmed, even though they were apart.

A knock on the door drew the women's attention away from their conversation. Jubilee sprang up from her chair with a forced enthusiasm. "That must be my carriage," she announced as she quickly donned her elegant cloak of sea green. It matched the shimmering hue of her silk gown, which was styled with a low-cut bodice and a tucked waistline that accented Jubilee's bosom and tiny waist. The rare beauty of the suffrage speaker had always drawn everyone's attention, especially unwanted advances from an abundance of attentive males. The cold attitude she conveyed usually halted the attempts at intimacy, but had not endeared her to their wives. Her appearance and unattachment was a threat to their own insecurities. Since returning from Wyoming, however, Jubilee had been showered with invitations to social events given by the wives of the politicians and powerful people of the nations's capital. As soon as Jubilee had informed her landlady of her sudden marriage, Miss Gurdy had made it her personal quest to inform all of Washington of Jubilee's romantic attachment while she had been out West. The high society of Washington was thrilled with the idea of the suffragette finding a husband in the wilds of Wyoming, but they were even more intrigued by her lack of information on the subject.

Jubilee's reasons for keeping an aura of mystery about her new husband was not because it added to her mystique. She allowed them to draw their own conclusions about the stranger she had met and married during her short visit to the Wyoming Territory because she did not want them to know the truth. Her refusal to talk about her marriage was reinforced each time she heard the speculations, which portrayed her groom as an influential Wyoming businessman, or a wealthy rancher, and even a daring adventurer who had made his fortune from one of the rich veins of gold or silver in the savage lands of the faraway Western territories. She despised herself for her haughty attitude, but how could she admit to those proper biddies that her new husband was the owner of a brothel and gambling den?

The ride to Congressman Wilson's home was a time of nervous anticipation for Jubilee, although she wasn't sure if she was actually looking forward to the party, or if she was anxious to get the night over with so that she could concentrate on the plan which was beginning to formulate in her mind. As the carriage rolled through the city streets, Jubilee became more and more aware of where she wanted to be, and with whom. Knowing Chance Steele was not in town meant that Washington no longer held the excitement it once did for her. She had lived in so many different towns and spots along the road while growing up that she had been enchanted by the clean, majestic appeal of the nation's capital when she had first come here five years ago. Every time she stopped to gaze upon the White House, she was overcome by a sense of pride for her country, and for the small role she played in a city so grand. Lately though, the beautiful tree-lined streets of the capital only seemed to lead to loneliness and despair. Each day increased her love for the man she had left in care of her heart. It was hard for her to believe that she was looking forward to going back to the blustery prairie, where nothing but wind and snow graced the walkways and icy streets.

"Marriage certainly agrees with you," Mrs. Wilson said as she eyed Jubilee's elegant gown, then focused her wide-eyed stare on the exquisite ring upon the woman's finger. A glint of envy filtered into her expression, but she did a quick recovery as she began to lead Jubilee through the crowd who was gathered in the elaborate ballroom of the congressman's mansion. "I want you to meet some of our out-of-town guests who just arrived today. They missed all your speeches about the Wyoming legislature's decision to pass the enfranchising bill, but they're anxious to meet you." The woman chuckled in a knowing tone laced with sarcasm. "Of course, they also want to hear all about the great romance which you found out in that savage land."

Jubilee imitated the woman's snide chuckle, but did not offer the reply the woman hoped to hear. Obviously, her marriage had once again been the subject of conversation among these snooty gossips.

"Oh," Mrs. Wilson said. Her smile dripped false sweetness as she motioned toward another woman who was standing nearby. "Here is one of my guests that I wanted to introduce to you." As they approached the woman, she turned and nodded politely at Mrs. Wilson when they stopped in front of her. "Mrs. Henderson, this is the famous Jubilee Hart whom I have have been telling you all about." Her introduction omitted Jubilee's new last name, but she gave Jubilee a glance which intimated the gossip she had already related to the other woman. She added, "Mrs. Henderson's husband is the governor of Mississippi."

"It's an honor to meet you," the governor's wife said with a sincere smile, and extended her hand toward Jubilee.

Without hesitation, Jubilee took the woman's hand. "The honor is mine," she replied, noticing how the other woman did not appear to have the affected attitude which most of the politician's wives possessed. She also noted the woman's beauty and guessed her age to be in her late thirties, or early forties. The woman had a quiet dignity, which was accented by her flawless peaches and cream complexion and thick auburn hair. Her gown of white silk was an understated design in elegance, but it was the look contained within her eyes of tawny gold which made Jubilee feel that she was wise far beyond her years. When she spoke, her southern accent was deep and slow.

"Mrs. Wilson has told me about your victories in the West, but I would love to hear the story first-hand." Her interest was sincere — very different from the banter one usually encountered at these functions.

The snoopy hostess frowned with disappointment when her husband choose this inopportune time to call her to his side. With promises to return, Mrs. Wilson obeyed her husband and left Jubilee alone with the governor's wife. Jubilee did not realize her feelings were so apparent, but Mrs. Henderson chuckled when she noticed the suffrage speaker's sigh of relief when the other lady was out of earshot.

"Mrs. Wilson is a generous hostess, but she can be a bit pushy," the red-haired woman said with an exaggerated roll of her sparkling eyes. She smiled again when she noticed how her remark had set the younger woman at ease. "Now, please *do* tell me all about Wyoming?"

Jubilee smiled with sincere gratitude, especially since she had been certain the woman would immediately ask about her new husband. "Well, first I must admit that I obtained no victories for my sister suffragettes in Wyoming, for the decision to grant women the right to vote was decided long before I arrived." Jubilee went on to tell the governor's wife the reasoning behind the generous gift the men of the Western territory had granted to their women. When she was finished, she was not surprised to learn that Mrs. Henderson was as enraged as she had been when Chance had told her the same story.

"That's outrageous!" the woman huffed in her heavily-accented drawl. "I hope those Wyomin' women give those men hell come votin' time."

Jubilee choked back her shock, and attempted to hide her mirth at the other woman's statement. Mrs. Henderson was a rare find among these high-society snobs. Jubilee excitedly told her of the women's plan to vote to close the saloons on the Sabbath, and by the time the two women finished chuckling over the many possibilities the new bill posed, they felt as if they had found a new friend in one another.

"Temperance is the one issue in which I have not become involved," the governor's wife said with noticeable uneasiness when Jubilee began to speak of her ongoing battle against the evils of alcohol. She attempted to change the subject with an invitation to further their developing friendship. "Please, let's not be so formal. How 'bout if I call you Jubilee and you call me by my first name." She blinked her thick lashes like a proper southern lady, adding, "My name is Faith."

"Faith," the name rolled off Jubilee's tongue without hesitation as an easy smile touched her lips. "I recently acquired a new last name," she said, feeling comfortable enough with this woman to talk about her sudden marriage.

Faith giggled, "Well now, I was wonderin' if you would mention that bit of interestin' information 'bout your trip to Wyoming. Heaven knows, Mrs. Wilson has talked of nothin' else. Why, you've got all of Capital Hill buzzin' about your marriage to a man whom you hardly knew."

A cloud settled upon Jubilee's face at the thought of being the constant source of gossip lately. "It was sudden, but I fell in love!" she added in defense.

Another deep laugh welled up from the Faith. "Well then, why in Heaven's name did you leave this irresistible man way out there on the prairie?"

"He has a business in Cheyenne, and he has . . . other commitments." Jubilee felt a rush of color come into her cheeks as she feverishly hoped she would not be asked about her husband's business endeavors.

A curious expression filtered across Faith Henderson's lovely countenance. "Then, why, aren't you *there?*"

All at once, every one of Jubilee's anxieties about tonight began to surface. She had the urge to tell this woman everything about the night she had become Mrs. Chance Steele, her embarassment over his occupation and her desperate desire to be reunited with the man she now realized she could not live without. And she probably would have begun to burden her new friend with a multitude of confessions if it had not been for the arrival of Mrs. Wilson, who immediately brought the conversation to a halt with a shocking announcement.

Chapter Twenty-four

"Are you sure this is the place?" Chance asked as he stared out the coach window. They had passed dozens of mansions and lavish estates before coming to stop at this modest boarding house in the center of a middle class neighborhood. The coach driver gave his head a definite nod, but Chance asked him to wait for a few minutes — just in case the man was mistaken.

As Chance passed under the gaslight, he glanced down at the small piece of paper he had carried with him for the past few weeks; it was the address Jubilee had recited to him in her room at the Railway Inn, while they had hastily packed for her return to Washington. Could he have made a error when he copied it down on the paper? The street number was the same, but he still could not conceive that this was where his wife resided. His tentative steps led him to the front door, yet even as he banged the curved iron knocker, he was certain he was at the wrong house.

"Good evening," the small elderly woman said in greeting when she opened the door. Her wrinkled face tilted up toward the man towering in the doorway. "I have no vacancies, if you're looking for a room."

"No, I'm — actually — I think I'm lost. I'm trying to find the Hart residence."

An odd expression overcame the old lady's face as her speculative gaze traveled down the entire length of the fancy dressed stranger. "Are you looking for Jubilee

Hart?" she asked in a guarded tone, while she continued her close surveillance of the man.

Chance nodded his head enthusiastically. "Yes, do you know her?"

"She's been living here at my boarding house for five years. I imagine I know her very well." The woman leaned forward and studied the man over the top of her wire spectacles. "And, I imagine you're Chance Steele."

Chance did not answer immediately. He was stunned by Jubilee's modest dwelling. The images he had constructed—of elegant mansions, servants, a life of privilege—were utterly false. He had never been so wrong about a person, and his success as a gambler depended on his instincts being correct.

Miss Gurdy did not grant him much time to mull over his obvious confusion. "She's not here right now," she stated. "Have your driver take you to Capitol Hill. There's a New Year's party going on at the home of Congressman Wilson—that's where you'll find your wife." The old woman did not offer any further information, but a satisfied smile came to rest upon her lips before she said goodnight and shut the door.

Chance stared at the closed door for a few seconds before his thoughts began to focus. He still could not believe he had been foolish enough to connect such an outlandish fabrication about Jubilee's life here in the East. His invented fantasies had created all the insecurities and torments he had been suffering for the past several weeks. He had come to Maryland to have a showdown with his bride, to learn if their marriage would ever have an opportunity to evolve. Since he had imagined her with a wealthy family and lavish lifestyle, he had also expected to encounter numerous relatives who would try to make him seem an unworthy mate for a woman of her position. Now it appeared that if he had not been such a coward, all the agony he had invented for himself could have been avoided by a few simple inquiries about her life.

As he settled back in the coach for the journey to Capitol Hill, he told himself that from now on he would not dwell on anything other than the love he and Jubilee had for one another. But as he walked up the marbled stairway which led to the front door of the politician's home, his uncertainty returned. He had a premonition that he was about to face a challenge inside the walls of that mansion that would change their lives forever. Still, he was unprepared for the unexpected discovery he would make when he saw his wife at the home of Congressman Wilson.

"If you'll just follow me?" Mrs. Wilson gushed when she had been called to the front entrance by the servant who was checking invitations at the door. Her speculations about Jubilee's groom had been grossly understated. He was dressed in a manner that suggested wealth, but there was a reckless quality about him which only served to accentuate his extraordinary good looks. "What a lovely surprise for your bride. Why, it must have been just awful for the two of you to have been separated so soon after your wedding?" Her prodding tone hinted heavily that she was hoping the man would divulge a tidbit about the impromptu marriage, but Chance gave her a patronizing smile as his only reply. With an exasperated huff, the woman twirled around. "I see your wife is still in the same spot where I last saw her." Although he was not willing to relate any added information, the arrival of the much talked about stranger was enough to make her smile as though she had just obtained the inside news on the scandal of the decade.

Chance located his beautiful bride at once through the crowd of guests. Her pale gold hair shimmered in the dim lights of the ballroom like spun silk, and her deep blue-green gown accented the creamy shade of her complexion. As he drew nearer, he felt they were the only two people in the room. It was like walking over the arch of a rainbow, and she was the pot of gold waiting at the other end. He wondered if his feet had touched the ground since he spotted her enchanting face from across the room. He briefly tore his eyes from his wife to glance at her companion, and the magic of the night shattered. He saw the face of Faith Barnett, and his heart twisted within his chest. A fiery hole burned through his soul when he beheld the woman whose memory had haunted him for the past sixteen years. Mrs. Wilson led him to within a few feet of the women, and he did not have time to hide his shock — his steps faltered, coming to a complete halt, but it was too late for retreat.

Jubilee and Faith swung around in unison when Mrs. Wilson called out to them, but the seconds which followed were filled with a strange silence of immense proportions. Jubilee was overwhelmed by joy when she saw the handsome man who stood behind the congressman's wife, but her happiness was quickly thrown off balance by the horrified look on his face. She was more confused when she realized he was not even looking at *her;* his disbelieving, wide-eyed stare was directed at Faith Henderson. When Jubilee glanced at the woman who was standing next to her, the same expression of undeniable shock was etched upon her countenance.

Faith had been about to take a sip from the long-stemmed goblet she held in her hand, but when she met the face of the man from her past, her hold grew limp and the elegant glass crashed to the hard ballroom floor in hundreds of shards. Still Faith did not look down at the broken glass, which was scattered across the delicate toes of her white satin slippers. "Chance! Dear God!" she gasped, while her mind was thrown into a kaleidoscope of panic. It had taken her years to bury the past, years of pretending to be someone of class and breeding. Here, in one brief instant, her delicate facade had caved in around her. Recollections of the time she had spend upon the riverboat as a whore, of her love affair with the dashing young gambler, and of the son she had borne and deserted, shattered through her being.

"Have you already met Governor Henderson's wife?" Mrs. Wilson asked of Chance Steele. She narrowed her eyes in a thoughtful manner as she noted how his reaction matched the odd behavior of the governor's wife. By the look on Jubilee's face, it appeared that the arrival of her husband was about to cause more than just another bout of idle gossip, and Mrs. Wilson dearly loved to be the bearer of such prattle.

Since it looked as though neither Faith Henderson or Chance was able to overcome their awkward silence, Jubilee decided it was up to her to make the first move. She stepped forward, placing herself between her husband and Faith Henderson. "What a—a surprise," she said, her voice hoarse, while her eyes sought some small sign of reassurance in his gaze. It was a vain quest, though, because he barely glanced down at his bride before looking past her to continue staring at the auburn-haired woman. She had no idea how, or why, her husband was so enthralled with the wife of the Mississippi governor, but she did know that she was being publicly humiliated again. One glance at the smirking face of Mrs. Wilson confirmed this, and convinced Jubilee that she had to get out of here before something even worse happened. She looked up toward her husband once more. Still, he ignored the unspoken plea in her expression. She did not think about her next action, because jealousy toward Faith Henderson, and fury toward Chance, made her blind to everyone else in the room. Her acute heartbreak was shadowed by her disgrace as she pushed past her husband and ran toward the door at the other side of the room.

Jubilee's sudden action snapped Chance and Faith from their shocked trance. As Chance watched his wife's frantic retreat, he realized the terrible error he had just committed. "Jubilee!" he shouted before he started to chase after her. He practically shoved Mrs. Wilson aside in his attempt to get past her, but his steps halted when Faith called out to him.

"Chance! Wait—please—I'm coming with you! We have to talk." She kicked aside the broken splinters of glass and rushed forward. As she grasped onto his arm, she turned toward Mrs. Wilson. "Please inform my husband that I will return shortly."

"But—but—" Mrs. Wilson did not have a chance to ask any further questions because the elusive Chance Steele was disappearing through the crowd, with the wife of the governor of Mississippi hanging onto his arm.

"I can't talk to you now, Faith," Chance said in breathless gasps as they reached the front stoop. "I have to find my wife and try to explain to her why I acted the way I did." He motioned toward the door of the huge mansion. Yet, when his eyes fell upon the trembling woman he had thought he loved for so long, he knew he could not desert her either. His shoulders sagged in defeat as he pulled her down the marble stairway. "You can come with me to find Jubilee, then we'll talk."

Faith allowed him to drag her to the bottom of the wide stairway, then she abruptly pulled away from him. In her silk gown, the winter chill was felt acutely. She crossed her bare arms over her chest and shivered. "I can't leave here, but please—I beg of you—just give me a minute of your time." The tears hovering in the corners of her golden eyes were not intentional, yet they were the deciding factor in Chance's decision.

"All right, we owe one another at least that much." His eyes met with hers as the recollections from which they both wanted to escape imprisoned them. Time had cradled her gently within its embrace, and she was still as beautiful as he had always remembered. Now, however, she was the epitome of the high social status she had acquired. But then, Chance remembered how she had once been the epitome of a riverboat courtesan, too.

Faith tore her eyes away from his face and gave a nervous glance up toward the front door of the mansion. To see Chance Steele after all this time was unbelievable, but to encounter him here was the worst nightmare she could imagine. "I—I don't know where to start," she said in a shaky voice as the tears began to flow down her cheeks.

All at once, Chance knew she did not have to say a word to him. For one crazy minute, he had thought that perhaps she was about to tell him how much she had regretted what she had done to him, and most of all, to their son. In that moment of insanity, he had been prepared to tell her that he forgave her. But then he glimpsed the look upon her face as she glanced up towards the mansion, and understood exactly what was going through her mind; he always understood his counterparts. "Don't worry, I won't tell anyone about your lurid past, Mrs.—ah—I must have missed your last name. But did I hear that you were now the wife of the Mississippi governor?" He tried to keep his voice in a civil tone, but it was a difficult task with all the emotions that were flooding through him.

Faith caught the cold undertone of his voice. Yet she could not dispute him, because his answer was the assurance she had sought. "It's just that I've worked so hard to overcome the mistakes of my past. If my husband was ever to find out—"

"Save your explanation," Chance interrupted as his impatience grew sharper. "We've both come a long way since those days on the riverboat, and I do not want anyone to learn of my past association with you, either."

Although he had not meant for his words to be so blunt, a dark red blush worked its way up through Faith's neck and cheeks. "Of course," she retorted in a defensive mode as she began to back away from him. "I'll make up something to tell Mrs. Wilson about our unusual reactions when we saw one another."

"I'll bet you can think of something to tell her."

She looked up again with a wane smile curving her mouth. "Still a betting man, I see." Her eyes remained fixed upon his face for a bit longer, until he forced himself to turn away.

He wanted to say so much more, wanted to grab her, shake her, until she remembered that they had a son, about whom she had not even bothered to ask . But the appearance of Mrs. Wilson at the top of the stairs kept him in restraint. "Better start thinking," he snapped, snidely. He bowed in his elaborate manner before he twirled around and strode toward the row of carriages which waited to transport departing guests from the party.

As the carriage carried him away from the exclusive area of Capitol Hill, Chance had time to think over the incredible irony of seeing Faith Barnett standing next to his bride in the rich surroundings of the congressman's mansion. It was almost as if fate was trying to tell him that he could never escape from his past. A crude, hard laugh rang out in the dark interior of the coach when Chance remembered what he had said to Faith about how they had both come a long way since the riverboat days. She was now the wife of a prestigious politician — obviously she had achieved a great deal. But he was lying to himself if he was foolish enough to believe he was any better off now than he had been sixteen years ago. The Second Chance Saloon had been built with money he had obtained from gambling, so could he truly consider himself a success?

When the coach jerked to a halt in front of the boarding house, Chance's whole body jumped in surprise. He had not yet thought of a way to apologize to Jubilee for his inexcusable behavior at the party. His stomach twisted into a knot as he thought of how rejected she must be feeling at this time. He just hoped she would forgive him for humiliating her in front of her important friends and associates. He quickly paid the coach driver, but as he found himself in front of the boarding house once more, he paused beneath the gas streetlamp to catch his breath before continuing up the walkway. His trip to Maryland had certainly not started out as he had planned. He only hoped the worst was behind them as he made his way toward the old brownstone house.

Chance did not have time to knock, because as he reached for the brass knocker, the door swung open. Jubilee's hurt was written across her face in bold script, but the fact that she had opened the door gave him a minute sense of optimism. "May I come in?" he asked in a low voice as he noticed the frowning elderly woman who

274

stood close behind his wife like a sentry.

Jubilee glanced back over her shoulder when she saw his gaze move in that direction. "It's all right, Miss Gurdy," she said. She smiled at the old woman with a look of gratitude, but it took the lady several seconds before she decided to leave the couple alone. Jubilee returned her attention to her husband as a wounded expression once again claimed her face. She stepped to the side of the doorway and motioned for him to enter. "We'll have more privacy in my room," she mumbled as she began to lead him up to the second story of the large brownstone.

While he followed her up to her room, Chance remained silent. Though he now knew it to be true, he still could not believe that his wife lived in this boarding house. She exuded an air of upper-class breeding, and he prided himself at determining a person's worth and abilities. Yet Jubilee's rich style and dignity had fooled him completely. Tonight, after he asked for her forgiveness, he hoped to learn all the things he should have known about her before he had permitted her to leave Wyoming. Maybe it was time he told her some of the significant things about his past too, he decided as she led him into her crowded room. A lamp on the table beside the bed cast a dim light throughout the interior of the room, and a softly flickering fire in the stone fireplace warmed the area, and gave off a rich glow of its own. Two huge armoires stood side by side against one wall, their doors open from the bulging array of elegant gowns. Several large trunks were pushed up against the walls, each of them overloaded with shoes, scarves and lacy undergarments. Chance smiled to himself. It was apparent his wife had a weakness for fine garments and accessories, which had led to his evaluation of her social class.

"You may sit there," Jubilee said as she motioned to an overstuffed chair, then seated herself on the edge of the bed.

Chance glanced at the table beside the chair, whose

top was filled with pictures and an assortment of mementos that were obviously important to Jubilee. He noted how the entire room was loaded with personal items and treasures which she had collected or purchased. He thought of his own living quarters at the back of the Second Chance Saloon where everything was polished, organized, and void of anything personal.

"How do you know Faith Henderson?" Jubilee blurted out without warning. In her urgency to know why he had embarrassed her at the Wilson's mansion, she did not have the patience to wait until he finished with his scrutinizing appraisal of her meager possessions.

Her question drained Chance of his curiosity, while his troubled gaze settled upon the beautiful face of his wife. "Faith and I were once lovers." He heard Jubilee's gasp when he announced what he knew she did not want to hear. However, he could not make up a lie when his relationship with Faith had been made so obvious by their reactions.

Jubilee clutched her hands over her breast. Light reflected by the flickering fire caught the shimmering facets of the diamond ring he had sent her as he noted how her other hand, which she had broken, appeared to be healed. His words echoed through her mind over and over again—he and Faith Henderson had been lovers. Painted-faced women, women like Ina Devine, passed through Jubilee's mind in distorted flashes. She did not want to think about her husband's past liaisons, which had to equal countless numbers of women who had been with him for a night or two. Faith Henderson was nothing like those woman, and it was obvious that she had been more than just a casual lover who had traipsed through her husband's unsavory past. "Do you still love her?" she forced herself to ask as she recalled they way he had looked at the beautiful auburn-haired woman.

The idea that she could think he loved anyone but her made Chance feel as though he had failed her completely. He had tried to give her so much of himself in the few times they had been together, but if she still had to ask him if he loved another woman, then he knew he had not given her enough. He rose from the chair and strode to where she sat on the bed before she had a chance to protest. Kneeling down before her, he clasped ahold of her hands as he began to speak. "I love *you*, and if I ever thought I loved Faith it was only because I did not know the true meaning of love . . . until I met you."

Their faces were only inches apart, and the heat of his his breath filled Jubilee with a raging fire that could not be contained within her slight body. She believed him because her heart would not allow her to do otherwise.

"When I walked into that ballroom, I had planned to sweep you into my arms and make all those stuffy old aristocrats green with envy." He pressed his head up against her breast and closed his eyes, and he became lost in the nearness of her. "I'm so sorry." It seemed he was always apologizing, he realized as he wished he could turn back time and fulfill his original plan.

Jubilee placed her hand upon the thick waves of ebony hair that covered his head. How she loved him, in spite of all their diversities. And how she longed for a normal life like other married couples. But how could they ever obtain this goal when his home was in the back of a saloon, and hers was this crowded room in a boarding house? "I'm sorry too, Chance."

The sorrowful sound of her unexpected apology sent a shiver through Chance's body. He pulled away to gaze at her face. From the side of his eye, he caught a glimpse of the ring again. When he had picked out the piece of jewelry for her he had wanted to impress his bride, and the family he had invented for her, with his expensive taste. But now the shimmering adornment seemed insignificant in comparison to all the other things he wanted to give her. Almost as if he could read her mind, Chance sensed what she was thinking when their eyes met again.

"It's time we began to take this marriage, and our future, seriously," he said as he rose to his feet and pulled her up with him. "The ceremony may have been a charade, but the end result is that we are husband and wife."

His declaration surprised Jubilee and filled her with hope. "I want to talk about our future too. But—" she was hesitant to tell him about her childhood and the reasons she could never live at The Second Chance Saloon. "I can't—I won't live in the back of a brothel."

When she paused, Chance feared that she would also tell him they had no future together. "You deserve much better, Mrs. Steele. And so does Jerrod." He tossed his head back and laughed with relief when she nodded in quick agreement. "As a matter of fact, so do I," he added.

Jubilee wanted to join in his mirth, but all she managed was a gasp as he pulled her up against him once again. "We'll have a real home, Jubilee," Chance said as he immersed his face in her silken hair. "I'm gonna buy that ranch as soon as the snow melts," he added, then began to kiss her ear since it was in reach of his eager lips.

"Were you serious about becoming a rancher?" Jubilee asked in a disbelieving tone. Though she remembered him and Jerrod talking about their plans to buy a cattle ranch, she still could not imagine Chance dressed in chaps and a wide-brimmed hat. But, living on a ranch was a pleasant idea, she thought, and the image of a rambling ranch house filled with dark haired children passed through her mind.

Chance stopped his delicious assault on her earlobe and tried to fake an offended attitude. "You still don't think I could learn to run a ranch?"

With a shrug, Jubilee's brows drew into a frown. "As I mentioned before, it *is* a lot different than running a saloon."

Her lack of confidence gave Chance a challenge he readily accepted. "I guess I'll just have to show you that I can be as successful on the back of a horse as I am at a card game." Chance felt her body grow tense, though he was not sure what he said to make her mood change. He remembered his vow to learn more about his bride, and he determined that now was a good time to ask her a few questions about her background.

"Why are you so opposed to gaming establishments?" When she didn't reply, he began to draw his own conclusions. Had she lost a member of her family in a drunken brawl in some saloon, or was she raised in a strict family of religious teachings which did not permit drinking or gambling of any sort? Why didn't she want to tell him anything about herself? When she still did not offer to answer his question, he attempted a different approach.

"You're going to think it's funny when I tell you where I was expecting to find you tonight." He didn't give her an opportunity to answer, but he went into a detailed description of the image he had of her lifestyle here in Washington D.C. He was wrong, however, because she did not find any humor in his account of the wealthy and prominent family he had envisioned for her.

All the frustration of her youthful dreams settled around her with an engulfing sense of loss. She had worked hard to project the high-class image Chance had of her, and apparently she had been successful. Yet, it did not change the reality of her life. "I'm a fake, Chance," she announced in a flat tone of voice. "You were so worried that you were not good enough for someone of my breeding, when the truth is that I'm not worthy of you." She scooted away from him when he reached out to her again, and when he opened his mouth to disagree with her, she raised her hand up into the air in a gesture of silence. "Did you have a home when you were growing up? I know you had a brother, but did you have a real family, Chance? A family who lived together and ate together and went to church on Sunday mornings together? Did you have all of those things?"

Chance ran his hand down the front of the elegant paisley vest she had sent to him for his Christmas present. "Ah, well, I—I guess my brother and I had a very good childhood," he replied. Her questions summoned up comforting memories of his life on the Kansas farm where he had been raised. His family had been a close-knit one. When his parents had been killed by a plague which had swept across the prairie, Chance had prayed for his own death too. Instead, he fled from the farm and sought solace in the excitement of the Mississippi riverboats.

"I never had a childhood," she spat out in a bitter tone. "I was too embarrassed to play with the other children because I was afraid they would ask me who my father was or what he did for a living. I spent my time hiding in the backroom of the hovels where my father gambled away the money my mother earned by scrubbing the dirty floors of the saloons where we were forced to live — until he was accused of cheating in a card game and we had to move on to the next pigsty." She exhaled the heavy breath which had lodged in her throat before she continued. "If you thought I came from a wealthy, upper-class family, it was only because I have learned how to hide who I really am so well." She turned and gazed at the dying embers in the fireplace, wishing she could toss in all the hurtful memories of those bygone days and watch them burn until there was nothing left but a pile of ash. There was no way she could change the past, but she craved a future which would shine as brightly as the flames that reached above the ashes.

"I never want to hide in the back room of a saloon again, Chance." Her voice projected the uncompromising determination of her quest as the flames in the fireplace took on a renewed vigor and began to burn in brilliant hues of orange and red.

Chapter Twenty-five

Chance leaned back against his pillow and observed his sleeping bride with grave concern. When he had believed she was used to living in luxury, he had felt incapable of providing for her in the style to which she was accustomed. Now, he had a great desire to give her all the things she had lacked in her life of suffering. This task seemed even more difficult. He thought of waking her so they could begin to make some decisions about their future since they had become distracted last night and had only managed to catch up on the love-making they had missed in the past few weeks of their separation. When he thought of the energy they had spent, he decided to let her sleep for a while longer.

As quietly as possible, he eased himself from the bed, then slipped into his pants. He did not bother to fasten them all the way as his attention was diverted to Jubilee's personal possessions which decorated the room. He tip-toed around the small, cluttered room studying the vast array of clothing and adornments she had collected through the years. She needs a real home to put all this stuff in, Chance thought to himself. He paused by the fireplace long enough to stack another pile of logs on top of the fading flames. When he turned around, his bride was watching his movements with a look of intent interest.

"Good morning," he said with a tempting twinkle his raven gaze. He began to grin when he noticed the way her eyes traveled down over his muscled body, pausing for a significant second on the exposed area between his unfastened breeches.

A slow grin creased her smooth complexion as she returned his greeting. "It *is* a very good morning." It was the dawn of a new year, and a new day, but it did not seem possible that he was here with her, when only yesterday she had been prepared to return to Wyoming because she had missed him so much. She glanced at the blazing fire, then added, "But it would be even better if you came back to bed and kept me warm."

"If you're cold, I could put another log on the fire," he teased.

"I'd rather you put yourself over here," she retaliated without wavering. A victorious smile claimed her lips as he obediently complied with her wishes. "Do you need those," she asked, pointing at his pants.

He shrugged nonchalantly and began to discard the article of clothing. "Is there anything else, Mrs. Steele?" His thin mustache curved up slightly with suggestive innuendo.

"Only one more thing," she whispered as she reached up and pulled him down to the bed. "Would you kiss me?"

Another shrug shook his broad shoulders. "I could, but is that all you want?"

A thoughtful pout settled on her face, but she did not have an opportunity to continue with her taunting invitations. Chance had enough of her enticing jests, and he had decided he was no longer a patient man when it came to seducing his bride. He scooted under the covers with her and wrapped her in his arms. Her entire body yielded to him at once, while her lips searched for the kiss she had requested. Their mouths devoured one another as their heated bodies ached with awakening desires. Each time they united in these moments of unabashed passion, it seemed they could not get enough of one another. Just as Chance was about to indulge his urge to make love to her once more, Miss Gurdy's gruff voice called out from the other side of the doorway. In unison, Jubilee and Chance groaned with disappointment as they were forced apart.

"There's a lady waiting down in the parlor to see you, Mr. Steele," Miss Gurdy shouted at the closed door.

"A — A lady?" Chance asked in a tentative voice. He knew at once who she was, and he could tell by his bride's expression that she knew who the visitor was, too. Throughout the night, he had attempted to reaffirm his love for her until he was convinced she would never doubt it again. He had also hoped that they would not have to discuss his involvement with Faith until he had figured out the least painful way to tell her about their past affair. Since he had determined that when the time was right he was also going to tell Jerrod he was his real father, he would have to inform Jubilee of this fact as well. With Faith's arrival here this morning, though, Chance was afraid the wounds he had healed last night would be reopened, and the pain it would cause his new wife would be even worse.

"She probably wants to apologize to you about last night," he rationalized as he dragged himself out of the bed and started to dress.

Jubilee's blue gaze narrowed. "Miss Gurdy said she was here to see *you*." She did not like the way she was acting, especially since she really had enjoyed meeting the governor's wife last night. She hoped Chance would volunteer to tell her about their relationship and what had happened between them that had torn them apart, but he avoided all mention of the subject. He only told her that he had not known the meaning of love until he had met her, but if that was the truth, then what had he shared with Faith Henderson?

Chance was hesitant to leave when he finished putting on his clothes. Jubilee's attitude on the subject of his involvement with Faith was apparent, although she attempted to hide her jealousy. "I won't be gone long," he said with a sheepish lowering of his head.

"You'd better go," Jubilee said flatly, pulling the bedcovers up under her chin in a prudish manner. Her mind could only imagine why Faith Henderson had come here this morning, and she did not think it was because she wanted to make amends for last night. Still, she could not imagine why the woman had traveled from Capitol Hill to see Chance . . . unless, perhaps, seeing him again had made her want to rekindle their past love affair. Jubilee shuddered under the covers as this thought raced through her mind. She did not feel any threat from Chance's association with the prostitutes who worked for him, but a woman like Faith Henderson was an opponent worth worrying about.

Chance nodded and turned toward the door. He remained unmoving for a second as if he was contemplating saying something else. Then, with a quick glance back over his shoulder, he gave Jubilee a weak smile and a brief announcement. "Don't forget . . . you're the only one I love."

No reply came from Jubilee as she watched him leave the room, but the moment he was gone, she cursed at herself for not reminding him that she loved him too. Why did she find the words so difficult when she had no doubts about her feelings? But if he was not sure of her love, maybe his visit with the beautiful Faith Henderson would induce more than just casual conversation. Jubilee threw the blankets away as she began to imagine her dashing husband drawing the lovely woman into his arms, but this was a pleasure reserved only for herself, and the thought of him holding another woman enraged her!

"Chance, I—I hope you don't mind that I came here?" Faith said as a blush colored her cheeks and she glanced downward as if she was suddenly embarrassed by her own question.

The gambler tossed his hands up into the air. "It *is* very awkward, especially after last night." He glanced toward the doorway, wondering if Miss Gurdy or one of the other residents of the boarding house was nearby. "Why did you come here?" He added with a note of impatience.

Her golden gaze raised up until it focused on his tense face as she considered the reason for her visit. After all these years, she could not bear to know that they had parted last night on such unfriendly terms. But her real reason for coming was because she had not been able to sleep all night wondering about the boy whom she had not been able to erase from her mind, even though she had tried diligently for the past sixteen years. "It's about the — our son," she finally forced out of her mouth. Since the time when she had dumped the infant in his father's lap and walked away, she had not admitted aloud that she had a son; saying the words now made her feel as though she had been transported back to that very day on the Mississippi.

"Our son?" Chance retorted, incredulously. "You gave up the right to claim him as yours a long time ago."

"And you're any better?" she fired back at him. "I'll admit there are no excuses for what I did, but you deserted him too." For a while after she had fled from the riverboat, she had tried to keep tabs on the boy's whereabouts and she was aware that Chance had given the baby to his brother and sister-in-law to raise.

Chance was taken aback by her knowledge of Jerrod, yet he still was not going to allow her to berate him when she was just as guilty. "I saw to it that he had a decent upbringing. Thank God for my brother and his wife, because the boy wouldn't have had a chance in hell with you or me."

Another deep rush of color came into Faith's unmarred complexion. She couldn't blame Chance for the resentment he harbored, but she hadn't come here to exchange degrading remarks with him. "I only wanted to find out if he's well and happy with your family."

The first instinct to overcome Chance was to toss another debasing comment regarding her sudden interest in the son she had deserted. But as the words hovered on his lips, he realized that he was being unfair. All the time that Jerrod was living on the farm with his brother and sister-in-law, he had been consumed with guilt. Had Faith lived with the same painful burdens? "Jerrod is a fine young man," Chance replied, deciding that Faith deserved more consideration than he was giving to her.

A relieved smile crossed her mouth. "Is he?" she answered in a wistful tone. "Do you ever go back to Kansas to visit with him?"

Chance was aware of the precarious situation he was in, and he was uncertain how he should proceed. He wanted to lie to Faith, but as time passed, he was starting to realize how all his lies and mistakes were catching up with him. He also wanted a new life, a new beginning for himself, Jubilee and Jerrod. Perhaps now was as good a time as any to start. "Jerrod is living with me in Cheyenne."

His announcement caused a stunned gasp to escape from Faith's mouth. After a moment of initial surprise, though, Faith began to fill with an odd sense of jealousy. It had been difficult to live with her impulsive decision to leave the boy with his father, but she had managed to cope because of her belief that he was living with two people who could care for him better than either of his parents. Knowing now that the boy was living with his father made her own desire to be a part of the boy's life quickly surface. Chance had been granted a second opportunity to make up for their drastic mistake of the past, and Faith felt she deserved another chance too. "I want to see him."

Her unexpected announcement made a shiver race down Chance's spine. He was not prepared for her to make such a startling revelation, nor would he grant her request at any cost. Inwardly, he violently raged at himself for not telling the boy about his true parentage before something like this happened. But he kept finding excuses to avoid the subject, because he was reluctant to face up to his past mistakes.

"That is impossible!" he retorted, making his position clear by his tone and his enraged expression. If she thought she could prance back into the boy's life, she was grossly mistaken. Now that the boy was his sole responsibility, he planned to do everything in his power to protect him from unnecessary pain. Informing the boy of his deception was going to be difficult enough, but to suddenly introduce him to a mother he never knew existed would be even more traumatic.

"He's my son, too, Chance. Surely he has asked about me once in a while?" she implored as she took a step forward. "At least let him make his own decision about whether or not he wants to see me." Another step forward brought her within an arm's length of where Chance stood.

Her words brought a new barrage of guilt down upon Chance. He shook his head in defeat as he allowed his eyes to meet with the haunting jewel-toned gaze of the woman from his past. She was wearing an expensively tailored suit of dark brown. The high collar and sleeves were adorned with elaborate swirls of gold braid, which perfectly matched her eyes. Chance was struck once more by how far she had truly evolved from those days when she had been the toast of the riverboat.

"What about your husband?" he asked in a harsh tone. "If you acknowledge Jerrod as your son, won't you also have to tell your husband the truth?"

Faith cringed visibly at his words. Admitting her past to her husband might also mean the end of her marriage. The governor was a good, decent man who lived his life by a strong moral code. To learn that his wife had been a riverboat prostitute could destroy his love for her. When Chance had told her their son was living with him, she had not taken the time to think about anything other than her own selfish desire to demand her share of the boy's life. But was seeing him worth losing all that she had worked to obtain for herself?

Her face filled with an indecision which bespoke of her inner thoughts, a look Chance could easily decipher. "Would it be worth it, Faith?" he asked in a sympathetic voice. He reached out and rested his hand gently on her arm. They had once shared something very special and the memory would always live on in the form of their son. Chance realized he no longer wanted to hate Faith for what she had done, nor did he want to continue to hate himself.

Faith stared down at the hand resting upon the sleeve of her woolen coat. When she had been a high-paid courtesan working on the riverboats, there had been an endless parade of men who had passed through her life, but only this dark-eyed gambler had possessed the touch which could induce magic. After she had become pregnant however, she was filled with resentment. Her only thoughts were of losing the dreams she harbored for a life of wealth and prestige. Chance was younger than she was, and lived a reckless existence at the gaming tables. Though she knew the young gambler was devoted to her, she was petrified of living the rest of her life on the riverboats, while she had one baby after another and watched all her dreams, one after another, pass her by.

When the baby was born she made the most difficult decision she had ever faced; even then she was a selfish woman who did not realize what she was doing until it was too late. She did not give herself a chance to love the baby, because as soon as she had recuperated from his birth, she handed him over to his father and fled from the riverboat. For a while, she hid out, afraid that Chance would come looking for her and persuade her to return to the riverboat with him. As the weeks passed, she began to feel a deep sense of guilt, which drew her back to the river. She discovered that the gambler had taken their son to Kansas and dumped him with his family before rushing back to resume his carefree lifestyle. She had hated Chance more than she had ever thought possible, until she realized that he had been more responsible toward the infant than she had been when she had abandoned him. At least in Kansas the boy would have a normal and secure upbringing. Her return had been shrouded in secrecy by the other courtesans, so Chance had never known of her presence. When she walked away from the riverboat the second time, she vowed to never return. Her exquisite beauty had aided in her quest to leave her past behind and pursue a life of power and money.

"When I came here today, I had only wanted to know how he was doing," she began in a strange tone of voice. "But—" Her frantic gaze flew up to Chance's face as she tried to find the right words.

"I understand," he said and was touched by a compassion he was not expecting to feel. "But you need not worry, Jerrod is going to do his parents proud."

"Je—Jerrod?" Faith said with a voice that cradled the name tenderly on her lips. That she had not even bothered to name him had always been the main source of her agony. At least now, her long-lost child had a name by which her tortured mind could address him. "Does he look anything like me?"

A poignant grin curved Chance's lips as he replied, "No, he's the spittin' image of his father."

A trembling sigh took her breath when she attempted to smile. "Well then, he must be a dangerously handsome young man." She could not help but experience a bit of disappointment, since she had always imagined that the boy was a replica of her.

"Everything has turned out for the best, Faith," Chance stated in a positive voice as he reached for her hand. After all the years of fantasizing about holding her again, and as much as he had focused on his hatred for what she had done, he was surprised by the way he felt toward her now. With her hand in his, he realized that the past was finally beginning to ease into the background as the bitter recollections began to fade. The new beginning he kept promising was within reach now.

Faith glanced down where their hands were entwined. There were still so many things she wanted to ask about their son, yet, she knew Chance was right— the best had happened for all of them. "You'd best get back to your lovely bride," she said in a low voice.

Chance met her sad smile, he felt the sorrow in her touch, then he shook his head in agreement as he released her and backed away. They had both paid their dues with years of suffering, and now it was time to forgive each other. "If you ever happen to be in Cheyenne—"

"I'll stop by to visit," she finished, then quickly added when she saw his expression grow guarded, "As one old, old friend to another." His easy smile was contagious and as their gazes met one last time, they were both filled with a deep sense of relief that their lingering hurts had finally been give a chance to rest. Faith drew in a deep breath. She turned without hesitation and walked away without another word passing between them.

Chance followed her to the parlor door and watched her depart from the boarding house with the soft smile still intact on his lips. He felt as though he had just been reborn, and his only need at this time was to hurry back upstairs to his beautiful wife. As he turned toward the stairs, though, his happiness disappeared as rapidly as the smile upon his face.

Jubilee stood, unmoving, at the bottom of the stair. She had not wanted to interrupt his visit with Faith Henderson, but her nagging jealousy had urged her down to the lower landing. She tried to rationalize her actions by telling herself that she was Chance's wife now, and she had a right to know what was going on in that parlor. Yet, when she had spotted the two of them holding hands and smiling at one another in such a personal manner, she had been staked to the spot by the spear which had shattered her heart. Her jealousy was replaced by acute pain, and she wished she had never left the security of her room to glimpse this touching scenario.

"How long have you been there?" Chance asked in a voice that hinted at his uneasiness. For a reason he could not explain, he felt guilty that his bride had witnessed his brief contact with Faith.

Jubilee opened her mouth, but nothing escaped from her dry throat. She shrugged in response, but still remained rooted to the spot. His question had made her feel as though he suspected her of spying on him and Faith Henderson. If that was the case, what were they trying to hide?

The distrust and pain Chance could see in his wife's face stole away his optimism for a perfect start to their new life. He knew he could not avoid the obvious any longer. "Let's go back up to your room," he said in a stern voice. "I have something to tell you." Without giving her time to make a move on her own, he took her hand and pulled her up the stairs with him. Her legs moved of their own accord, but the seriousness of his tone and expression made Jubilee wish they would never reach the top of the stairway. He did not release his firm hold even after they had entered her room. Instead, he led her to the chair where she had told him to sit last night. He knelt down beside her, still holding her hand tightly in his.

"I had planned to tell you about this last night, but as usual, I was too cowardly." His grip upon her hand tightened when he felt her tremble. He looked into her eyes, willing them not to turn away from him. His worries were in vain, because she could not tear her eyes from his face. She waited in agony for the words she expected—the admission that he still loved Faith.

"I guess I should start at the beginning," he said with a heavy sigh. "You're assumption the night we dined with the Crowlys at the inn—that I had learned my trade on the riverboats—was correct. After I left my parents' farm in Kansas, I got a job working on the river as a cabin boy. My interests were quickly captivated by the debonair gamblers who worked in the saloon of the lavish boat." A wistful smile rested on his lips as his thoughts traveled back through time. "Ah, and I knew I could be even more dashing than any of them if given the opportunity. I was a Kansas farm boy, Jubilee — surely you can imagine how exciting those men in their elegant attire and with their polished manners, must have looked to me?" She did not offer her opinion, but he had not expected one and he rushed on. "And I was a diligent student. By the time I was twenty years old, my reputation was renowned up and down the Mississippi as the fastest card shark. I was the most charming of the riverboat gamblers. I suppose it was fate that I should meet the most elite of the riverboat courtesans in my adventures."

He paused when he saw the confusion come over Jubilee's pale face. After meeting Faith at the party last night, he could understand how difficult it was going to be for his wife to believe what he was about to tell her. "Faith was that woman, and she was as accomplished in her line of work as I was in mine." He felt Jubilee's hand go limp in his, while the color totally drained from her cheeks.

"Faith was a — a prostitute?" she gasped as her voice returned with the shock of this discovery. She wanted to dispute him, yet, something in his gaze told her that she was about to uncover those strange emotions she had always glimpsed behind his outward facade.

"It is rather hard to believe," he replied. "But then, we all make mistakes; some of us just make worse ones than others. Faith and I have certainly made more than our share."

Jubilee's terror expanded as she wondered what he meant. "Was it a mistake that you parted?" she asked, feverishly hoping he would not agree.

"No, it was a mistake for us to have met." He noticed the strength return to her hand as the relief his words brought sank into her worried mind. "For a time, we had a beautiful love affair, heedless of any conscience or thought to what lay beyond our moments of passion and —"

"I don't think I want to hear anymore," Jubilee burst out as she yanked her hand out of his. She could accept their past liaison, but she did not wish to hear the intimate details.

Chance immediately recaptured her hand in his and continued. "You have to hear the rest because it affects you too." When she began to shake her head in a negative manner, he rushed on. "It does, because Jerrod is not my nephew. He's mine and Faith's illegitimate son."

"Dear God," Jubilee whispered in a barely audible voice. "Does he know?"

"No," Chance admitted as his guilt over his reluctance to tell the boy returned. He took this opportunity to relate the rest of the story to his stunned bride, telling her of Faith's desertion, and of his own. He spoke of the years he had anguished over his decision and of his belief that the boy was better off with his brother and sister-in-law. As she listened in silence, he related everything to her about the past sixteen years, even the conversation which had just taken place in the parlor with Faith Henderson.

When he took a deep breath and fell into a quiet contemplation of his long admission, Jubilee finally spoke. "You were correct when you told Faith that everything had turned out for the best." She reached out the hand which he did not hold and cupped it under his chin. He was still kneeling beside her and their eyes met on the same level. "Our decision to marry turned out to be the best of all." A soft smile floated across her lips. "And now it's time to get on with that future we still have to plan."

Chance exhaled a sigh of gratitude for her understanding, then he rose to his feet and pulled her up with him. His arms slid around her waist as he drew her up against his taut body. "I still have to tell Jerrod, but now that I know you're going to be there to give me the strength I need, it will not be so difficult."

"I won't be there, Chance," she said in a firm voice.

His entire being filled with dread at the sound of her determined words. "What are you saying?"

She repeated her statement. "I won't be there when you talk to Jerrod. This is something you must do on your own, and when you've accomplished this long overdue task, we can get on with our lives." He opened his mouth to dispute her, but she pressed her finger against his lips. "This is the beginning for us, Chance. You will return to Wyoming and straighten out your relationship with your son, and I will stay here and finish up my commitments to my job. Then when we have put all this behind us, we will only have to concentrate on our marriage and the home we will make for Jerrod—and the rest of the children we will have together."

Chance felt as though he had been run over by a train. In all the craziness of the past few weeks he had never taken the time to think about the possibility of having children with Jubilee. He was struck by the realization that she could already have conceived his child. This thought only served to fuel his urgency to fulfill his obligations to her and Jerrod. But the idea of leaving her behind was too painful for him to bear. "I'm not leaving without you," he replied.

Jubilee caressed his face with her hand. "It will take me a couple of weeks to tie up the loose ends with the suffrage committee, and though I've already started looking for a replacement to take over my position, I still haven't found anyone who is suitable." She glanced around at the array of belongings she had crammed into this small area. "I will have to pack all this up and arrange to have it shipped to Wyoming."

Chance listened while she talked about the things she had to accomplish in the next few weeks, but his sorrow at their parting no longer seemed so desperate. For the first time, she spoke as though she had no doubts about returning to Wyoming. He sighed with resignation as he realized he could not stay in Washington until she had finished up the last of her duties and had found a replacement. Howard Crowly was still breathing down his neck about the mortgage note he held on The Second Chance Saloon, and the old banker would like nothing better than for Chance to be away when the next payment was due. The profits from the saloon were the only assets Chance had to use to obtain a home for his expanding family and he could not allow anything to interfere with this quest. Even Abigail Crowly presented a problem for the saloon keeper which he still had not figured out how to handle. On Christmas Day, the elderly female had waged another protest against the saloon. Alone, she had marched up and down the walkway in front of the establishment, sign in hand, shouting words of damnation to every man who had entered the saloon.

"You're right again, I need to return to Wyoming and tend to my own business," he said in a disappointed tone of voice.

Jubilee took this opportunity to repeat her determined vow. "I won't live in that saloon when I go back." She wanted to add that she did not even want that business to exist when she returned to Cheyenne, but she knew this would be an unfair request. Although she hated the idea of her husband owning the establishment, she also understood that it would take time for him to proceed with his proposed plan. He had said he would buy a ranch when the snow melted, so surely they could stay at the inn, or rent a house in town until then?

"I would never ask you to," he replied as he recalled the tragic revelations about her childhood. Since he was already holding her in his arms it seemed like an appropriate time for their lips to unite in a kiss which would seal all their hopes and dreams for a future that had never seemed more perfect.

Chapter Twenty-six

"This coat is real interestin', Uncle Chance," Jerrod said as he studied the cold weather gear they had just purchased from the trading post at Fort Russell. "We look just like a couple of soldiers. Maybe those Sioux Indians who live around here will leave us alone if they think we're in the army."

"We don't need to worry about seeing any Indians at this time of the year," Chance answered as he glanced down at his own long overcoat made of tanned buffalo skins. "They don't travel this far south of the reservation until the grass is high enough in the spring time to feed their ponies."

Jerrod shook his head in amazement. "Lordy, Uncle Chance, are we really gonna buy us a spread and start raising cattle?" In his enthusiasm, he did not give his uncle an opportunity to reply before he returned to his interest in the Indians who inhabited the Wyoming Territory. With an uneasy glance, he looked toward the front gates of Fort Russell. "Think we'll have any serious problems with them Sioux when we buy a ranch out there?"

Chance gave his head a nonchalant shake, and refrained from discussing the threats of living in the vicinity of the Sioux reservation. An Indian Treaty of 1865 had removed all the Arapahoe and Cheyenne Indians from the area where the Union Pacific Railroad was laying tracks, and in 1868 there was a treaty signed here at Fort Russell, granting the Sioux a hunting reservation to the north of the fort. Most of the tribes did not cause any trouble during the cold winter months, but the Sioux were known to be ornery come spring and summer. But Indians were just one of many adversities in this harsh land, so Chance did not allow himself to dwell on the possibilities of Indian attacks. "Fort Russell was established to protect the settlers in this area," he replied in a disinterested manner as he motioned for Jerrod to mount his horse.

"These buffalo shoes are a might awkward," the young man said as he struggled to fit his leather-bound foot into the stirrups, then pulled himself up into the saddle. All through the winter he had observed the soldiers who came into Cheyenne wearing their winter gear, and he had wondered how they were able to walk around in the heavy animal hides. "A fella can't move none too swift in this get-up," he added when he finally managed to situate himself in his saddle. Though he didn't voice his thoughts outloud, he was wondering if the heavy gear would hinder their riding abilities in case they should encounter any Indians.

"You've got to dress like this if you're gonna be a rancher out here in this country. We may not look too savvy, but every time we ride out on that snowy wind-blown range, we're going to be grateful to have these warm coverups." The acreage they were riding out to see was a sizable chunk of land northwest of Fort Russell. Chance had ridden through the property last summer and knew it was the perfect location to start a cattle ranch. But at the time, he was too involved with building his saloon to consider buying the land. He worried that the spread would sell if he waited until summer, and when Jubilee returned in a couple of weeks he hoped to have the deed already in his hand.

"What in the devil are those?" Jerrod asked as he stared at a strange looking herd of animals who were grazing nearby.

Chance chuckled at the perplexed expression on his

son's face. "Those are Texas Longhorns. They're a hardy breed and can tolerate the weather in this area better than most cattle. We'll be raising longhorns on our ranch, too. You mark my words, boy, cattle ranching is going to thrive in this area now that the railroad can ship the cattle in and out of Cheyenne." He glanced out toward the open plains with a sense of certainty about his prediction.

Jerrod had been riding his horse slightly behind his uncle's mount, but he gave his horse a gentle kick and urged him to speed up. "I've been wanting to tell you something," Jerrod announced when he came abreast of the other man. He took a deep breath as if he was not sure how to begin. "I—I just wanted to thank you for taking me in after ma and pa died."

With a sideways glance Chance gave the boy a quick nod of his head. He had two reasons for riding out to look over this land today, and to tell the boy the truth about his parentage was one of them. He had rehearsed the words a hundred times, but now that Jerrod had presented him with the perfect opportunity to say them, they seemed to freeze in his throat. "I would never turn my back on my—my brother's boy." Chance cursed inwardly at himself, but the time was not right, he reasoned. They rode down into a snowy gully lined by bare-branched cottonwoods. The endless Wyoming wind kept the land barren of snow in most areas out on the open flat lands, but there were patches of ice and snow in the lower crevices along the prairie.

"The southern border of the spread starts about here," Chance said as he motioned toward the crest of the ridge they were beginning to ascend. "It's unfortunate you and Jubilee have only seen Wyoming during the winter, because in the summertime these sagebrush flats are knee-deep in green grass, and the hollows fill with fluffy white cotton that blows from the trees." As the horse's hoofs reached the top of the ridge, Chance waved his arm out over the vast expanse of land that lay below, while he desperately tried to avoid the subject he most dreaded. "Every color of flower you can imagine grows out in that sod, and even a few kinds of cactus." He pointed towards a cluster of gray trees, whose barren forms appeared to be dead. "See those poplars? During the months of April and May their branches become burdened with big red flowers and you can smell their sweet scent for miles around."

Chance pushed back the wide-brimmed hat he had just purchased at the post and smiled with satisfaction as he looked beyond the prairie, toward the towering blue mountains far off into the distance. He was reminded of the royal blue gaze of his beautiful bride. His vague dream of owning land became a consuming urge he knew had to be fulfilled before any more time was wasted. In spite of Jubilee's worries that he was not cut out to be a cattleman, he had no qualms about taking on the hardships involved with ranching. However, he was still deathly afraid of telling Jerrod that he was his real father.

Jerrod halted his horse beside his uncle and looked out at the land as a low whistle emitted from him. "I think it's beautiful now, so it must really be somethin' come summertime."

Chance's aspirations expanded as he drew in a deep breath of the crisp air. "I'm going to buy this spread," he stated in a definite tone, along with a firm nod of his head. A creek bed was visible by the uneven row of leafless willows that lined its frozen shores. Chance pointed toward a swell in the land on the other side of the creek, adding, "Up on that plateau is where we'll build the ranch house." He began to imagine how it would be the first time he brought Jubilee out here, which aroused thoughts of the sons and daughters they would have someday — thoughts he had not been able to get out of his mind since he had returned from Maryland. He glanced at Jerrod and was overcome with the pride he already felt toward this young man. Their ebony gazes met for an instant before Chance turned away. His sights wandered out towards the plains again as he envisioned the Steele dynasty spread out below them for as far as the eyes could see. This land would be the legacy for his children, and for their children. He was vaguely surprised to realize how the excitement of the card tables and the lure of the saloon life no longer appealed to him.

Jerrod began to nod his head in agreement while his dark eyes remained on the older man's face. He wanted to say a few things that had been welling up inside him ever since he had come here, but whenever he attempted to talk to his uncle about his gratitude, the man always managed to change the subject. "I wish you'd let me tell you how much being here with you, and having you include me in all your plans, means to me. Saying thank you just doesn't seem like enough."

A deep sigh rumbled from Chance's throat. He sensed he was not going to find any easy escape this time, nor could he keep looking for one. "There's no need to thank me. I don't deserve it."

A puzzled expression overcame Jerrod's smiling face at the tone of his uncle's voice. Still, he needed to talk about his feelings and he wasn't going to be detoured this time. "Me and Pa always talked about you, mostly about the exciting life you led on the riverboat. I think sometimes he was a little jealous though—of the way you were free to come and go." Chance gave his head a vicious shake as Jerrod quickly added, "Oh, he loved Ma, and nothin' would have dragged him away from that farm. It's just that you were—" he hesitated while he tried to find the right words.

"Irresponsible," Chance volunteered. "Selfish and—" he began to fill in the words he felt would fit his own description.

Jerrod quickly interrupted. "I don't want to hear you talk about yourself like that. Pa told me how tough it was for you to stay on the farm after Grandpa and Grandma died, and we all understood how hard it was for you to come back to visit too."

Chance stared at the boy for a few seconds before

tearing his eyes away and dropping his head down with a sense of shame. During the years Jerrod was growing up, Chance had only visited his family a couple of times. They were brief stays, because he felt like an outsider as he watched his brother and sister-in-law raising his son. He felt even worse learning now how his brother had smoothed over his absence with noble excuses. Chance threw his leg over the saddlehorn and dropped down to the frozen ground, then gestured to Jerrod to dismount. When the young man was standing at his side, Chance turned so that their eyes were in direct contact. He was struck with a sense of melancholy when he noted how they were almost the same height, and he realized it probably would not be long before he was looking up when they spoke to one another. The years he had missed when Jerrod was growing into manhood had never seemed more relevant, but those years were gone forever. He planned to do everything possible to make Jerrod understand why he had abandoned him and why their future together was so important.

"It was difficult after your grandpa and grandma died," he began. "But that wasn't the reason why I hardly ever came around when you were growing up." The gambler drew his gloved hand down the front of his heavy overcoat. "My visits were sparse because I was too ashamed of myself to face you or your parents."

Jerrod shook his head in confusion. "There are worse things than being a gambler, Uncle Chance."

"You're right, there are worse things, such as being a coward and a liar." Chance saw the boy start to disagree with him, so he held up his hand to gesture silence. "Let me finish before I turn tail and run again. You're ma and pa — they —" he paused, trying to remember the carefully planned speech he had rehearsed. But it had fled his mind and left him with a blank void.

"What about my ma and pa?" Jerrod demanded. He did not like the way his uncle was talking about himself, nor did he want him to start berating his parents.

301

"They never had a bad word to say about you."

While trying to skirt around the issue, Chance realized he was filling Jerrod with all sorts of misconceptions, and there was only one way to straighten everything out. "They weren't your real parents, Jerrod," he said after a heavy sigh. He saw the look of disbelief filter into the boy's dark eyes as he rushed on without giving Jerrod chance to speak. "I'm not lying to you, boy, so hear me out."

Jerrod's eyes narrowed with distrust as he studied the older man for a moment. As a child, he had idolized this man and the exciting tales of his exploits on the Mississippi. Since coming to Cheyenne to live with him, the young man had decided his image of his uncle had been underestimated. His uncle was everything his parents had said he was; a kind, generous man who lived life to its fullest extent. To Jerrod, it didn't matter what his uncle did for a living. His parents had taught him to judge a man by the way he treated other people, and in Jerrod's eyes, his uncle was a great man.

"I know what I'm about to tell you is not going to go down easy, but it's not easy to talk about, either." When Jerrod did not make any attempt to move or speak, Chance began to relate the story he had spent so many agonizing years trying to hide. Exposing his well guarded secret to his son, while observing the pain that washed through the boy's expression, was more difficult than Chance had imagined. In spite of the chill of the wind, he found himself drenched in sweat as he related the same story which he had told Jubilee when they were in Washington together. Jerrod made no attempt to interrupt him, and when Chance finished speaking, he waited for the questions which he was certain Jerrod would want to ask him. But the boy only turned away and stared off in the distance in silence.

Chance's worry intensified as the seconds turned into minutes, while Jerrod's quiet mood filled the air with a tense stillness. He knew he could not rush the boy as he tried to digest the startling truth about his birth, yet

Chance felt he would lose his sanity if he didn't know what was going through his son's mind. He had omitted telling him about his recent encounter with Faith, and now he debated whether or not he should divulge this information. When the young man finally began to talk, Chance decided it was best to leave things as they were.

"I guess keepin' this a secret all these years was hard on everybody," the boy said without looking at the other man. "And I reckon it took a lot of courage for you to admit to it now." Jerrod turned and focused his moist gaze on the man whom he had believed to be his uncle for the past sixteen years. "But that don't change anything. The fact that Pa was not my father, and that some prostitute on the riverboat gave birth to me, does not mean that she was my mother. As long as I live, nobody will ever take the place of my ma and pa in Kansas—not even you, Uncle Chance."

Chance drew in a burdened sigh, and slowly nodded his head. "I'm not trying to take my brother's place, because I'm not worthy of that position. I might have been responsible for your birth, but beyond that, my brother and sister-in-law will always be your true parents." When Chance glanced back at the boy, he was sure some of the agony had eased out of Jerrod's expression. He also became aware of what a good man his son was shaping up to be as he listened to the mature words Jerrod spoke.

"When you first started to talk, I was sure you were lyin'. But the longer you talked, and I began to put things into perspective, I knew you were telling me the truth. Then I started wonderin' why you were telling me this, especially now, after Ma and Pa are gone. For a time, I was afraid you were telling me because you were hopin' to take Pa's place. But now I understand." An easy smile curved the boy's lips as he added, "You've come a long way from being that young gambler who was unable to face up to the responsibility of raising a son, and I admire you for admitting to your mistake. But I respect you even more for lovin' me enough to allow me to hold on to the memories of the two people who deserved the right to be my parents."

Chance was taken aback by Jerrod's mature insight, but the boy's reference to how he had come a long way since his riverboat days filled Chance with more pride than he had ever known. He recalled how worthless he had felt after meeting Faith at the mansion on Capitol Hill. The words his son had just spoken, however, made him feel as though he could conquer the world. He draped his arm over Jerrod's shoulder and drew the boy to his side. While the savage Wyoming wind whipped around the bottoms of the long overcoats they wore, both men turned to gaze out at the sprawling prairie where they would lay the groundwork for the future generations who would carry on the Steele heritage.

Chapter Twenty-seven

Jubilee opened the newspaper again and re-read the front page article for the third time before she wadded up the entire paper and shoved it into her bag. She glanced around the Cheyenne depot, but was disappointed when she did not see any one with whom she had become acquainted during her first trip to Wyoming. However, no one knew she was coming in on the train today since she had wanted to surprise her husband. Now she wished she would have returned a few days earlier, so she could have been in on the upheaval which had occurred prior to her arrival.

Esther Morris had recently been appointed the nation's first female justice of the peace, which was another victory for the suffrage issue. The article briefly acknowledged Mrs. Morris's achievements, but it also went on to describe how a grand jury in Laramie, which had been composed of nine men and six females, indicted all the saloons in the territory for not closing to observe the Sabbath. Cartoons of the event depicted women in the juror's box in frilly dresses and ruffled bloomers, bouncing squalling babies on their knees, while their ears were stretched towards the lawyer who was presenting evidence. The reporter commented on how it might be a long time before another woman was invited to sit on the jury, then he went on to suggest that come voting time, husbands would be wise to forbid their wives to leave the house. It was apparent the men of Wyoming, and undoubtedly men all over the country, were turning the passing of the enfranchising bill into a joking issue.

As her fury toward the men of this territory flared, Jubilee quickly arranged to have her baggage and trunks sent to the inn. She then hurried off in the direction of The Second Chance Saloon, where she expected to find her husband. Though her first intention was to satisfy her ravenous desire to hold and kiss him, she was also anxious to find out his feelings on the unfair treatment of women in the Wyoming courts. A thaw had set in on the prairie town, bringing with it a warm current of wind. The frozen streets had been converted into rivers of mud, which also oozed over onto the narrow wooden walkways. As Jubilee carefully made her way through the slippery mess, she found herself comparing the "Magic City of the Plains" to the cultured city of Washington, D.C. She shook her head as she lifted the hem of her skirt above her ankles in an attempt to keep the garment out of the mud. Had she really been anxious to come back to this awful place? She sighed with relief when she managed to bypass a gooey puddle of thick muck, which appeared to be more than just a minor mud hole. But she had only taken a few more steps when a buckboard rolled through the deep puddle and splashed brown mud across the entire walkway. The driver called out his apology as the wagon rolled past, but Jubilee gave him the most debasing look she could muster. In disgust, she glanced down at her expensive gray suit, which now had a splattering of thick mud spots. For a moment she debated whether or not she should go back to the inn to change, but when she looked toward the muddy street again, she realized it would be futile. She wiped away a glob of mud which clung to her cheek, while cursing under her breath. When she had arrived in early December for the suffrage rally, she had thought there was nothing worse than the freezing wind and piles of snow that blanketed the ground. Now, as her high-heeled boots were sucked down into the bogs of mud, she realized there were even worse conditions for these hardy settlers to deal with out here in Wyoming. As she trudged toward the saloon she began to speculate on what the next few months would be like once the spring runoff from the snow-covered mountains started to flood across the flat lands. She was beginning to understand what Chance had meant when he told her the reasons behind the legislator's decision to grant women the vote; on its own, Wyoming could not entice any sensible-minded woman to settle here.

Once she had finally managed to dodge the larger mud holes, and had made her way along the slippery walkway, Jubilee found herself staring at the front door of The Second Chance Saloon and she was invaded by an eerie sense of dread. Her aversion to gaming houses would never go away, and the pain of her past would always surface whenever she was confronted with an establishment of this sort. Even her love for Chance Steele could not make the torment go away completely. Her gaze traveled up towards the curved sign, with its paintings of lascivious forms of pleasure as she attempted to force herself to turn the handle of the front door.

"Well, I hope you're back because you discovered you couldn't stay away from me for long?" Howard Crowly chortled as he came up behind the mud-spattered blonde.

The sound of the man's hateful voice caused Jubilee to fill with a mixture of rage and fear as she twirled around. "You're the one reason I wouldn't have come back," she spat as she gave him with a contemptuous glare. She could not believe he was so bold as to approach her after what had happened the last time they had encountered one another. She was even more amazed to see that he still had the guts to frequent this saloon. "What are you doing here?" she demanded, suddenly feeling protective of her husband's interests.

A smug smile settled on the banker's face as he answered, "Your husband asked me to come over here to-day. He thinks I might be interested in buying this—" Howard's taunting gaze moved towards the sign, then back to Jubilee as his face contorted with a cruel smirk. "This house of pleasure. But I doubt I'll find his asking price satisfactory. Unless, of course, the offer is too good to refuse." He raised one brow in a suggestive manner, which left Jubilee no doubts as to what he was thinking.

"He's going to sell the saloon?" she asked. Her joy over this prospect made her oblivious to his leering grin.

"He has to find a buyer with enough collateral to assume the bank note as well as a tidy sum of money to cover the overhead of such large business."

Jubilee tossed her head back with an indignant gesture. "That should not be difficult in an area as prosperous as Cheyenne." She glanced up and down the street which was lined with thriving new businesses.

Howard's evil grin remained intact when he replied casually. "True. But I must approve the buyer, unless, of course, it is someone with enough money to buy the whole establishment outright without assuming the loan." He saw her face light up with the possibility, so it pleased him to add, "But that is very unlikely. And rumor has it that your husband is quite anxious to sell because he has found a chunk of land he hopes to buy." He leaned down until his face was almost touching hers as he added, "Still, there might be something which will persuade me that this brothel is worth purchasing." He winked as he straightened up and gave her entire body a crude swipe with his eyes. A patronizing expression crossed his smirking face as he noted the mud splattered on her elegant gray suit and across her smooth complexion. "You just might make a good rancher's wife after all," he added in a flat tone and a disgusted roll upward of his eyes.

She could no longer ignore his insinuations as all the animosity she harbored for this man was reborn. "If you think I'm ever going to give into your ludicrous advances you must be more insane than I thought."

"How badly do you want your husband to sell this place?" he asked, motioning toward the descriptive sign hanging over the doorway. "I'll bet that you'll start thinking along more sensible lines eventually." His evil grin broadened when he noticed the way Jubilee cringed as she stared up at the picture of the voluptuous saloon girl.

But his words had also set Jubilee to thinking. "Did you say you were willing to *bet?*" she inquired, and her eyes lit with the fire of challenge. She smiled back at him when he gave her a curious shrug. "I'd be willing to make a friendly wager, Mr. Crowly."

Crowly stared at her for a long moment, then chuckled. "Do you know — you're starting to sound like a gambler. Marrying one must have had a profound effect on you." He winked again. "What other tricks have you learned from the proprietor of this whorehouse?"

Jubilee's cheeks flamed with heat at his foul words, but she forced herself to remain calm as she continued to try to lure the banker into a bet. "About the bet?" she repeated. "What would you say to a game of cards to determine whether or not you will buy The Second Chance Saloon — at a fair price?" she quickly added.

The old man shook his head and continued to chuckle. "That's very good, Jubilee. But even an old fool like me would not be stupid enough to play with a professional gambler such as Chance Steele for something as important as what you're proposing." His next round of laughter was cut short by the sudden opening of the saloon door.

"Jubilee!" Chance shouted as he rushed through the door and reached for his muddy bride. "I wasn't expecting you until the end of the week." He drew her close, but as he started to bend down to greet her with a welcoming kiss, his eyes traveled over her disheveled appearance. At once, he turned towards Howard Crowly. "What did you do to her?"

Crowly gave the man an impatient huff. "I didn't touch her, but she was providing me with a good laugh."

In confusion, Chance looked toward his wife for an explanation. A taunting expression, much like Crowly's, met his inquiring look. "I was just trying to make a bet with Mr. Crowly," she offered as she narrowed her blue eyes in a teasing manner. Her previous anger over the newspaper article was completely wiped out of her mind as she shifted her priorities to the deal into which she was about to enter.

"I don't think that would be a wise idea," Chance retorted, not bothering to ask what she intended to bet. He did not want his wife involved with the old man in any manner, but he especially did not want her entering into a wager with the unscrupulous banker.

As he held up his hand and let it slap down against his thigh, Crowly laughed again. "But wait until you hear this," he chortled. "She wants me to play you in a game a cards to determine whether or not I should buy the saloon — at a fair price, of course." A barreling laugh ripped from his mouth when he was unable to contain his mirth. But before the gambler had a chance to offer his own opinion of her absurd suggestion, Jubilee made another unexpected announcement.

"I didn't say I wanted you to play my husband for the saloon. What I had in mind was for *you and I* to engage in a game of cards." She kept her unwavering gaze leveled at the banker in spite of the loud gasp which came from her husband.

"You?" Crowly said with another chuckle. "Are you serious?"

"No, she's not serious," Chance interrupted as he gave his wife a look of disbelief. But as he stared down at her, he became aware that she was dead serious, and he wondered if she had gone insane as well.

Jubilee tossed her blonde head back and graced the old man with a sly grin. "I've played a few hands of poker in my time. The odds might be a bit more even between you and me." She could see the stunned expressions on both men's faces with this revelation. Though she had not touched a deck of cards in over a decade, she knew she had not forgotten her father's diligent teachings. The only activities she had ever shared with her father were the occasions when he had taught her how to play cards. By the time she had left home at age fifteen, she knew all the tricks of the trade. "Do we have a bet," she challenged again as she held her hand out toward the old man.

Crowly tilted his head to the side in a thoughtful manner. "Let me think—if you win, I agree to purchase this saloon at a fair price, right?" Jubilee nodded her head, while Chance's gaping face grew more uncertain. "But what if I win?" His leering expression made his thoughts obvious, but before he had an opportunity to voice his terms, Jubilee finished her terms of the wager.

"If you win, then we'll take whatever offer you make for the sale of the saloon."

Chance threw his hand up to his head in a gesture of shock. "Are you *crazy?*" he asked, turning his full attention toward his wife. "He won't pay a dime over the mortgage note, and where will that leave us then?"

"You sound as though you have already placed all your bets on my opponent," Jubilee replied with a defensive pout. Crowly's rumbling laughter rang out again, but she did not look away from her husband's confused, angry face. They stared at one another for several more seconds until Chance began to shake his head. *I can't believe this is happening, he thought.* His hand moved instinctively down the front of his brocaded vest.

"You really are serious." His voice contained a sense of defeat in its tone as he envisioned himself handing over the keys to The Second Chance Saloon to the gloating banker, while he, his wife and son were tossed out into the street without a penny to their name. Yet he also realized that he could not talk his wife out of going through with her destructive plan. Chance wondered if she felt this was the only way they would ever be free of the saloon. But if this was so, wasn't she aware of the terrible consequences? He started to explain what the loss of the saloon would mean to their plans to buy a ranch, but as he did, she lightly pressed her finger to his lips.

"Trust me," she said, her voice quiet with serious intent. "I know what I'm doing." Chance fell into a silent stupor as he studied her smiling, unyielding countenance. *I must be the crazy one,* he decided, because he was beginning to trust her. "Are you going to shake on this bet?" he asked as he backed away and glared at the banker.

Howard Crowly wasted no time in reaching for Jubilee's hand before she changed her mind. He continued to snicker as he kept trying to comprehend his good fortune. Playing a game of cards was going to prove to be a waste of time, he thought as he followed the pair into the saloon; Chance Steele's silly bride had as much as handed him the deed to the saloon on a platter.

"Is there trouble, Boss?" Walker said as he strode from behind the bar and gave Crowly as hateful glare when the trio entered the saloon. He carried a shotgun in one hand, making his meaning clear as to how protective he felt towards his boss and his boss's wife. Jubilee forced back the fright she felt at the sight of the gun, along with the horrible remembrance of the morning Chance had shot Howard Crowly.

"Jubilee and Howard are going to play a game of cards, Walker. Why don't you cut them a fresh deck?" the saloon owner announced. He bowed slightly and motioned for his wife to pick out a table of her choice.

With a calm smile, which belied the trembling in the pit of her stomach, Jubilee walked to a table in the far corner of the room. She attempted to divert her thoughts away from her intense nervousness as she reminded herself to have a talk with her husband about his silly habit of bowing. That may have been a gallant practice on the riverboats, but she had seldom encountered a rancher who indulged in such habits. "Is this a good table?" she asked Crowly in a coy manner.

He answered her with a disinterested shrug of his shoulders, since he was already busy thinking about his new business venture. He no longer cared that Abigail still refused to let him come back home, because by tonight he would be taking up residence right here in Chance Steele's living quarters. With a smug sigh, Howard pulled out a chair and plopped down in anticipation of the events that would quickly follow this ridiculous game, and a slight edge of doubt started to creep through his elated being. He watched the opening actions of his female opponent.

While Chance began to open the new deck of cards Walker had handed him, Jubilee took off the short gray jacket which topped her matching skirt and pink shirtwaist. She shook the jacket, then carefully draped the garment over the back of the chair. Without glancing at the men who were observing her unhurried actions, she unbuttoned the tiny clasps which adorned the wrists of her silk shirtwaist and began to roll her sleeves up to her elbows in narrow folds. When this was accomplished, she daintily smoothed down the back of her skirt and she sat down in the chair. A knowing grin touched the corners of the gambler's lips, but he did not say a word about her nonchalant behavior. Watching her was like watching a mirrored image of himself when he was preparing to play a game that held high stakes. A true professional threw his opponent off guard before the game even started by using slow, deliberate movements which would provoke the other player's sense of impatience.

It was not until Jubilee had seated herself and took the time to look around the huge expanse of the elaborate saloon that she was overwhelmed by how much she had just put at stake. Still, her panic was contained within her thudding breast, and was not evident upon her calm countenance. Ben Hart had taught her all the tricks of the game, but many his teachings had focused on the shady side of the deal. Jubilee, however, did not intend to cheat in order to win this game. She had com-

313

plete confidence in the honest skills she had learned from her father, and she was not the least bit worried about Howard Crowly's knowledge of cards. He spent too much time on the second floor of the gaming house to pose a real threat at the card table. As Jubilee's confidence increased, she noticed how her opponent's decreased. She had always felt that the only thing she had learned from her father was to avoid men who reminded her of him. Yet, as she glanced up at the handsome gambler who had stolen away her heart, she wondered if she had not learned a few lessons which would prove to be valuable.

"Name your game," she asked in a blunt tone as she settled her gaze on the banker again.

Howard's expression reflected his increasing uneasiness. "I — I —" he stammered with indecision and glanced toward the saloon owner as if hoping to receive some assistance. But Chance only reciprocated with a patronizing smile. He was thinking about the scared little girl who had hid out in the back of the barrooms where her father worked. Apparently, she had ventured out from her hiding places long enough to give close attention to the activities that were going on at the gaming tables, too.

"We'll make it draw poker, with an imperial trump," Jubilee said when the old man continued to stutter with uncertainty. From the side of her eye, she noticed her husband give his dark head a positive nod when she chose the professional's favorite poker game. Her father had always played poker with an imperial trump, or cuter, as it was sometimes called. This meant a 53-card deck was used, which included the joker, who could also be played as an ace.

"I'll cut the deck," Howard retorted in a rush of words as he tried to sound as if he was as polished at cards as he was at demoralizing women.

Jubilee pushed the deck to his side of the round table. "It's all yours," she said. Then, as he divided the cards in two and restacked them, she added, "I *never* cut a new deck. It's bad luck." A satisfied grin consumed her pretty face when she noticed his hand shake as he attempted to push the cards back to her for the deal. By the time Jubilee had dealt the first hand of five cards each, a ring of spectators had surrounded the table. She was struck once again with the idea that she could not do anything in this town without an audience.

"I need a drink," Howard said as a visible blanket of sweat broke out upon his upper lip and forehead.

Chance motioned to Walker to fulfill the man's request, then added, "Bring my wife a sarsasparilla." When she glanced up from her intent study of the cards she held in her hand, their smiling gazes met briefly. The unabashed love shining from his eyes fueled her optimism.

Jubilee focused her unwavering sights on her opponent and acquired an innocent smile. "Do you want to open,"

"I'll take two" he announced with a cocky tilt of his gray head and a sinister grin. He reached out and plucked the top two cards from the deck, then settled back in his seat with his evil expression still intact. As the audience attempted to glimpse his cards, Howard clutched them against his chest in a gesture of indignation. "Your turn," he said to Jubilee. A frightening glint began to emit from his eyes.

Refusing to be upstaged, Jubilee returned his glare with her own cunning look as she eased the next couple of cards from the top of the deck. "I'll take two cards, also." She noted how the old man's smile remained intact, but the glimmer in his eyes began to dim. When she glanced down at her hand, her excitement threatened to burst from within her. "Place your bet," she demanded, keeping her voice steady and quiet. She hoped the stakes would not exceed the meager savings she carried in her velvet purse — approximately seven hundred and sixty-two dollars.

Howard dug into his vest pocket and pulled out a wad of money that caused Jubilee's anxiety to abound.

She had an unbeatable hand, but if the bets were too high, she would have to fold. In a second of panic, she glanced at her husband, and could tell his thoughts were running along the same lines as he stared at the roll of money the banker had produced.

"I'll bet one hundred dollars," he replied as he tossed out a crisp one hundred dollar banknote. Once again, he leveled his icy stare at his lovely opponent as he anticipated her next move.

Inwardly, Jubilee kept telling herself to remain calm. If Howard sensed her panic, all would be lost. She forced herself to grace him with a placid smile as she opened her purse and pulled out a handful of crumpled greenbacks. Taking her time, she counted out a hundred dollars and coins, which she laid on top of Crowly's bill. "I'll meet your bet, and I'll raise you—" she glanced down at the money she still held, while she debated whether or not she should attempt to trick him with caution or flamboyance. "I'll raise you another hundred," she added, deciding to play it in the middle. She tossed out the remainder of her bet. A round of whispering echoed through the crowd, which had grown larger with the addition of the courtesans and the patrons who had begun to filter into the establishment.

Crowly frowned when Jubilee placed her bet on top of his. He had expected her to dole out her bets in meager sums of tens or twenties. With a discreet glance at her purse, he wondered how much money the bag contained. Perhaps she had already exhausted her total, he hoped. She quickly pulled the draw string shut when she noticed his inquiring gaze. "I'll raise you . . . another hundred," he stated, and carelessly tossed out two more bills.

A tension filled moment passed as Jubilee pretended to ponder her next move, although she had no doubts that she would continue to bet until she was out of money. She laid her cards face down on the table and carefully re-opened her bag, removing two hundred dollars in small bills. "I'll raise you another hundred."

Excited murmuring rose from the crowd. Crowly counted the money she had just placed on top of the pile as if he did not trust her. When he was finished, he grabbed two more hundred dollar banknotes from his roll and threw them on the table in a manner that suggested he was beginning to grow flustered.

When he did not offer to say his bet outloud, Jubilee began her final strategy. "Let's see," she frowned and drew in a deep sigh. "You just raised me another hundred, so I'll—" her frown intensified as she contemplated her hand again. She yearned to look up at her husband, but she did not want to break the hold she had on Howard's attentive eyes as he watched, and waited, for her next move. She had three hundred and sixty-two dollars left, which meant she could begin to decrease the size of her bets, or she could make one more exorbitant bet. "I'll meet your hundred and raise you another . . . two hundred and fifty." She had been expecting an outburst from the crowd, and she was not surprised to hear a loud gasp from her husband. But she refused to allow her attention to be diverted from her opponent. An elated feeling began to come over her when she kept her steady gaze on his face and observed him break out in another profuse layer of sweat.

As he made an concerted effort to avoid looking in Jubilee's direction, Howard considered her ploy. In his hand he held two aces, the imperial trump, and two jacks—a full house; a good hand worth betting on, but not a great hand. If she held four matching cards of any kind, she was the winner, hands down. He forced his eyes to settle upon her face, but as he studied her angelic expression, he slowly became aware of the fact that he had been conned. With a nervous glance at the sea of faces who waited for his next move, Howard wiped away the perspiration which drenched his brow. It was obvious everyone was enjoying watching him squirm, he realized as he looked back down at the five cards that were beginning to curl around the edges where his sweating hands held them in a tight grip. He still had plenty of money to keep raising the woman's bets, but an inner sense told him he had already lost. After another long pause, which fueled the tension in the entire room, he finally drew in a ragged breath. "I'll call."

Jubilee's tough exterior began to crumble with the relief she felt over her opponent's decision. If Howard had raised her bet, she would have had no choice other than to fold, nor would she have ever been able to forgive herself for entering into this bet. As the group around the table waited in hushed anticipation for the players to show their cards, Jubilee finally allowed herself to glance up at the tall man who had stood beside the chair like a silent sentry throughout the game. The slight smile which flashed across her lips, was the clue he had been waiting to see. The corners of his dark mustache curved with overwhelming relief, and he gave his head a reassuring nod.

Jubilee's triumph flooded over her whole being as she looked back at the banker. Before she had even laid her cards down, Howard groaned with defeat, but when he glimpsed the four kings and one ace she placed down in a neat fan, his despair exploded. There were only two unbeatable hands in draw poker: four aces, or the hand she had just revealed. An instant of madness overcame Howard as he thought to accuse her of cheating. But as this possibility passed through his mind, he caught the movement of Chance Steele's hand as it slid down the front of his vest. He threw his cards down on the table as a rousing round of cheers began to circulate throughout the now crowded saloon. The glowering face of the banker turned toward the large group of spectators, while he became aware of how many enemies he had made in this town. There was not one friendly face directed at him, nor was there any sympathy over his loss.

"Let's head on over to the bank and draw up those papers right now," Chance said, skirting the table with his wife in tow. He found it difficult to keep the smile off his face as he announced with a deep bow to Howard Crowly, "Congratulations on your purchase of The Second Chance Saloon."

The spectators fell into a stunned silence. However, Jerrod wasted no time in confronting his uncle. "But Jubilee won! How come he gets the saloon?"

"Ah, do you want to answer that?" the gambler asked as he smiled down at his lovely bride.

She nodded her head with excitement as she addressed Jerrod, as well as everyone else in the room. "If I lost, Mr. Crowly could have bought the saloon for the cost of the mortgage his bank holds on this property." Another chorus of startled gasps and low murmurings followed until Jubilee began to speak again. "If he lost, he had agreed to pay off the mortgage and purchase the saloon at a price which would also provide Chance with a fair profit."

Since it was well known to all of Chance's clientele that he had been wanting to sell his saloon, they immediately realized Jubilee had claimed a true victory for her husband. However, no one was anxious to have the new owner take over the establishment, and there was no attempt to hide their unhappiness as the banker began to follow Chance, Jubilee and Jerrod Steele out of the saloon.

As the threesome wound their arms around one another's waists and made their way down the muddy street, they portrayed an invincible force of impending success and eternal bliss. With a roguish grin, Chance leaned toward the beautiful woman who walked between him and his son. "Well, Mrs. Steele, since you have such a doubting attitude toward my ranching skills, it looks like I'm going to have to start proving to you that I can rope cattle as good as you can play cards." His smile broadened when he noticed that she had caught the taunting twist of his words.

While they followed Howard Crowly down the street, Jubilee was oblivious to the mud that oozed over the tops of her dainty boots. Nor did she notice how the wind whipped around them, or the threatening dark clouds that had begun to gather over the prairie again, signaling the end of the brief warm spell. The rugged Wyoming Territory was the most beautiful place she had ever been, and she never intended to leave here again. She turned her enraptured face up toward the handsome raven-eyed man who held her in his tight embrace as she retorted to his teasing remark, "I'm willing to bet you can prove me wrong."